THE · SWALLOWS · UNCAGED

A · NARRATIVE · IN · EIGHT · PANELS

The *Swallows* *Uncaged*

ELIZABETH McLEAN

Freehand Books gratefully acknowledges the support of the Canada Council for the Arts for its publishing program. ¶ Freehand Books, an imprint of Broadview Press Inc., acknowledges the financial support for its publishing program provided by the Government of Canada through the Canada Book Fund.

Canada Council   Conseil des Arts
for the Arts   du Canada

Alberta
Government

Freehand Books
515 — 815 1st Street SW   Calgary, Alberta   T2P 1N3
www.freehand-books.com

Book orders: LitDistCo
100 Armstrong Avenue   Georgetown, Ontario   L7G 5S4
Telephone: 1-800-591-6250   Fax: 1-800-591-6251
orders@litdistco.ca
www.litdistco.ca

Library and Archives Canada Cataloguing in Publication

McLean, Elizabeth
[Imagining Vietnam]
The swallows uncaged : a narrative in eight panels / Elizabeth McLean.

Originally published under title: Imagining Vietnam. Exeter : Impress Books, 2012.
Issued in print and electronic formats.
ISBN 978-1-55481-264-6 (paperback).
ISBN 978-1-4604-0528-4 (epub).
ISBN 978-1-77048-569-3 (PDF)

I. Title. II. Title: Imagining Vietnam.

PS8625.L424I63 2015   C813'.6   C2015-903663-1   C2015-903664-X

Edited by Barbara Scott
Book design and illustration by Natalie Olsen, Kisscut Design
Author photo by Eric McLean
Printed on FSC® recycled paper and bound in Canada by Friesens

I'll never know them,

those outmoded figures

— the same as we are,

yet completely different.

My imagination works to unlock

the mystery of their being...

I imagine the void

of their exhaustion, empty moments

through which I spy

their life's core.

ADAM ZAGAJEWSKI

CONTENTS

Prelude ix

PANEL 1 *The Black Stain* 1

PANEL 2 *The Mongolian Stake* 39

PANEL 3 *The Queen of Mulberry* 77

PANEL 4 *The Story of Joseph and Mary* 113

PANEL 5 *The Sisterhood of Concubines
and the Brilliant Speck of Yellow* 151

PANEL 6 *La femme et la mer* 203

PANEL 7 *Dear President* 239

PANEL 8 *Orange County, Canada* 259

Acknowledgements 305

Author's Note 308

Prelude

Picture a Vietnamese screen. You unfold it across the floor and eight panels come into view. You step back to take a look, and in the midst of the lush topical setting you see men, women, and children in various postures. You ponder who they might be and what they might be doing.

Digesting the history of Vietnam is like that. You plough through a blurry grove of wars won and lost, catch some dates and names of generals who wrote poetry, of emperors who roused the country with bold reforms, and of adventurous Westerners who for 400 years meandered through the land. Some milestones, customs, and personages lodge themselves in your mind and stir your imagination.

You telescope the last 1000 years of the history of Vietnam into a few singular episodes that were heroic or compelling, and want to tease some stories out of them. You begin to feel for the ordinary people who lived behind the curtain of history and they tempt you to recreate the family clans they begat, the humiliations they endured, or the love affairs they fancied. The hard spine of history holds, the eight-panel screen comes alive, and you succumb to the pleasure of writing fiction.

The Black Stain

1

In the early centuries of the Christian era,
Việt clans that worked the rice paddies in
the Delta of the Red River lived under the
yoke of the Emperor of China. But they
kept their own observances, spoke their
own dialects, and, unlike the Chinese,
chewed betel nuts and blackened their teeth.
In mid-tenth century, the rebellious clansmen
drove out their Confucian overlords, and
around 1010 founded the kingdom of Đại
Việt under the Buddhist Dynasty named Lý.
Its first monarch, King Lý Thái Tổ, laid the
foundations of future Vietnam.

HE CAUGHT HER UNAWARES in the hollow of the black-mangrove ravine. She was heading home, treading over the mangled roots that sprawled on the trail like crab legs. A gust of mint-scented air swept by and she caught the sound of rustling in the grass — ferrets and hares returning to their burrows for the night. But then she heard twigs snapping and footsteps on crisp leaves. She whirled around and there he stood, against the last of the light, a tall man not of her village, whorls of matted fuzz hanging from his chin.

She stared at him, her body stilled, her wits running. No family lived anywhere near that stretch of bog and the village drum had given no warning that a stranger was inside the gates that day. She had just delivered the family's gift of rice to Teacher Cường's hut and he had not mentioned any visitors. Was he a demon? A beast in human form? A savage from China? If he were a man, he would not dare approach a girl who was not his betrothed. But if he were an evil spirit, he could carry her off in an instant.

She dug her toes into the mulch and crossed her arms over her chest, her heart hammering. He moved forward slowly, wearily, looking more like a real man with every step. If he tried to speak to her, should she answer? Talking to strange men was absolutely forbidden. She resolved to say only — and only if he asked — that her name was Lan, that she was of the Nguyễn clan, and that this was her village. She waited because she was a girl and he was her elder and had the right to speak first. He was close now. The flesh of his face had the yellowish tint of a rotten pumpkin, and the slits of his eyes were narrower than those of her people. When he parted his lips to speak, she had to muffle a scream — his teeth were white. Like the teeth of a rat. If he was a man, he was not a Việt man.

"I am Confucius, your Master," he said sternly. "You've been talking to me in your head. Speak up now." Her teeth, also shamefully white, had locked, and she could not utter a single word. "Where is your family?" he demanded. She pointed back to the light flickering over the fishpond beyond the second dike. "That's... my brother Toàn, baiting frogs... with a torch."

He hooked his thumbs on the cord of his cloak and waited.

She lifted her chin and took a deep breath. "Master, I've tried to talk to you to ask about Senior Sister Sen. She was widowed last lunar year when the great flood came. She's waiting to hear her future. Father hasn't spoken, but Grandmother says that virtuous widows must devote their lives to the memory of their husbands. Is it true?"

"Are you betrothed?"

"Master, I am not," she gasped. Did he know that she had recently become fit for betrothal? She could not quite read his face in the dusk and the silence lingered till he spoke again.

"Have you asked Teacher Cường about my commands for widowed women?"

"Master, Junior Sister has no right to ask such questions. Brother Toàn is Teacher Cường's disciple, so he could ask him. But Brother Toàn defers to Father, as is befitting." She was sure she had given the correct answer and lowered her head to listen.

"A woman's virtues are four: *Công, Dung, Ngôn,* and *Hạnh,*" he said, opening his palms. "Care of the family and exemplary housekeeping come first; this is what women are born for. Neat and pleasant appearance is mandatory because it brings honour to the husband. Also, a gentle manner and polite language which show her respect of others. The strength of her character is revealed in her obedience to her elders. At home, her deference is to the father; when betrothed, to her husband; and if widowed, to her son. The wife owes obeisance to the husband even after his death."

He paused for a moment and continued in a harsher tone.

"Senior Sister has failed to bear a son and must defer to her father. Father's duty is to weigh the good of his family and of his community. He will be guided by Teacher Cường, who knows the rules. Your duty is to obey."

Lan wanted to explain that Sen had no son because she had been betrothed for only a short time. That Sen's husband had drowned and the in-laws blamed Sen for not moving fast enough to save him, and called her an evil comet who brought flood in her wake, and, when they found out that Sen was not with child, said she was no better than deadwood, and refused to feed her, and now Sen was back home and despondent, and her parents had to bear the shame of having their daughter returned... and it was just heartbreaking to watch Senior Sister suffer. But when Lan looked up, she faced a tangle of mute boughs; the white-toothed stranger had vanished.

She glanced down the ravine and saw Brother Toàn walking along the top of the dike. She took the shortcut across the swamp that used to be a duck pond, her legs sinking in the sludge, her eyes casting about for the flickering lights of evil spirits she knew were lying in wait to drown young girls. Only a few sunrises earlier, after Grandmother had chastised her for dawdling in the market for too long, Lan had asked them to carry the old woman off. Then, ashamed of her insolence, she had changed her mind and begged them not to. Were they still angry with her?

Her home, at the foot of the gully, was a rugged hut on stilts. A mossy boulder formed the back wall and three wooden logs held up the floor. The palm-leaf roof and the rickety scaffolding were sealed with mud and straw. She ran up the chiselled pine log that was the wobbly gangplank to the hearth and gasped, "I saw Master Confucius. He spoke to me."

Sen narrowed her eyes and Grandmother swung around irritably. "Get the mat ready. Help the young widow with the fish pot."

Lan opened her mouth to repeat her message but Sen pressed two fingers to her lips. The sisters dragged the cauldron down the log to the grass where a dinner mat was waiting, and Sen turned her face away from the hearth and whispered, "Do as you're told and keep quiet. You'll get Grandmother angry again and we're about to eat."

"You don't understand. I've talked to Master Confucius. He says you may be allowed to be betrothed again. Father will decide with Teacher Cường's help."

"The spirit of Master Confucius wouldn't stoop to talk to a person of low rank — not to a female child, her teeth unstained..."

"His teeth were also unstained... because he was Chinese, right?"

"Oh! Shut up..."

Grandmother was approaching with a bowl of rice in her hands and family members were emerging from the pitchy hollows between the rows of guava trees. Toàn came in first, lifting the cover of the basket to show his brown-speckled trophies. In the third lunar month, frog meat was at its best, and their chubby backs shone in the fading light. Grandmother accepted the catch with a bow, her face softening as she lowered the basket into a pail of damp moss. Tomorrow, she would stab the frogs between the eyes with a spike for an easy kill, slit their bellies neck to tail to scoop out the guts, chop off the heads, and pull off the skins. Then she would grill the flesh with bamboo shoots and saffron — the family's favourite.

Father and Mother came down the path stooped with fatigue. Sen rushed to them and gently lifted the bars off their weary shoulders. Lan sprang forward with two water gourds. The sisters watched in silence as their parents poured the water into their throats and over their heads. Every spring, all delta farmers bent over the sodden paddies from before sunrise to after sundown, planting and transplanting rice seedlings, hoping for enough rain in the summer for the vital autumn crop not to fail. At home, Grandmother looked up to the sky and read the future in the shadows on the face of the moon, in the ghoulish formations of the clouds, in the direction and rustle of the wind. Father brushed the driblets of sweat and water from his eyelids and pointed to the dark puffs tumbling over the horizon. "These clouds will bring us rain."

Grandmother stared him down, "Folly! The northern wind will bring drought." Lan bit her tongue, as she so often did when she heard Grandmother dash the family's hopes with warnings of floods and plagues and famines to come.

Father crumpled at the head of the mat, between Toàn and Grandmother, and tucked his knees against his neck, his grimy fingers still holding on to the water gourd. His body, more muscular than that of other village men, bore the imprint of his Chinese ancestry. His face had the shape of a rabbit snare: wide at the top and tapering down to a narrow chin. His eyes were like two slits on the piece of bark that was his parched face. Mother's face was very Việt — a smooth oval capping thin and bony shoulders — she, a timid bride of a hillside tribe, swapped for a sackful of salt twenty lunar years earlier. She crouched on her haunches, further along the mat, her fingers clamping her mud-splotched knees. With her pale eyelids meekly down, to Lan she looked like a sleeping sparrow. Sen and Lan squatted at the far end of the mat, a respectful distance from the senior members of the family.

At the evening meal, Grandmother usually allowed her daughter-in-law to serve the rice, so Mother lifted her shoulders, cupped a few pieces of a torn banana leaf in her palm, filled them with rice, and passed them one by one to her husband, her son, and her mother-in-law. She served her two daughters last — Sen first, Lan second. The family followed the same order reaching out with their chopsticks to the salted aubergine and grilled sweet potatoes. They drank a broth of carp bones left over from a previous meal. Grandmother, as rigid as a plinth of limestone, watched with pleasure as her son and her grandson relished her cooking.

Lan could hardly swallow because she ached to tell her family about her amazing encounter. But she could not say a word because the evening meal was always eaten in silence, in deference to the exhausted paddy workers, and to the ancestors believed to be silently sharing the food with them. The family gulped their rice by the quivering light of coconut lamps: two shells filled with groundnut oil, wicks stemming upwards. By the time the hushed ritual ended, dusk was thickening and sleep was calling.

They followed Father up the chiselled log and he and Toàn curled up by the hearth, their heads sharing a rolled-up grass mat which was their headrest. The women slept together on a straw mat on the other side of the hearth, Grandmother right next to it, then Mother, Sen, and Lan pressed against the wall. Grandmother's carp-scented hair remained pinned on top of her head in a bun and she wheezed through her nose. Mother's splayed hair smelled of raw mud; her breath would go steady in seconds. Lan wiggled close to Sen till their shoulders touched. She longed to whisper kind words into her sister's ear and give her hope that Teacher Cường might grant permission for betrothal, so that she could have a son, and then more sons, and Junior Sister would come to help with the babies... as they had always planned. But

Sen was already asleep, and the dark hour was not the time to chat. Only the toads and the cicadas thought otherwise.

Listening to the creatures' chatter in the murk, it occurred to Lan that perhaps her maternal grandparents might want to hear about her meeting with Confucius. She sealed her eyes, emptied her head of any earthly thought, and called out their names repeatedly in a whisper. She did not have to wait long. Grandfather appeared first, acknowledged Lan's kowtow with a wave, and said, "I know, I know." His wispy beard was longer than it used to be in life. He said that Master Confucius had been pleased with Lan's comportment, and that Teacher Cường would be coming to dinner with the family soon. Lan asked if she could speak to Father about Sen's widowhood and Grandfather said, "It would be incorrect for Junior Daughter to speak to Father. Only Brother Toàn can do that. Speak to him." Lan was so happy to have Grandfather's permission to speak to Brother Toàn that she reached out to brush his arm, but he quickly vanished and the good Grandmother took his place. She wore the same grassy robe in which she had been buried five lunar years earlier and looked just as frail. Silently, she stroked Lan's arms with her palm as she had done when Lan was little, till her granddaughter's arms and then her head went to sleep.

ON A SCORCHING AFTERNOON two sunrises later, Lan sat cross-legged under the raised floor of her hut, Grandmother rumbling around the hearth above her head. In Lan's lap was a stone mortar, by her side a basketful of silvery paddy crabs. She had to grind the crabs with the pestle into a paste for soup. A paddy crab was no bigger than a bee, but grinding its crusty shell was as hard as crushing rocks in a quarry. Lan could only work on one fistful at a time, pounding till her arms had gone numb.

Nearby, in the shade of a guava tree, Toàn had settled down to carve a shoulder bar. He clutched a sturdy trunk of bamboo between his knees and was paring it with a stone chisel, the shavings flying away over his head, the thinner chips settling on his hair. Was the bar for her? Surely she deserved one of her own now that she was sturdier and had regular errands. A Việt girl who had her own shoulder pole and her teeth stained was a grown-up. Since the family had lost their pigs and chickens in the flood, they had had to barter tuber vegetables for pork, and carrying the heavy roots of taro and cassava to market had recently become Lan's chore. Brother Toàn had laughed at her. "In the Confucian order," he explained, "traders stand below scholars, farmers, and artisans, because they're crafty and deceptive." She did not care. To escape from Grandmother's shadow to the market, to plunge into the sea of straw hats and shoulder poles weighed with pomelos and squealing piglets, to be able to talk to women from families other than her own, was a gift from the gods.

She took her first break from pounding the crabs just after Grandmother had come down the chiselled log with a rattan rucksack on her back and disappeared among the guava trees. Toàn also rested his chisel and mopped his forehead with a clump of grass. When Grandmother was out of earshot, Lan put down the pestle and called out: "Brother Toàn, do you know that Teacher Cường will be coming to have dinner with us? What an honour for Father and for our family. All the villagers will be envious."

When he did not respond, she continued in the respectful tone she knew he expected, "Does Teacher Cường think that Sen cannot be betrothed again, do you know?"

"I don't know."

"At the next lesson, can you ask him?"

"Father will ask him when the time comes. It hasn't been that long."

"Grandmother says Sen is a widow, just like herself. But Sen is too young to be a widow. She must have another chance to bear a son. She's so sad. Father hardly speaks to her. Grandmother only tells her what to do and lashes out at her whenever —"

"Listen to me, Junior Sister. Grandmother has outlived all our other ancestors. You must honour her wisdom. If you don't show respect she'll punish you. You should know that by now."

Lan pouted. "I do know that. But what I don't know is why Sen must stay a widow forever."

"Because these are the rules, the Confucian rules. No man can override them."

"I know. But Teacher Cường is a man of wisdom... He can consider... I mean take into account that Fate has been mean to Sen and... contemplate the future of our clan... he can help Father decide."

"Teacher Cường is a learned man, no doubt. But why should the village have to feed him when we hardly have enough for ourselves? Or why must I do errands for him when there is more than enough work around here?"

"But Teacher Cường's son is very young and his parents are very old. They need food and help with chores. Teacher Cường is the *thầy đồ* of this village. He's your spiritual father."

"Teacher Cường is not my father in any way," Toàn protested. "And I hate those lessons. If Father didn't insist I'd drop them today."

"Oh, Brother Toàn! You cannot defy Father's will. He wants you to be wise, to learn the rites and the observances of our clan."

"Father is twice the man Teacher Cường is. I can learn all I need from him."

"Father cannot write ideograms. Isn't that what Teacher Cường is teaching you?"

"He's trying. He's always talking about the great honour of

becoming a Mandarin and serving the Monarchs. I don't care about any of that. Father's ancestors were common people and worked the paddies just like we do. I want to be a farmer like Father... like Grandfather who earned this land for us with his soldiering. Father will be buried here because his father is buried here and I want to be buried in this village with them. I can serve the Monarchs as a soldier if we are invaded again. I don't need any Chinese ideograms."

"But Father expects you to be a teacher, so that people will pay you homage and bring you food. Teachers don't have to do any soldiering."

Toàn swung his legs sideways, pushing a pile of bamboo shavings away. "Father wants dignity for our family. It's hard for him to live with the shame of having his daughter returned. He gave her away to a family richer than our family to raise his rank in the hierarchy, maybe even become an elder one day. But nothing has come of it. Fate punishes people who leave their birthplace."

Lan flew at the chance to talk about Sen again. "If Father had been less hasty... I mean if he had waited to find a suitable husband in our village, Sen wouldn't be a widow. And would have a son by now."

"Sen is a soursop. She frets and grumbles and complains. She annoys Father and Grandmother all the time. She irritates me no end."

"That's the way the gods have made her. And she's your senior... by a year. It's hard for her —"

"She's a girl and should know her place. She tries to help herself to as big a chunk of fish or taro from the bowl as I do. That's not correct. And because of her, Father is burdened with two hungry daughters again and must scheme to find men who will pledge to feed them."

"You can speak to Father and he'll ask the matchmaker to find someone in this village. Our clan needs sons. You said —"

"I want to give this village many sons. You must have many sons too, Junior Sister. It's your duty. That's how we honour our ancestors who gave us life."

"That's what Confucius says, right?"

"Oh, hush! You know more about Confucius than a girl needs to know. Your head is too big for your own good. Don't meddle in what belongs to men."

SHE HAD BEEN BORN — a tiny wizened clump capped with a coconut-sized skull — just before the rainy season of the Year of the Rooster, during the reign of the Lý Dynasty. Her parents farmed a snippet of land tacked on to a village one sunrise away from the bend of the river. She was their third living child and the Second Daughter. Two older boys had been stillborn. Too premature to have a soul, their remains were buried under the rice shack to protect them from scavenging animals.

When she was little, her family called her a runt — a foul moniker aimed to repel evil spirits. But when they saw that Fate had ordained she would live, her name was entered in the village register as Lan, or Orchid. Senior Sister Sen was Lotus. Brother Toàn was the second living child but the First Son. First Son was everything. He could eat all the food he wanted and come and go as he pleased. Even though she was his elder, Senior Sister had to defer to him in all things and she seethed at the obligation.

Lan understood Sen's rancour and tried to be a dutiful Junior Sister, deferring to Sen even if it meant that very little food was left for her. She herself looked up to the family's cherished boy and admired how he kept the hut patched, and the hoes, scythes, and hunting bows sharpened. When food was scarce, he vanished for a day or two and emerged from the forest with a wild beast hanging around his neck. When dikes had to be repaired, he carried the biggest boulders, and when a new hut on stilts had to be erected to save the family from the misery of another flood, he hauled the heaviest logs. They could not have managed without him, and Lan eagerly joined her parents and Grandmother in prayer to beseech the village guardian spirit to keep the family's heir away from war. Sen joined them because she had to, and scowled throughout till Grandmother, exasperated, chased her away with a broom.

Lan loved to be near Toàn. Two sunrises after Sen had been dispatched to her husband's village with a dowry of rice and pork meat and the family had no food left, Father found Lan under the mulberry bush crying her eyes out for the sister she thought she had lost forever. He told her to get up and help Toàn bait eels. She followed her brother across two rice fields, wading up to her knees in mud, to where two streams emptied into a marshy lake. He carried bamboo trunks on his back, she a wicker basket filled with a gooey mixture of stale rice and crabs. By the shore, she stuffed the hollow stalks with the gruel, and he carried them to the water and angled them among the reeds. Then, sitting side by side, they watched two squeaky shorebird mothers teach their chicks to fly.

The next morning, they returned to the lake. Toàn peeked into the trunks, closed one end of each trunk with a clump of grass, lifted them gently from the mud one by one, and tilted the open end down letting the squirming eels pour into the sack Lan held open for him. She loved being his helper; he would have never taken Sen with him.

Back at the hut, Grandmother lifted the eels from the sack and dangled them on a stick for a moment before dropping them into a cauldron of boiling water. Some time later she fished them out and laid them on the grass. When the eels were cool, she dusted them with wood ashes and ordered Lan to scrub off their slimy skin with a piece of chinar-tree bark. Cut up and grilled in pork fat with chopped root of banana tree, the tidbits were delicious — crunchy on the outside, chewy on the inside. The family, now smaller without Sen's hungry mouth, munched with pleasure and forgot that the spring crop had been meagre and the fall crop was a long time away. Lan felt like the family's saviour.

But the following morning, when she was getting ready to help Toàn again, she heard Grandmother tell Father that leaving a young girl alone with an older brother was not correct. Thereafter, Grandmother kept her by the hearth till, three sunrises later, Father ruled that she was old enough to take vegetables to market. Lan was beside herself with joy. The very next afternoon he told her to deliver a sack of rice all the way to Teacher Cường's. "That's because he knows I'm a grown-up," she told herself. For that, she thought him the best and the wisest father of all. Father and Brother Toàn — two good men. And Brother Toàn the best of brothers.

All she needed to be fully happy was to have her teeth stained. Grandmother resisted, claiming that her youngest grandchild was much too headstrong and needed to grow up a lot more. But not too long after Sen's return to the family the stubborn woman had a new reason to keep Lan away from her brother — and was forced to change her mind about Lan's teeth.

On a spring day, running home after delivering the midday meal to the paddies, Lan suddenly felt cramps in her belly. She rested under the crown of a flowering apricot tree, drawing her knees to her chin. Sticky red rivulets were oozing down her thighs. She had seen such stains before on Senior Sister's legs. Flustered, she smeared the dribbles with her forefinger, her heart swelling with pleasure. It had been a long wait but finally she would be like her sister — a grown-up. Grandmother would have to stain her teeth, and Sen would not be able to call her a white-toothed dormouse any longer. Elated, she scooped up a fistful of apricot petals, wiped her mucky calves, and glanced along the dike to see how far she had to go. It was far, but she knew where to look when she got home.

Near the family hut, a straw basket wrapped in a banana leaf would be sitting among the branches of an old fig tree. It had been there before Sen's betrothal and came back with Sen when she was returned. The lid was fastened with a loop and stick clasp, and under it, crowded like newborn rats, laid a dozen packets of fluffy hemp and silken cotton-tree down, each tied with a thread of dry reed. Lan had admired them in secret a few times but dared not touch. Now, a flush of goosebumps swept over her at the thought of putting one between her legs. She ran all the way home.

Grandmother smelled her right away. "So, you have come of age." Lan's cheeks flared; she would have wanted to keep the secret to herself till dinner time.

"I knew it would come soon, just from looking at you. Go and clean up."

"I've cleaned up a bit already. I'd like to wait till Sen gets home."

"The young widow cannot do anything for you. She is not a model of good behaviour. Do as I say. Go to the pond and wash your legs. Then come back and get to work. The fish needs to be gutted."

"I'm a grown-up now, like my sister, and —"

"Ho, ho! You are still the runt of this family." The old woman's voice crackled like a tree snapping in a squall. "You will obey your family elders till you are betrothed. Then you will be released into the keeping of your mother-in-law. In my father's house, I was taught with the whip to behave like a virtuous woman. I taught your sister with the whip and will teach you the same way. I will not allow a runt to defy me."

"But I'm not —"

"I will tell Father that you have come of age; he will decide what needs to be done."

"My teeth must be stained. Father isn't the one to decide when. You are the one who performs the rite."

"Father will have his say. You will wait."

"I've waited enough. You said… after the flood waters go down. You said… after the dikes are rebuilt. You said… when I grow up a bit —" Lan imitated Grandmother's haughty pitch.

"Hold your mouth, Junior Runt. I will stain your teeth when I am ready. Now get to work."

"I'm begging you, Grandmother. I'm a good person… respectful of my elders… trying to do everything correctly… my errands. I don't want to look like an animal any longer. Like a corpse, or an ugly Chinese. Please!"

"I will speak to Father. You need to learn absolute obedience first."

"I've been obedient," Lan yelled and kicked the grass.

Grandmother's mouth flew open — her teeth like scorched wood, blistering blacker than black because she was furious — and the firecrackers flew out. "Disrespect… for your elders is unseemly… I have given birth to three sons… You are the runt. I will teach you deference… obedience…"

She grabbed a broom of dried twigs and swung it hard, striking Lan's back, swiping and scourging. Lan kept her arms and her eyelids down, hoping the submissive posture would calm Grandmother. But Grandmother only paused to turn the broom around so she could whack Lan with the wooden handle. Lan ducked. The handle slashed the air with a hiss and hit the dust. Grandmother hurled the broom across the yard and ran to the wall. She pulled down a rattan whip and — her chin quivering like a beheaded snake — swerved at Lan.

Lan knelt down, pulled off her grassy vest, and crossed her palms over her nipples. She knew the whipping would be severe. Father and Brother Toàn were not around to restrain Grandmother's flying arm. Mother would not dare interfere with the senior woman's will. Sen might try to beg mercy, only to earn some welts on her own back. Lan sunk her knees into the earth to endure the lashes without toppling over. Then she sucked her cheeks between her teeth and swayed forward and backward with the whacks. She peed down her thighs, and — erect and defiant — whimpered like a dog until the strokes weakened, then missed their aim, then finally stopped when Grandmother was spent.

She rose unsteadily, kowtowed three times, and said what the correct conduct required, because not to do so would risk having to live with white teeth forever. "I thank you for being my guide and a model of good behaviour, and promise to be respectful of your resolve to teach me to be a virtuous woman." She made another deep kowtow, picked up her vest, and took Grandmother's curt shrug as permission to leave.

She crumpled under a mangrove palm that crowded out the rushes just past the water wheel, sank her legs into the water, and tried to rub the crusty stains off her calves. Then she bunched up a lotus leaf and stuck it between her legs. From the pocket of her vest she pulled out a betel nut she liked to chew because it gave her teeth a reddish tint, which in some measure made up for the shining black she had been denied. She gnawed at the nut in rhythm with the lashes still echoing in her head. Her back was on fire. But her head was cool and as hardy as a paddy crab. She would get her teeth stained somehow... she would pester Brother

Toàn to speak to Father about Sen... she would call on the spirits to carry off Grandmother and avenge all the beatings she and Sen had suffered...

The still water of the pond was blanketed with water lilies, their purple blossoms fully open. At the far edge, a swarm of children waded in to pluck snails and paddy crabs with their bamboo ladles. Their bare backs glimmered like lacquer as they flocked around the tallest boy, who had a basket hanging around his neck, as if to admire a find. The bigger boys shoved aside the little ones, who jostled their way back in, and all of them shouted and squabbled and then burst out laughing and spread out again. The ripples spread out with them, bringing a whiff of carp roe.

A pair of white egrets, their heads bald and their backs fluffed with jasmine-white plumes, stood motionless at the shallow end. In unison, their bills stabbed the water with a quick lunge. Lan watched the impaled fish flutter and glisten in the sun and felt more sadness. She had pitied the giant birds ever since she was quite small and Brother Toàn had taken her into the tall grasses to show her their nests. The bluish eggs were hidden under the mantle of feathers and twigs. But nearby, in full pitiless view, laid the punctured red-veined carcasses of the chicks that had been killed by their older and stronger siblings.

Beyond the clump of reeds she saw Sen walking alone by the second dike, her shoulder pole weighted heavily, her silhouette forlorn. A full lunar year had passed since she had become a widow, since the river had swollen its banks, poured over the dikes, and swallowed the paddies. The God of the Mountain had tried to raise the hills and save the villages, but the God of the Water had proven quicker and angrier and would not be mollified with prayers.

The family had had little warning of the deluge. From the hill behind the water wheel, Father saw rippling waves scale the second dike and ran down, shouting to the women, "The waters, the waters!" In the courtyard, he corralled the family's two precious pigs and shoved them into a wicker basket used to store dry grasses. He dragged the basket to the carambola tree, the sturdiest tree around, and hung it on the lower bough. The animals, cramped and frightened, squealed pitifully.

Seeing Father go after the pigs, Lan tried to chase down the chickens but Grandmother called her back and threw two rope hammocks in her arms, yelling, "Run to the tree!" Mother rummaged around to salvage some raw rice, taro roots, and nuts, then waded precariously across the yard, holding the basket above her head. Lan pulled her up onto the branch. Toàn had enough time to rescue the pouch of fish hooks inherited from his grandfather and to throw some chisels and hunting gear into a sack — the waters swishing around his knees.

For several days, they lived in the carambola tree, Father and Toàn sleeping in one hammock, Grandmother, Mother, and Lan in the other. During the day, they gazed at dead chickens, clumps of thatch, wooden utensils, feather brooms, animal dung, and bloated bodies of rodents spinning in the current. At first, they fished out all the flabby carcasses and hung them on the branches to dry, hoping to roast them. But the wood was too soggy and the wind too strong to make a fire.

Then the heavy rain began. Lan, perched astride a crusty bough, watched the billowing clouds shape themselves into dragons and fiends. They surged down the river of the sky, their giant paws reaching down onto the flooded paddies and dissolving in the rippling whitecaps. The air around her felt laden with pain. Grandmother crouched unsteadily above Lan's head, tied to her son's waist by the rope. From behind the screen of sodden leaves Lan heard Mother pray aloud. Toàn lowered his legs into the water, still hoping to catch any edibles floating by.

All he caught was a splintered branch thick enough to carve. Restless and bored, he chiselled a crude water buffalo with no tail and a firebird with one foot. He gave the puppets to Lan to play with, and to please him she tied them to a bamboo string she had shaved off the pig basket and launched them on the waves. But all she could think about was, "Where is my sister? In her husband's village? Also in a tree?"

On the third sallow dawn, she heard the slats of the pig basket begin to sputter as the hungry pigs thudded about inside. She shouted, "Brother Toàn!" and he slid down from his perch, hooked his knees over a branch, and leaned out on his backside to pull the slats together. But the animals scuffled in panic, tipping their narrow prison dangerously from one side to the other, and the basket fell apart before the family's eyes — the churning waters carrying off the pigs, their chubby legs going down with the broken strips, their squeals gobbled by the current. Only the lid was left swinging at the end of the twine.

When the flood waters receded and Sen came home, she told the family that her husband had lost his life in exactly the same way. He was asleep in a makeshift hammock and the branch of a young pine gave way. When he hit the water, he cried out to Sen, who was dozing against the tree trunk, and she sprang for his outstretched hand and screamed for help, but his parents were stranded with their pigs on a ledge some distance away. Petrified, Sen watched her husband wriggle and clutch, his body entangled in the netting and the swirling debris, the waves carrying him away, his cries and her screams growing faint.

The horror of the flood was still vivid in Lan's memory. So was the shock, shortly after the waters had ebbed, of finding Sen at the foot of the chiselled log, muddied and defeated, begging Father to take her back — the joy of seeing her again sinking in the sorrow of knowing she had been discarded. Lan had felt then like the same helpless child she felt like now. She spat out the betel and scanned the watery skin of the pond, willing the husband's remains to appear. If by some miracle the waters had brought them all the way from his village and she found them, they could be given a proper burial, and his soul would not be condemned to eternal wandering, and Sen would have to show gratitude, and two families would rejoice, and Lan would be singled out for praise. But the gleaming surface of the pond surrendered nothing, the ripened lilies motionless as if moulded in clay, the ivory birds and young crab pickers gone.

TWO SUNRISES AFTER the spring transplanting was finished, Father stood at the edge of the lane to welcome the esteemed *thầy đồ* with a line of poetry he knew — *floating on the wing, I rise to meet my guest, forgetful of the wailing of the wind.* Toàn, his body and face tense, kowtowed to his master and led the way to the spot under the guava tree where a newly woven straw mat — Mother's work — laid on the grass. In its centre Sen and Lan had placed polished stoneware jars filled with fish brine, pickled apricots, and salted sesame seeds. A basket of freshly picked coriander greens rested on a bamboo rack at the rim.

Lan was delighted to see that Teacher Cường had brought his son Anh, a pasty child no older than four. The boy's mother had died the day after he was born, and there was a shadow of an orphan in his eyes. The paternal grandparents were raising Anh in his father's hut. Toàn said that during the day the boy meandered around the schoolroom, rolling and unrolling study mats on the floor and rinsing brushes, sometimes tickling the students' soles as they knelt over their tablets. Now, timid among strangers, he clung to the tassels of his father's robe.

Father beckoned the venerable visitor to his place of honour at the top of the mat and squatted on his right. Toàn took the spot on the other side next to the little boy. Mother had brushed her men's hair back with duck grease and they wore indigo blue vests over their loincloths. Father promptly filled three small gourds with rice wine and proposed a toast. "May your presence bring blessings to this family, and may good health and good fortune attend to you always." Teacher Cường raised his gourd up high. "A new Emperor is on the throne, His Majesty King Lý Nhân Tông— a young boy who reigns jointly with his mother, Queen Ỷ Lan. May the Gods shower them with blessings." Father and Toàn bowed their heads. Lan, sitting between Mother and Sen and watching the men from the distance of the upper level of the hut, felt her heart swell with joy — that the *thầy đồ* had honoured her family with his presence, that Father was so gracious, and Brother Toàn so poised, so very much Father's heir. If only Teacher Cường would talk about widows. There was so much more she wanted to know about Confucian wisdom than what she had been able to overhear when Toàn reported to Father on his lessons.

All four women wore their best hemp tunics and pink blooms of bindweed in their hair. But they would not sit with the men below, or eat with them. They would eat separately, up by the hearth, and only after the men had finished. Grandmother had prepared red sticky rice, cooked with the pits of momordica melon to give it the festive red colouring. The rest of the meal would be what the family could afford — steamed taro garnished with garlic buds, grilled sweet potatoes speared on a stalk of sugar cane, convolvulus greens boiled in ginger water, charcoaled chestnuts, and fried green bananas. Fortunately, Teacher Cường adhered to Buddha's First Precept not to harm another living thing, so no meat would be served. Meat was scarce in this household. Several sunrises had passed since a piece of pig tripe had been put on the mat, dozens of sunrises since they had eaten the last castrated cock. Lan could still relish the memory of its fleshy meat, and the fullness she had felt after the Lunar New Year's feast. And what generous portions the family had put on the Altar for the Ancestors!

For today's special meal, Grandmother had reclaimed the honour of portioning the rice, and scooped it out generously. Her bearing, Lan noted, was uncommonly meek, her face dutifully servile, and her eyes cast at a deferential angle. Mother, timid as usual, stepped down with the vegetables, her hands trembling as she placed the leaf-lined serving basket of roasted garlic and honey-glazed taro in front of the men, then quickly followed Grandmother up the chiselled log.

Compared to Father and Toàn, Teacher Cường looked pale, as befitted a man who worked indoors. His cheeks were puffy, and his double chin folded and unfolded as he talked. His long pigtail, tipped with an ornamental yellow gourd, wiggled across his chest. His arms were short, and he had to lean forward to reach the food, which he did immediately, plucking a chunky slice of sweet potato. As he munched on it he launched into a lecture on surrendering oneself to a higher spirit and the promise of the afterlife. Father and Toàn listened in silence, and when Teacher Cường concluded with, "Yes, yes, after a life of good deeds, you can be reincarnated as a superior being," Father asked, "How can a man change into something he is not?"

"Because Lord Buddha has shown us that any bad man can become good if he opens himself to the Buddhist Dharma."

"But it is Confucian wisdom that has ruled our families and villages since the beginning of time, ensuring peace and order." Father's voice rose at the end, inviting his honoured guest to confirm.

Teacher Cường fingered some chestnuts, and said that Confucian rules promoted harmony in the community. But Lord Buddha's teachings allowed individuals to reach a state of liberation and peace. "A social ethic is one thing," he said, "but personal enlightenment quite another." Lan saw Brother Toàn grimace. Like her, he probably could not understand the difference but knew better than to question his master. Like her, he probably hated to see Father lectured to. Should not Teacher Cường talk about Confucius? Should not Father ask him about the rules for widows? She frowned.

Grandmother stepped down from the hearth to serve the men more rice, and Father waved her to stay and eat with them. She accepted the honour with a deep kowtow and squatted by her grandson, her face glowing. As Grandmother reached for the honey-glazed taro, Lan felt her stomach grumble. Would any of the men's food be left for them? She was sure that Brother Toàn would eat small and salvage some nice morsels for Mother — who would share them with her daughters — but Grandmother might not.

She glanced down at little Anh sitting at his father's side and felt sorry for him. He had no mother because his father had no wife. Teacher Cường was the senior member of the Nguyễn clan in the village. To remarry, he needed a Nguyễn woman. She mused for a moment, knotting her fingers. Why not Sen? A widower and a widow, would it not be a suitable union? She cast an eye at Teacher Cường again — his puckered face and sweaty neck — and thought of a tree mushroom after the rain. His body was loathsome but then Sen, no longer a virgin, was an unworthy woman. The union would keep her in the village, wipe out the shame of her return, and relieve the family of the burden of feeding her. Teacher Cường's family would gain a daughter-in-law beholden to them for taking her in. She would have to work hard and dare not be as surly as she was at home. A perfect match!

Just then Teacher Cường belched and raised his head to commend Grandmother for her cooking, his eyes moving beyond her to take in the three women sitting by hearth. Mother and Lan swayed lightly but Sen was a perfectly-behaved widow; she never looked up or fidgeted.

Father began to say something about the heavy debts he had incurred after the flood to buy rice seedlings but did not finish. He turned to his son and then to his guest with an anxious expression. "Will the Chinese armies try to retake our land?"

Teacher Cường resumed his lofty tone. "The Song Dynasty has not forgotten its humiliating loss of the Việt territory. Chinese soldiers have raided our villages from the mountains in the north... A call for more conscripts is bound to come from the Capital. Only teachers and students will be exempt." Mother looked at her son, her face shrunk with foreboding.

Lan did not care about raids. She cared for Brother Toàn remaining a student so that he would not be conscripted. She needed him to talk to Teacher Cường about how suitable a bride Sen could be. She wanted assurance that life was well ordered and things could be arranged genially in her clan, one fitting measure at a time. It was fitting that Senior Sister be betrothed first, then Junior Sister, when her time came. But if Sen was left behind and continued to irritate Father and Toàn, Grandmother would find a way to do away with her. Such solutions were not unheard of in the clan, and she shuddered at the thought and sealed her eyelids, willing it not to be so. When she opened her eyes, she saw Grandmother was staring up, reading her thoughts word for word.

The meal over, the women stepped down to join their men in the kowtows of farewell. Father and Grandmother would take the honoured guest home. Brother Toàn was staying back. Lan tiptoed up to him and whispered over his neck, "Teacher Cường needs a new wife and the little boy needs a mother... from our village. Sen would be just right for both of them, don't you think?" He grunted but did not deny it. "Father would be vindicated... the whole family would..." He sighed and stepped forward and then Mother pulled Lan away from him.

AS SOON AS SHE caught sight of Grandmother's clay powder-pot with dry areca nut peels scattered around it, Lan knew. She gazed at them, numb and stirred, determined to stay poised and show gratitude. "Father ruled the time has come," Grandmother startled her from behind. Sweeping Lan aside, she pulled a scorched coconut shell and a stone chisel from her basket and began to scrape the charcoal powder from the shell into the pot. Lan watched, panting and swishing her tongue around her teeth, trying to let them know that they were about to lose their shameful whiteness.

After the evening meal, Senior Sister Sen, by custom Junior Sister's caretaker for the ritual, led Lan to the rice shack's wattle wall and laid her firmly on the ground. Sen knelt down by Lan's side, tied her hair behind her back, and gently stroked her cheeks till Brother Toàn brought a torch to Lan's face. Lan was suddenly scared and reached out to cup her sister's knee, but a stern voice commanded, "Hold your head back. Don't move and don't whimper." Grandmother dipped a cluster of areca nut peels in the charcoal powder and began to scour Lan's teeth with a steady circular motion, mauling every crack and crevice, the coarse grounds scraping Lan's gums, which began to bleed. "Don't gag or swallow," Grandmother warned when she saw tears dribbling down Lan's cheeks. More tears seeped down the back of Lan's throat but she swallowed only when she absolutely had to. She sealed her eyes tight and tried to breathe through her nose.

When the right side of Lan's mouth was done and Grandmother moved to the left, Sen slid into the vacant spot and guided Lan's hand to cup her other knee.

The first batch of peels was quickly used up and Grandmother turned to pick up a fresh cluster. Lan jerked with relief and tried to straighten her sore back but Sen pinned her chest to the ground. Lan's tongue was stinging and her eyes burning but she reassured herself that she was now more than halfway through the ordeal. Just then Grandmother muttered, "Your teeth are stony… like gravel. I may have to scour twice if the stain is to take… blighted nuisance." Lan's head was going up in smoke.

Presently, the scraping stopped and Grandmother barked, "Open your eyes." Her sweaty face retreated, and her hand came forward holding a gourd. "Spit out, then rinse your mouth." Lan spat and gulped. The rinse, made of lime juice and rice vinegar, stung to the very core of her teeth and set her throat on fire. Her eyes streamed sour tears. She closed her lips to hold back the howl but Grandmother cried, "Open," and thrust chunks of lime into her mouth. "Keep them in all night. You will sleep alone tonight. In the rice shack. If bad spirits find you there, they will leave us alone." Lan was frightened again; she had never slept alone before. And why would bad spirits be looking for her? She wanted to ask Sen but could not open her mouth. She let Sen help her to her feet, ring her arms tightly around her waist, and steer her to the shack. At the doorframe, she heard Sen whisper, "The most painful part is over. Soon, you'll look like me."

She lay in the murky shack listening to the hum of the night, terrified of being snatched by the spirits, alert to any sound that could be twigs snapping under footsteps. Her body hurt, from her scraped teeth to her toenails. Breathing through her nose or rubbing her cheeks did not help; there was no way to ease the pain. Feverish and dazed, she stared through the slats of the wattle wall and walked her eyes down the lanes of the stars that also seemed on fire.

A woman's shouting woke her at sunrise. She sat up and spat out the lime wedges, now marinated in blood. She gagged, clamped her throat to stifle vomit, and strained to hear more. That raspy and shrill voice, was it the matchmaker's? That fiery woman who had brokered Sen's betrothal two years earlier? She peeped through the cracks and could not see anyone but, all ears, heard Grandmother's muffled voice coming from behind the mulberry bushes, "It's been agreed... family." She forgot about vomiting. A betrothal was being arranged, for sure. Father must have sought Teacher Cường's consent when they walked together after the dinner. Or perhaps Brother Toàn had talked to Teacher Cường after his lesson and convinced him that Sen would make a good wife. Wild with hope, she shoved away the hanging jute rags that blocked her exit, swished her scorched tongue over her swollen lips, and crawled out of the rice shack, looking for Sen to tell her the good news.

TWO SUNRISES LATER, famished from living on green broth, Lan was allowed to rejoin the family. At noon, Mother put a tall heap of rice and grilled fish in front of her and said, "You must eat it all because you won't eat for days. The stain needs time to take." In late afternoon, Grandmother told Lan to lie down again by the wattle wall of the rice shack and to open her mouth wide. Lan hooked her thumbs over her belly button, hoping not to throw up the big meal. Holding a small piece of banana leaf between her fingers, Grandmother smeared Lan's sanded teeth with the viscous mixture, containing shellac, lemon juice, and rice liquor, that would stain Lan's teeth red. The syrup tasted sour and singed Lan's swollen gums. Her eyeballs burned behind her dry lids but she had no tears left. She let her body go limp and groaned inside, but kept her courage, musing how beautiful she would look for her sister's betrothal.

A coat of Grandmother's black paste followed the next evening. It contained cooked shellac and powdered iron, root of licorice and peel of pomegranate, cinnamon bark and sandalwood sap, anise and cloves, and other ingredients Grandmother would not divulge. She had simmered the mixture for hours, checking the colour and the pungency, tasting and spitting away, and adjusting the quantities now and then. At the end, she added some rice flour to turn the black liquid into thick paste.

Lan's family stood in a semicircle to watch the solemn ritual. Senior Sister Sen, once again the chief helper and guide, held Lan's shoulders pinned to the ground. Grandmother loaded a gob of the paste on a flat wooden stick, hooked her little finger against the corner of Lan's mouth to get the teeth bare, and smeared the teeth on both sides, blowing in some air to help the paste dry. Lan stayed rigid but calm. If a drop inadvertently fell on her tongue, she kept it firm and rubbed her thumbs together to take her mind off the ache. When the teeth were thoroughly coated, Father bent down to look and nodded his approval. Lan, grateful and jubilant, beamed at him. Sen lifted Lan up and said, "Grandmother did everything right. Just keep your mouth closed." Grandmother dealt out the final command, "Both of you go and lie down. You can sleep together again."

Back in their sleeping spot, Sen laid her Junior Sister in front of her and guided her right fist to Lan's chin to keep the singed lips from opening. Then she snuggled behind her and rested her arm on Lan's shoulder to hold it in place. "The first time it hurts badly but you took it well," she said. "I cried and squirmed and Mother could not hold me in place. Grandmother was livid and wanted to whip me. You also cried — for me — remember?" Lan had no strength to nod. "You're a grown-up and you look beautiful. You've been a dutiful Junior Sister." Lan jutted back her bum to acknowledge the praise. "I've been thinking," Sen continued. "Father hasn't paid Teacher Cường for Toàn's lessons. That small sack of rice he sent with you was just a token. When you first told me that the matchmaker was here I didn't believe it. But maybe you were right. Maybe Father is trying to pledge me to Teacher Cường to settle his debt. I want to be a pledged woman. I want to count for something. I don't want to eat Father's food any longer." She lightly jabbed Lan's ribs with her elbow and snickered, "And as Teacher Cường's betrothed I could use my rank to put Brother Toàn in his place. The snotty heir would finally get his comeuppance."

The rest of the family were climbing the chiselled log for the night and Lan had no strength left to think. But when she drifted to sleep, she dreamt about Senior Sister's betrothal; about the neighbours bringing ornaments; Mother, indispensable again, making festive garments; Sen laughing again. Teacher Cường's family and Sen's family sharing a feast — his pigtail adorned with colourful pods. Little Anh gobbling up sugar cane and beaming at his new mother. She dreamt about herself, Junior Sister, grown-up and beautiful, chanting a wedding ditty with the others, her charcoal mouth open wide.

Three sunrises later, after two more coats of the black paste had been applied and allowed to harden, Sen sat Lan down on the grass, fed her some thin rice gruel, and said, "It's done. Don't faint now. Swallow slowly." Lan had not eaten solid food in quite a while, and suddenly craved it badly, especially blackened meat. She recalled the meal that had sealed the betrothal with Sen's in-laws, for which Grandmother had roasted honey-crusted geese stuffed with berries, and grilled chunks of pork in her special way that made them as delicious as dog meat. Ah, to suck on one such charred morsel again. Sen's hands, cradling the coconut shell of rice soup, were right in front of her, and Lan reached out and placed her palms on top of them.

Mother's voice pulled them from her trance. "You must not go hawking in the market for now. Don't step any farther than the pond," she said to Lan.

Lan looked at Mother, surprised and hurt — why should she be denied her favourite errand, especially after days of pain and hunger?

"But I'm well. I can do my chores and show the market women my teeth."

"Father said."

How very much like Mother it was, Lan thought wearily. Always passing orders from Father, her own wishes — if she had any — quelled and buried. But why would Father want her confined? To give her a new chore now that she was a grown-up? Mother's eyes were aglow and she just stood still for a while, taut and earnest, before moving her arm forward as if wanting to touch her younger daughter. The arm hung there for a long moment hesitating, and then Mother let it fall. She did not look at Lan again but turned and walked away, dainty on her tiny feet.

GRANDMOTHER COMPLETED THE coming-of-age ritual a few sunrises later with a final coat of coconut-milk glaze, which gave Lan's teeth a lovely glossy sheen. The rainy season had just begun and Lan could admire her reflection in the puddles, her heart throbbing every time. But she also felt an odd heaviness around her — in the bend of the sodden branches of the bamboo saplings, in the soughing of the wind, in the clipped talk of family members. She tried to talk to Brother Toàn but every time she came near him when nobody was looking, he walked away.

After the midday meal, she followed Sen to the rim of the first dike to gather some algae for Grandmother. Together, they perched precariously on top of it, letting their legs swirl in the water. On the other side of the dike, rice seedlings quivered on their fragile stems, submitting to the stroking of the wind. Dank mist, trailing all the way to the bamboo fence that belted the village, made the air tremble. The horizon was a purple ribbon.

Lan nudged her sister with her foot, hoping for a kick back, but Sen did not respond. Lan nudged her with her hip. No reaction, just a chilly stare straight ahead. Lan followed the stare and saw Brother Toàn emerge from the bushes dragging a fishnet too big to carry. When he came close, she asked, "Brother Toàn, has the matchmaker been back to see Father, do you know?"

Sen's back stiffened and she snapped, "Yes, Brother Toàn. Tell us what you know. Senior Sister wants to hear it," the word *Senior* very strong.

"Father must consider things women don't understand," Toàn said sharply.

"Women understand what can be done when the family is in debt," Sen shouted. "Father could give me away as a pledged woman and still save the family's honour. You're Father's heir. You can tell him —"

"It is Father's right to rule on the women in this family, not yours," Toàn shouted back. "He cannot offend the gods or the villagers. He cannot lose face."

"Well, you've had some long lessons with Teacher Cường. Did you get a pledge for your sister... one of them? Am I to suffer the bane of widowhood?"

"If I must suffer the life of a teacher, you can suffer the bane of widowhood..." Toàn snarled.

"The bane of... but —" Lan stammered, dazed. She needed someone to hold on to but Sen was no longer at her side. Tufts of whitish puffs were blocking her view and Mother was nowhere to be seen. Brother Toàn's twisted face soared through the haze and faded away. She ran to Confucius, to hear a word of... counsel... wisdom? His face came into light — the skin with the same tint of a rotten pumpkin, the matted beard in place. But his lips were sealed.

Toàn hurled a stone into the water, and turned his back to his sisters. "Enough," he said. "Even if I wanted to change things, Father's word is the law for us all. You must know that. You're both grown-ups now."

BACK AT THE HUT, they waited out a shower, and when the sky cleared Mother took Sen to see the rodent traps Toàn had been setting up by the third dike to give the family more meat. Toàn followed Grandmother to help her bring back two baskets of guava fruit she had left at the very end of the lane. Father motioned to Lan. She put down her fish scraper and walked behind him toward the water. Just before a felled mangrove, he turned and began to climb the hill with the big boulder near the top. She followed. At the summit, he leaned against the massive rock, his face glistening with sweat. The muscles of his neck furrowed and when his mouth opened, his black teeth mirrored hers.

"It is my duty to rule on my daughters' future," he began. "You are homely but good-natured; your kindness is your saving grace. Your Senior Sister has been punished for her bad temper. She'll be sent to work for a family in another village."

Her eyes were downcast, her bare feet moored.

"I have arranged a betrothal to Teacher Cường. It is a righteous decision that will benefit both households. It puts my daughter in the care of *thầy đồ* who will educate my only son and shield him from conscription. You are young and chaste.

You must bear him many sons, mindful that your Senior Sister will not have any."

She jerked her arm out to halt Father's words but they were closing in on her.

"My decision puts you with a family of superior rank. Teacher Cường is devoted to knowledge and order. He will quench your maverick spirit. On account of his eminent position, the village betrothal tax will be waived. I have had Toàn arrange for, and I have accepted, an indemnity from Teacher Cường's family for our loss of daughter. The compensation must be repaid with hard work. You will submit to the rule of your mother-in-law and obey your husband."

Father swished his betel between his cheeks and his voice softened. "Your obedience to this contract is a repayment to your parents for your life, and the fulfillment of your duty to your ancestors and to posterity."

She lowered her head. Her tongue was a dry cornhusk. Her teeth were on fire. Father concluded, "Your vow to your husband will be till you die." She kowtowed.

She was in her thirteenth year and understood that Father had done his duty. She swished her tongue around her teeth and they felt soft to the touch. Her throat let out a cry, but it rang whiny and reverberated low. When the echo came back, the message was the same: "Your vow to your husband will be till you die." There was a silence, and then a voice, "Thank you, Father."

SHE LIVED A LONG LIFE as a dutiful wife and was widowed when she was thirty-five. A short time after Teacher Cường's burial, the family to which Sen had been indentured in a distant village released her from service, saying that, at forty, she was too old to carry water from the river or mud to repair dikes, and should

go and live with her widowed sister. At the gate to a tidy courtyard, hung up with scrolls of hieroglyphs, Sen was met by a stout
woman whose strained but still perky face transmuted from a
murk of confusion, to a shimmer of recognition, to a timid grin.
"You're my Senior Sister, right? You've come from far away?"

Sen stepped over the threshold and embraced Lan guard-
edly. "How have you been, Junior Sister?"

Lan looked frail but her voice rang strong. "I've had a fruit-
ful life... five sons... three already married, two at home... three
daughters... many blessings..."

Twenty lunar years later, when Lan died, it was Sen who
stood in the same courtyard handing out the mourning hats
of raw hemp and rough-grass shoes to the mourners who filed
by. She waved her walking cane at Lan's great-grandsons — two
dozen comely heirs who would carry the Nguyễn torch into the
future — shepherding them to the bier to watch as a black turban
was placed on her sister's head. A bowl of fragrant rice stood by
the hollowed trunk of the sandalwood tree that was Lan's coffin.
The mourners filled a dozen baskets with their offerings of salt
and silk, and lit joss sticks around the tablet bearing Lan's name.
On the first anniversary of her death, her First Son would place
the tablet on the Altar for the Ancestors in his home.

The cortège wound its way through the black-mangrove
ravine to a temporary burial site, where her soul would wait to
be judged. The men and boys followed the coffin on foot, but the
women lay on the ground along the route, chanting lamenta-
tions. Lan's daughters and daughters-in-law, her granddaughters
and great-granddaughters, had tied a piece of rough hemp to
their mourning clothes over their hearts, to show that their
hearts had been broken with grief.

Three lunar years later, when Lan's skeleton was exhumed,
her teeth had turned white again. Senior Sister Sen summoned

the dead woman's two surviving daughters to the final ritual of committal, always performed by the deceased's female kin. Together, the three women washed Lan's bones and laid them parallel in a small box to be interred with her husband's bones. At the burial ground, Teacher Toàn, stooped on the arm of his First Son and clutching a gift of rice in one hand and a puppet firebird in the other, said a short verse for his Junior Sister — *the mighty wind soars and takes you away to the valley.* Then he beseeched his old master, the venerable Teacher Cường, to receive his wife in his tomb. A Buddhist monk swathed in gold chanted prayers. The sullen gale wailed a lament.

The Mongolian Stake

In 1225, in the absence of a male Lý heir, the crown passed to the Trần Dynasty, whose kings would prove their mettle battling the Mongol armies of Kubla Khan. His grandfather, Genghis Khan, had already vanquished much of Central Europe, the Middle East, and the Far East. Kubla's horsemen invaded Đại Việt from their stronghold in China in 1257, 1284, and 1287. Three times in one generation Việt men had to march to war.

Ngọc at Dawn

MINUTES BEFORE SUNRISE, Ngọc is a lonely sentry on the mound by the duck pond. She is scanning the fields of maturing rice stalks, watching for any stirring that would give away the movement of enemy soldiers advancing on her village. Her eyes follow the curve of the land from the left, where the roof of the pagoda meets the sky, to the far right, where the lake that irrigates the village's crops lies in slumber. The rice fields are slowly coming awake with a ripple, and the mist coating the water is just beginning to rise. The watchwords rumble in her head: "Is this the day the giant dogs will come?"

The enemy will charge from the east, from the river shore. If they are foot soldiers, they will crawl on their knees, and only the quivering stalks will give them away. Ngọc must not miss that sinister rustling, that ominous dance in the heart of the golden sea. If they come on horseback, the trunk of the man and of the horse will show above the tips of the ripening kernels. The animals will rumble and snort, the riders grip their swords. When they get closer, the cracking of their whips and the rattle of their foreign tongue will smack Ngọc's ears. The air will swell with fear and she will run for her life. But not yet. Not this morning. This morning all is calm. On a grassy knoll behind her, the village's water buffaloes, their hinds melded into one grey slab, calmly chew their cud. Above and beyond them, the red flowers of kapok trees glow like lanterns.

Not long ago, the hour before the sunrise was the time when Ngọc and her husband came together in the alcove of Mother Hương's hut on stilts. His arm would reach out and his nails

41

would scratch the mat. Ngọc would pretend not to hear and keep him waiting, then swiftly roll into him and hug the back of his neck. He sucked the tip of her nose and nuzzled his good leg against her legs. Then he clamped her hips — his biceps as taut as drums — and hovered her above him like a butterfly. She arched her back and let her hair spill over his eyes. He nibbled her nipples and made her sway. She held on to the slope of his shoulders and whispered, "Good morning to you, Husband Hành." He pressed his thumb to her lips for quiet.

That was before the war — when Ngọc could bask in the glow of being the only woman in the village to lie with her husband at night. The Việt custom was for the men of the family to share a mat at one end of the floor and for the women to sleep together at the other end. Young couples took their lovemaking to the lime bushes after dark. But when his father fell on the battlefield, Hành ruled that he would not lie alone. His mother and daughter, Thu, would share a mat by the hearth, while he and Ngọc would sleep in the alcove. Mother Hương skipped a breath but said nothing for once and Ngọc's idyll lasted for two years. Until Second Wife was brought in.

Now that she is almost certain that her village is safe for one more day, Ngọc pulls up a wayward lotus plant from the pond and rolls the stem between her fingers as tenderly as she would her husband's flesh. She lifts the pale petals of the bud and peels them back to the very centre where the purple dew gleams like a gemstone. Guiding the tip of the bud to the cleavage between her breasts, loving its cool, she rubs it hard till the white liquid squirts out, then brushes the tender bristles against her nipples, stroking around and around, feeling her nubs ignite, letting her neck keel back, dilating her mouth for air. When her neck feels firm enough to hold up her head again, she droops her shoulders and returns the spent shoot to its bed. Most days, before the family awakens, before her crusty mother-in-law takes charge of the day and the morning wind begins to sough in the pomelo trees lining her lane, Ngọc shares a spell of passion with her Hành far away. The edge of the duck pond is her military post and her surrogate marital lair all in one.

At this very moment, she imagines, her Hành is probably tossing and turning on the sleeping mat somewhere by the shores of the Bạch Đằng River, crowded with other men under one roof, or maybe no roof, his mat on stony ground, or maybe no mat. His spear and dagger press against his chest and his crossbow rings his head, his fingers at the ready. His hardship, his distance from her, make her blood swell. "Good morning to you, Husband Hành. Where are you?" she whispers, stroking the air, touching his hair. "In a dream I saw you drive the iron drum to battle in a cart hitched to a water buffalo. With the roll of the drum you were summoning good spirits to the fighting men, or maybe you were passing orders from the general. You're my hero, Husband Hành. Stay safe and come back to our village."

Ngọc has been Hành's lucky wife for ten years. For him she rinsed her hair in lime-scented water so he could bury his face in it and gasp. For him she rubbed her body with chunks of coconut so he could sniff it off her arms at night and swoon with pleasure. To him she sent searing glances when they planted rice seedlings in the paddy, and he returned them with a twinkle. Even their silences, serene and mellow, bound them together like clustered pomegranates. Mother Hương frowned every time she saw Hành and Ngọc play hide-and-seek by the lake, and recoiled when they batted their eyelashes at each other. Once Ngọc overheard her telling her son that his wife was more seductive than a sorceress.

For the last ten of her twenty-five lunar years Ngọc has tried to be a dutiful daughter-in-law because Hành has expected her to be. When she left her parents' hut for her marital home, she carried a gourd filled with water to wash her mother-in-law's feet on arrival. Over the years, she has learned to live with the willful and ornery woman and the deadly snakes she breeds in a pit right by the house to have her own weapon against the Mongols. Her scornful asides, her nasty scrapes with village women, the reek of her sweaty body seldom washed. The stony weight of her voice.

Ngọc's name means "Pearl," and she has acquired the sheen of a pearl in her husband's eye in spite of failing to give him a son. Having delivered just one daughter, she knows she has fared better than the custom dictates. But now that Hành has taken another wife, she fears that her sheen is losing its glow, that onerous trials lurk over the horizon. What sacrifices will she have to make to survive them?

In recent months, Ngọc has already made two painful sacrifices. The first one, just hours before Second Wife and her sons arrived, was thrust upon her by Mother Hương, who walked into the marital alcove, collected Ngọc's garments into a basket, and said to her son, "The young boys, even though they aren't yours, will lie here with you. They must grow into manhood by your side." Hành stood respectfully silent, but Ngọc's blackened teeth rattled like stones — two offsprings of Second Wife's previous marriage would replace her by her husband's side. She was still reeling from that loss when an order came from the Capital and the village men left for war. Within three short months, Ngọc had surrendered her beloved — first to Second Wife and her sons, then to the general. She had had no time to prepare herself for either blow and was shocked to feel the bonfire of anger erupt in her heart at having her life torn asunder.

JUST OVER ONE LUNAR YEAR EARLIER, well before the talk of Second Wife or another war, three Buddhist monks arrived at the village gate one evening. "By the will of Their Majesties," they said, and asked to speak with the elders. They waited on the bridge suspended over the moat, jumping it up and down, testing the sway of its jute ropes. With their grey robes floating around their skinny legs, they looked like cormorants poised to fly. Curious village men ran to the shallow end of the moat, calling out, "Where are you from? Are our Kings well? Are you staying with us for long?" Howling dogs circled about and children stuck their heads out from behind their fathers' backs to peek at the travellers. When the elders emerged from the pomelo alley, the crowd stilled.

Ngọc scaled the pole to the attic, and stuck her awl between the strands of the roof's straw weave to pry them apart and watch the excitement. The visitors talked with great agitation, and the elders listened motionless, as if cast in limestone. When one of the monks swung his arm high and pointed to his bulging biceps, the crowd applauded. Then, the elders led the monks toward the guest house and the men and dogs followed.

At the hour of the evening meal Hành burst into the hut, his hair untied, his sweaty arms whacking the air. He slid into his place at the head of the mat, breathing heavily, his eyes casting about as if he had entered an unfamiliar place. After Mother Hương served him his rice, he stilled his fists on top of his knees without touching the food and said, "The monks have been sent by the Kings. They'll train all able men in wrestling. And in martial arts. They'll make us all fighters. They claim that any man... any man... can fight barehanded or with weapons. He just needs the courage and the skill."

Mother Hương snapped, "A lame man cannot be a soldier."

Ngọc lay on the mat that night and thought about her gentle husband's ability to swim like an eel and dive like a spear. Dozens of times she had watched him lunge into the water fearlessly, stay down much longer than seemed possible, and resurface a good distance away with a catfish between his teeth. When village men played "chase the duck" — five men after four ducks in the water — Hành was seldom the one left empty-handed. He was also a master oarsman, gripping the oars with his palms like a bear and pulling his weight better than the rest of the crew. But on solid ground, he was a man with a limp. His left knee, mangled during the escape from the Capital when he was an infant, had not healed properly. The village men called him "lame deer." Yet he could gird a pig in a jute bag, hoist it over his back, and carry it to market like anyone else. And like his father, he groomed and trained his cocks into fervid killers and they brought him much glory in the pit. "He can be a soldier like the others," Ngọc contended silently.

The second evening after the monks' arrival, all the village men were late for the family meal, and Hành, no less agitated than before but very hungry, gulped his food hurriedly before telling his women the exciting details. "When we quit the paddies just before sunset, we saw boys running toward us shouting orders from the elders: 'All men go straight to the Đình.' We squatted on the tiled floor around the stony cranes and turtles. The monk with the big biceps stood in front of the effigy of Cao Sơn, unfurled a scroll, and read from it an excerpt on the art of warfare — a stirring piece. Then he called on us to form an armed contingent to complement the royal troops. Our regent King Trần Thánh Tông, and his heir, King Trần Nhân Tông, who govern jointly — the son guided by the father — have knowledge that the Mongols will return in force. A martial art school has just opened in the Capital for conscripts of the royal family, and General Trần Hưng Đạo has ordered that thousands of recruits be trained. We shook our fists and hooted till the walls of our communal house shook and puffs of dust fell from the rafters. We chanted prayers begging our venerable guardian spirit to give us courage and in the courtyard every man stuck a burning joss stick in the sand of the stony urn. All of us are ready to fight!"

Mother Hương, who had been nervously sipping her herbal broth while her ears twitched, rose to her knees to have the last word, "A man without a son has no business being a soldier."

The next sunrise, after love, Hành said to Ngọc, "I've been a cock fighter long enough. I want to be a real fighter, like my father." She spun toward him with open arms and he rolled into her, consumed by fresh desire. After he rolled away, he fell to his knees before the Altar for the Ancestors. From the way his body curved in total surrender she knew that he was not mouthing his usual prayer for a son, but a plea to the spirit of his father to bless his life as a soldier. Every day afterwards she prayed for him, not expecting another war to come soon, not allowing that it might take his life.

But now that the prospect of being a barren widow has become real, regret, dread, and a vague hatred tug at her heart incessantly. Hành's death, she is coming to realize, will not just make her a widow — it will bring a lifetime of woe, reducing her to the lowly servant of Mother Hương and of Second Wife.

WASTING NO TIME, before the evening meal, the monks assembled all the able men of the village on a clearing shaded by the foliage of the pomelo trees to train them for war. Ngọc climbed the pole to the thatched roof, hauling her work with her — a bin of rattan splints, which she whittled with her awl until they were thin enough to weave into baskets and fishing nets. From her solitary perch, sometimes with her daughter, Thu, in her lap sharing a sugar-cane chew with her, she would fix her eyes on her husband — head shorn, feet bare, loincloth around his hips — as he and the others practised the basic movements of parrying and kicking. The men lined up in a low-hip stance to perfect blow-striking; they staged fights with scimitars and metal rods, and races while holding heavy stones. They threw spears at straw scarecrows. When they did a drill of slamming their fists against tree trunks, Hành slammed with such ferocity Ngọc let out a shout of glee at his dogged prowess.

Down below, preparing food around the hearth, Mother Hương did not see any of the drills. "Serves her right," Ngọc thought with rancour, remembering how the older woman had denied that Hành could ever be a soldier and how she cast stern glances at Ngọc whenever she was brimming with pride at her husband's growing swagger. She had also denied Ngọc the pleasure of cooking the evening meal for Hành after his father had died. Cooking was a rite of homage to the husband, and Mother Hương could have relented. She did not, and gutting ducks and chickens was all she allowed Ngọc to do. But Ngọc had found her own way with the ritual. Whenever she and Hành went bathing together, they made a fire first and left a heap of stones to bake in the embers. After the bath, Ngọc roasted on the stones the tree mushrooms she had collected and hidden in the bush, and dropped the crispy tidbits into Hành's mouth one by one.

Of course Mother Hương had every reason to be stony. For two long lunar years following her betrothal, Ngọc had had to report her monthly bleeding to the old woman and watch her wrinkled face curl with disappointment, then with displeasure, and ultimately, with indignation. When Ngọc finally announced the good news, Mother Hương said only, "You took far too long to live up to your wifely duty." The day Ngọc went into labour, Hành had gone to help with the clearing of trees felled by lightning. Mother Hương received the infant alone, and since she neither lifted it up nor cried with joy, Ngọc knew it was a girl. For a moment, she feared that the letdown woman might smother the newborn. More than one village family had dealt with an unwanted baby girl that way. But Mother Hương allowed Hành's daughter to live. Ngọc vowed to give her a boy next time.

Only there was no next time. The barren years went by, even though Mother Hương made Ngọc drink muddy and acrid teas and eat chopped mushrooms spiced with miracle salts. Once, she slaughtered a pregnant pig as a special offering in Ngọc's name. Twice, she sent Ngọc to the festivities honouring the Goddess of Fertility, where the shamans threw about a piece of sacred bamboo promising it would bring a male child to the woman who caught it. Ngọc missed it both times. She had disgraced her mother, her grandmother, and her husband's family.

Her comeuppance came when Mother Hương announced at the evening meal, "Before a soldier leaves for the front, he needs to sire an heir. War could come any day —" Hành jerked up his arm to stop her but Mother Hương tilted her head and said into his ear, "Your father would not forgive me if I failed in my duty... a second wife must be brought in." Ngọc dared not say a word because at the evening meal only Mother Hương and her son conversed, and because she knew the older woman was right: Hành was an only son and his lineage could not be secured by a daughter. Upon marriage, Thu, almost seven now, would move to her mother-in-law's home and bear sons and heirs for her husband's lineage. Hành needed a second wife — the thorn-barbed words scored Ngọc's heart.

The next sunrise the monks took the soldiers-in-training to the limestone mountains darkening the horizon to practise rock-climbing. They had barely left when two royal runners arrived and hung the trees with parchments carrying orders from the Kings. The village herbalist, who doubled as teacher, read them aloud: *All able men — dig tunnels and gorges, to trap the enemy and link villages together. All able women — stock food and water in mountain caves to have a hiding place.*

Ngọc threw herself into the work. For weeks she and the other young wives carried food and water to the older men who were not in training and who took to hacking at the earth with axes and mallets, digging pits and ditches the Mongol horses would fall into. They hewed out trails that circled around and led nowhere, or ended in ravines where the enemy riders would be trapped by Việt men lying in wait to drop rocks on them. At night, Ngọc wove tree-twig rugs to cover the traps and hide them from the enemy. When the work was done, the entire village came to admire the grid of cleverly camouflaged trails and decoys, and the men and women yelled together, "You come here, Mongol dogs, and you will get your bone."

When the soldiers returned from the mountains, Hành's soles were as rough as lizard's hide and his toes hardened to a grip like bear's claws. Late into the night, Ngọc rubbed his coarse skin with pig grease and kissed his lacerated ankles, loving the music of his moans, hating the thought that her time as his only wife was running out.

THE BLEAKEST MOMENT of Ngọc's married life came the day the three newcomers arrived on foot, looking dusty and dishevelled: two boys, about Thu's age, carrying small bundles of family belongings, and their mother a few steps behind them clasping the withered forepaw of a hare. Ngọc stood in front of the family hut, between her husband and her mother-in-law, hands behind her back, fingernails stabbed into the flesh of her palms, eyes lowered. She raised them long enough to note that while Second Wife was younger, she had pockmarked cheeks, frightened eyes, and a shrunken, worn-out look. Ngọc had told Thu to wait till the kow-tows were exchanged to play a tune on her wooden flute to welcome her stepbrothers to their new home. While Thu played, the boys did not look at her at all. At dinner, Mother Hương filled Second Wife's rice bowl before she filled Ngọc's, the one and only time that Second Wife would be served before First Wife. They ate in silence and after the meal Hành ushered his stepsons to the alcove and helped them unroll their frayed mat next to his marital mat.

That was in late spring, and now it is almost fall and Hành is gone to fight the Mongols. Ngọc craves to hear his voice again, and, seeing the sun rise above the water, she casts Second Wife from her thoughts and goes back in memory to what Hành told her about the enemy from the north. "Their horses are taller than our Việt workhorses; they look like giant dogs — ten times big-ger than our dogs," he reported when he returned from the patrol that collected Việt bodies during the previous invasion. "The rid-ers spur them to gallop until the beasts foam at the mouth and shoot their arrows skillfully, but on top of a giant dog they are a visible target. And our ground troops also aim well." And then he showed her three Chinese hieroglyphs tattooed on his arm, and in a victor's voice read to her what they said: "Death to the Mongols!"

At the time she felt tender-hearted with him, but today she feels disconsolate and defeated. It puzzles her why the chestnut-skinned horsemen would want to roam the earth and trample on her land. How can they not stay put on the sacred grounds their forebearers walked and are buried on? Have they been cursed by the gods? Mother Hương has the answer: "They're a horde of thugs. They suck the milk from the tits of their oxen and shear their goats to weave the hair into clothing. The general will take care of the brutes!"

THE GIANT DOGS and their awesome riders have shadowed Ngọc from the very beginning of her life because she was born the year the Mongol horsemen attacked the Capital for the first time. Ngọc's father fled with his three wives — the youngest one pregnant, seven children, and four goats and their kids, to his sampan on the Red River. He helped deliver Ngọc on the floor of that boat, and she spent her earliest days in a mossy cave offshore, where young mothers breastfed their babies and the older children too, if there was no other food for them. The royal family with their newborn heir, also born on the river, was hiding nearby.

Now, thirty lunar years later, the chestnut-skinned riders are threatening to take her husband's life and ruin hers. Sometimes, Ngọc has a wild wish to get a glimpse of them galloping along the dike. But she knows that if they appear she will have to obey the drum's "Abandon the village" command and run to the caves. In the stillness of the morning, with no Mongol menace on the horizon, she turns her thoughts to the adversary at hand — the two women at home who are a threat here and now.

The arrival of Second Wife has relieved Ngọc of having to scour the pigpen, gut the chickens and fish, and — a real boon — catch lizards for Mother Hương's odious snakes. These foul chores have now become Second Wife's chores. But Ngọc is determined not to allow Second Wife to relieve her of the connubial duties. She is sure that she can give Hành more nighttime pleasure than that worn-out, pockmarked woman who will spend much of her time bringing babies into the world. Ngọc will work around her pregnancies and confinements, stepping in whenever her husband wants her. That way, even if Second Wife brings forth a son, Ngọc will keep a tender spot in Hành's heart. "Mother Hương will favour the wife with the fertile womb, but I will put up a fight," she vows. "I will bite and scratch and whack, if I have to. Second Wife will find out that my fists are also made of lizard's hide."

The prospect of Hành not coming back is more terrifying. When a short time after he left for the war Second Wife displayed her stained proof that she was not with his child, Ngọc nearly fainted with relief. But Mother Hương howled to the sky and turned into a hag overnight. She slithered around like a snake — her tongue flickering — cursing her step-grandsons when they got underfoot, smashing pots against the wall beams, and damning the invaders at every turn. Ngọc had never seen her so wild.

Mother Hương has always run the household like a hardened general. Now she is at war, and Ngọc is in ashen panic when she realizes that if Hành does not return his mother will blame her for encouraging him to become a soldier and for causing the rupture of the family's lineage. To the end of her days, she will blame First Wife for all those barren years, not Second Wife, who in those same years gave birth to two sons and has barely had a chance to prove her fecundity in her new home. The young mothers of the village, glowing in the abundance of young sons, will always look down on the ill-fated family with three widows under one roof, inflaming Mother Hương's fury even more.

Without Hành, Ngọc's cherished shelter could become a fenced-in pen. Her status as First Wife will no longer matter. The homely Second Wife will triumph because she has her two male trophies. When Thu leaves for her husband's family, Ngọc will be left at the mercy of Mother Hương and of Second Wife and her growing sons. Will Mother Hương treat her spitefully and put a whip to her at will? Or will she declare her the family's curse, release the latch of the pit, and let the snakes do away with her?

Such fears throb in Ngọc's head as the sun clears the bamboo fence that marks the boundaries of her village and of her life. She fears for her future with the paralyzing rage of a rabbit caught in a snare. Before her, the fields run to the sky and dissolve in the morning mist, forming stripes of rainbow pink, gliding into mauve, shading into grey, and then the blue of the sky taking over. Against it, the rice plants stand like an army of iron reeds poised to thwart any Mongol riders. She turns to walk back and at the old gatepost bends to lift the corner of a grassy cover. It masks a trap into which a Mongol horse will fall if it manages to come this far across the quilt of ponds, swollen creeks, and submerged rice fields of her Việt countryside. The hole is deep, and arrows are embedded in the soil at the bottom, their tips pointing up. Ngọc shudders at the thought of the carnage that might happen there. She shudders again, dreading her own battle — the one she will have to fight at home.

Mother Hương in the Morning

Upon awakening, Mother Hương's first thought strikes her like an arrow. "What is General Trần Hưng Đạo's battle plan for today?" And then, "Is he being served a decent breakfast?" She thinks like a wife and mother, a caretaker of men. She pushes her sleeping granddaughter's head to the side, glances at Second Wife tucked in slumber around her sons, and at the spot where Ngọc was lying before she left for the duck pond. She twists her hair into a careless knot, scratches her armpits, and ambles toward the hearth, her cracked heels catching on the earthen floor.

She parts a mound of rice husks with a twig and blows at the embers to fan a spark to life. From the water pot kept only half full, she pours a few drops over her fingers and grimaces at the meagre fistful of rice and mushrooms at the bottom of the morning basket. On General Trần Hưng Đạo's orders, villagers in Đại Việt keep only small rations of food and water by the hearth. The rest has to be hidden, out of sight and out of reach of enemy soldiers should they enter the village suddenly. Mother Hương sets the earthenware pot to boil and rests her spine against the bamboo shaft that holds up the thatched roof and the mud wall of her hut on stilts.

In the serene stillness of the morning, she can picture the general in one of the stalagmite grottoes by the sea. His knotted trunk looks like an overturned tree ripped out of the soil, the matted strings of his grey hair creeping like wild roots around his neck and shoulders. His knees brace a coconut shell filled with rice as he reaches with his wooden chopsticks to the common soldierly bowl of grilled seaweed. Mother Hương imagines her son, Hành, on the general's right, eating rice with his fingers from a torn piece of banana leaf, eating ravenously because it could be his only meal of the day. His skin, like that of the others around the circle, glistens after the morning swim. The men eat in silence, in communion with their mothers and wives far away. In the early hours of the morning their hearts need to fill with home.

Around the jagged entryway to the grotto, they have stacked their swords like bamboo poles — tips pointing upwards. They have sunk their axes into a dead tree trunk, and stabbed their daggers in the soil. Their spears lie flat on the ground like freshly scythed rice plants. Mother Hương lets the piercing image fade and begins her morning prayer:

> *May the enemy soldiers and their giant animals suffer*
> *May they wilt and die in the muggy heat*
> *May their boats fill with water*
>
> *And let our soldiers be victorious*
> *And let my son be saved*

Her last wish is for the general: *May his wisdom be eternal, his valour unwavering.*

Her husband and brother dead, her only son on the battle-field, Mother Hương is at the helm of a manless household. She hates her burden as much as she hates the Mongols. She believes wholeheartedly that it is against the law of nature for a woman to be in charge. The general must bring her son back. If he does not, the brutal family yoke will be hers for life.

SHORTLY AFTER Mother Hương gave birth to her son thirty lunar years ago, the Mongols and their Chinese henchmen attacked the Capital of Thăng Long for the first time. Throngs of terrified men, women, bawling children, and squealing animals ran west to escape murder and pillage. Her husband dragged a wheelless cart that bleated piteously beneath the load of their belongings; his parents, right behind him, lugged their brittle bodies over ruts and puddles. Mother Hương tramped down the sodden track at the end, her infant on her back. Resting under the stars for the night, the family could see an orange rainbow arch the sky. The fires swathed Thăng Long in charcoal and the wind brought the fumes westward, parching the throats and eyes of the escapees. Mother Hương had no way of knowing that her future daughter-in-law had just been born up the river.

It was the youthful Prince Trần Hưng Đạo who saved the Capital — and without a single battle. First he ordered the in-habitants to flee and take their food and animals with them, so that when the enemy entered Thăng Long, they would find it empty. Then he left the Mongols alone to suffer their fate. His soldiers, hiding in the countryside, booby-trapped the invaders' supply trails with well-concealed ditches, and with noose-like snares spiked with blades to injure the horses. They burned the Mongol food wagons with fire arrows. In quick strike-and-run raids, small bands of Việt men snuck up on the sleeping enemy at night with dogs and stones to sow panic and traumatize the men and animals. But they did not confront the enemy in an open field. Driven mad with harassment, wilting in the fervid summer heat, and felled by unfamiliar tropical diseases, the dispirited Mongol soldiers began their miserable trek back to the coast. There, they found the boats they had left behind punctured or sunk, their soldier-guards nowhere to be seen.

When a military runner brought the news that the enemy was gone from the Capital, Mother Hương returned and, impressed beyond measure with the guile of the shrewd commander, vowed to raise her son to follow in his footsteps. Whenever Hành's tiny head poked through the bundle hanging across her chest, she imagined his adult head rising out of a uniform.

Now that the clever prince is general, will he save her son's life again? Will he return him safely to be the master of the household? Mother Hương's husband fell by the shores of the Bạch Đằng River during the previous Mongol invasion. The three-year period of grief has just ended, and she has burned her mourning garments and come out of seclusion. But she continues to talk to her husband daily because his spirit is all she has. In the evening, she kneels down in front of the Altar for the Ancestors, lights the incense sticks, and makes a votive offering of rice, fried pork, and bananas to the gods. As soon as she can discern her husband's head in the whorls of smoke, she kowtows and tells him that the people's loyalty to the Kings has not wavered, and that his son is in the trenches with the general, who is holding the line with the enemy from the north. In the hollow of the Altar, her husband's shadowy face advances and retreats, never coming close enough for her to touch. When she asks what she can do for the general and his troops, he says what he has always said, that when men are at war, the duty of women is to wait and pray. Mother Hương wishes to be given something to do, but to press her husband would be disrespectful. So she listens reverently, caressing his image with her eyes, waits for the round of incense to burn out, and lets him go.

Then she is alone with her burdens, which are many. Ngọc, the flawed daughter-in-law she never allowed herself to love because Hành loved her too much, has not borne a single son to help fill the painful void left by the men who have died fighting the Mongols. Other women have — plentifully — and now the village is brimming with radiant grandsons and heirs — not one of them Mother Hương's. These days, Ngọc is always out some-where, whispering endearments to her husband, because Ngọc is bent on holding Mother Hương's only son in her grip even when he is away. Second Wife, who has increased her new family's burden by two small mouths and has not yet become pregnant, likes to work the paddies and takes her boys with her. Only Thu, sprightly and playful like her mother, lingers by the hearth lis-tening respectfully to her grandmother wail: "Three women and three children under one roof, and no man to rule the household. Only the general can save us."

Mother Hương's confidence in the general is absolute. She trusts his simple and practical strategy of "empty hut and garden." If the enemy appears, run!

> Abandon the village and hide in the hills and forests.
> Leave no food or water behind, or booty or spoils to plunder.
> Set fire to the yellow grass. Open the dikes and flood the
> green meadows to deny the feed to enemy horses. Take away
> from the invaders all provisions and comfort. Leave them to
> sweat in the heat and swelter of empty villages.

"The man is clever," Mother Hương mutters. "He has a mind and a heart." Five lunar years earlier, well before the second invasion, two village elders went to the Capital, to a rally of noblemen, military men, and wise men, called by the Kings who wished to know if their subjects were ready to fight the Mongols again. The elders reported back that men from all corners of Đại Việt had lifted up the roof of the Royal Citadel cheering their Monarchs, calling for war. That in his "Proclamation to Officers and Soldiers," General Trần Hưng Đạo had cried, "I can neither eat nor sleep, my heart aches, and tears trickle down from my eyes; I am angered at not being able to tear the enemy to pieces, pluck out his liver, taste his blood."

Then two lunar years later, on the eve of the second invasion, the very young King Trần Nhân Tông, terrified of the mighty Mongols at the gate, summoned General Trần Hưng Đạo and asked, "Must we fight the foreign devils again? Our people have borne agony enough. Must they suffer anew?"

The general kowtowed. "Your Majesty shows great heart… but if you wish to surrender, Sir, I beg you to cut off my head first." The King had to bow to the grit of his royal cousin, who once again let the Mongols in, left them to squirm in heat and hunger, then chased them down the river to the sea. When the royal family returned from hiding and the Kings ordered the rebuilding of the torched Capital, the general advised that the walls of Thăng Long could wait, but the starved and bloodied people could not. Their loyalty was the first wall to uphold. The solemn words were repeated around the temples and pagodas. Mother Hương sings them like a mantra to this very day — *The walls of Thăng Long can wait, but the starved and bloodied people cannot.*

Seeing her husband enthralled with the burning images and the general's knife-edged oratory, Mother Hương remembers blurting out shamelessly, "Your son is lame. You're old but fit enough. Go to war and bring honour to your family." He was one of the first to enlist and later one of the first to die. Mother Hương was left with her infirm son, who she believed could never be a soldier. But less than three short lunar years later he was.

SHORTLY AFTER her son and the village men began their military training, wanting to distract herself from thinking about war, Mother Hương took to weeding the village's *thuốc nam* garden. One day, when she was on her knees among the beds of mangosteen, white rose, mulberry, and galangal, she came upon a nest of newborn cobras. They brought memories of her twin brother with whom she had scavenged the countryside for frog eggs and bird nests, trying to outdo him in rare finds. He had taught her that snake wine was valuable because it made men more virile. With a twig, she moved the wormlike infants from their grass-cushioned pit to the pocket of her vest, and took them home. Within days they died, but Mother Hương told Ngọc to get a shovel and help her dig a pit under a clump of kumquat trees. She lined its bottom with stones and sturdy elephant grass, and fenced it with bamboo stakes to keep small rodents out. Then she wove a willow-twig trunk and started stocking it with lizards, toads, and slugs.

From then on, whenever she worked in the thuốc nam garden, she kept a lidded basket nearby. When she spotted a young cobra sunning in a furrow, especially the regal white cobra, she crouched low, prodded it with a stick till it lifted its head, swiftly ringed the thumb and forefinger of one hand around the stiffened neck, slid the palm of the other hand under the coil, and popped the snake onto the basket. When it rambled inside, she giggled like a little girl.

By late fall, when the men returned from training, she had half a dozen cobras to show her son. When Hành noted how greedily they ate before settling down to hibernate, his mother gloated, "Wait till you see how well I can sell them in the market."

In the third month of the new lunar year, the cobras shed their skins and were ready for mating. Mother Hương took the first batch of eggs as a good omen for the fertility of her household and proudly showed them to two older women who happened to pass by. "These snakes can kill us. You should breed them beyond the village gate," they warned, but Mother Hương knew better. "I was breeding snakes when I was half my grand-daughter's size," she lied. "You know nothing about snakes. I do."

In the market, she bartered cobra meat for the salt, shrimp, or seashell necklaces that travelling vendors brought from the coast. She gave the necklaces as gifts to the women in the village she had been rude to. When word came that the Mongol armies were heading south again and her son had been hurriedly con-firmed as a recruit, her parting words for him were, "When you bring home victory, there will be snake wine to welcome all the soldiers." She did not tell Hành that at the back of her mind she had planted her very own war strategy: if the Mongols came close, she would set her cobras on them.

NOW THE SOLDIERS are gone to war and Mother Hương's anguish is aggravated by boredom. The village is an empty shell. The Đình is silent. No disputes are judged; no council meetings or communal feasts are held. The roof of the Đình slopes sadly, the lovely clay tiles — the pride of the village craftsmen — dulled. The once fearless lions sculpted at the roof's upturned corners look defeated. Once a week, Ngọc and Second Wife polish the urns and statues of the Đình, but the aged elders hardly ever go there. Only the women come. Every day before sunset, Mother Hương, her two daughters-in-law, and the rest of the womenfolk of the village stand before the effigy of Cao Sơn, praying that the guardian spirit keep their soldiers from being clawed by a tiger or a bear. That the Mongol spear not find them. The beady eyes of the giant cranes and turtles stare at them mournfully.

Worse, there are no cockfights. Wife and mother of champion cock fighters, Mother Hương so loved watching the combat roosters go at each other with their feathers, caked in magenta and turquoise, stiffly pricked up. The metal spurs (in place of the amputated real ones) pointed like darts. The crimson combs jiggling. The hot-tempered ivory roosters attacking mercilessly with the phoenix kick, while the men chomped their betel nuts to the bone, shouting, "Blood, blood," and the women egged on the men and their cocks from a distance. Mother Hương the sole woman in the inner circle, because after Hành took his fallen father's place there, she demanded a spot by him to light the incense stick that timed the fight, and the cock fighters relented.

"By what right do the Mongol devils hold sway over the earth?" Mother Hương hollers while threshing rice, her throat choked with rage, her arms cutting the air like a battle axe. "Who gave them permission to trample over our lands? That pig-headed Kubla sitting on the throne of China — how dare he demand from our Kings the right of passage through Đại Việt? Just to conquer more lands in the south?" She flicks her finger at the spittle around her mouth and yells: "Thieves and plunderers all of them! The general will make Kubla pay with his neck!" The women working around the common courtyard rest their beating rods, kick the husks to the side, and squat down to take a break from threshing. They wait to hear what else their headstrong neighbour will say. On the subject of the Mongols she speaks for them all.

MOTHER HƯƠNG NEEDS to hope against hope, because if her son does not return to father an heir, the rest of her life will be a torment. She bit her tongue when Hành first brought Ngọc to his sleeping mat because she thought he was trying to show that, with his father dead, he was taking seriously his obligation to posterity. Every morning, she listened to the young couple's morning rustles, and giggles, and thumping. Sometimes the partition of the alcove shook. That no son and heir had issued from such labouring was a grievous mystery. Her own couplings had been outdoors, her body pinned to the grass. She had strangled every moan because she knew from her mother that it was improper for a woman to show carnal pleasure, that she must heighten her husband's gratification by throttling her own.

When Thu turned six and no other baby had arrived, Mother Hương quietly told her son, "It's Ngọc's duty to find you a second wife, but I wouldn't trust her with the task."

Hành sighed with relief. "It's been on my mind... even though Ngọc..." They agreed she should seek advice from the oldest elder in the village. The man knew of the family's plight and told Mother Hương of a widow with two boys in a neighbouring village, in a family with too many grandsons to feed.

Two sunrises later, Mother Hương crossed the bamboo fence carrying, in a fancy snake-shaped wicker basket, a gift of fresh snake meat wrapped in a lotus leaf. Two village boys met her at the fence to help carry her other gift — a live piglet trussed up with twine and decorated with rosebuds knotted around the neck and the tail. In mid-morning, an older man met them in his courtyard, looked over the gifts, and said he would be glad to get rid of his widowed daughter-in-law, provided she would be kept even if she only gave birth to girls. Mother Hương agreed to make a payment of five sacks of rice over the next year for her new daughter-in-law and her two sons. Those boys would grow into sturdy men and protectors.

Every day after Second Wife arrived, Mother Hương prayed that she was with child. The day she found out she was not — and Hành had left by then — she ran to the forest and ranted at the sky. What on earth was happening to her life? First her husband dead, now her lame son gone to war. Why had she waited so long to bring in a fecund woman, allowing Ngọc — a lowly daughter of a third wife — to bewitch Hành for so long? Stupidly putting the family's bloodline at risk. Why had she not forbidden Hành to train for war and given Ngọc a sound flogging to stop her flattery? If Hành dies, how will she manage the crippled household? How will she rein in his two widows? To quench their passions, she'll have to work them senseless in the paddies. At home, she'll have to crack the whip. Will her son's spirit restrain her flaying hand? And what about her own life amidst spiteful villagers? Villagers who have little regard for widows, even war widows.

Such terrors grip Mother Hương's chest as her home fills with the morning light and she catches a glimpse of Ngọc on her way back from her military post. Her throat is dry from rehashing her woes but the flame has died, the water is unboiled, and there is no time for tea. Hungry piglets are squealing below. Before sliding down the bamboo pole, Mother Hương stiffens her spine and summons up the face of General Trần Hưng Đạo. Staring him in the eye, she commands, "You be brave and pitiless!" Then, remorseful of her effrontery before the great warrior, she kowtows and implores, "Bring my son home. I beg you."

Hành in the Afternoon

The scorching sun high above his head, Hành wades into the cool ripples of the Bạch Đằng River. He is about to probe its floor for patches firm enough to support the weight of a steel-capped log. Every day, at low tide — the water up to his hips — he feels around the tangled weeds and loose stones of the riverbed with his lizard-hide soles and toes. When he finds solid gravel, he hacks out with his dagger a hole big enough for the thick end of a log to fit in. Then he guides the men of his platoon to the spot, and they bring in the giant spear and pound it into the hole at a slant — pointing inland. The trunk has to be set low enough for the steely tip to be hidden below the surface, but high enough for it to pierce the hull of an enemy boat as the tide carries it out to sea.

At high tide, the water well above his head, he leaps from a boulder, soaring in the air like a combat rooster, and — the dagger held between his teeth pointed down — he dives to the bottom to make sure the logs are holding firm against the swelling tide. All the while, he kicks his legs lightly to keep himself down as long as possible. When his ears begin to ring and he knows he has only a few seconds of air left, he marks with a wooden stake the logs that are loose or set too low, so that rocks can be hauled in to steady them. By then his lungs are racked with pain, and he swings his body around, points the dagger in his mouth upwards, and pushes off the river floor, his good leg and his bad leg kicking furiously. He loves every moment of his singular challenge.

Well before Hành's arrival at the start of the rainy season that had just ended, soldiers of the Bạch Đằng River platoon had set up camp at the mouth of the river, in the rushes between the ocean and the grey lagoon, where the sea breeze twirled the tall grasses around them and licked their sun-baked backs. Day after day, they felled trees with their axes and skinned the trunks with their chisels. They hewed the tips of the naked logs into sharp points, and capped them with pointed hats of steel to make them into giant arrows. In the evening they trimmed the cut-off branches into even lengths and fastened them with twine across two parallel bamboo poles to craft narrow one-man rafts. Bronze-winged jacanas and red-crested kingfishers flapped overhead and squawked hungrily before swooping down to spear any salty scraps of the sea. At the water's edge, white ibis birds alighted to peck on the sand fluttering away from the foamy ripples. Every now and then, over the waves, the bannered tips of the Mongol boats came into view.

Hành had been transferred to the elite royal unit because of his reputation for being as skillful in the water as a sword-fish. Before sending him off, the men of his village contingent had tossed him in the air a dozen times hooting and yelling, "Hey, hey, lame deer, make us proud!" For two days he walked in pouring rain behind the military runner, alternately elated and petrified, reluctant even to contemplate what Fate had in store.

By the seashore, he joined this elite Bạch Đằng platoon of fishermen-soldiers who farmed the ocean for a living. They have lived along the sea for so long they can feel in their veins the pulse of the currents and of the undertows. They can read the face of the moon — the ruler of tides. New to big waters, he watched in awe as they mounted bamboo fish pens on stilts, waited for the tide to rise and wash the fish into the pens, then waited some more for the tide to ebb and leave the fish trapped inside. "We're getting ready for a daredevil mission," they explained to Hành as they gauged the height and the length of the waves at high and low tide. As if on command, the water swelled, contracted into ribbons, and surged into the tunnel of the river to meet them.

"We need to arm the bed of this waterway," his commanding officer interjected, "and you will be our 'bottom man.'"

Hành's head and limbs crackled with excitement as he shouted, "Yes!" only to be corrected at once, "Yes, Commanding Officer."

Life in the royal unit is very much to his liking: disciplined, ordered, and manly. All day, the soldiers work diligently, and at night, far away from their women, they share stories of hand-to-hand brawls they have fought and wrestling matches they have won, and their plans to groom their sons for the wars to be won.

Before sleep, he wanders among the tall grasses hoping to meet the ghost of his father, who fell somewhere near this site, or to catch a glimpse of General Trần Hưng Đạo, who often takes a walk before dark to see how the work is progressing. How thrilled Mother Hương would be to see her hero up close. Hành has left her behind hopeful for a grandson, and maybe her wish has been granted. He does not know. His mother and his two wives are where they are meant to be; he sees no need to worry about them. Their work is nowhere near as important as his, which is to be an elite diver, a key man in a daring plan, and maybe even the champion of a heroic mission.

His hero is General Trần Hưng Đạo, whose story, which he heard from his fellow soldiers, is so gripping, so instructive, that he takes it as a guide to his own conduct. The general, a scion of a powerful Trần family, was two years old when his pregnant sixteen-year-old mother was taken away to be betrothed, as Second Wife, to her husband's ten-year-old brother, who was the King. The boy, who had won the crown for the Trần clan through an arranged marriage to his playmate, a child princess of the ruling Lý Dynasty, was too young to father an heir. By betrothing a Trần princess, already pregnant with a Trần baby, to the boy Trần King, the ruthless family would quickly seal its claim to the throne with a Trần heir. The soldiers told Hành how the general watched his heartbroken father grieve the loss of his wife and unborn child, and how he resolved to avenge his parents' honour not at court but on the battlefield. "They say he speaks bluntly to the Kings on military matters, but stays away from any Trần rivalries. He's ordered his own sons to steer clear of all court intrigues because fighting the Mongols is a greater cause," they told Hành and he thought with relief, "So even the royals have to struggle and make sacrifices to have an heir. They just make their women do what needs to be done." When he asked them how many sons the general had, they said, "Oh! Many," and he felt a raw pang of envy and resolve in his chest.

Within a week of Hành's arrival on the river-mouth site, the entire Bạch Đằng River platoon was summoned to the general's bamboo-and-twig tent, where they heard him announce that if his battle plan was successful he would end his soldiering and go back to writing poetry and studying history. Go back to his youthful concubines waiting at home. When the soldiers cried out in disbelief, he shouted back, "Forty years in the trenches is a lifetime!" They fell silent, respectful of their general's wish. They knew that he had already sent word to the Royal Family to evacuate the Capital once more — men, chattel, and livestock — so the Mongols would find nothing to loot. That he had ordered his land commanders to steer the Mongol horsemen into combat only in thick forests and muddy swamps where horses were least effective. The enemy had to be ambushed on water, he told his troops, because water was their weakest side. "All we need is one clean tidal cycle, a steady flow in, and then a strong ebbing of the tide out to the sea," he said. High above his head shone his strongest adversary — the moon. He knew how fickle it could be, so he clasped his palms, lifted his head, and mouthed a plea: "Let the tide not come low! Let the tide not come late!"

Unversed in military strategy, Hành wondered how effective mining the river with steely stakes would be against the Mongols, and how many Việt soldiers would have to die in the general's devious scheme. But his mat-mate explained that the saying "Fight the long with the short" had always guided the general's life. "He never allows his troops to face the enemy head-on when it's stronger in men and arms. He's a stalk-and-ambush man — like a wily cougar." Long after the mat-mate had fallen asleep, Hành ruminated how he also needed to be patient and cunning. If he resolved that having a son was his greatest cause, he could bend his wives to his will. But his heart also belonged to the general's cause, which was calling on him to lay down his life for his country.

"If the mighty moon can be made to play into the crafty man's hands," Hành tries to convince himself now, "I can make it play into mine." He is becoming very proud of his own exploits. Away from his wives, he has had to rein in his carnal longings, and without his mother at his heel, he can think and act decisively on his duties as a soldier and as an heir to his father's heritage. Elated to have excelled as the "bottom man," he aches for more trials to come his way. The general's longevity is his great consolation. "The cougar has survived countless wars — forty years... All I need is to survive just this one."

The general's new order for him is that on the day of the battle he is to steer a one-man raft close to the Mongol boats as the tide carries them out, and with his crossbow shoot burning arrows at them while not letting himself be hit by their spears. He is ready for the mortal challenge. But in his head, he also hears his father's order: "My only son must fulfill his duty to posterity before he surrenders his life on the battlefield." The dual obligation tears at him mercilessly. If he dies for his country, his living villagers will honour him as a hero. But the dead of his lineage will curse him for having failed to repay the filial debt he owes them.

"How righteous Mother Hương was," he concedes, "to rule that a second wife be brought in. But why did she not do it sooner so that I could be sure to father a son before leaving for war? Why did I, the man of the house, allow Ngọc to hold me in her grip for so long?"

Some nights, when he gives in to the temptation to think of home, he resolutely calls up the faces not of his wives but of his stepsons. He lets himself bask in the memory of their heady musk on his sleeping mat, of their boyish pranks around the hut, and of their wiggly bodies, one under each arm, as he carries them home from the paddies, swinging them around till they shriek with fear. "I'm a battle-ready army man, but I need to sire sons of my bloodline," he tells himself, his body taut, his knuckles locked. "Second Wife must save me from ignominy. If she fails in her duty, I'll take a third wife." One morning, he crafts a prayer: "I'm not afraid to die, but I will strive to stay alive. You spirits know it. Give me the wisdom to best the enemy. Save me!"

ON THE GENERAL'S ORDERS, the elders of the three villages closest to the mouth of the Bạch Đằng River have read the stars and the moon and chosen the time when the tide will come in strong and move out stronger. It is the sunrise of that auspicious day, and Hành's platoon, their heads camouflaged with twigs and grasses, is burrowed in the trenches. When three burning arrows pierce the sky, giving the signal to begin, a squadron of Việt junks sails toward the mouth of the river, pauses in full view of the Mongol vessels coasting out at sea, and retreats behind the bend. With the sun at its zenith, the junks move forward again, let the enemy watch them manoeuver their craft as if getting ready to charge — then pull back once more.

The Việt junks emerge for the third time just as the tide is about to swell, and this time the enemy takes the bait. The chestnut-coloured arms of the Mongols pull their oars through the soaring current. Their vessels ram the waves into the tunnel of the Bạch Đằng River in pursuit of the Việt junks, now seemingly in retreat on the sweep of the incoming tide. Buried in a sandy trench, shielded by the sun-warmed rocks, Hành trembles at the sight of the fleet of Mongol boats choking the river from shore to shore. His spine is like a steel-capped arrow ready to soar, but momentarily his heart halts. How on earth will the river hold all the blood about to be spilled?

The Women at the End of the Day

The last piece of war news Mother Hương has heard comes from an itinerant salt vendor who said that the Mongols had entered the mouth of the Bạch Đằng River and would be heading inland soon. The village women wait by the fence, holding their children close, ready to run for the caves as planned. At sunset, they feed the children cold rice cakes and light no fires, out of reverence for their soldering men fighting to hold the enemy back.

In late morning, children climbing up to get at the ripened fruit at the crown of a pear tree spot a convoy of men spilling out of the horizon, and run down the centre alley of the village shouting, "They're coming, they're coming!" Instantly, the village drum booms out the frightful "Alarm! Alarm!" cry. Ngọc, who has just beheaded a chicken, flings the dripping bird in the air and darts into the courtyard looking for Thu. Mother Hương springs from the pigpen and squeezes Ngọc's arm in dread. They run with the others, the children leading them to the east. Over the edge of the bamboo fence they can see the line of hammock-bearers scurrying across the meadows, fading away in the greenery, reappearing closer. The women know. They pause long enough to let out a shriek and run back: to get the fires going and the water boiling, to fetch the bundles of hemp and herbs and rinses from storage. Ngọc slides into the secret dugout by the back wall of the hut and rummages among the bundles. Mother Hương kicks over two wooden pails to empty them of the soaking snails, her mind drumming the supplies she needs to dress gashes, stabs, burns, broken bones... She yells to Ngọc not to forget the torches and when she turns she sees Second Wife flying toward her across the paddy screaming, "I'm here! I'm coming!" Her boys, some distance behind, are braving the sludge, wailing, "Mummy, wait!"

Drenched in mud and blood, the men are being lifted out of the hammocks one by one. Some are morose and listless. Others moan softly, relieved to be touched by the hands of caring women. Some are dead. Mother Hương stands guard at the gate, her hawk eyes searching for the face she yearns to see. She points the hammock-bearers to a ditch, which drains the water from the pond during the rainy season, where the dead bodies can await burial. Ngọc, turned into stone, cannot bear to look at the dead but scans the faces of those holding on to life. There are so many and they all need her. She runs to the spot under the trees where the wounded have been laid, throws a fistful of crushed soapnut-tree seeds into a pail of water, and begins to pass a mossy sponge over the crusted blood and dirt. Mother Hương, who has saved a gourd of duck fat just for this hour, is right behind her, smearing grease on burned flesh. On her heels is Second Wife, who has placed her boys at the head of the line with palm leaves to fan the soldiers' faces. She herself is ready to lay poultices of moss and peat on open wounds. The women move in tandem, washing, greasing, dressing, pausing to stroke a shattered chest, then on to the next casualty, and the next.

As darkness falls, the children light torches and the flames move along with the women. The scent of herbal oils fills the air but cannot veil the stench of scorched flesh. From afar the wind sends doleful sounds of penned animals crying for their evening feed.

Mother Hương holds a wooden splint to a soldier's badly crushed arm with one hand and wraps a banana leaf around it with the other. She fastens the cast with a piece of twine and asks, "You stopped the Mongols on the river? They aren't heading this way?"

"The Mongols will never come here again," he says. She aches to talk more and ask about her son, but cannot linger, and how would this man — who is not from her village — know Hành? As she moves down the line, she hears some snatched sentences: "... out on the tide... the river on fire... all the way to China." A group of boys drags in a pot of freshly cooked rice and Ngọc portions it out to the hammock-bearers, lotus leaf by lotus leaf. She listens as they talk about "black smoke rising over the ocean... bodies of scorched sea hawks on the sand." With so many wounded men around her, she cannot bring herself to ask about just one.

Eventually, well into the night, after most of the men have been attended to, Mother Hương wraps some dry leaves around a tuft of yellow crabgrass, and twists the bundle into a small torch. With the feeble flame lighting her way, she staggers away from the blood-splattered site, across the pumpkin field, and through the thicket of pine saplings that lengthens into the main alley of the village. At the Altar for the Ancestors she sinks to her knees. Her blackened teeth rattle as she tells her husband what she knows: "Our soldiers lured the Mongol boats into the riverbed over the steel-tipped stakes... and our ground men fought them off from landing on the shore... then the tide carried the Mongol boats back impaling them on the stakes… and our soldiers shot fire arrows at them." She can tell her husband nothing about their son, so she whispers with a fading breath, "Our soldiers were brave… victorious!" She pulls herself up, intending to light a joss stick of thanksgiving, but her torch has burned out.

Ngọc is the last to come home at dawn. She finds Second Wife already snuggled against Mother Hương in deep slumber, and, too exhausted to push her away and reclaim her rightful sleeping place, she curls up at the edge of the mat. But sleep does not come. She remembers her grandfather telling her once about their ancestors playing a similar trick of iron-tipped stakes on the Chinese invaders long ago. How she laughed with him and cheered the cleverness of their Việt people. The battle scene then must have been the same as now — the horses, at least ten times bigger than dogs, plunging through water streaked with ribbons of crimson, the shipwrecked enemy clinging to planks of driftwood, their heads jerking on the waves. She strains for the head of her husband among the crowd of rafts but cannot see him. The hammock-bearers told her that the chestnut-coloured devils were done for, but that many more wounded will be coming.

Mother Hương wakes amidst the sour sweat of her two daughters-in-law and the reek of her own laden body. A dull thud rattles her chest. Is it the beat of her heart or the echo of a crossbow ejecting arrows into the air? She tries to doze off again, hoping to see in her dream the mangled Mongol boats on the run toward China. But what she sees is her son, astride his narrow raft, his legs slicing the water like oars, his arms shooting fire darts. She runs to the water's edge just as a furious wave drinks in his wobbly craft and carries it away from her into the open sea. She wades forth, shouting with all her might,

"Turn around! Come back!" — but the roar of a thousand voices drowns her out. Only her two daughters-in-law hear her, and First Wife Ngọc turns her face sobbing to the mat, leaving Second Wife to pull Mother Hương into her. She steadies the trembling body and runs the hare's paw over the quivering cheek, "Hush, hush. You stay calm, Mother Hương."

END NOTE: The victory over the Mongol fleet at the Bạch Đằng River in 1288 is a pivotal event in the history of Vietnam, on a par with the victory at Dien Bien Phu in 1954, which ended France's colonial domination, and the battle of Saigon in 1975, which terminated the American intervention. General Trần Hưng Đạo remains a revered figure. Several of the wooden stakes, now over 700 years old, are on display in the museums of Hanoi, Bach Dang, and Ho Chi Minh City.

The Queen of Mulberry

The Lê Dynasty took the throne in 1428 and advanced Đại Việt with impressive reforms. Its longest ruling monarch, King Lê Thánh Tông (reigned 1460—1497), a poet and historian, ordered the law codified in the esteemed "Hong Duc Code" which recast many Confucian tenets to include Việt customs and traditions. He also opened up the Imperial Examination, allowing talented sons of commoners to vie with the sons of the well-born for the coveted careers in the state bureaucracy. The Examination kept the men in the Capital for months.

THIS IS WHAT I DARE REMEMBER: under the verdant thicket of the mulberry grove, First Wife and Overseer Dũng pursue their wanton pleasures. Sprawled on the grass, they elbow the branches away and he rings her chest with his arms and spins her through the trees. They roll down the furrow like a watermelon. He stops the tumble when she is on top of him and slithers his palms down her spine, kneading and nipping her thighs and groaning like a cougar. She snuggles his neck and arms with her chin, her hips throbbing. He rubs his chest against her nipples and moans, "My precious blossom, my lady moth." She presses her fingers to his lips to still his gasps, to better hear the sounds from the village. Lest they bring vigilant signals, lest they be caught. When she hears her children call, she tears loose, slides her robe over her head, and flies out of the grove like a winged fairy who need not worry that her hour of reckoning will come.

MY SILKWORMS HAVE no more patience with my absences than my children. In the morning, when they hear me coming, they curl up their heads to meet my hand. I scatter mulberry leaves over their writhing bodies. They take the pulpy flesh into their tiny mouths, sucking on it softly till only the naked lace-like netting remains. I lift the wiry remnants away and strew more fresh leaves for them to crawl over. Snug in their shallow wicker baskets, they swell like ashen embers, pearl grey and pudgy. Late in the day, I come back to bid them good night, holding my torch high so as not to startle them. They lie motionless and spent, and I savour their calm.

The life path of my silkworms begins in a mound of silvery eggs that look like tiny heaps of sand. The eggs swell till a black larva emerges from each shell and lies very still. Several sunrises later it sheds its scaly crust and turns into a caterpillar that never lies still. After eating ravenously for days and nights, it spins a strand of silk around itself, a golden cocoon. My servants drop the cocoons into hot water to kill the worm entombed inside, then leave the soggy globules on the grass. When the globules are dry, they unwind the softened threads, discard the tiny corpses, then spin the threads into strong yarn... and weave... and when they bring the finished cloth to me I design lovely garments for myself and for sale. My life with my silkworms has been better than my life with Husband.

BEFORE HE LEFT for the Capital, Husband instructed his properties' overseer, Ông Trần Quốc Dũng, to take care of me, First Wife, his precious son, and his two daughters, and to read Husband's letters to me. Husband had hardly left and the rainy season had not yet ended when Overseer Dũng came to the house holding a scroll in his hand and telling my maidservant that he had to see me. I scrambled for a gown and coiled my hair in a jumbled knot. When I stepped out he stood there drenched in the morning dew, kowtowed three times, and said, "Husband may be away for a long time. Maybe the entire spring. Maybe through the summer too. Overseer Dũng is a humble servant. In Husband's absence, his duty is to see to First Wife's happiness. To take away any household worries." He turned, and walked toward our giant almond tree, and I followed instinctively, as I would have followed Husband.

The tree, weighed with leaves and buds, was like a thatched roof. We sat beneath it and the lower branches combed our hair.

He told me about unruly servants — how he gave them two warnings and, if they did not heed them, a whipping — and about other household matters. "I expect at least three dozen piglets to be born this spring and about that many bales of silk to take to market by the fall." His voice was haughtier than when he talked to Husband. Never before had I faced him so close or been given such details. His gaze was scorching. My face was becoming a glowing ember and the fan in my hand fluttered by itself.

"Husband will not return for a long time and his mother can come here only in spirit. First Wife is Queen of the household and can tell Overseer Dũng what her pleasure is," he said.

My pleasure? This could not be. My pleasure could come only from being a dutiful wife to Husband and seeing his children bring him pleasure.

"First Wife's Husband will soon be Mandarin. She is entitled to make demands." He reached for my fan to help me cool myself, as he used to do for Mother-in-Law, and his hand brushed mine. I fastened my fingers around the fan's handle until his arm retreated. He brought Husband's scroll close to his face and read it briskly:

> On the third day of my journey to Thăng Long, late in the
> afternoon, a fierce wind sent the grasses and the leaves
> swirling around. The downpour began at sunset. Before
> Husband's very eyes, the leafy crater that was to be his bed
> for the night turned into a puddle. Thunder rumbled
> through the night and lightning scorched the sky, leaving
> Husband cold, despondent, and at the mercy of wild beasts.
> In the morning, the ground was covered with steamy haze;
> the path to the east seemed to be going in circles. Thankfully,
> three bonzes happened by and pointed the way. They will
> deliver this letter.

Husband wet and cold in a storm and going in circles in the mist? How he must have been riled by his impotence. How lucky I was to have been harvesting leaves in the mulberry grove at that time, and away from his anger. Overseer Dũng chuckled, rose, kowtowed deeply three times, and quickly walked away.

THE MULBERRY GROVE has been my refuge since Husband brought me to his house ten lunar years ago, a place to cry in loneliness for my parents and my home. Father had always disdained the shiftless peasants, but when he was approached by one who owned some land, he had me betrothed to his First Son, aiming to give me a lifetime of security. When I arrived in Husband's house, Overseer Dũng kowtowed to Husband first, and then to me, and held his head down as we passed. The back of his neck was sinewy and sweaty. I tiptoed around my new home, observing that the brooms stood packed in a narrow nook and the hearth was ringed with stones — all of them white and sternly uniform in size — and the many chopping-and-cutting tools were aiming their grim blades at me. An austere kingdom.

Later in the afternoon, as is the custom, Mother-in-Law walked in to receive me, her face as flat and grey as a stone tablet. She lurched at me, and pulled me in and out to have a look, overpowering me with her bulk exactly the way her son would do later that night.

Was it Husband's callousness that made me fall into infidelity as soon as he left, and in a shameful moment of recklessness dishonour my parents' noble design? When a gloomy reverie comes over me, I see my head sticking out of a wooden cangue that weighs down my shoulders, telling all that I am a vile adulteress. My hand cannot reach around the yoke and my Junior Sister has to feed me. She is a woman of cold stares. Her censure frightens me more than that of Mother-in-Law, whose vengeful ghost follows me step by step.

At home, I was raised into goodness. Mother taught me that virtue seals a woman's honour and makes her superior to men. She was a gentle soul and had a talent for carrying a tune. Often strangers — sellers of pearls or royal runners — stopped at her door to rest and listen. When she finished her chore and her song, she would ask about their trade and linger to hear their stories. She never failed to give them good cheer for the road — some spiced mango chunks or her deliciously crisp banana fritters.

But Mother-in-Law was not a welcoming woman. The only visitors that stopped at her door were striped wild pigs coming out of the forest to mix with her pigs around the trough, or wood grouse that alighted among her chickens to scavenge for grains. After another scolding from Mother-in-Law, I would watch them snort and peck in the courtyard, trying to fool myself that they were my confidants, my mates, the silent witnesses of my turmoil. Until she chased the intruders away. The mulberry grove has been my one faithful friend. Its white blooms, gentle and innocent, tease my nostrils with perfume, tempting me to breeze through them with my eyes closed and my hair to the wind. By late spring the pollinated blooms become succulent berries pricked with black hairs. The day the second scroll arrived, Overseer Dũng found me in the grove and startled me. My palm closed around a ripened cluster and purple juice seeped through my fingers as I motioned him to read:

> *The first decree after arrival commanded us to memorize*
> *the names of the Living Members of the Lê Dynasty,*
> *which we must never say or write. In place of these*
> *Venerable Names we must use blank space, add a stroke*

to the word, or make a different phrase — even in casual conversation. The Examiners can fail us if we use the tabooed appellations. Husband's ink-pot and brushes survived the journey well.

Our living quarter is a barren yard, well-fenced and well-guarded. The ground is furrowed with muddy ditches and the bamboo slats under Husband's mat sink into the bog. Some 300 candidates are here, sons of Mandarins and landowners, but also of lowly country teachers and other commoners. Many commoners are not correctly attired, mangle the language, and display their lowly ways. Yesterday, one of them, instead of summoning a servant, tried to wash his own garments.

In the afternoon, we were shown around the Examination Compound and the enclosure for the Examiners' lodgings nearby. From there, we could see the big dike along the Red River that protects the Capital. It is an earthen wall shielded by a bamboo hedge and a moat. The apricot trees are in bloom, as they must be at home. The banner by the lake says, "The King looks for talent." Husband's pride swells knowing that he is among the talented. Tomorrow, we will be given our Examination Tablets.

THE FIRST SUNNY DAY after the rainy season, I was squatting at the doorway mending my daughter's straw-and-silk doll when Overseer Dũng came out of nowhere holding a scroll tied up with the now-familiar red cord. He motioned to the almond tree but I told him to wait and called out to the children to come to me. "Read the letter to all of us," I commanded and he obeyed.

*In Thăng Long, the huts of common people are made of
clay and paddy husk pasted over bamboo or timber columns.
They must not be higher than the Royal Dwellings. Many
are grouped according to the trade of the tenants. The Bakers
Alley adjoins the Examination Compound and we salivate as
the delicacies are carried by.*

*The alleys bristle with noise and commotion but all hustle
pounces aside when Mandarins are carried by. Their
palanquins are ornamented according to rank. The ornate
palanquins for senior Mandarins look like floating pavilions.
The sable bearer leads the way and the parasol carriers provide
escort, so that one can see the cortège from far away. It is an
awesome sight. Husband's Venerable Mother was correct
when she cried, "Oh, the grandeur of the Mandarin's life!"*

*The First Segment of the Examination will begin at sunrise
and today a candidate who sneaked in a "helper" to assist
him with the composition received his just punishment.
His head was clamped in a bamboo head-hold as he was
flogged and we jeered. His name will go on the List of Those
Who Disgraced Themselves and he will be expelled.*

*After the flogging we took a walk in the alleys, among
rumbling carts and rickshaws, and hawkers weighted with
shoulder poles selling candied ginger and "Hands of Buddha"
cakes, which I have never tasted before. They were delicious.*

THE CHILDREN GIGGLED at hearing that their father liked the
cakes. Overseer Dũng chuckled with them, pleased to have
brought us good news. Then he turned to me: "Do I have your
permission to take the children to catch crickets? It is the season." The children answered before I did and it took me only a

moment to decide there would be no harm in it. Husband had often allowed him to take the children fishing and they had had too few outings in recent months because our family was in mourning for Mother-in-Law. I did not think of being included until I heard him say, "Your mother will come and watch you."

He pulled some netting off a hook, motioned us to follow him, and led us to a quarry overlooking the river that cuts through our village. There, he settled the children along the crevice of a craggy boulder and told them to have their sticks ready. I was left standing at the far end. Overseer Dũng's grassy vest, soaked with sweat, clung to his body like bark to a trunk. He scooped water from a puddle with his hands, poured it into the crevice, and cried out, "Watch carefully, they'll be coming up!" Almost immediately, scores of insects crawled to the surface, plump and shiny, their carapaces crusty black, their gangly brown legs scrambling. The children prodded them with sticks into the netting. When there was a quavering heap of them, Overseer Dũng tied a knot, threw the netting over his back, and led us home.

He stepped over the threshold to the big anteroom at the head of the procession and walked straight to the hearth at the far end, as if it were the right place for a man to be, the stupefied cook and her daughter scurrying back to the mud wall. The children exuberant in his wake, First Wife in the children's wake, not saying a word but cringing at what Overseer Dũng might do next. By the hearth, he crouched down with the children — something Husband would not dream of doing — opened the netting, lifted one big cricket, snapped off its head, wings, and hind legs, and stuck the long nail of his little finger into the neck cavity to scoop out the guts. The children gagged as the slimy muck poured out. He chuckled with pleasure again, clamped two fingers firmly around the cricket's empty chest, and slid them down to force the rest of the innards out the back of the abdomen.

The cook and her daughter watched from a distance, mortified at seeing a man soil his hands by the hearth. They sent me a puzzled look. Overseer Dũng caught it and quickly ordered: "Clean up the offal and steam the carcasses." The two frightened women rushed to do so at once. He looked at me triumphantly, pulled a metal wok off the ceiling hook, and reached for the pig-fat gourd. He fried the crickets himself, adding some lime leaves that sat in a basket and some kumquat juice that the cook handed him with trembling hands. His fingers danced like moths around the fire and beads of sweat trickled from his forehead to his neck. His skin was darker than mine and leathery. But oh so luminous! The children watched him with their mouths open; they had never seen a man touch a wok. Beads of sweat dripped down my temples too, even though I was quite away from the flames, and my grassy robe was clinging to my body.

We squatted around the hearth, eating the crickets with our fingers, the children crowding and touching him from all sides as they would have never dared touch their father. Their mother also overcome with desire to touch him as she would have never dared touch Husband. Her head giddy with pleasure and with foreboding. Overseer Dũng looking straight at her and saying, "I must go back to my duties now." And after licking his fingers, turning to the children with a wink, "I'll have some new fishing nets for you soon."

On leaving, his kowtows were so respectful, and I gathered the leftover crickets into a gourd and placed the offering at the Altar for the Ancestors. At the evening ritual of mourning, the children lit joss sticks and scattered jasmine blossoms around the tablet bearing their departed grandmother's name. Changed into a more somber gown, I led them in prayer, singing loudly enough to blot out Mother-in-Law's shrieks of censure for the unseemly levity of that day.

JUNIOR SISTER IS VISITING when Overseer Dũng brings the fishing nets. Her home is at the rim of the village, by the paddy, where animal butchers and other landless peasants live. But she knows everything. She knows that Husband will be away for months taking his Examination, that he has charged Overseer Dũng to take care of us. But when she sees the children prance around him, a scowl comes on her face. Oh, how I hate her caustic looks. Does she have to be so high and mighty? To remember every transgression? And hold grudges forever? Even when she was little she was willful and obstinate. In our parents' house it was my duty, as Senior Sister, to whip her after she stole ivory beads from the servants or drowned the cat they had been saving for a festive dinner when it ripped her thumb. The whipping — a dozen strokes with the same bull whip my parents used on me — was meant to teach her a lesson, and I meted out the punishment faithfully. Sometimes, I added a stroke or maybe two, which, as Senior Sister I had the right to do. She wouldn't know, because it took her a long time to learn to count beyond her five fingers. But even though it happened long ago, she's always just waiting to pounce, to avenge the beatings and vent her bile because our parents chose a rich husband for me and cast her off to a lowly animal handler.

She complaints that her husband has too little land, that I spend too much time with my silkworms and have too many silk gowns, that her four sons run her ragged and since I only have one son and my daughters hardly count, I should visit her more often and not wait for her to come to me. Especially now, when I no longer have to work in Husband's shop.

"Just once you should try wearing my grubby vest and working by the hearth and with the filthy animals all day. Just once. No Overseer Dũng in my household. Just two slothful servants — no respite," she bewails.

"You have a concubine to oblige your husband — that is a big respite," I retort.

Junior Sister smirks. She has shared the yoke of her husband's lust with his concubine for years, but has six children with him while the concubine has just one. Maybe she gets little respite?

She is right about Husband's shop. I no longer work there and miss it terribly. More than I miss Husband. When I stopped nursing my third child he brought me in one day, when Mother-in-Law was suffering from the heat, to tidy up a heap of scrolls he had tossed in the corner, and when he saw how swift and helpful I was, decided I should come most days to keep his records in good order. There were many land transactions in the district — people wanting to buy but not pay the full price, landless peasants looking to rent. Husband knew how to read and write, so only he could record the details. My duty was to greet the visitors, pull out any prior scrolls, dust them with a hand broom, and lay them open on Husband's mat. I put the rolled-up scrolls of big transactions into a trunk, those of smaller clients into clay urns. I taught myself to recognize clients' scrolls by folding the corners in my own special way, or inserting light and dark chicken feathers in them, or memorizing the shape of the ideograms at the top. Mother-in-Law did not understand transactions and preferred the hearth to the shop. She was glad to have me under Husband's yoke all day; she welcomed the chance to raise my children her way.

When a Mandarin came in, I greeted him, took off his shoes, scraped the mud off the wooden soles, polished the leather straps to a shine, and put the shoes back on his feet when he was ready to leave. Mother-in-Law spent her last years dreaming that her First Son would earn the right to wear footwear and enjoy all the other privileges reserved for Mandarins. When she stopped by the shop, she talked incessantly to the clients about how she would make his ceremonial tunics — in red and blue silk — and stitch his formal undergarments with her own hands.

Overseer Dũng came to the shop at the end of each lunar month to show Husband the household accounts. The first time he crossed the entrance when I was there, he kowtowed to me deeply. My eyes were cast down looking straight at his bare feet — knobby and soiled. On the way out, he kowtowed again, and I noticed his muscular shoulders and the sheen of his sun-scorched skin stretched over the furrows of his ribs. His body looked less harsh than Husband's, and his manner... well, I had not known much kindness in my marriage. He must have known of my unhappiness because some months later, on the way out, he lifted his head and said quietly, "First Wife works hard for a hard-nosed man." It was startling to hear a man, a servant, disparage his master and praise my effort. I trembled at his daring but felt its warmth. Now, as he hops with my children in the courtyard, I see no impropriety in it, but Husband surely would and Junior Sister surely does. And when he shows off the fishing nets, pre-tending to catch the children as if they were fish, she grimaces in disapproval. I see her scrambling for words to reprimand him... but then she says nothing.

I know that she and Husband share an invisible bond. She has always admired his cleverness at enriching himself, and he has always admired her swift verdicts. More than once he has said that she is much wiser than I. By custom, both being married, they must keep a distance from one another and from anyone else of the opposite sex in the family. They cannot speak face to face even at village gatherings. But I've suspected for some time that their servants carry messages back and forth.

Junior Sister's skin is pockmarked with boils, like the rind of an unripe soursop. Her heart is like the soursop's stone. If she knew of my infatuation she would be the ruin of me. She would never comprehend how an esteemed First Wife, consort of a future Mandarin, could risk her rank and her life by succumbing to a ravenous thirst for a willful servant twice her age. Oh, how thrilled she would be to see me caught. How quickly she would send her servant with the spiteful news, urging Husband to show no mercy.

Mother-in-Law would have been equally merciless. She was so determined to see her son become Mandarin. To please her, Husband went to the Regional Examinations. When he returned with the roll of papyrus under his vest, she fell to her knees and shrieked like a frenzied stork. But she had barely thanked the gods when death took her. She went to the meeting of the Burial Society and never came back. Villagers found her in the bushes a few steps off the trail, her arms and chest covered with snake bites. The village sorcerer said the venom had gone to her heart. Her body was so rigid that during the Ceremony of First Offering — to give her that last material meal and pay her way to the otherworld — Husband had to pry her teeth open with a shell to put in the rice and the coins. He left the other observances of mourning to me. "I'll pay obeisance to my parents' memory by becoming Mandarin," he said.

The written work on the Confucian Canon has been submitted — all fourteen tablets. We had to write a commentary on one part of the Spring and Autumn Annals. Husband's submission argued that the story of the State of Lu points to the evils of arrogating the power of one's Superiors, and teaches obedience to the Monarch and his Emissaries. First Wife is commanded to pray fervently that the Examiners will reward Husband's effort. If they do not, Husband will have disgraced his Venerable Parents and come home in shame.

HUSBAND'S VENERABLE FATHER was brash and greedy. Two years before my betrothal, the reckless man procured a tract of land too big for one family to handle, and had to hire men to plant it. But the flood swept away his paddies the very first spring, and when the men were not paid they ran away. "I came to his rescue," Overseer Dũng boasted to me after we had become lovers. "Took him to train with my brother who is an artisan — sculpting and painting wooden puppets for the Water Puppet Guild that stages shows on ponds and lakes. The haughty man's fingers were nimble enough, but his tongue was vile and within months the Guild expelled him."

Overseer Dũng did not belabour the rest because everybody knows it. On his departure, Husband's father received or took money from the Guild, and used it for a bribe to secure a position as the agent in charge of distributing the rice gifted by the King to the victims of famine. Almost immediately, the victims protested that they were not getting the rations they had been promised. They refused to pay taxes and accused him of corruption. He countered that he had not received enough royal rice to gratify one and all. The district Mandarin would not hear such an allegation against the King and withdrew the appointment. The disgraced man ran to the river. That was the last time anyone saw him; the shame of his demotion has trailed the family like the stench of a rotting goat.

As a boy, Husband revered his father, always standing humbly before him and listening to him with utter respect until dismissed. He dared not cough or yawn in his presence, or touch his clothes or personal utensils. "But Father beat Husband for no reason," Overseer Dũng told me. "Just to vent his rancour. And Mother stood aside praying he would spare her. This rarely worked." Later, when Husband beat me, she did not interfere. Overseer Dũng knows that too.

A restful interlude after the strain of the First Segment.
Some candidates long to leave and be with their wives and
families again. But they fear the humiliation of handing their
empty tablets to the guards, and the shame of seeing their
names on the List of Quitters. Husband will not be a quitter
but will remain here as long as it takes to be successful.

The long break before the Second Segment is a time to
take stock of one's strengths and plan for a life of comfort
and influence. My First Son, still very young, will one day
be grateful for my ambition. Not having him by my side is
painful. First Wife's duty is to see that his character and
comportment do not deteriorate in Husband's absence.

FROM OUR CHILDREN, Husband demands abiding reverence. His
son has been taught the rites of filial observances, but performed
them reluctantly. Husband always blamed me for the children's
failings. When he left for the Capital, I was freed from his scru-
tiny. I shed my carapace, spread my wings, and flew straight into
the fire.

Ah, the shimmering memory of that first time: it is a dark
and cloudy morning, Husband far away awaiting the Second
Segment, the children with their fishing nets at Junior Sister's,
the servants on errands. First Wife and Overseer Dũng sit in the
alcove facing each other across the mat, a bowl of lychee fruit
between them. He reads her Husband's scroll, then peels one fruit
and offers her the white pulp that glistens between his fingers.
She does not take it but lifts her chin and opens her mouth. He
leans back, tosses the fruit across in a graceful arch, and it falls
on her waiting tongue. She catches the second one the same way.
The third one falls short, her open lips too far to reach, and she
tilts forward, her palms alighting on his thighs. She fans out her
fingers and begins to rake his flesh.

Abruptly, the sky lights up and thunder growls in the trees. The rain comes down like a mudslide, and First Wife walks over to lower the rattan screens on both wall openings. When she turns back, Overseer Dũng has removed his garment and is sitting with only his loincloth on his hips. The coarseness of his body shocks First Wife more than its nakedness. She has only known Husband's body, which has the lustre of a glazed teapot. Overseer Dũng's chest is pockmarked with scars — the chest of a man who has jousted with animals and wielded tree logs and scythes. Tiny white blotches — as small as the footprints of a rabbit — are splattered around his navel and on his hips. First Wife cannot see them clearly because her eyes are clouded with silver sparkles.

Overseer Dũng holds out his palms, fingers twitching, and she crumples onto the mat. He peels the garments off her arms and pulls them over her head but she does not feel unclothed because her skin is aflame. The storm roars outside as their two bodies fold into a scroll.

That day seems so remote now, yet I can still feel the rub of his skin as it scours mine.

OVERSEER DŨNG SAYS First Wife is Queen and I want to believe him. One of the lullabies my mother used to sing to me was about Queen Ỷ Lan, wife of our great sovereign King Lý Thánh Tông of long ago. He had built the Temple of Learning in the Capital and she had started the first silk mill right next door to it. She had learned the art of silk weaving from the wives of Chinese Mandarins who came south to build our citadels and fortifications. But when the King left for war with the Kingdom of Champa, his Queen put silk weaving aside and ruled the country. The Mandarins obeyed her every command. With Husband away, can First Wife be Queen and exact obedience? Can the spirit of Queen Ỹ Lan protect her? Provided she fulfills her duty and prays for Husband's glory as ardently as Queen Ỹ Lan prayed for her King's victory?

Any moment, my blissful interlude can come to a horrid end. If Husband fails one Segment, he will come home promptly, unexpectedly. The din of men who gossiped in the shop about goings-on in faraway lands reverberates in my head. In China, they said, adulterous women were buried alive, made to face their lovers in death as they had in life, the cuckolded husband their inviolable judge. Rarely, the husband might show mercy and spare the life of the lover, but never of the wife. At that time, I accepted that the punishment was just. Now I feel for these women, and at times, in a dream, the weight of wet bog chills my chest and it hardens into a lump. My heart clatters and my nostrils fill up with dirt.

The magnificent Royal Citadel, which houses the Royal Palace and the Court Hall where His Majesty holds audiences, is ringed by a brick fortress and a moat. Ming and Mongol armies have levelled it and it has had to be rebuilt time and again. The main gate is wide enough for a caravan of elephants to pass through. Across it are two hills thickly covered with trees, to prevent evil spirits from flying into the Citadel in a straight line.

Senior Mandarins live in grand quarters inside the Citadel, but the lesser ones live outside the wall in well-appointed brick residences and go to the Citadel only when summoned. Husband's fervent ambition is to have a house there one day. Some of Husband's land holdings could be sold to pay for a suitable dwelling in the Capital.

Husband's most Venerable Parents longed to have their First
Son become Mandarin and live in the vicinity of the Citadel.
More than a good effort is required to earn the privilege.
One must get to know influential people. The price is worth
paying. First Wife is commanded to pray for Husband's
success in the Second Segment.

THE GHOST OF Mother-in-Law visits me often, thrusting into my face its upper limbs which have swelled into ghastly fingerless knobs. Or walking through me as if I were a cloud. My feet grip the rocky edge of a limestone cliff and my arms clutch the air. Mother-in-Law's orders — "Do the honourable! End your life!" My mouth falls open to speak the words she wants to hear but no sound comes out. Any moment now she will nudge me off the cliff. When I look down into the abyss, I see the ashen ghosts of my ancestral women jutting their straw brooms at me and echoing Mother-in-Law's orders: "Jump... jump now!"

THIS MOMENT I WILL CHERISH: On a sweltering day, Overseer Dũng leads First Wife away from the village in search of a gust of wind that will relieve the red heat of the fifth lunar month. They pause in the river cove, concealed from the other shore by tall reeds. He has brought his new fishing basket — cylinder-shaped, smelling of freshly cut willow twigs, and taller than his legs. When she squats on the sand, he says, "Close your eyes." She closes them and he slides the basket over her — the bottom rim ringing her hips, the narrower upper rim haloing her head. "Would you like to be my fish?" he whispers. The scent of coconut milk and honey comes off his skin like opium and his breath is scorching her cheeks. She pokes her fingers through the slats, blindly seeking his skin.

"All creatures like to roam freely. It's a pity to see them trapped," she says to him.

"The clever ones never get caught. They know how to stay free," he laughs.

She wiggles inside impatiently and pleads. "Let me out!"

The basket does not move and she opens her eyes.

"You let me out now," she commands and he pulls off the basket and scoops her up in his arms. "You're a good catch for me," he cries triumphantly, carrying her to the water where he releases her and she is free.

That happened just before Husband's torturous Second Segment, and my body still thirsts for my lover's body. To suck lychee fruit from his hand and have him fan my face. Mothers teach us about virtue. Mothers-in-law about obedience. But Fate has sent me Overseer Dũng, who has taught me about desire, and now my destiny sways on a silken thread.

JUNIOR SISTER KNOWS NONE OF the secrets of my life with Husband, or of the shop. She knows nothing of Husband's outbursts when deals fell through or landowners tried to defraud him. In a rage, he hollered, whipped the offender's scroll against the floor, and kicked the ground. There was nothing to do but try to stay out of the way. Then walk home in his wake, his fury not yet spent, remembering to keep the children quiet and servile at dinner.

Even when not enraged, Husband demanded that my comportment be correct at all times. When he was teaching me how to usher clients, if I took a step he deemed too big, he rammed his heel into my toes till my eyes watered and the steps were just right. If he thought my posture was not perfectly erect, or my feet not scrubbed to the bone, he would not speak to me for days. Sometimes he would take offence for no reason that I could fathom and also not speak. But the silent interlude always ended the same way. In the middle of the night, he would reach over my daughters' heads and pull me off the mat. I had to follow him to the bushes. There he would thrust his daemons into me, crudely and painfully, over and over again, until he had his release.

Serenity has reigned in my home since he left. I take big steps when I want to and allow the children to make noise when they play. At night we lie together. With my son sleeping by my side, I can tousle his hair and hold him close at will. But I catch him looking wistfully at the empty mat on the other side of the floor where he used to lie with his father and listen to tales of his heroic ancestors. Little boys need their fathers. My daughters cling to me as before but are happier knowing that Husband will not take me away at night. They have always known that married life is an ordeal; now they also know that when a woman's master is away life is favoured in many ways. Queen Ỷ Lan would have known it too. Did she yield to the witchery of a lowly Mandarin? Did she suffer the torment of frightful dreams?

> His Majesty is a student of history and surrounds himself with men of letters. He has ordered itinerant traders and vagrants expelled. Only those pursuing respectable professions can live in the Capital.

> His Majesty's poems, which celebrate "the rivers and mountains of the Celestial South," are very much admired. When He is away at military manoeuvers, his Mandarins have his verses engraved on rocky cliffs to surprise and delight him on his return. His Majesty works very hard but also likes to amuse himself. Apparently he is quite lustful.

IN THE SOGGY FURROW of a paddy, a condemned woman is kneeling on the ground. Her shackled arms cramp her belly and a brawny man wearing a tattered loincloth is flogging her naked back with a cane. With each stroke she hunches onto herself, slowly, till her head drops onto her thighs. The man lightens the stroke. Nearby, under a banana tree, the presiding Mandarin shoots up his arms and commands, "Don't slack off, soldier!" His blue tunic folds around his shoes and the tassels of his high hat flutter in the wind. He taps his hand on his rattan rod, counting the strokes as the soldier's arm flies. "Forty!" The soldier drops the whip and yanks up the victim abruptly, as he would a dead crab, to show that he is not slacking off. He cuts the rope belting the woman's arms and leads her by the neck toward the bamboo grove where two elephants are waiting. Her back is a slate of crimson. Her teeth must be clattering, because the soldier stuffs a clump of straw into her mouth. The Mandarin reads her sentence from a scroll. "Adulteress." Mother-in-Law leans in, repeats the sentence after him, and rubs her palms. I wake up with my fingers in my mouth and my maidservant bending over me, saying, "Your limbs were clattering like arid bones."

The sun has not yet cleared the tip of the mulberry grove when Overseer Dũng arrives and waves the maidservant aside with Husband's scroll. It is probably the same scroll he brought a few days earlier but the maidservant does not know this. Behind the partition, we drink mint tea from one cup — he from one side and I from the other. We tilt the cup back and forth and let our noses touch and our breath mingle. Then we turn the cup around and he drinks from my spot on the rim and I from his. He peels a tangerine and holds a segment in front of my open mouth for a long moment before slipping the sweetness in. We wait for the maidservant to leave on her morning errands; I don't want her to see any of my wrongdoing.

"What if you made me with child while Husband is away?"

"Ah! Woman's fears. As if you were a common girl. You are Queen. Don't you know that only common girls are made to suffer? Let me tell you what happened last year in a village where some of my ancestors are buried. An unbetrothed girl had done wrong. The elders had prescribed a whipping, but the Mandarin ruled that a woman with child could not be battered. Instead, he ordered her head to be shorn and smeared with lime. Whenever she stepped out, villagers covered their noses and spat at her."

"But she was allowed to live?"

"No. When her shame began to show, she was tied to a wooden raft and sent adrift to the sea. Her father kicked the raft onto the waters."

"The elders know Husband has been away too long to have fathered my child."

"And you must know that no one of a family in mourning can be put to death. Why worry? Mother-in-Law is protecting you from the grave. And when Husband becomes Mandarin, you cannot be made to suffer humiliation in public. Fate will shine upon him. In the Capital he will take a new wife and leave this household in my hands."

"You are counting on that?"

"And on my standing in this village. I own no land, which is a curse, but I can read and write... breed animals... take a whip to a lazy chattel. A wise landowner needs me, the district Mandarin too. If I prove myself clever, one day I'll be an elder."

"You cannot hold back nature. Only shamans can. If I am caught with child —"

"You cannot be made with child if you are held above me. Men know the mysteries of nature; women are better off not knowing these tricks."

"I know from my moths. They always lay eggs on time."

"Ah! Lady moth. You are Queen. I hold you above me for a reason. You must trust your Overseer Dũng."

He rests his head on my knee, waiting for me to stroke his hair. But that common girl sent down the river weighs on my mind. Did she regret her wrongdoing? Was the moment of lust worth death?

> The Second Segment required us to write a Royal Decree, and Husband's composition assumed a suitably imperious tone. It was addressed to the Emperor of China and directed that he abandon his dream of ever retaking Đại Việt. It restated our willingness to continue paying the tribute but also called on Việt people never to surrender to the enemy.
>
> Later, in a dream, a group of Ming Emissaries appeared and demanded a higher tribute, but Husband dismissed them with a regal wave of hand. It was a daring gesture, and made Husband yearn for a chance to face the real Ming Envoys one day.
>
> An older candidate named Chiến has become a good companion. He is writing the Imperial Examinations for the second time. Husband has helped him with the composition of the Second Segment, hoping that he will repay the favour. His great uncle is a Mandarin who lives on the rim of the Citadel. Much benefit can be derived from getting into the good graces of Chiến's family.

THE GRIM DREAM RETURNS. This time there are two mahouts handling the elephants: Mother-in-Law is with the bigger elephant, Junior Sister with the smaller one. Both prod their beasts forward. The smaller one balks, but the bigger one lumbers toward the condemned adulteress. She skids on her knees trying to get away, rolling her head in terror. The elephant coils its trunk around her and swings her up like a tree trunk. She whirls in the air and hits the ground with a thump. The elephant kicks her and pins her down with its front leg. Her neck snaps with the sound of a branch rupturing off a dried-up tree. Mother-in-Law turns the giant beast around and it tramples the body over and over again till the corpse is as flat as a shrivelled cobra. Except for the head, whose hair lies limp in the puddle. Junior Sister stirs her elephant around and it thumps over the woman's head, which cracks into a reddish pulp like a momordica melon. She twirls her rod above her head. "Good riddance!"

I am still shaking when my maidservant enters to say that Overseer Dũng's Third Wife and her youngest daughter have arrived. I tell her I am not ready yet; I need time to wake up and compose myself. Overseer Dũng has three daughters with this wife and the four women do sewing at home. His other wives and daughters work the spindles and the looms. When I step out into the roofless ledge that runs along the side of the house, the youngest daughter, the one who usually does the cutting, unties a roll of raw silk and lays out a gown pattern on the floor. She needs my orders for the seamstresses to stitch a dozen gowns to take to market.

The blanched cloth refracts the pale light of the rising sun but my eyes cloud over with red. I cannot bear to look at raw silk now. The girl raises her tiny head from shoulders as bony as the featherless wings of a fledgling sparrow. Why has she not been betrothed yet? She is old enough. She used to help Junior Sister with her sons when they were infants. Junior Sister, not one to give compliments, said she was a good worker. Perhaps Overseer Dũng finds her more useful at home, in the family business.

The mother squats close to her daughter, cooing, "We have prayed for Husband's success every day. It will be such an honour for the entire clan — a pathway to influence for centuries to come. First Wife will shine in the Capital with her beauty."

I suspect she is taunting me. How dare she? Husband does not need his servants' prayers to succeed. I want to dismiss her but then hesitate, my empty stomach tying knots. She knows that Husband has made it through the Second Segment. What else does she know? The daughter gives me a bland stare that women often put on to hide a scheme. I order them to leave.

Yesterday, we stayed up late saying goodbye to four candidates who have decided to quit. One of the quitters said that life in the Compound was a dog's life and that he would rather seek adventure in the army.

We fed the quitters with the sap of a milk tree, grilled fish we bought over the fence from the hawkers, and fleshy jackfruit from a tree on the other side of the lake. They left with good spirits in their wake, but think of their heartbroken parents.

We await the Poetry Segment with trepidation.

JUNIOR SISTER ARRIVES and congratulates me in venomous tones. "Husband's appointment to the Mandarinate is assured. He might be made tax collector in our district. Or he might meet people with influence in the Capital and obtain a position there. And then he'll leave you in the village and take a second wife there. You're a spent wife —"

"Oh, shut up your stupid mouth," I shout. I will not allow her to blabber on like this in my home. "I am First Wife and I know land transactions. Husband needs me more than your husband needs you."

"Don't be so sure," she snaps. "Ten lunar years is a long time. He's ready for a new wife... he needs another son —"

"You with your soursop face. And that horny ram for a husband. Six litter in six years. What else can he do? What else can you do? I will find Husband a new wife when I want to. Before the betrothal, I will drill her, and prod her, and hustle her until she obeys me completely."

Junior Sister will have to learn that Senior Sister is Queen, and as willful and pitiless as when she wielded the whip. She had better believe that queens command authority. If I put my mind to it, I will join Husband in the Capital. Unburden myself of my ugly sister and her carping forever. And of my servant-lover too. Dismiss him and return to a blameless life. A lowly overseer must obey his Queen's command.

Husband's hands and feet are swollen and his chest is covered with red blotches that itch and burn. The flies are merciless, even at night. We have been promised an ointment but there may not be enough for all. It has not rained for days, our throats are sore and our heads ache. The suffering affirms the sacrifice Husband is making to honour his Venerable Parents and repay his immense debt to them.

His Majesty has ordered that the names of the top three laureates of the Court Examination be engraved on a stone tablet so that they become known to the future generations. Some of the more talented candidates are offering to help the weaker ones for a fee. A lot is at stake here.

OVERSEER DŨNG HAS NOT been to see me in several days and the longing for him takes my breath away. The sun has gone to sleep but in the shed my moths are out of their cocoons and ready to mate. The male's enlarged antenna curves up so that the tips of its wispy hairs can sniff out the scent of the female. The awkward torsos tumble, the sticky bellies brush one against the other tenderly. With the tiny duct, which is their nose, they leisurely sip each other's nectar. In twos, they roll as one, the hind wings enmeshed, the forewings entangled. When they find a restful pose, they lie still till the early rays pierce the dawn and warm up the sky.

In the mulberry grove, Overseer Dũng would hold on till he heard me chirp, till I sang like a meadowlark. In broad daylight, his antenna in full view, he looked like a giant moth. Our loins fluttered like wings as he waited for me to crest, his arms gliding up and down my sides, until his final thrusts pushed me over the edge and brought me plunging to earth.

For the Poetry Segment Husband wrote about the wind and how it sweeps our woes away. Many other candidates also chose nature for inspiration.

Husband hopes that the Examiners will not judge the idiom of the "river talking to the fishes" as too frivolous. All through last night, these lines circled around Husband's head, which was drowning in sweat. Remembering how the wind gusted through my mulberry groves helped. The temptation to gather the brushes and leave for home can barely be resisted...

I PRAY EARNESTLY THAT Husband gets through the Poetry Segment. If he fails and comes home early to discover my betrayal, he will have me tied to a raft like that lowly servant girl. I know it. He will kick the raft onto the waves himself, and stand on the shore with a look of utter disdain, the elders applauding his righteousness. Junior Sister will not shed a single tear. And Overseer Dũng? He will be in hiding, listening to the villagers' chants urging evil spirits to chase me to the otherworld, where Mother-in-Law will wield her scythe at the hag who dishonoured her First Son.

*About half the candidates have failed the Poetry Segment.
There is more room for the rest of us now. At night, the ghost
of Venerable Mother hovers over Husband's head shouting
that failure would devastate her, as she has always counted
on her First Son to make up for Father's shortcomings.*

*The worst that can happen is that Husband will be relegated
to the List of Mediocrities. But if he succeeds and there is a
Mandarin in the family, our clan will be exalted and the lives
of all our descendants elevated. Husband's duty is to struggle
toward that end.*

*It rained all night and our trousers, crusted with mud, scrape
our ankles till they bleed. The water, dotted with corpses
of rodents, laps against the trees, bringing foul odours.
On account of the flooding our meals are often late and sometimes come not at all. We have to trap birds at night and roast
them over the fire. The peacock-pheasant roasts very well.*

*Tonight we'll sleep in a sitting-up position, hoping not to
drown in the puddles. At sunrise, we'll walk in circles trying
to shelter our fears. The critical Segment Four is near.
My friend Chiến bites his toenails to the bone. Husband's
courage has not failed him, but he agrees with the others that
the price of advancement is very high.*

*Overseer Dũng has written that First Wife is worried that
Husband's First Son's moral growth may suffer from being
deprived of his father's presence and guidance. That she
wishes he could be brought to the Capital. Indeed. Husband
will attend to this matter soon. For now, to commiserate with
the hardship Husband has to suffer, First Wife is commanded
to abstain from amusements and forbid the children any
frivolities.*

AT TWILIGHT, the servant-lover sits in front of me in the mulberry grove, succulent berries overhanging his head. He pulls a stem of grass, chews on it, and reaches for my hand. I hold it back. "You have been scheming, Overseer Dũng," I say as sternly as I can. "You have been writing… What else have you written to Husband?"

"I can read your mind, you know. What dutiful mother would not want to see her son in the Capital? To sit at his father's side amidst all the splendour."

"You must not speak for me. But I do want my son in the Capital." I have to stop myself from screaming at his disloyalty. "You can take him there immediately."

"I will take him there immediately. This is what Husband has ordered me to do."

"And when you return you'll keep away from me. Husband will be Mandarin soon and our wrongdoing must end."

He pulls his knees to his chin and locks his arms around them, the muscles on his arms like granite. "You are Queen and in command of me."

"You must not call me Queen any more. You bewitched me and now you must let me be."

He glances down the path running between two rows of mulberry saplings. "Queens are irresistible. Even sorcerers are drawn to them like moths to fire. But before a lover is discarded, must he not be paid?"

Ah, this brazen servant wooer. Has he not trampled on First Wife's honour and used her body for his pleasure? Has he not sipped her nectar to the brim?

"The duty of First Wife is to bring in Second Wife," he says, as if I did not know. "You offer my youngest daughter to Husband. That will be my payment, and I will let you be."

So he has thought of the payoff. Did he know from the

beginning what he wanted in return? Have I been but a pawn in his scheme? I rise and he stays down — disrespectfully.

"You have been well paid, Overseer Dũng. When Husband settles in the Capital, he will need First Wife by his side. Later, his peers — the Mandarins — will offer him their daughters — girls more suitable to his new standing, and I will choose the Second Wife for him."

He snorts, gets up, and walks away without a kowtow, leaving me to ponder what he might do.

A few days later a man stands in the doorway. I stare at his face and recognize Overseer Dũng's Younger Brother. He has been travelling with the Water Puppet Guild for years and comes home only for the Tết. Why is he home now? He kowtows deeply and says, "There's good news for you." I keep staring as he unrolls the scroll and begins to stammer, licking his lips after every word:

Just thirty of us have advanced to the Fourth Segment. The Essay was on the intricate subject of the prerogative of the Monarch to collect taxes during famine. My counsel was that the King must collect what is due or the State will fail.

We have to wait three weeks because, to ensure fairness, our Essays will be graded by more than one Examiner. The tension in the Compound tears us apart, the candidates — win or lose — making deals to exchange favours in the future. Some say that all of us will be awarded the coveted title, but others say the King will select a handful of Mandarins.

I FEEL FOR HUSBAND. The tension in my home tears me apart. I must send my son to the Capital so that I can follow him promptly and forget my Junior Sister, and my former lover, and never have to deal face to face with his wife and daughters again... I feel for myself...

My servants have spread the autumn rice on a long quilt of overlapping banana leaves. The harvested grains pave the courtyard and the path leading to the mulberry grove. Millions of tiny grains slumber under the full moon. I sink my feet into the pearly sea and the grains lodge between my toes. They rub and scratch and titillate.

The line of my wayward footprints comes to an end at the edge of the grove where my misdeeds are concealed. My heart swells, my nipples harden, and I know that it would take just one wisp of hot air for the fires to flare up again. The cinders will take some time to cool. But I have put my past to rest and my ache is only for a well-favoured future.

Overseer Dũng's Younger Brother arrives to tell me that my son has left to be reunited with his father. "He's in good hands... will be well cared for on the road. Elder Brother has seen to it..."

I hold back a sigh of relief. It will be easier not to have Overseer Dũng here, not to see his vengeful face. By the time he returns I might well be gone. Younger Brother holds another scroll and I tell him to read it. He seems more nervous than he was the first time and stammers badly:

> *The King has personally selected the top three scholars for the honour of "Tam khôi"... The three will receive gifts of rich clothing, an ornamental hat, and a horse, and will be escorted to their villages in a festive procession of soldiers and musicians.*
>
> *Alas... Husband and his friend Chiến were not among them. We accepted the verdict with humility. But the following morning, five candidates were awarded the title of Mandarin... including Husband and Chiến. The Fourth Segment was brutal and we were exhausted. The title will suffice to secure a suitable appointment.*

FATE HAS BEEN MERCIFUL. Husband must bring me to the Capital to reunite mother and son; this is the law. While I am there, my silk women will go on spinning the harvest of the mulberry grove, their looms purring with pleasure. From the cloth they send, I will design lovely garments, richly gilded and embroidered, for the women of the royal family. I will make my life in Thăng Long shine.

I will find Husband a new wife — a diffident daughter of a rich Mandarin — to take over the burden of his miserly lust at night. But in broad daylight, that Second Wife will submit to me — First Wife — consort of a Mandarin — the Queen of Mulberry.

When the time comes, I will find husbands for my daughters, men strong in body and of tender heart — if such can be found. And before I am very old, I will pass on to my daughters the account of my infidelity, of my daring. They will hear the story of bliss and hurt. They will learn that women must be like the limestone mountains — alluring, rugged, and eternal.

First Son has arrived in the Capital under the care of Overseer Dũng and his youngest daughter, just in time to have the great honour of seeing his father reach a superior grade in the hierarchy, and petition His Majesty to restore the honorific grade of the Mandarinate on his unjustly maligned father, the boy's grandfather. When the glorious time comes, my father's soul will be summoned to listen to the reading of the Royal Warrant. He will take delight in his First Son, and his First Grandson who will inherit the Mandarin's mantle.

As esteemed Mandarin, Husband will be charged with reviewing land records for the Ministry of Punishment. Apparently, some Crown Holdings were awarded preferentially.

A fitting payment must be made to secure the fine position
but Chiến, whose appointment is with the Ministry of Rites,
says the situation will allow Husband to gain familiarity
with Court procedures and open the way to advancement.
To expedite the payment, Husband has ordered Overseer Dũng
to return home at once and have the mulberry groves sold.

In the Capital, Husband's concubines will attest to his
superior rank. Overseer Dũng's daughter will remain here
as Husband's Second Wife. Overseer Dũng's ancestors have
been in Husband's family's service for three generations.
Junior Sister, who had that girl caring for her sons some time
ago, was astute to point out to Husband that Overseer Dũng
has earned this reward. She has given good counsel. First
Wife is a spent wife. Husband is on a path to a grand career
and must leave past entanglements behind.

The Story of Joseph and Mary

By the end of the sixteenth century two rival clans, the Nguyễn and the Trịnh, had come to control the kingdom of Đại Việt. Both clans governed willfully, raised their own armies, and fought brutal battles, in defiance of the power of the Lê Monarchs. Eventually, the Trịnh Lords tightened their grip over what is now northern Vietnam, and the Nguyễn Lords fled southward. In the ensuing decades, thousands of landless northern peasants followed them to the south. There, on the seacoast, they came face to face with European traders and Christian missionaries.

NGUYỄN THỊ MAI WOBBLED PRECARIOUSLY on the edge of a rocky outcrop, her skinny body splayed against it like a runaway kite, forehead, limbs, and toes pressed to the stone. Rivulets of sweat dribbled down her neck and spine. With her fingertips, she pawed the craggy surface of the cliff for lumps and bulges she could not see because her eyes were shut. Close by, her father, his two concubines, and two housemen were strung to her along one long rope that looped their waists. They guided their feet over slippery ridges and rocky shards one foothold at a time. Overhead, flocks of sooty swallows flapped their wings and sent down shrieks and bird droppings.

The climbers were harvesting the nests of *chim yến*, a split-tail sea swallow — black on top and grey on the belly. Its sturdy legs ended with well-pointed claws, which hooked easily to scraps of rock, like any bird's. But chim yến was unique because it built its nest with layers of seafoam laced with seaweed and glued with the bird's own saliva. Fastened to a rock, the slimy paste hardened into a yellowish scab that formed the outer shell of the nest. When soaked in water and then boiled, the shell dissolved, yielding a broth with magical curative properties. Swallow-nest soup was said to relieve back and joint pains and to cure lethargy. It was a lucrative commodity.

An itinerant Chinese merchant looking for a chim yến supplier met Mai's family shortly after their arrival in Phai Phô from the North and urged them to head for the shore. "Chim yến birds fly low to catch termites and dragonflies to feed their young, but build their nests high on windy cliffs and in airy grottos to be safe from predators. All you need is two nimble feet and a rope. Get up there and scoop the nests. You will make a fortune."

In the third lunar month, when the young birds had fledged, Mai's family would load their junk with bamboo rods and scaffolding, ropes and cords, hand nets and baskets of food, and head off to the cliffs of Chàm Islets. There, they waded in shallow water through one cove after another, climbed over mounds of limestone, descended on ropes into crevices, and crawled through narrow crannies to get to the foot of a cliff dotted with the nests. The father and Thu Trang, the older concubine, scaled the heights first, with the family's two housemen in tow. All four dislodged the scabs with poles tipped with scraper blades, and threw them into the rattan baskets hanging on their backs. Mai and the younger concubine followed below, plucking out with their scrapers or fingernails the jutting bits and pieces the others had missed or abandoned. Mai hated every moment of the arduous expedition. She was afraid of heights, so going up she had to fix her eyes on the dark cloud of birds screeching overhead. But descending at the end of the day was a horror she concealed from her family, for fear of having such childishness ridiculed.

Back home the nests were piled on the grass and Mai would wipe them off with a hemp rug to remove any dirt or sand. Then the younger concubine scraped off with a chisel any feathers or feces embedded in the crust. Finally, both girls polished the nests to a shine. A good day's harvest could yield as many as six dozen nests, and the cleaning and polishing took days. When the sparkling nests lay in rows across the yard, Thu Trang, as the senior woman in the household, sorted them by size, shape, and luminosity — huyết, hồng, quan, thiên, bài, địa, vụn. The best-looking huyết Mai put in a sandalwood trunk to be sent to Phú Xuân, where the Nguyễn Lords held their court, in the hope that the gift would earn favours for the family.

Just after their third harvest, Mai's father had paid a man who knew hieroglyphs to write a petition asking the Lords to grant the family a concession to export the nests to China. After a long wait, the man came to say that the petition had been denied, because the rulers claimed — or their Mandarins did — that the family's harvest was small and the bird-nest export tax would have to be paid first.

The less perfect nests Mai had to sell in the alleys to passersby or Chinese merchants who were always on the lookout for a deal. No matter how much she managed to bargain for them, she would face Thu Trang's wrath. "You've given them away for a pittance. Because of you we'll need to get up there a second time around."

When food was scarce after flooding, Thu Trang would send Mai and the younger concubine to the paddies to scavenge for carcasses of hare and mongoose and rats. "And don't come back empty-handed," she would warn them at the gate. One year the girls dragged in a drowned wild hog that fed the family for days, but received no praise for their effort. Since Mai's mother's death, Thu Trang had become very willful, her bad temper directed mainly at the younger concubine. She put her rival to work at the hearth, then resented that a girl so young could cook so well and took a whip to her at any lapse. If Mai got in the way, she would catch a swipe as well.

The younger rival swallowed her tears and tried to please Thu Trang. Mai did not. She was lost in a family with two concubines but no mother, and having menstruated for two years was ready for betrothal. When she contemplated being a wife and mother in her own home her heart flitted like a swallow in a cage. Every harrowing day on the cliffs, she reckoned, brought her one day closer to leaving home. Her evening prayer was: "May Father have me betrothed as First Wife, like Mother was. And may my mother-in-law not be tyrannical." Squatting in an alley, waiting for a bird-nest buyer to come along, she would furtively eye men in the crowd and dream, "Perhaps one richer than my family will stop today — looking for a bride."

IN THE FADING PALLOR of the evening light, Father Pedro Antonio de Vasconcelos knelt on unhusked rice strewn on the earthen floor of his hut. The coarse grains gleamed like a halo around the folds of his cassock as he prayed for the safe arrival of the shipwreck now being towed toward the mouth of the Thu Bồn River. That morning, a fierce tempest had struck the coast of the territory of Đàng Trong, ravaging sea vessels and their crews, and filling his humble shelter with salty spray and the wind's low howl. His fingers kneaded the beads of his mother's rosary, while his lips mouthed the hallowed words: *Hail Mary full of grace, the Lord is with thee; ... blessed is the Fruit of thy womb, Jesus.*

In the year since his arrival, it had become Father Pedro Antonio's habit to use the morning penitence and prayer to ask the Heavenly Father to bestow His grace on him — to allow him to bear this strange land with humility, to help him master the tones of the Việt tongue, to grant him the joy of his first conversion. But in the evening, he beseeched God for mercy on his fellow men — on the sailors at sea, on his Christian brethren persecuted to death in Japan, and always on the hapless heathens of the hamlet of Phai Phô.

During his three-month training in Macao, he had been told to expect "a dismal horde of heathens living in a primeval state, indifferent to privacy or propriety, and desperately in need of deliverance." As he stepped down the ramp of the boat, staring at him was a rabble of short leathery-skinned men, their muscled torsos shielded by the scabbard of uncut hair, their skulls round, their eyes and teeth black, their faces mulish. Around their necks hung strings of seeds, animal teeth, beads, and feathers — fetishes to ward off evil spirits. He listened to the rattle of their tongue, to the swelling tones and monosyllabic shrieks bursting out from their black mouths, and thought, "These dark creatures warble like frightened birds." He tried to look at the horde with compassion, eager to tell them — in their own language — about Jesus, and to bring them into the Saviour's fold.

But so far, he had made little progress with the Việt language, and the only person he could converse with in Portuguese was his dead mother. To her he recounted aloud his daily walkabouts in Phai Phô and his awe of the savage land. At sunrise he celebrated Mass, setting the liturgical cloth and the sacred vessels on top of the truncated tree shaft that stood in front of his hut, and preached his homily in Latin and Portuguese, also aloud, to the caged emerald-green parakeet he had bought in the market for company.

Holy Mary, Mother of God, pray for us sinners, now and at the hour of our death. There were less than a dozen of the fifty-five beads remaining, and Father Pedro Antonio's knees were on fire and his back hurt. When he slumped his shoulders forward to ease the strain, his stomach growled, reminding him that it was almost dinnertime. But his Việt boy-cook had run away to help with the sea rescue, so the dinner bowl of swallow-nest soup would not be there tonight. The Jesuit raised his face to the Lord looking down on him from a wooden crucifix, crossed himself, and concluded hastily: *Glory be to the Father, and to the Son, and to the Holy Ghost. As it was in the beginning, world without end. Amen.*

He hoisted himself up, rubbed the rice grains off his knees, and crumpled onto the tree shaft that was his chair. His only friend, Miguel de Roussado, was out there on the waves, helping to tow a shipwrecked vessel to shore. For weeks, Father Pedro Antonio had shared his dinner with the young trader, trying to make him do what a Christian man must do — take his chosen native woman for a wife by way of a Christian marriage. If he used his authority well, and prevailed upon the young man, he could convert the woman's family into the Christian faith, and do so discreetly, without attracting undue attention to his proselytizing. In the long year gone by he had converted no one.

The Jesuit crossed his legs and reached for the water-stained Việt—Portuguese—Latin Dictionary written by Alexandre de Rhodes, a fellow Jesuit from Avignon. The spirited French-speaking brother had arrived in Đàng Trong in 1624, bent on learning the native tongue, and had been stunned by the coarse stresses, the sharp intakes of breath, and the rapping tones. "They hardly resemble human speech," he wrote in his daybook. "And Việt writing done in Chinese hieroglyphs?" Presently, he set out to transcribe the Việt language in his Latin alphabet. His dictionary had been Father Pedro Antonio's send-off present in Lisbon. It was shrivelled now and strands of yellow grasses protruded from between its covers. He had held the dictionary in his hands as often as the Holy Bible, marking with blades of grass the pages with difficult-to-pronounce words, to return to them again, and again, only to forget the words overnight. How would he ever convince the natives to take Jesus into their hearts without speaking their language?

But the Lord showed his mercy. Only last week, Miguel agreed to take Father Pedro Antonio to meet the family of the young woman they had talked about. "There are six potential converts for you there, Padre," he promised.

They arrived at a tattered bamboo fence, where they found a woman kneeling on the ground washing the feet of her master. He pushed her away, rose, and with a friendly sway of his arm ushered the visitors to a mat spread on the grass. Then he motioned to the woman and a girl standing by the hearth. A minute later, the woman emerged carrying a heavy pot without a spout, the girl gourd shells stacked in one hand and a basket of plums in the other. The girl set the shells down, her hands grubby but steady, her face sunny and alert. Briefly, she cast a curious glance at the pallid visitors. The woman, her face hidden under her matted hair, poured some yellow liquid into the gourds with her shaking hands, and fled to the hearth without looking at the strangers.

The three men had no common language other than the play of gesture, posture, and contortions of face. The host's eyes moved rapidly between his two guests, and Father Pedro Antonio wondered what the man thought of them — one with a full head of bark-brown hair cut to his neck, his upper body swathed in a light cloth extending into sleeves, tucked at the waist into the bottom part which separated into two leg covers, and the other with only a few strings of dry grass hair, his body encased from neck to foot in one dark frock, cinched at the waist with a silver chain from which a wooden cross dangled. He must have thought that these two strangers, both equally pallid, had come from two very different tribes.

Father Pedro Antonio and Miguel reached for the plums, munching and sucking and rolling their heads to show how delicious they were. Their barefooted host stared at the boots on Miguel's outstretched legs, and began to finger one, chuckling with admiration at the sturdy Portuguese leather, the metal knobs, and the artfully braided laces. The woman and the girl cowered by the hearth, not sharing in the feast of plums. Were they the host's wife and daughter? And who were the two men sitting with a young girl by the fence over the heap of bird nests? Whoever they were, Father Pedro Antonio was glad to have it confirmed that there were indeed six heathens in the household.

As he recalled the auspicious visit now, the Jesuit realized that he had already forgotten the names of his host and his two women. He had not been able to pronounce them anyway. "I don't need to remember their Việt names," he thought. "Upon entering into the faith, converts will take Christian names." A lonely evening looming before him, Father Pedro Antonio stretched his legs, lengthened his spine skyward, and three names came to him as if by divine revelation.

Joseph. A perfect name for the head of the family. The man's lustrous black hair brought hazy memories of Father Pedro Antonio's own father, who died at sea. The son's one vivid memory was of craning his neck over the casket and kissing the hair because his lips could not reach the waxy face. He was eight years old.

The woman had to be Magdalena, because when he had first seen her, his mind had gone to St. Luke's story of Magdalena washing the feet of Jesus. With her hair drooping over her sullen face, she reminded him of a painting he had seen when, shortly after his ordination, he was summoned to perform the last rites for a dying patriarch — a painting of Magdalena grieving under the cross for her emaciated saviour.

The young daughter simply had to be Mary. The girl was fresh and innocent, and one day would become a dutiful wife and bear a son in a dwelling not very different from the stable in Bethlehem.

Father Pedro Antonio shifted his body and felt his heart compress. If he managed to convert these three, he would send the good news to his superiors in Macao and, for once, look forward to their reply. He patted his knees with both hands, then stood up and lifted his arms to the heavens. He danced around the tree shaft in small steps, the way he had seen the natives dance at the Spring Festival. As the day's last rays slid into the water, he sank to his knees to thank his loving God for watching over him this day and every day of his missionary crucible.

THE SALT-ENCRUSTED ROPE of the rescue boat cut into Miguel de Roussado and jerked him sideways. He screamed into the wind and bit his lips in pain. His mouth flooded with a sweetish sap and he shoved his fingers between his teeth and retched red. A few seconds later, another churning wave bounced off the gunwale and crashed into his face. He spat the suds overboard and retched again. From the prow, the Chinese flagman was yelling orders to his oarsmen, but Miguel could not hear his words over the wind. He loosened the rope that was chafing his groin, pressed his back to the backboard, and splayed his feet against the walls of the boat to save himself from being washed overboard.

The months following the Lunar New Year were the height of the trading season. Filled to the brim with goods to barter, dozens of vessels — their food and fresh water rations nearly gone — swept in on the bulge of the northeastern monsoon and waited at the mouth of the Thu Bồn River for a pilot boat to guide them upstream to the shelter of Phai Phô. But if a vessel were wrecked by a sudden squall some distance from shore, the worn-out crews needed help. Miguel had volunteered for the rescue mission because he had come to crave the stab of physical exertion and wanted to test his skills alongside the Việt oarsmen. And still deeper in his heart, he fancied that by risking his life to save the sailors, he was repaying his God for allowing him to see the world.

Across the rippling whitecaps, he caught sight of the ashen cliffs of the shore and strained his water-clogged eyes to spot some long dark shadows on them. Would one of the shadows be the swallow-nest girl? She could well be hanging on one of those cliffs, also tied by a salty rope, scraping the surface of the rock with her cheeks. Her vest, soggy and transparent, would be pasted to her slender frame, her hair twisted into a knot, her neck bare.

She was the girl Miguel desired. He had lived alone in Phai Phô for over six months and was ready for a home and a steady bedmate. He could take the girl by the custom of the country — ask her father's permission and reimburse him for the loss of daughter — or by the rites of Christian marriage. The native way was simpler, and when the time came to return to Portugal, the girl could be left behind. The vows made before the Christian God would have to be sworn for life... for life in Đàng Trong? He needed to find the strength — somehow — to resist the admonitions of his Jesuit friend.

They were approaching the mouth of the Thu Bồn River now, and the Chinese flagman had stopped yelling. But Miguel's two choices continued to collide in his head while his edgy passions cried for release. Even in the bowels of the rescue boat, with chilly water dousing his chest, the thought of the swallow-nest girl spread out on the cliffs turned his body into a torch.

MIGUEL DE ROUSSADO had left his parents and seven siblings in a village, nestled amid the granite peaks of Serra da Estrela, on the west coast of Portugal, shortly after he had had a dream in which the Black Madonna bade him to retrace Vasco da Gama's voyage to India of nearly two centuries before. When he recounted the dream to his father, who had always longed to sail the seas, the old man decreed, "You cannot dispute the command of the messenger of God." In a blessing tinged with envy he ordered, "Go with God, and bring us a fortune, you lucky bastard."

The lucky bastard was hired as a deckhand by a captain with a cargo of silver bought from Spanish seamen who had hauled it from Peru. The captain wanted to take the silver to Asia and barter it there for the cotton or silk that was in great demand in the capitals of Europe. When he realized that Miguel could read and write, he made him double as a navigation aide.

After a seven-month ordeal of seafaring, on a stopover in Phai Phô, the captain made him another offer: "Stay here and scout for good deals in silver and copper for me." Miguel calculated: a trading scout instead of a deckhand; a chance to stay on dry land for a while and head home with a fortune and wild stories to tell. Why not?

With a year's advance pay tucked in his satchel, he rented a cubicle in the waterfront row of straw-thatched huts on stilts that had once sheltered Cham seamen. Itinerant merchants and the crews of pilot boats slept there now. At night, he dreamed of hiring vessels and native sailors to take him across the sea to China, of lining up silver buyers and becoming a rich middleman. During the day he ambled about fingering gems, jewels, and bronze drums, looking for deals that would be most profitable. The bustling mob in the alleys left him dizzy. He was particularly awed by the puny Việt coolies who carried loads on their backs that were twice their size. At night, worn out by the sun and vaguely dispirited, he hid in the shade of the verandah on the upper level and watched Chinese sailors trail Việt street women with catcalls.

One evening, he saw three men follow a food stall girl who had served him his midday meal. They were sticking a rod between her legs to trip her. When she fell to her knees right below the verandah, Miguel slid down the ramp and pulled her away from her tormentors. Within seconds the men punched him to the ground. Unable to rise, he dug his elbows into the earth and thrust his legs at them. They kicked back and a bare foot landed a blow on his cheek. He howled, clutched his head to protect it from more blows, and rolled away in the dirt. He came to a stop at the feet of an Asian man covered from head to toe in a hemp-coloured cloak. From the folds of the cloak, the man flashed a dagger, twirled it above his head, and began to scream words — or threats — in Việt. The assailants ran, and the girl vanished into a side alley. The man bent down and said in perfect Portuguese, "I'm Hisao. Can you get up on your own?" Miguel probably could, but was stunned to hear his native tongue and stayed down.

The next day, his rescuer, who turned out to be a Jesuit lay brother from Japan, came to check on him and translated the eviction notice Miguel had found under the mat. "Makes no sense to risk your neck around the pier," he advised the grateful trader.

Miguel moved to Cù Lao Chàm, an island of rocks and clumpy soil that shielded Phai Phô from the sea. His body sore from the brawl, he hired a servant to help him build a shack of mud and stone, and a cot of bamboo trunks and jute rope. He had the cot raised on logs and feathered with coconut leaves. Lying in it, he dreamt of Portugal rising over the horizon. His baffled servant slept on the grass and feared that his master might fall off and hurt himself. The master never did, even though he tossed and turned a lot because his dreams were sensual.

The women of Phai Phô were a marvel and a puzzle. Miguel's mother only left the family cottage without her husband at her side on Sunday night — to attend her second Mass of the day alone. His sisters were not allowed to go to town unless accompanied by one of their brothers. Here, in Đàng Trong, unchaperoned women were everywhere. They swarmed like moths around their stone-and-wood firepits set up in handy spots along the pathways, enticing sailors and tradesmen to their steaming crocks. They sold pepper, cinnamon, sugar, silk, and pottery in the stalls and sheltered alleys, calling out to Miguel, "Come, come! Buy from me!" In the floating market of the Thu Bồn River, they steered their junks toward him, offering clusters of pomegranates and passion fruit, and sometimes tossing a garland of blooms his way.

And how easily they took charge of bewildered foreigners! The evening after his captain had sailed away, when Miguel could no longer join the crew for a meal prepared by the ship's cook, he had strolled with hunger pangs for a good hour, dreading the prospect of ordering his first Việt meal and eating it alone. By a roadside eatery, a wispy youngster stepped in front of him. Her teeth were tiny and, unlike the blackened teeth of the older women, oyster white. She gripped Miguel's arm firmly and pulled him to a patch of grass, where she pressed down on his shoulder with her other hand to make him sit. A few moments later, she swayed toward him like a bamboo sapling, carrying a hot pot in a basket. She removed the lid, pulled the skin off the fish with chopsticks, split the flesh open, lifted the backbone, and stuck it in her teeth. Then she draped his fingers around the chopsticks, and moved his arm up and down to his mouth to show him how to eat. Charmed by her manner, and aroused by the intimacy of her touch, he kept his eyes on the naked fish. But the heat she stirred in his body was almost as intense as that of the hot pot, and his wobbly fingers refused to bring the chopsticks together.

A week after moving away from the pier, he sought out Hisao, who had promised to show him the Chinese Quarter, where good deals could be made. They walked to the west end of Phai Phô, where the alleys bristled with colour and vigour. Buddhist temples and ornate wood-and-brick houses were lit with lotus-shaped lanterns, their walls adorned with beamheads of dragon or fish. Huge meeting halls, painted red, were roofed with the yin-yang rows of convex and concave tiles and festooned with porcelain figurines in brilliant hues. "The first Chinese runaways came here a decade ago, to escape the bloodshed when the

Ming Dynasty lost the throne to the Manchus," Hisao explained. "The meeting hall is where the men talk trade and make deals."

"But why are there so many Việt women in this Chinese pack?"

"Because a Chinese merchant is smart. The minute he steps on the shore of Đàng Trong he takes a 'temporary' Việt wife."

"You mean a servant — a helpmate?"

"No, like a real wife. He gives her a roof over her head and all the food she wants and she cooks and launders for him. He teaches her about trade and learns from her a few words of the Việt language. When the groom leaves on a trading voyage, the bride stays behind with a satchelful of coins, knowing what to buy at off-season prices. If the groom decides to take his wealth and go home for good, the bride needs to sell herself elsewhere. Girls from the hinterland are the easiest prey because they're very poor and want to help their families."

"Do you have a woman to cook for you?" Miguel asked.

"No, I have a man cook, a young boy, also from the hinterland."

Miguel marvelled at the ease and benefits of the casual matrimony. Lonesome for Portugal, lusting for a woman, and vaguely fearful of competing for trade with the nimble Chinese, he was desperate for a moment of pleasure, of abandon. He politely declined Hisao's invitation to stay in the Chinese Quarter for the evening meal, and the minute he said goodbye to him went back to the waterfront and the row of grimy huts that was the brothel. After that, whenever the left-behind Việt "brides" brushed by him in the Chinese alleys and longing rippled in his head, the brothel brought him deliverance.

One scorching day, seeking refuge from the sun, he ducked under the bridge and saw a girl dozing on the ground. Her body, folded inside layers of colourful cloth, was tucked against the stone wall, her face a mask of calm. What looked like the usual array of crockery filled with Việt medicinal herbs was spread before her. He bent down and picked up a jagged crust — a small container. It was empty. The girl shook awake, blinked in dismay at his pallid face, then briefly bared her teeth in a smile and quickly lowered her eyes. Now in his fourth month in Phai Phô Miguel no longer recoiled at the sight of black teeth. He smiled back. She pointed her forefinger to the crust in his hand and then to the flock of birds skirling overhead. He did not make the connection and instead of looking up looked down. The girl's feet were scored with scabs. He felt for her. And he was curious about the craggy object. Hisao might know what it was. He slid the object inside his vest and offered the girl a coin. She took it, still too shy to look up, and he bowed to her courteously. Walking away, he felt her eyes burning his spine. He looked back just once and she was folded against the wall again like a multi-coloured sail. "Could I beat a Chinese merchant to her favours?" he mused and promised himself to come back.

When he stepped into the light on the other side of the bridge, where the Japanese Quarter began, his eyes fell on a crowd of Việt men crouching on their haunches under the boughs of a sprawling banyan tree. In front of them, on an overturned wooden pail and holding a crucifix in one hand and a manuscript in the other, stood a European man. The belted robe of his religious order only just covered his bare feet. His mouth was moving and his body swaying back and forth, as if to propel his words. When Miguel moved closer he realized that the preacher was trying to speak in Việt, twisting his mouth around the awkward tones and circling the crucifix in the air to keep up his rhythm and his courage. The Việt men mumbled and simpered, then one of them stood up, spewed some harsh-sounding words at the wooden pail without lifting his eyes to the preacher, and walked away. The others followed him. The preacher raised the crucifix and made the sign of the cross over the departing flock. When he tumbled off the pail, he nearly fell into Miguel's arms. *"Escusa,"* he muttered as Miguel caught him by the sleeve. He looked into the preacher's face and saw that he was crying.

"IS THIS PERSON ILL, or was his face painted this way?" Nguyễn Thị Mai asked her father. The family was walking in the main square of the Chinese Quarter, aiming to rent a stall to sell their first big harvest of bird nests. Leaning against the stone of an ancient water well was the pallid man who had bought a bird nest from her. She recalled the coin between the fingers with cut-off nails. With her father at her side, Mai was less timid about looking at the man's face. Under a dark cap, it shone like sea sand. Ringing the man's neck, around which no hair could be seen, and drooping over his shoulders, was a black cape. Việt traders scrambled about, showing the man their wares — whale bones and scythes and animal pelts. The man's legs were encased in leathery sachets with metal knobs, and braided up with twine. He must be a nobleman. Simple people like her went barefoot.

Later that evening, Mai's father climbed the hill to the sorcerer's tent, which was adorned with feather charms and fish-bone amulets, to ask about the pallid intruders. He brought his explanation to the family: "Several pallid people have been seen in this hamlet. They've come from across the sea. They don't paint their faces that way. Nor are they ghosts of their dead ancestors. Their deathly appearance cannot be healed by Việt spirits."

That night, Mai lay awake fancying that the pallid stranger must be a whale in human form. How else could he have crossed the immense waters? When she had first glimpsed the horizon from the shore, the sea — so howling, so endless — frightened her. Now she reasoned that the sea must end somewhere and this is where the eerie seafarer had come from. From a strange land far away. But why had his hair been cut to his neck and his fingernails pared? He must have committed a terrible crime in his native land to have been maimed so severely in punishment.

Mai's exile to Phai Phô had come as a result of her father's punishment. He had supported a village chief who was leading a peasant revolt against a rogue Trịnh Lord, and when the revolt failed and the ill-fated leader was seized and garrotted, his destitute and defenceless supporters fled to the South, overrunning the lands of the ancient kingdoms of Khmer and Cham. Uncertain how well he would fare there, the father took with him only his first wife and his youngest daughter, leaving his other five children and his parents behind. The three runaways walked for two months to reach Phai Phô, which at first sight appeared peaceful and thriving. But within days Cham sea pirates attacked a vessel carrying Việt gold and only two sailors survived the carnage. Mai's mother nursed them in an abandoned hut the family had moved into. When she fell ill and died, Mai cared for the men, who recovered and stayed on to help with the swallow-nest trade. Her father took a runaway from the hinterland named Thu Trang to cook for the family and to be his concubine. A short time later, he took another concubine, a girl as young as his daughter, and Mai found herself sharing the sleeping mat with two women who fought constantly. Motherless and unhappy, she kept her turmoil to herself. A runaway from the North, she found solace in knowing that a pallid man had also left his native land. She lulled herself to sleep pretending she was a newborn sea turtle being carried by big waters to a distant shore.

THE EVENING OF Father Pedro Antonio's hapless attempt to deliver a homily in Việt, he and Miguel sat on the ground in front of the bamboo-and-mud hut which was the Jesuit's chapel, vestry, and living quarters all in one. Around them swarms of fireflies glinted in the grass. The men sat cross-legged before a banana leaf filled with nut meats and chunks of grilled fish.

"You know," the host began, "when I look at fireflies I imagine that they are the dimmed eyes of my Lisbon parishioners obeying my call to fall on their knees before the Lord. At the Igreja Sao Roque in Lisbon, I was the church's choice to replace my ailing superior. But my widowed mother insisted that since the Lord had given me the gift of oratory I must join the Society of Jesus and follow in the footsteps of St. Ignatius and St. Francis Xavier to spread the faith. I prayed that God give me strength to disobey my mother. But she promised the Society a large bequest upon her death if they chose her son for an overseas mission. I wept but had to obey, for the love of Christ, for the triumph of Christendom."

Father Pedro Antonio threw a nut meat in his mouth and bit on it hard. "So here I am. Risking my neck preaching to the natives, trying to master the dreadful tones. The missionaries who were here before me didn't have to learn them. They said Mass for the Portuguese sailors, heard their confessions, and went home. Now, thanks to Father de Rhodes and his dictionary, my superiors in Macao want me to convert the natives — in their language. I can't... I know how to preach but I can't..."

"Well, Padre, even the great Father de Rhodes was not perfect. Do you know that once he asked his men to cut down all the bamboo trees, but mistoned one syllable and his words came out as an order to kill all the children? The natives ran into the bush in horror."

A brief smile appeared on Father Pedro Antonio's face and he slapped his palms on his knees in relief. "Can you make yourself understood in Việt?" he asked Miguel.

"A little. I keep my ears open to catch the tones and often use the one phrase I have mastered, *Đây là cái gì? What is this?*" I have a Japanese friend who has lived here for some time and speaks the language well enough. He helps me." Miguel hesitated for a moment, then added with a grin, "And very soon I will take a Việt girl for a wife and she'll teach me."

"Well, her family will have to be converted first."

"Not necessarily. I can take her by the custom of the country — like the Chinese."

"You're not a shabby Chinese runaway; you're a noble Christian man. You owe it to your Maker and to your parents."

"This is not a Christian country, Padre."

"Not yet."

"Well, Padre, I need a woman here and now. I cannot be celibate like you and your kind. A temporary wife will do for the time being."

"There is no 'for the time being' for a Christian man. That would be a grave offence against the Ten Commandments. That native girl... If her family came into the faith you would earn grace in the eyes of the Heavenly Father which would count on the Day of the Final Judgment."

"But if her father finds a Việt man or a Chinese trader before you are successful, a dutiful daughter cannot refuse. I can take her by the custom of the country now and convince the family to be converted later."

"No! Their dark souls must see the light first. Marriage and commerce will follow soon enough."

"I'm sure her father will see the benefit of trade before he sees the benefit of salvation." Miguel was becoming impatient.

"As an ordained servant of God I must forbid you to sin with a heathen woman. Take me to her family and in six weeks I'll open their hearts to the word of Our Lord Jesus Christ. That Japanese friend of yours, can he interpret for me?"

"Probably... He's a Jesuit layman himself and he speaks Portuguese and Việt fluently."

"Perfect! Now, let me hear your confession. It will lift the burden off your shoulders and give me the joy of granting the forgiveness of sins — in Portuguese."

Miguel had little to confess but his visits to the brothel and taking God's name in vain now and then. Father Pedro Antonio pronounced his absolution and thought what a gift from Heaven his chance encounter with Miguel was. What might lie ahead for them — two prodigal sons from Portugal lost in the wilds?

ON A MUGGY SPRING DAY Miguel and Hisao walked down the boardwalk, wading through the jubilant crowd of traders, sailors, musicians, and jesters gathered for the opening of *hội chợ*, the annual trade fair in Phai Phô. Five-coloured pennants soared in the wind. The fairground was the place to make trade deals, but the first day was always reserved for contests, games, and amusements. At the very tip of the pier, a crew of Italian sailors was inciting two fighting roosters with hoots and whistles. Further down the embankment a quadrangle of the meadow had been roped off and patterned into a chessboard for human chess to be played. Miguel was stopped in his tracks; he had never seen the game staged outdoors with live players. Before him on the grass, men richly costumed as chess pieces stood in their assigned positions, waiting for their masters to tell them which way to move. A small rook, decked from his ankles to his turbaned head in yellow, was pushed by the agent of one master to advance a single spot to his left, and the opponents at the other end of the chessboard countered by moving a chess-warrior decked in green. Next a man in an ornate Mandarin costume was made to step one spot up, and at the outer edge of the chessboard the tallest player wearing a royal crown of twigs and ribbons found himself checkmated.

As the sovereign was run off the board, Miguel clapped with the others till his eyes caught the body of a lamp dancer swathed in white silk and pink lotus blooms. She was tilting and balancing a gourd of groundnut oil on her head, the wick nearly scorching her hair. But she did not spill a drop as she swayed her arms and hips sinuously to the beating of drums. Miguel felt a jolt of desire and let his hips sway with her.

"It's amazing how the native women move..." he said, but Hisao was looking at two boy-rooks pulling off their yellow costumes in the tent for chess players.

The two men had become companions ever since the taciturn lay brother from Japan had saved Miguel's life on the pier. Over the several walks and meals they shared, Hisao told Miguel that he was a foundling left on the pier of Nagasaki and raised by a Portuguese harbourman and his geisha. When his adoptive parents caught him in the garden nuzzling a boy under the rose arch, they put him in the hands of a Jesuit seminarian who was to convert him into righteousness. When that proved unsuccessful, they put him on a cargo boat and told him not to come back. Hisao had survived three years in Đàng Trong as a roving helper, tutor, or go-between for deals of all sorts, and, in the process, taught himself enough of the Việt language to "translate" — with what accuracy Miguel could not be sure. He was so grateful to have him for a companion and a street counsellor that he turned a blind eye to what Hisao called his "oddity." And Hisao never pushed the matter.

They left the fairground and sat on the grass in the eatery by the water. Hisao, in fluent Việt, ordered the girl-server to bring some gingered grilled fish and rice-flour dumplings instead of steamed rice, explaining, "I hate their lousy rice. Japanese rice is superior but impossible to find here." Then, he lowered his voice.

"I know you need to trade and make deals, but let me warn you. The natives are a dishonest lot. They'll agree on a price and deny it later. Try to pay you with forged coins. Often, they won't show up at all. They use two scales, you know, one for buying and one for selling. And they speculate like the Chinese — buy up goods and store them to get a better price later."

He paused and portioned out the dumplings.

"In any case, you must know that the Nguyễn Lords are first in line for anything and everything. What they don't want is left for you to sell. Their storehouses burst with gold and silver, tortoiseshell, paper, sugar, and rhinoceros horns. *Mùa mậu dịch*, the spring trading season — right now — is the best time to make deals."

"I need a Việt partner, a man who knows this country and speaks the language. Who can take me around the entire territory of Đàng Trong and to China," Miguel said.

"Do not count on going to China. Việt merchants want to do business but they also like to hug their shore. They have little curiosity about the world. Look at the *ghe bầu* they build." Hisao pointed to the wooden barges with their tall leafy sails crowding the shore. "Every one of them can carry 100 tons. But the Việt won't venture to other lands."

"Well, for now I can trade around here... bird nests for example. I bought one from a Việt girl. I went back quietly and followed her home. That girl could pave my way to a good deal."

"You like Việt girls?"

"I have been thinking of what you said about taking a Việt wife, about how these women can help with trading. I mentioned her to a Jesuit priest who lives on the outskirts of this hamlet. He insisted that for him to bless the union with a Việt woman, her family would have to be converted. But he cannot speak Việt. Do you think you could translate for him?"

"I've heard of the Jesuit. A high-minded and aloof man. He has little gift for languages... or for converting. Why don't you just ignore him and take the girl the Chinese way?"

"I owe the Jesuits a lot. They taught me to read and write — in the vestry of my parish church in Portugal. Without them, I wouldn't be here. I can at least introduce you to him. There is no harm in that, is there?"

"As you wish. I can tell you now that the infidels won't listen. They resist change. A Confucian man is loyal to the powerful. Stories of the Bible hold little power over them. They don't want to understand our God."

"Well, if Father Pedro Antonio fails to bring that family into the faith, he won't be able to blame me for taking the woman the Chinese way. But you can help him try. Yes?"

IN THE SIXTH WEEK of proselytizing with Joseph and his women, Father Pedro Antonio and Hisao were walking toward their hut when they saw a large fire at the end of the alley. The stench of burned animal hide overlaid the evening air. When they came close, the flames lit up the face of the woman Father Pedro Antonio called Magdalena, who stood by the spit poking the slab of meat with a rod. "We've bartered a basket of swallow nests for the hind of a male boar," she said haughtily. "You've done well," Father Pedro Antonio acknowledged and felt a gust of hot air singe his face.

They settled on the ground close to the spit, in a circle as usual, Joseph in the middle, his two concubines and his daughter, Mary, on his sides, Father Pedro Antonio and his translator facing them, the Holy Bible in a straw covering on the grass. The preacher opened the holy book to St. Matthew, Chapter Thirteen, and was about to begin his lesson when Magdalena rocked back and forth on her bum, narrowed her eyes, and asked, "If we agree to be what you call 'baptized,' will we change into Portuguese persons? Will we look like pallid people?" Hisao gulped before translating.

Father Pedro Antonio also gulped — Hisao must have mistranslated the previous lesson about the holy water cleansing the sinner. "No! No!" he cried. "Nobody's appearance will change. You'll always look like Việt people. But you'll enter into Christian law and your souls will be saved and go to heaven. That's what I want to talk to you about today — your afterlife." He spread his fingers over the Bible.

"One of the lofty mysteries of the Christian religion," he began, "is that it promises an afterlife for the true believer who's led a righteous life on earth." He pointed to the sky. "Far above where the flocks of chim yến are flying is a place of eternal joy, where the soul, which lives beyond the death of the body, will dwell forever in the House of the Lord. But for the sinner, a place of torment... of pain... is waiting. It's called Hell."

He waved his hand at the flames smouldering beneath the boar. "If you put your hand into the middle of that fire, and hold it there... can you imagine holding it there forever?" he asked. His listeners stared at the spit. "Hell is even hotter than that. It's like a dungeon..." Hisao grimaced and the preacher simplified, "It's like a huge cauldron of flames that scorch the flesh endlessly — the flames of Hell having no light — there is an abyss of fire and brimstone... the cruel company of fiendish tormentors..." Hisao tugged Father Pedro Antonio's sleeve to signal that the words were too knotty, but the preacher closed his eyes and quoted St. Matthew from memory, *"The Son of man shall send forth his angels... And shall cast them into the furnace of fire: there shall be wailing and gnashing of teeth."*

He paused to let the family listen to the sizzle of the scorched meat, as the flames, incited by dripping fat, hissed and sputtered. "In the eternal darkness of the dungeon," he intoned, "and in the company of devils, the human soul is condemned to the everlasting misery of guilt and anguish, and the wretchedness of eternal suffering." Convinced that he had created the required amount of terror, Father Pedro Antonio opened his eyes. Joseph's face had gone grim and Magdalena's ferocious. The younger concubine rubbed her eyes, ready to weep, and Mary, the youngster of the group, had shrunk into herself and was chewing on her knuckles. Father Pedro Antonio pointed to the spit again. "Only by becoming followers of Jesus will you be saved from such a horrendous fate."

Magdalena jumped to her feet, grabbed the meat rod, and gave the roasting boar an angry smack. With an outstretched forefinger, Father Pedro Antonio ordered her back to the grass. Now that his listeners appeared to be sufficiently convinced of the agonies of Hell and the glory of eternal salvation, he felt ready to move to the blessed state of Christian matrimony. "In the Garden of Eden, God, being perfectly just and the maker of laws which conform to natural reason, gave Adam one wife." He thrust his forefinger in the air twice, "One man, one wife. And the man shall 'cleave to his wife and the twain shall be one flesh.' A man who wants to avoid the terror of Hell must choose one woman to marry and remain faithful to her for life."

In a tomblike silence the two concubines turned to their master with questioning eyes.

"How is it possible to live with one wife? What if she is barren? Or lazy? Or gets sick? A man with many wives is a rich man... What would others say if they saw me with one wife? They would look down on my impoverished household." Joseph was genuinely puzzled.

Father Pedro Antonio said patiently, "To a true Christian marriage is a sacrament." He saw Hisao struggle with the word and clarified, "It's like a solemn vow before God. With prayer and obedience to God's laws, you'll have more children with the woman you choose to marry."

Joseph leaned forward, dug up some dirt with his long fingernails, and poured it from one shaking hand to the other. He looked stunned. Magdalena said that the boar was ready to serve, but Father Pedro Antonio waved her down once more.

"Having many concubines need not be the proof of man's riches," he said. "In the eyes of the Christian God man's virtuous conduct is a higher treasure. In any case, having more than one wife is sinful and will bring damnation in Hell. Is it worth sacrificing eternal glory for the sake of trivial customs and conveniences?"

Joseph lowered his restless hands to his lap, looked at the two concubines sitting by his side, and asked, "If I marry one, what will happen to the other? Both are mine."

Father Pedro Antonio said firmly, "The other will not be excluded from salvation. She'll also be saved from sin. A husband will be found for her and she'll receive many wedding gifts."

"She cannot have another husband..." Joseph burst forth, but Father Pedro Antonio ignored his protestations.

"'For what is a man profited, if he shall gain the whole world, and lose his own soul?' Whatever your sacrifice on earth, it will be given to you a thousand-fold in the heavenly kingdom." The words rushed out of him. Hisao sliced the air with his hand again to slow him down, but the preacher could not. "When the body is dead, the soul will stand before God to be judged. He will reward the good and punish the wicked." Hisao shut his eyes.

The fire of the spit had died down and there was only the light of the moon. Joseph was still alert but young Mary and the two concubines looked exasperated and worn out. All four listeners kept glancing at the boar with hungry eyes. "And the miserable sinners will be torn from their families, their wretched souls condemned for eternity," the preacher cried. Hisao gestured frantically one more time and then fell silent. "And the Kingdom of Heaven on earth will come but not before there will be earthquakes, and the sun becomes black and the moon blood-red… and all souls… will stand together on that supreme day…" He raised his arms to the heavens and boomed, "Repent, ye sinners!"

Joseph also raised his arms, gripped Father Pedro Antonio's right hand and stabbed his forefinger at the preacher the way he had seen him do, and spat out — and Hisao sprang alive and translated — "My women cannot belong to anybody but me."

ON THE LAST DAY of the Lunar Year of the Dog, which was on the eve of the Lunar Year of the Pig, which was in early February of the Year of Our Lord 1656, a Việt man wearing a vest edged with rabbit fur stood in front of his hut between his concubine and his daughter, both women swathed in red silk. Father Pedro Antonio lifted the silver chalice he had brought from Lisbon and sprinkled holy water around the family — now reduced to three. The younger concubine had refused to come into the faith and had fled to join the two former housemen at the new water-well construction site in the Japanese Quarter. The Jesuit walked across the cleanly swept yard to the wall of the hut and took down the parched rib of a whale — the idol the family had been worshipping since coming to Phai Phô — and put the bone on the ground. From the folds of his cassock he pulled out a wooden cross and hung it in its place.

He anointed Joseph, Magdalena, and Mary one by one "in the name of the Father, and of the Son, and of the Holy Ghost," pronouncing their Christian names softly, almost affectionately. "You are the children of the true God and Saviour now," he chanted as he hung a pendant of Agnus Dei around their necks, the Lamb of God and the cross beautifully carved in sandalwood.

Two weeks later, Miguel stood beside Mary, who was crowned with the traditional turban of red brocade edged in black, twisted and braided into layers of coils. Her gown was a five-panelled chiffon-and-gauze tunic held at the waist with a sash of purple satin. Hues of crimson overlapped at the front of it, concealing her bare feet. Her eyes, as pitch-black as her teeth, beamed from a face that was pure sunshine. Miguel wore his mother's black cape, still redolent of the sea winds that had gusted over it on the voyage from Portugal. Under the cape shone a white silk chemise that Mary had hastily woven for him. He stared straight ahead like a hawk taking in the mountains.

Father Pedro Antonio, in a white silk soutane with a gold-embroidered stole around his neck, bound the couple's hands with a garland of jasmine blooms and heard them repeat their vows in Việt and in Portuguese. The bride, who had been coached by Hisao, pronounced her Portuguese phrases laboriously but correctly, but the nervous groom fumbled his Việt tones badly. Hisao held the handbook of liturgy open to the right page. Almost three years had elapsed since Father Pedro Antonio had performed the sacrament of marriage in Lisbon and he did not want to miss any words. When he came to "let not man put asunder," he caught a cloud of melancholy in Miguel's eyes. His own eyes burned like embers. He had converted three heathens. He had saved a Portuguese trader from sin. If only his mother could see him now.

The newly married couple turned and walked toward Joseph, who unexpectedly kowtowed to Miguel, as if Miguel was his new master rather than his new son-in-law. The son-in-law, his head leaden with the gravity of what had just taken place, failed to return the kowtow. But he stayed close to Joseph, weary of facing Father Pedro Antonio again, his pulsating head still trying to fathom how the holy man had managed to mediate the betrothal so swiftly and smoothly and haul Miguel to the altar with neither one of them missing a step. Aching to set his body in motion and dissipate its tension, he ran to the gift basket and opened up a blue Japanese parasol that was his wedding present to his bride. He twirled it between his palms, letting the plum blossoms vibrate, and watched the faces of his new family open up in smiles. Only Hisao, who had moved to the back, looked forlorn.

A fancy lacquer fan was another gift for Mary, and when Miguel put it in her hand she cooled her face with it gracefully, as the consort of a Mandarin would — as the stately wife of a high-ranking man that she had just become. She glowed with exuberance, looking forward to having her own home, to roasting a boar on her own spit, and to discovering — very shortly — if her husband's skin was pallid all the way from his head to his toe.

Finally Miguel turned a silver-rimmed piece of looking glass toward his new family and saw them scramble forward to see the reflection of their faces so much more clearly than they would in the puddles of rainwater. Earlier in the morning he had looked at his own reflection in that mirror, and flinched at seeing a man very different from the one who had left Portugal a year and a half earlier. He looked much older and very crisp-skinned. Every ray of Phai Phô sunshine seemed to have left a mark on him. It would take half a year for his family in Portugal to receive the news of his betrothal and he was grateful for the time lapse. He knew what his mother would do when she learned that her son had married a dark-skinned pagan who ate off a mat spread on the grass and heaped her food with sticks. She would collapse on her sewing stool sobbing — as she always did when struck by a family calamity — and spew wrathful threats to the sky till spent, only to end by beseeching Jesus's mercy on the miserable sinner who had caused her pain. He figured it would take him just as long to believe that he was married to a Việt woman.

His mind raced back to the turbulent weeks preceding the Christian union he had had no intention of entering into. He had gone to Joseph's hut bearing a deerskin satchel, which he shook vigorously to let the coins clink until Joseph's eyes grew as large as wild hazelnuts. He brought out from the satchel a fistful of rare *ten-liang* silver pieces, and fifty plain coins each of zinc and bronze, which was his payment for Joseph's loss of a daughter. Joseph took only a quick look at the largesse before acting out with his arms, his legs, and every other muscle of his body what he wanted the pallid man to know — that trusting in Miguel's good character and intentions, he agreed to allow his daughter to become his temporary wife. Then Joseph picked up a swallow nest from the grass and added, with more blistering looks and head shakes and animated gesturing, that Miguel would now take him as partner in the swallow-nest trade, help him buy a concession from the Nguyễn Lords, and share his personal riches with the family for the duration of his stay in Phai Phô. Miguel used his entire Việt vocabulary to convey that he was honoured to accept. Before leaving, he added, combining mime and words, that he would ask Hisao to come to Joseph's hut in the next few day to confirm the temporary union in words properly translated.

A few days later, when he arrived at the hut, Joseph's concubine and daughter were carrying bowls of grilled sea fish, sap-glazed root vegetables, and nuts-and-berries studded rice to the dinner mat pinned down with four bird's nests at the corners. Joseph was already squatting, along with Hisao, and — to Miguel's surprise — Father Pedro Antonio. Had the Jesuit relented and decided to turn a blind eye to Miguel's Chinese-style marital arrangement with a native woman? The two women joined the men at the mat, Mary glowing, Magdalena smug and almost smiling. Miguel had not known her to smile before. Joseph hastened to explain — and Hisao translated painstakingly — that his two women were joyously anticipating their exalted rank as first and only wives for life, as was the Christian married custom, and that the rite of baptism would take place forthwith. Momentarily puzzled, Miguel leaned back and said that no baptism was necessary for Mary's betrothal by the custom of the country. But Joseph wagged his finger in the air and shouted, "Christian way... one man, one wife! My women like..." Father Pedro Antonio raised his arm to speak, but Miguel cut him short and in loud words began to explain that a few days back he had offered Joseph many coins as payment for the loss of his daughter. Joseph thrust his chest at Miguel and shouted, "No loss daughter... Christian marriage good..."

In the chaos of the moment, Hisao had shrunk back and dropped his head to the ground, and Father Pedro Antonio, his arm still in the air, said it was clearly God's will that Joseph's family come into the faith and seal their commitment with a Christian marriage. Hisao mumbled the translation and Joseph roared with laughter. Miguel, his agitation cresting, sidled up to Father Pedro Antonio and hissed, "How did this happen?"

Father Pedro Antonio explained in a hushed voice that after the failed instruction on Hell he and Hisao had gone for one last visit and found only Mary at home. She asked to hear again about the Christian custom of "one and only wife," and at the end said she liked it very much. So much that she thought that her stepmother would want to marry her father the same way. The two women must have convinced — or coerced — their master, because the following Sunday Joseph barged into Father Pedro Antonio's hut in the middle of the Mass, demanding that the preacher confirm that the trader Miguel, if he became his Christian son-in-law, would bring him riches in life and in afterlife.

"Some assurances may have been lost in translation," Father Pedro Antonio added apologetically, "but did these natives not deserve the blessings of a singular union? Will you not profit from having a woman blessed by God in a Christian home? Will you not find the fulfillment you have yearned for and also earn the promise of the special grace that awaits those who make sacrifices to clear the path for Jesus in the jungle?"

Remembering his father's admonition never to argue with a man of the cloth, Miguel mustered in response: "I'll need some special grace soon because after paying Joseph for his daughter's hand and the Nguyễn Mandarins for the licence to trade bird's nests, I'll have no riches left." Then he looked at Magdalena, who was elated at her clever advancement from a hinterland runaway to — soon — first and only wife of one man for life, and at Mary, the radiant girl he desired, whose motive he understood even better later, when he heard her rhapsodize about the joy of being married to a man whose mother lived too far away to rule over her.

YEARS LATER, when his son was ready for his First Communion, Miguel watched with great pleasure as his three daughters adorned the boy's long hair with orchid blooms, and recalled how in the days after his marriage he had grown his own hair long to look more like a follower of Christ. Most statuettes given to the natives had Jesus's hair fall from under the crown of thorns to his waist, and Father Pedro Antonio had often been asked by prospective converts why pallid people would want to cut their hair short and alter the appearance given to them by their God. Miguel very much liked the ruddy look of his long-haired Việt—Portuguese children.

Alas, at the family celebration of the Communion he was bitten by a scorpion and for several days lay swollen and nearly paralyzed while Mary covered his limbs with a steamy cloth and clapped a hot wooden spoon against his soles. When a mud plaster prescribed by a Portuguese doctor failed to cure him, and the local medicine man had chased Mary away with curses for betraying her ancestors with a pallid alien and converting to his repellent religion, she secretly took three silver coins from her husband's satchel and offered them to the sorcerer. He performed a restorative dance behind the wall when Miguel was asleep, alternately tapping his knees and the beams of the house and twirling his tiger-rib wand to the tune of a healing chant. Before he left, he told Mary to feed the sick man roasted maggots. She did, and put the looking glass to Miguel's face every morning to convince him that he was getting better. He always turned his head away. He hated to see his lips, stained red from the betel leaves Mary had made him chew to keep his mouth healthy. The day he finally stood up, Mary tried to bring the glass to his face again and he swung his arm to push it away. The glass shattered into silvery chips on the stony hearth and Mary cried. But Miguel thought it might as well be gone. He hardly recognized the Portuguese man in it.

Father Pedro Antonio, who on account of his declining health had come to live with the young couple shortly after the betrothal, had barely changed. The Jesuit lived long enough to baptize all four of Miguel's children in fluent Việt, which Mary insisted be spoken at home. But he continued to be tormented by back and joint pains that the swallow-nest broth could not relieve. "You should put yourself in the hands of the 'surgeon of the country' who is skillful with bleedings," Magdalena urged him when she visited. He resisted, but when the pain got too severe, he gave in. The surgeon took out a clay-tipped goose quill and flicked the pointed nib into the vein of the Jesuit's arm. He let the blood drip for much of the afternoon, till the patient's cheeks turned the pale yellow of rice stalks dried by the sun after threshing. Then he pressed the vein shut with his finger and made Miguel spit at it to build up a dressing. The bleeding stopped and the gash dried up. But the patient died.

His body was entombed in the courtyard of the Catholic Church, a stone's throw away from Hisao's lowly burial ground, which lay outside the fence — for in the end, Hisao used his dagger to cut short his troubled wanderings upon this earth, and Father Pedro Antonio had to deny him burial in the consecrated ground. Feeling vaguely remorseful, Miguel tried to argue, but the Jesuit was adamant that the canonical law was very explicit on the subject of suicide.

After Father Pedro Antonio's death, Mary went back to worshipping at the Altar for the Ancestors that she put in the corner of her home and adorned with fruit and flowers. Miguel did not object because the Jesuit's successor in the diocese of Phai Phô had told him that it was a social rite more than a religious rite, and that the natives had made enough adjustments for now. And when Miguel and Joseph got back from a trading voyage along the coast and stopped at Joseph's house to store their wares,

Miguel saw that the whalebone was hanging from the thatched roof again. He was relieved that Father Pedro Antonio had been saved the distress of seeing it there. Over the years of his marriage to Mary, Miguel had come to accept the earnest continuity of native ways, as he accepted the trees that sprang from the Việt soil and came into bud by his bamboo-log house.

Years had passed since he had last heard from his parish priest back in Portugal who, before he retired, had written that Miguel's father and two sisters had died of influenza, that his brothers had all married, and his mother had entered her seventy-fifth year. Miguel did not reply. His Portuguese family seemed too distant to be real. And he shied away from the Portuguese clergymen and traders visiting Phai Phô lest they look askance at his merged family. Now and then he went to the churchyard to check on the headstones of his two friends and sometimes imagined his own headstone sprouting there one day. But he never entered the nave. At home in the evening, while Mary worked her loom, he would bring down from the roof beam Father Pedro Antonio's rosary and stroke the beads one by one without saying any holy words at all.

The Sisterhood of Concubines and the Brilliant Speck of Yellow

In 1802, having successfully put down a country-wide peasant uprising, the Nguyễn clan saw one of their own mount the throne of Đại Việt. The feat was accomplished with some help from the French, who had increasingly explored the country's shores looking to establish trading posts. The first Nguyễn Emperor united the South and the North under the name of Việt Nam and moved the capital to the central city of Huế. He and his successors lived in the Forbidden City of the Huế Citadel in whose heart, girdled by a stone wall, laid a compound for the royal concubines.

1847

BEAUTIFUL NGUYỄN THỊ CHÂU SQUATTED on the grass with her back taut and her hands folded in her lap, exactly like the backs and hands of the five other newcomers to the Forbidden City who squatted near her. But her head rose well above theirs. On the other side of the mat, Concubine Quỳnh of Grade Four waited for her charges to be perfectly still before beginning the story she wanted them to hear:

"In the early years of the reign of Emperor Minh Mạng, a prolonged drought blighted our land. The fields and meadows shrivelled into dust and the riverbeds narrowed into muddied grooves. The Emperor ordered his senior Mandarins, imperial astronomers, and local wise men to determine the cause of the calamity. Three lunar years later, when no one was any wiser and the land still lay withered, the Emperor took matters into his own hands. He issued a decree unheard of in the chronicles of Chinese or Vietnamese dynasties."

Concubine Quỳnh's voice rose to a lofty pitch as she quoted the Emperor's chilling words: *"There are too many women inside the walls of the Forbidden City. The foul smell wafting from their quarters hinders the flow of the wind and poisons the air. The Gods are manifestly displeased. They must be mollified before our Kingdom is ruined. Since the women are the cause of the calamity, let one hundred women be expelled!"*

Concubine Quỳnh always told this story when the novices were still daunted by the thick walls of their Compound, still desolate with longing for home. They needed to hear about the banished women of long ago to begin to accept that they would live in the Forbidden City for life. That such ill-fated expulsion would not happen again. She paused to watch as the novices lowered their heads to reflect on the gravity of the incident.

"The one hundred women were wronged," chirped a young voice.

"They were not wronged; they were doomed; it was their Fate."

"The Emperor was wise. My father says no woman is worth more than a bowl of rice."

"The doomed women," said Concubine Quỳnh, her thin voice getting graver, "who had never expected to see the outer walls of the Citadel again, were ferried back to their villages. When they arrived, their parents — who had unquestioningly believed the centuries-old proverb, 'A daughter sent to the Palace is lost forever' — thought they were seeing ghosts."

Beautiful Nguyễn Thị Châu heard an echo of her father's triumphant cry: "My daughter will live at the Palace for the rest of her life!" She could never return and break her father's heart.

"The returned women's grief did not end there," Concubine Quỳnh continued. "Their families blamed them for failing to please the Emperor and bringing shame on their clans." She gazed at the novices with a faint smile. "All the women of the six pavilions of the Đoạn Trường Palace have been exalted to serve Emperor Tự Đức, the fourth Monarch of the Nguyễn Dynasty, for life. You have not seen him yet, but he is our Son of Heaven and yours is an ennobling and enduring honour."

Châu's heart swelled with pride. Three months earlier, her father had delivered her to the Citadel in Huế in a dragon boat adorned with royal standards and garlands of purple lotus. The village women had laid the blooms at her feet when they came to the water's edge to wish her well. Châu's mother and sister stayed home because her father had ruled they were too emotional to say goodbye at the pier. Châu had sailed the Perfume

River sitting on a platform raised high so that villagers on both banks could see her. Peasant women interrupted the washing of their garments and vegetables to kowtow to her. Their small daughters threw strands of jasmine toward her, dreaming of making the same journey one day. Fishermen trailing alongside in their junks called good wishes to her — the proud daughter of a Nguyễn Mandarin on her way to the Royal Palace. Châu sent back the wave her mother had taught her, while taking her last look at the land that she fancied lay at her feet now. She turned her head to the sun, which shone just for her, and to the birds who sang for her alone.

The boat docked across from the massive Flag Tower, above which the red and yellow royal emblem flew — a mighty dragon vanquishing the serpents and reptiles that squirmed around it. An ornate mahogany palanquin sat on the grass, its convex roof draped with red cloth crimped and tied to the four corners with colourful ribbons. Two logs ran along the sides of the box and at their ends, staring ahead, waited four men clad in long grey coats. Were these the eunuchs who would carry her over the moat and the ramparts into the grounds of the Citadel?

She stepped into the palanquin and, realizing the finality of her passage, grew cold, and colder still when her father kowtowed to her for the first time in his life. He was offering homage to the chattel of the Emperor. She wanted to thank him again for having procured this great distinction for her, and assure him of her eternal devotion, but he spoke first: "I command you to worship His Majesty, to bear him a son, and bring honour to your family." By then Châu's heart was throbbing and she kept her eyes down to hide her panic. It took all her strength to keep her back erect as the eunuchs carried her through the granite South Gate onto the grounds of the Forbidden City where her new life would be.

Months earlier, Châu's father, approaching his tenth year of service at the Citadel, had begged the ailing Emperor Thiệu Trị to mark the occasion by allowing him to offer his daughter to his eldest son and heir. The plea was granted. What a masterstroke for the father! What honour for the family!

Alas, on his deathbed, the Emperor had ruled that his pleasure-loving eldest son was too reckless and dissolute to rule, and had designated his younger son, who was more respectful of the country's Confucian mores, to inherit the throne. Poisonous court intrigues followed — the older and the younger brothers squabbling, their supporters scheming and sparring. Châu's father would not allow his triumph to be foiled by the royal reversal. Through his faithful Citadel servant he conveyed a promise to generously reward the eunuchs carrying his daughter to the Forbidden City if they delivered her to the pavilion where the younger brother's women lived. Châu knew from her mother about the plan and quietly marvelled at her father's cleverness.

The eunuchs set down her palanquin at a doorway arched with a bougainvillea awash in pink blooms. A petite woman stepped away from a gathering of women at a loom, stretched her arms to block Châu's entry, and said, "The Heir to the Throne is small in stature and prefers small women." Châu gasped with relief to know that she had been delivered to the right place — her father had told her that the younger prince was not as tall as she was. But she was also aware of the burden of her height and smiled at the woman, whose voice remained chilly. "The Heir to the Throne is a poet who likes his women to know poetry. Perhaps you belong elsewhere?"

Châu stiffened her spine and raised her head high. "I am a Mandarin's daughter. I am to bear the Emperor a son," she replied.

"We are all Mandarins' daughters!" the woman shrieked and the others joined, laughing callously, spitefully.

The snub shocked Châu. Had not her father boasted that given his Nguyễn provenance and his influence at Court, his daughter would be favoured for the Monarch's pleasure? Had not her mother bragged that her daughter's Nguyễn beauty and charm would make her a prize for the Emperor?

She was made to sleep at the threshold of the hostile pavilion. In the morning two eunuchs, carrying burning torches, led her to a bamboo shed without any window openings. There a man holding two wooden spatulas ordered Châu to remove her garment and lie down on the mat. She obeyed slowly, buying time, knowing what was to come. Naked and trembling, she pressed her spine to the mat. The shiny pupils of the two eunuchs standing over her were aimed right at her belly. "Don't open your eyes until you are told," the physician ordered and she locked down her eyelids.

Two scabrous palms cupped her knees. As the physician parted her legs, a gust of his breath skimmed between her thighs and her own breath stopped. His hair grazed the inside of her legs and the nibs of the spatulas stretched her flesh. She felt the gaze of the physician burn through her vagina and lungs and up into her throat. Her nostrils filled with the smoke of the torches.

A moment later, from the distance of the threshold, she heard the physician's voice commanding her to get dressed. She lay still for a moment, waiting for her damp cheeks to dry and her clogged chest to clear, then opened her eyes to the murk, sat up, and hugged her knees. She had passed her first test. Her father would soon be told that his daughter had been confirmed chaste and could stay where she was.

A FEW DAYS LATER, on Coronation Day, the junior concubines
were allowed out of their enclosure to watch the pageant from
the back of the crowd of spectators. The magnificent Palace of
Supreme Harmony loomed in the distance, the orange bricks
of its massive roof singed by the sun's rays into dazzling red,
the ivory-inlaid portals garlanded in the royal yellow with
pendants and twigs of flowering acacia. All around them, the
air crackled with the ear-splitting peals of bells exalting the
new Monarch. Châu could not believe the number of grey-
coated eunuchs and uniformed military men who were milling
about. Just ahead of her, rowdy soldiers hooted and boasted
about their victory over the French navy. "What is a *navy*?"
she wondered. "What does *French* mean?" she asked the senior woman who was their chaperone and was told, "The Son of
Heaven knows. You don't need to know." Through the tangle
of banners, palanquins, and parasols, she craned her neck for a
glimpse of the golden robe and the nine-dragon hat of the new
Emperor Tự Đức, but even with her height and on her tiptoes
she could see only the yellow royal banner being hoisted up the
Flag Tower.

She was vaguely worried about the new Monarch because
she had already heard rumours that the prince passed over for
succession had begun to conspire with Court Mandarins and
Việt Catholics to depose his younger brother. Would the stigma
of having been originally pledged to him taint her life in the
Forbidden City? Three days after arrival, when Châu was intro-
duced to the younger prince's First Wife, the woman said, "Ah,
you are the stick meant for the snake." The other women of the
six pavilions of the Đoạn Trường Palace emulated this disdain
and barely spoke to Châu.

One day, after sitting alone on her sleeping mat all morning, she burst out, sobbing, "Why are you so mean to me?" No

one answered and she raised her voice. "My father will have you punished for this."

Her housemates just dropped their chins. Later, when she reached for her evening cover, three rancid peacock turds fell out of its folds. She leaped back screaming but the others pretended not to hear. With the new Monarch on the throne, would such unseemly taunting stop?

But then, two weeks after the Coronation, an arm shook her from the afternoon nap and a voice shouted, "Get up, get up and run to be washed," in a tone so commanding that Châu sprang to her feet in an instant. By the water well, two eunuchs she barely knew pulled off her garments and scrubbed her all over with seaweed as they rained lime-and-ginger elixir over her head and shoulders, and squeezed the water out of her hair till it hurt. The taller eunuch, who had silvery hairs sprouting from his chin, dried Châu's skin with a clump of moss and finally explained, "Your father has been appointed the Minister of Royal Accounts. To mark the occasion, you have been summoned to the Son of Heaven's chamber." Châu raced back half-naked. Her torment-ors... let them squirm with envy.

All twelve of her housemates were squatting on the ground of the Sixth Pavilion where the newer virgins lived, and with them was a senior concubine. On a lacquered tray behind her lay a spray of white jasmine and next to it sat three purple mango-steen shells in which perfumed oils glistened. Without saying a word, the woman began to rub Châu's arms and thighs with the fragrances and a pungent lemony scent filled the chamber. When Châu's skin shone like dew, the concubine dusted it with the reddish powder collected from stamens of hibiscus blooms. Two ladies-of-the-palace Châu had not noticed before stepped forward with a tunic of pale blue silk, a matching turban, and a choker of tightly woven ivory dream-beads. Châu frowned.

Light blue made her look sallow. But she donned the tunic without a word of protest, and when the ornament was clasped around her neck, the senior concubine said, "This choker is the emblem of a virgin's diffidence." It scraped her skin but Châu did not complain. This was the moment she had been waiting for. Within hours, she would no longer be a virgin but a chosen woman of the Emperor of Việt Nam. In spite of having been meant for his disgraced brother. In spite of being tall and not a poet. The covetous eyes of her housemates were upon her as the senior concubine pinned the narcissi above Châu's ear with a fishbone and said, "You will follow me to the Khon Thái Residence. First Wife must look you over."

The graceful low-roofed villa, coasting on a carpet of diamond-shaped tiles embossed in blue and green, stood right behind the Cấn Thành Palace where the Emperor lived. Châu kowtowed to the tiny woman at the top of the stairs who was half-hidden under a flouncy parasol, and who, although no more than a couple of years her senior, managed to look both birdlike and commanding. Châu awaited her instructions for the correct behaviour in the royal chamber. But the woman the concubines always referred to as the Most Treasured Lady gave her only a cold glare. From her novice's training Châu knew that to put a question to a senior woman without being spoken to first was an unpardonable offence. The Emperor's First Wife was merely exercising her prerogative to look over the first-time woman about to be taken to her husband's bed.

Momentarily disheartened and twitching her fingers nervously, Châu was led back to the lawn that looped around the six pavilions, where her housemates were in an uproar. "A virgin has been summoned," they cried. "It hasn't happened in months... It's a good omen." They fluttered around Châu like swallows feathering their nest, suddenly friendly and eager. "We can tell you what you must do to earn the Son of Heaven's favour. We know from the women who have been with him." They beamed at her and laid their hands on her as if she were a good luck charm.

"The first time, you'll just stroke the Son of Heaven's soles or plums," said one, and Châu thought of the testicles of her family's goats. "There will be more adept women doing the pleasuring so just keep your ears open. You can learn a lot from listening to the groans," added another. Older concubines were arriving from the other pavilions, and one who must have been over twenty explained with authority, "The eunuchs decide how much Yin the Son of Heaven needs from a female to balance his mighty Yang — more Yin in the spring and summer, less in the winter. They keep count of his ejaculations so as not to deplete his prowess with too many."

Châu had only a vague notion of sexual pleasure from watching the family dogs mount each other and yelp. She knew nothing of ejaculations. A concubine who often played her harp to entice the eunuchs (and whom Châu suspected of having put the peacock turds in her gown) added, "If the Son of Heaven needs to fortify his Yang, the eunuchs will select a woman who orgasms fiercely; if not, they'll take a more serene one from the list they keep. Only if he wishes to take a virgin will you be put to him at once — probably blindfolded. It's a sign of the reverent surrender of a virgin to her Sovereign."

By the Hour of the Cock, the ladies-of-the-palace had served dinner on the grass, but Châu was too overwrought to eat. By the Hour of the Dog, dinner bowls had been cleared and the women around Châu had lost their sparkle and their smiles. They fumbled with their long fingernails and kept glancing toward the gate to catch sight of the Son of Heaven's eunuchs. Châu pinched her neck around the itchy choker till one of the women said, "Patience is what you must have." By the Hour of the Pig, with no stars and no moon in the sky, the grounds had turned pitch dark and some of the women had walked off to their mats. During the rest of the night, Châu thought up two reasons for the silence from the Cấn Thành Palace — the Son of Heaven was not well, or he had to deal with important matters of state. She felt slighted but also strangely relieved, and said a silent prayer for her Monarch.

In the morning she woke with the wilted narcissi lying on her cheeks like monkey tails. Instead of walking around her, her housemates casually stepped over her long legs. Her turn had come and gone and now there would be more opportunity for them. "You're not the first to be left out to dry," said one. Châu kept her head down and thought what she dared not say aloud: "My time will come. I am of the Nguyễn clan and my father is a royal Minister. He will not allow his daughter to be shamed." But shame was swallowing her. The eunuch with the silvery hairs on his chin walked to her side and helped her to her feet. In the Sixth Pavilion, she threw herself on the mat, ripped the dead narcissi from her hair, and turned to stone.

1852

That year the disowned prince starved to death in prison. The eunuchs brought the news to the concubines, saying that the Son of Heaven had shown his elder brother no mercy for his seditious schemes to enlist royal troops to his vengeful cause. Châu felt liberated, relieved of guilt, hopeful that the stigma of having been meant for him had also died. A few days later, she had the proof. She and eleven other virgins were led to the Khon Thái Residence where the Most Treasured Lady announced that on the occasion of his twenty-third birthday the Son of Heaven wished to commend their exemplary conduct and convey his wish that they continue to serve as a good example to the more impatient and unruly women. His Majesty was awarding them upgrades — Châu was elevated from the Ninth to the Eighth Grade and allowed to move from the Sixth Pavilion to the Fifth, where the more senior women lived.

She had barely settled into her new Pavilion when she fell ill with malaria and was moved to an isolation shed. There she found Eunuch Vinh, the one with silvery hairs on his chin who had witnessed her night of shame five years earlier. He had been assigned to her care and she could not have been happier. She had seen him briefly during the time of spring and fall festivals when even those eunuchs not assigned to work in the Women's Compound could enter it to offer good wishes. Over the years she had learned that a concubine with a eunuch friend fared better in many ways: she had a counsellor, a deliverer of news about life outside of the wall, and a listener to her tales of woe. Châu felt very ready to have a eunuch as a friend.

For days she lay listless, feverish, and convulsed by fitful jolts, as Eunuch Vinh washed her with clumps of seaweed the same way he had on that fateful afternoon years ago. One bad day, after vomiting into a watermelon hull all morning, she asked him to stay longer. He squatted by her side, fanning her head with a palm leaf till her quivering body stilled and her eyes cleared. "If I die, take to my father my pledge of reverence," she begged him.

"You'll recover. You're like your father, too strong to die."

"Have you seen my father around the Citadel? I've been wondering — he was able to place me in the Forbidden City but not to have me taken to the royal chamber. He could have paid the Son of Heaven's eunuchs to have me summoned. He is a Nguyễn and he has the means."

Eunuch Vinh tilted his head. "We are the property of our fathers. We must revere them for their wisdom in all things. I revere mine for granting me the honour of offering him happiness." He saw Châu's eyes narrow with curiosity and explained. "I was only a child when he ruled that I should provide for the family by making myself *giảm lat*. It was in 1836, the year Emperor Minh Mạng — you know the story of the women he banished?"

"I do. One hundred women were expelled."

"Well, with the one hundred gone, there were still some two hundred concubines left, crowded and restless, scheming to be summoned, scraping and complaining. The Emperor's First Wife had been unwell for some time, not willing to oblige her husband, not able to handle the harridans. She kept taking her grief to him till he became so annoyed that he issued an edict commanding that all eunuchs in the kingdom be sent to work in the Citadel."

"There couldn't have been two hundred concubines? There're a hundred of us now and we're cramped," Châu said, glad to feel her sore head working again.

"My district, which is north of here, sent seven eunuchs — some self-castrated, some incomplete from birth. At the gate, they were examined for the absence of their organs, and with dozens of others from different districts commanded to bring order to the women's quarters and relieve First Wife of her burden. My father was envious of the annual payments the parents of 'the seven' would be receiving from the Court for the surrender of their sons. He said that more eunuchs would be wanted in future years, and that, being frail and lazy, I could best repay my filial debt to him by preparing myself for the call. He allowed me to grow up a bit and get stronger, and helped me with the chisel. I repaid my debt. You are repaying yours. We are helpless children at the mercy of Fate."

"When you finally arrived at the Citadel, did you know of the Emperor's woe?"

"I did not. At the South Gate, a royal doctor examined the scar where I had amputated my organ and took me to a tutor to verify that I could read and write. When the tutor read my composition he said, 'You're good enough to work on the Book of Fecundity.' He led me to a room with stacks of tablets leaning against the walls, and explained they were the records, by the hour, day, month, and year, of the Son of Heaven's copulations. The names of the concubines summoned to the royal chamber, and the district they came from, had to be recorded precisely. Every summoned woman had to be kept in post-coital isolation to see if her monthly bleeding stopped and her belly swelled. The birth of the royal offspring had to come nine months and ten days later. Any undue deviation from the term could bring the accusation of adultery and the punishment of death.

"I spent several days reviewing the copulations, and one day when I was alone I opened the ledger of royal births. The ledger was blank. 'Not possible,' I thought. 'I must have picked up the wrong tablet. The Son of Heaven should have had several sons by now.' I was new and too scared to ask. But not too scared to look up other tablets. Perhaps the records for royal sons were kept separate from the records for royal daughters? Not so. Very grudgingly, the unspeakable truth dawned on me: our almighty Son of Heaven had failed to fulfill the most sacred of his filial duties — to perpetuate the royal lineage with an heir.

"When I arrived I was told nothing," Châu said, rising on her elbows for the first time in days. "Women kept being summoned. When they wailed after failing to conceive, some eunuchs taunted them. Why?"

"Because we eunuchs are responsible for the Son of Heaven's carnal life. It would be blasphemous to fault the Monarch. So we blame ourselves for failing to select the most fertile woman at her most fertile time... But there are always whispers that the Gods are punishing the Son of Heaven for having stolen the crown from his brother. By now, only the Queen Mother holds on to her illusions that her son will one day father an heir."

"Should not the royal physicians give a reason... or a cure?"

"They are also frightened. Our Son of Heaven is the grandson of Emperor Minh Mạng, who followed his physician's recommended regime of 'five copulations per night' without fail and could impregnate three concubines before the morning light. Even now, decades after his death, the Royal Family and the Mandarins remember him as the 'Insatiable One.' All of them despair that the aphrodisiac potions he willed to his heirs have proven useless to his diminutive grandson."

"And we concubines despair because we have no children to love. We have to cuddle ducklings to feel any warmth. There should be a child in our midst for our motherly care and amusement. Even a crippled or a dim-witted boy would do."

"It is very hard on you, I know. I would give anything to have a son, to raise him and have him worship me when I am dead. You're a woman. You were born for the day your belly would swell. But it never will. You're over twenty now, too old to be summoned. You know that, don't you?"

"Why are we not expelled then?" Châu cried. "Sent home to love our parents?"

"We're all chattels of the Son of Heaven; we'll always live here. More young girls will be arriving soon. The Son of Heaven must reward the Mandarins who support his dealings with the French. Bringing their daughters to the Forbidden City is the best way. They will replace the women we've lost to malaria. Maybe you should try to adopt a novice woman? Treat her like a daughter? Teach her the etiquette of the Court. I can recommend you to the Most Treasured Lady... Otherwise, you'll perish from boredom."

"I've perished already... Father wouldn't recognize me..."

1854

When the country girl Hồ Thị Thu Hiền was chosen by her district Mandarin to be the betrothed of his youngest son, her father sacrificed not one but two castrated roosters in thanksgiving. For twenty years he had toiled as the Mandarin's carrier, boat rower, and messenger, but never dreamed of receiving such a lofty reward. His only daughter was a good cleaner and food preparer for the animals in the pen, and for her widowed father and his four sons. But she was also a daydreamer who had to be whipped to finish her household chores.

A week before the betrothal, a felled tree crushed the future son-in-law. Humiliated by Fate, the father hoped that the Mandarin would find another use for his daughter. For some time, he had been baffled by her "dreamings" — muttered rumblings about the radiance of the lakes (which for him were just bodies of water to row through) and the warbling of the birds (which for him was an annoyance), about the fragrance of flower buds just after they open (which he was indifferent to), and about seeing her mother's ghost amidst the clouds (it had never appeared to him). She spoke her thoughts aloud while the pots overflowed and hungry pigs squealed. Ashamed, and fearful of ridicule, the father never spoke to anyone about the silliness.

But the Mandarin was like a father to him, and it was incorrect to hide his daughter's oddity from him any longer. He kowtowed as low as his sore hips allowed. "I humbly beg your forgiveness for not having disclosed it earlier." The Mandarin did not become angry but thoughtful. He straightened his back and licked his lips. "Dreamings, you say... She talks in verse?" The father did not know what verse was but the Mandarin did. "I will order the village teacher to write down some of these dreamings and we shall see."

One evening after her chores were done, the eldest brother led Thu Hiền to his school for the sons of the servants of Mandarins. Not quite sure how to behave in the walled-in courtyard no village girl had ever set foot in before, Thu Hiền kept her head down till her brother told her to squat in front of the teacher and recite the dreamings she had been stringing together by the hearth. She looked up to the cut of the sky beyond the high wall, and began with her favourite — about a wounded dove and its silverfish friend: "Do not fly away my feathered love / Your broken wing will perish in the storm / Come, come to the silvering river..."

"Not so fast," the teacher commanded; he could not keep up with the stream of words. When he had filled half a dozen tablets, he repeated the last verse, "'The pomelo tree floats its perfume, my hand on the white-speckled vine...'" and rested his quill with a sigh. "I wish I'd made up these lines." Thu Hiền stayed mute because she did not know how to respond to praise.

Several months later when her father called her back from the patch of lemon grass, she dropped her hoe and ran to him, resigned to hear again what other chore she had neglected and how many lashes would teach her to remember. But with his sons at his side, the father gulped three mouthfuls of air before emitting the fateful words. "I've been honoured with the greatest imaginable benevolence. Emperor Tự Đức has seen my daughter's dreamings and summons her to the Forbidden City to be his concubine."

It took Thu Hiền a few seconds to realize what the words meant — she was being banished from the family to which she belonged body and soul, sent away from her ancestors whom she worshipped and from the tomb of her mother, who had always loved her dreamings. She had secretly hoped to become the betrothed of the teacher who admired them. She prostrated herself and flailed her arms against the grass. "Let me stay, Father! I beg you!" Her brothers rushed at her with their fists but their father stopped them, shouting, "She's the Emperor's chattel now!"

A few days later Thu Hiền stood before the Mandarin who looked as pleased as a cougar after a kill and said, "The Emperor is a poet, and your duty will be to delight him with your special gift."

Thu Hiền kowtowed and wondered, "What does 'poet' mean? What 'gift' is the Mandarin talking about?" She was a girl and a daughter. Her life duty was to cook and clean and bear children. Then a glimmer of recognition lit up her heart: she had been summoned for her dreamings. Perhaps the Emperor had them too?

CHÂU WAS RINSING her hair late one morning when Eunuch Vinh walked up to her and said in a low voice, "A new concubine has just arrived from Quảng Điền — from the same district as you. She'll be your first. Run!" Châu twisted her sopping strands into a coil, pinned it down with a chicken bone, and hurried to the Đoạn Trang House at the far end of the Women's Compound where the lowly ungraded novices were held. There she saw a tall and thin girl kowtowing awkwardly, her eyes fixed to the ground, her lips too tightly compressed to issue a word of greeting. Châu was swept by a yearning to touch this forlorn colt, to hug her and inhale the familiar smell of home weeds and grasses, the sweet fragrances of chrysanthemums and sunburned thistles the girl surely had on her skin. And to hear her talk in the familiar home-country dialect Châu had not heard or spoken in years and though she had lost. But letting a newcomer talk was not allowed; it would only elicit tears and wails of longing for the family left behind. "The tutor must establish her authority without delay," was the iron rule the Most Treasured Lady had emphasized a month earlier, when she had granted Châu her permission to become one.

"What is your name?" Châu squatted on the grass first and patted the ground beside her. She waited for the girl to squat and for her lips and hands to stop twitching. "I am Châu. I am also from Quảng Điền, but have been here for seven years. It will take six months of my instruction to teach you the etiquette and the protocol of the Forbidden City. Only then will you receive your Grade." The girl's cheeks were as concave as orange peels because she was sucking them in nervously. "You'll memorize many rules and learn the ranks of the women here. Have you memorized anything before?"

After a long silence, a voice as soft as a swish of air said, "I'm Thu Hiền. The Mandarin said the Emperor is a poet." Châu corrected her at once, "In the Forbidden City, the Emperor is referred to at all times as Thiên Tử — the Son of Heaven. And yes, the Son of Heaven is a poet and we hold his verses in our hearts."

Thu Hiền's virginity confirmed, the first day after the end of the rainy season she squatted on the grass in front of the Đoạn Trang House holding her back respectfully taut. Châu sat on a bamboo stool so that her head would be higher than her pupil's. After suffering years of boredom, Châu was thrilled to be given something to do and determined to justify Eunuch Vinh's and the Most Treasured Lady's faith in her. Her pupil was a simple illiterate peasant girl, not of the Nguyễn clan, but Châu intended to mould her into a model concubine.

She began by having Thu Hiền memorize the bad-omen words that were never to be heard within the walls of the Forbidden City — bile, blindness, blood, death, leprosy, scourge. "They ruin the air and bring misery," she explained. "Only words invoking beauty, serenity, and grace are allowed. In the language of the Court, the Son of Heaven does not get up in the morning but 'rises to meet the sun.' He does not go for a walk but takes 'an imperial promenade.'" There were hundreds of such phrases, and Châu could still hear in her head the thud of her own teacher's reprimands from years ago. "And your inflections must be purged of the coarse country slang. Here, we must intone in the refined accent of Huế."

Next, Châu spent a week going over courtesy phrases, pointing out how they varied according to the ceremony and the seniority of the personage addressed. To refer to members of the royal family by their proper names was an unpardonable offence. "The official title of the Son of Heaven's First Wife is *Hoàng quí phi*. Can you repeat that?" Thu Hiền did, but mangled the vowels terribly. Spilling out of Thu Hiền's mouth, the august title sounded crude but also — Châu felt a pang in her chest — so much like home. "You must never speak to the Most Treasured Lady or look her in the eye without being spoken to first. If you do, I will get the blame." Thu Hiền promised.

Châu liked her from the beginning. The girl was sombre but keen to learn. Probably five years Châu's junior, she rewarded her teacher's nudges and praise with the innocent smile of a child. Sometimes the two of them laughed over Thu Hiền's blunders, and Châu would cast a glance over her shoulder to make sure that nobody was watching, because it was incorrect for a teacher to banter with her charge. But she loved sharing a light moment with a girl as yet untainted by the intrigues of the Compound. "She is sweet and uses her head well. She doesn't have to be prodded in the ribs with a cane as I was," Châu thought as her eyes moistened.

In the third month of training, Châu went over the rites of the royal birthdays, anniversaries of accession to the throne, devotion rituals, and spring and autumn festivals. "Only concubines of Grade Four and higher join the royal entourage.

The rest of us," she felt the pain of belonging in this category; she was only Grade Seven now, "stay in the Compound to make lotus wreaths and hand fans. Once we reach Grade Five, we'll be included in the spring outing of dragon boats down the Perfume River. And every year there are many betrothals. The Ministry of Rites is in charge of the requisite tributes. The animals given as gifts to the young couple must be tied with red strings — the water buffaloes too. The pigs must have knots of red ribbon around their ears and their cages. It takes us days to wash the red stains of momordica seeds off our fingers."

At night, lying alone on her mat, Thu Hiền went over the day's lessons, baffled and worried. Not leaving the Compound for the spring festival till she reached a higher grade? Last spring in her village she had sat behind her father and her brothers in the boats they were racing to the temple, which stood at the fork in the river. A pig trussed in red ribbons? She tried to make a dreaming around this image but the Huế tones she was learning to master made it sound odd in her mouth.

At the beginning of the fourth month of training, a concubine senior to Châu took over the lessons. She watched Thu Hiền walk out to her and said, "Your posture is terrible. Hold your head and shoulders up. You are no longer slouching over the hearth." She had Thu Hiền practise tiny steps — each no more than the length of her foot. She also grimaced at Thu Hiền's fingernails, once kept short for housework, and not yet grown long enough to grace the fingers of a royal concubine. She called Thu Hiền's hand gestures "jerky" and demonstrated how to move her arms "like a swan moving its neck." Thu Hiền understood because she had seen many swans sail in her dreams and could imitate the motion once she got used to it. "The eunuchs must judge you graceful — or you'll not be summoned," the woman said. Finally, she smiled her approval, "You're ready to have your teeth re-lacquered."

Within days, Thu Hiền's first concubine gown was delivered — a green silk tunic to be worn over loose white pantaloons. Two ladies-of-the-palace parted her hair in the middle, wound it around her head in a coronet, and pinned it down with a black cloth spiralled into a ring to rest on the crown of the head. She paraded the outfit in small steps in front of her two teachers, and paused to recite a new poem composed by the Son of Heaven:

> Mosquitoes rain on banana and lotus leaves trembling in the wind
> Odious mosquitoes fly into the houses and flutter everywhere
> We do not need smoke to get rid of them
> Let the cold weather come and chase them away

Châu's head was bursting. She was indifferent to poetry but this graceful charge of hers was reciting it beautifully in the refined accent of Huế. Only a trace of the country slang remained in her voice. The clumsy country girl from her own district of Quảng Điền was now a well-finished alumna. Châu could not have been more proud if Thu Hiền had been her own sister. She ached to give her a hug. But with the senior concubine present, she could not.

The very next day, in the courtyard of the Most Treasured Lady's residence, Hồ Thị Thu Hiền was awarded the title of *Tài nhân* — concubine of the Grade Nine. Châu, not wanting anyone to see her cry, hid behind the other senior women invited to the investiture, and watched her charge receive a hair ornament and a tray piled with additional wear in red and blue. When Eunuch Vinh and a helper stepped forward with a hammock to carry Concubine Thu Hiền to the Sixth Pavilion, Châu was momentarily panicked that she was losing her. She stepped around the assembled women, caught up with the hammock, and said the first thing that came into her head: "Your entitlement has been set at 200 ligature coins and thirty *vuong* of rice per year. You can send it all to your father, but you should keep some to buy jewellery or to pay for favours. There are other things you need to know. I'll seek you..."

The hammock moved on. Thu Hiền was puzzled. She had never had any entitlements or any coins. And what kind of favours would she need to buy?

HOW HAPPY THU HIỀN WAS to leave the isolation of the Đoạn Trang House behind. How eagerly she wanted to run and chat and set her mind to her dreamings again. But the images and the voice would not come. She had not seen any open country — a rice paddy glinting in the sun, a duck alighting on the lake, a water buffalo fording the river — in over five months. She looked at the peacocks foraging on the grass around the Sixth Pavilion and felt her heart constrict, knowing that their brilliant plumage was a jewel to the eye but a millstone on the body — a dazzling cage.

She missed the men she had left at home. They were swarthy and muscular and told her what to do. Here, the loathsome eunuchs fluttered in and out like fleeing storks, their movements sinuous, their voices high-pitched. She would stare at the flower-crest embroidered on their dove-grey coats to avoid looking at their barren chins and the translucent yellowed skin that in her eyes made them look ill. Châu had advised her more than once that if she could not make any new dreamings she should dictate some of the ones she still remembered to Eunuch Vinh. For a small gift of rice, he would transcribe them and take them to the Palace. But whenever she imagined squatting near him, her head felt like a stone hacked out of a rock.

Inside the grassy quadrangle girdled by a wall five metres tall, she felt severed from life. There was no cooking or cleaning to do. She tried to pray to her ancestors, but their graves were far away. Sometimes, she felt as though her body was floating above the ground, never to touch it again. At night, silences hung in the air, infrequently interrupted by the sounds of mandolins, flutes, and gongs that scaled the wall from the direction of the Royal Theatre where, Châu had told her, visiting troubadours played for the royal entourage. Thu Hiền listened to the revelry and fancied a day when on that very stage she would recite her dreamings to the Son of Heaven, who would sit on a dais of gold within the reach of her arm. "Why am I not able to make some new dreamings for him?" she agonized. Having Châu's friendship was the one thing that was real and brought her comfort.

That year the rainy season brought a sudden flooding that drove the concubines from the low ground of their pavilions, and Thu Hiền stood just outside the Compound's wall holding to the railing of a small bridge that arched over a brimming brook. Châu pulled her arm and pointed to the brilliant speck of yellow in the distance. "Look! The Son of Heaven!" On higher ground, a gnome-like figure stirred amidst a dozen specks in brilliant colours. The multicoloured entourage was making its way to the South Gate. Thu Hiền tried to lock in memory the golden speck glistening like a precious stone against the soggy greens of the foliage behind it. "On his way to the Perfume River to bathe with his favourite women," Châu added and furtively put her hand in Thu Hiền's hand.

"One day, we'll be among them... you think?" Thu Hiền whispered back and squeezed Châu's hand.

For a day or two, Thu Hiền fantasized that perhaps the miraculous sighting would lead to new dreamings. She had seen other concubines shout out their laboured lines about the Son of Heaven's perfection to the eunuchs who passed by, sometimes staging elaborate word-and-dance plays hoping that they would be singled out for the Palace. She detested the foolishness. She was beginning to doubt that the Son of Heaven had summoned her to the Forbidden City for her dreamings. And even if he had, she had none to offer after months in this sterile place. Listening to the Compound chatter, it had not taken her long to realize that if she were summoned it would be to perform something else entirely. The thought disgusted her — she had seen her brothers do things with the girl sent to clean up the family yard after the seasonal slaughter of pigs. She need not have worried. The Mandarin who had sold her to the Emperor had drowned during the spring runoff and there was no one else to plead her case at the Palace.

1862

The winter was long and tedious, and the Son of Heaven and many of his retainers were felled by bronchitis and torpor. The day after the season's last monsoon had spent itself on the rocky seacoast and a balmy breeze flew in from the Perfume River, Thu Hiền squatted on the grass in the far corner of the Compound, admiring the festive red ribbons she had just knotted around the necks and horns of four goats tied to a post. She was about to weave more red strings through the slats of a cage of five piglets when Châu walked up to her. Recently elevated to Grade Six and assigned some supervisory duties in the Compound, Châu did not like to leave her women idle. "These animals and a coffer of sandalwood filled with gems and rolls of silk will be the Son of Heaven's wedding gifts to a niece," she said. "Your ribbons look lovely... It's too bad you could not compose a dreaming to celebrate the occasion, but at least you've made something beautiful with your hands."

Suddenly, Eunuch Vinh burst through the gate, raced toward them, and between heavy breaths blurted out, "I've just seen the Son of Heaven... He left his mother's side... shame-faced like a scolded child. The Queen Mother... wringing her hands... sobbing, 'Oh, my spiritless son! Oh my beloved Nam Bộ! The loathsome French have wrestled it from him... French missionaries will preach their Christian barbarity in the land of my childhood... French ships will sail the Mekong River...'" Eunuch Vinh crumpled to his knees.

Châu and Thu Hiền had no idea where the Mekong River was or what missionaries were. Concubine Quỳnh had told them that Christianity was a barbaric faith sowed by the followers of a convict who was rightfully put to death.

"The Queen Mother called up the ghost of Emperor Minh Mạng, who was so steadfast in stamping out the unnatural religion, and begged him to put a curse on his grandson for his shameful capitulation. The eunuchs and concubines dutifully mirrored the Queen Mother's anguish and twisted their hands and lips in pain." Eunuch Vinh ended his torrent by speaking directly to Châu, "It's a calamity for your father; you had better pray for him," and ran away shaking his head in grief or dismay.

That night, when Châu curled up on the sleeping mat, she ringed her knees tightly to her chest. Her eyes watered. How could the French be a calamity to her father? What had he done? She had not seen him in fifteen years.

Seeing her distress, Thu Hiền lay down behind her and pressed her breasts to Châu's back. When she heard Châu's breath quicken, she pushed her hips into Châu's hips and began to sway back and forth. For a few minutes they rocked in unison, gasping softly. Touch by touch, Thu Hiền moved her palm to cup Châu's breast, her fingers feeling for the nipple, Châu's moans of longing and her own as gentle as a swish of autumn leaves on the ground. Their bodies fused, and when Châu reached back to hold them together longer, Thu Hiền blew soft gusts of air into the small of Châu's neck. Within seconds, she heard Châu's cry of pleasure and barely smothered her own.

They had to be cautious. Last time two "sisters" had been heard pleasuring each other, the eavesdropper tattled to the eunuchs, who informed the Most Treasured Lady, who ordered that the sinning women be housed in separate pavilions. Caressing one's own body was the safest way to gratification, a long-established code of silence protecting the aroused woman. Massaging the feet and neck of another was also allowed. The older or more bashful women fondled straw-and-rag male dolls to sleep. But those concubines who craved the pleasure that can only come from lovemaking often sent seductive signals to other women in the Compound — and to the eunuchs too. The more defiant were rumoured to be spending nights with their eunuchs outside the wall, but Châu demurred, fearing that, if caught, her upgrades would be revoked or stalled and Thu Hiền taken away from her. She had made it very clear to her sister that while Eunuch Vinh was a confidant, all her carnal tenderness was reserved for Thu Hiền alone.

Three days later, Châu was splashing her legs in the puddle in front of her pavilion when she smelled the sage spice of Eunuch Vinh's coat and heard his voice behind her. "Your father has been dismissed for his wrongful advice."

She jumped to her feet. "Is he gone from the Citadel?"

"He'll be leaving soon. Five other Ministers have also been banished. They've angered the Son of Heaven by advising him to resist the French intruders."

"Why haven't you told me before?"

"Because it's hard to know. The Court is divided... Some Mandarins are mesmerized by the French. Your father and his clique curse the foreign devils. But the Son of Heaven apparently favours the faction that calls for negotiating with the foreigners."

Eunuch Vinh waited for two ladies-of-the-palace carrying some laundry to pass by, and continued in a low voice. "Just about the time you arrived, the French first asked to put trading posts on our land. Your father didn't like them from the start and urged that they be chased away. Years later, when the Son of Heaven allowed them to bring in military men to protect their outposts from pirates, your father insisted Việt soldiers could protect them just as well."

"My father would not dare dispute any command of the Son of Heaven."

"Your father has always spoken... forcefully. I've heard it from a eunuch who transcribes the royal correspondence in French. Your father wanted the foreigners expelled. He warned the Son of Heaven about their awesome weapons — rifles — that can fire metal bullets and hit targets ten times farther than any arrow shot by a Việt soldier. But the Son of Heaven listens to those who say that the French only want trade. They have pointed out to him that the royal troops are needed to put down peasant uprisings... And the French pay well for the land they lease. The Court needs the revenue. Your father's pigheadedness has brought him — and you — no reward. He's lucky to have saved his head."

Châu's own head was bursting. It was too much to absorb. For fifteen years, she had lived 500 steps from the Cấn Thành Palace but had known nothing of the Court's affairs or her father's struggle. Now she realized that she should blame herself no longer for failing to scale the royal bed. Her father's opponents would have paid off their collaborators to keep her away. And her father had not abandoned her; he had sacrificed her to keep the French away.

She berated herself for questioning his commitment to her advancement in the Forbidden City, for not praying for him as often as she should — in the last few years hardly ever. Yet all that time he had stood for a cause, risking his Emperor's displeasure and his own walk of life while she merely pursued her own advancement in the Compound. As concubine of Grade Six she no longer poured her own tea but had it poured for her by a junior woman, and received other small gestures of respect customarily accorded the more senior women. She had also been granted permission to bring Thu Hiền with her to the Fourth Pavilion. The affairs of state were beyond her reach but she did know every fraying tendril of wrangling in the Women's Compound. There were so many grievances there. Perhaps, like her father, she should be brave enough to tell the Most Treasured Lady about them — even at the risk of disapproval? "Please come tomorrow and bring a writing tablet," she whispered to Eunuch Vinh and waved him goodbye. Puzzled, he promised he would.

The next day, Châu dictated the list she had composed in her head overnight:

> 1. Because of the anxiety in the Forbidden City that the foreigners will invade our country, concubines of the Grade Seven to Nine have not had an outing for three months and have become fretful and belligerent;
>
> 2. Concubine Hà, Grade Seven, deserves to be punished for using unbecoming language again, and beating up Concubine Linh, Grade Six, who inadvertently soiled her gown;
>
> 3. Seven concubines have been ill for some time — three with dengue fever which causes them to vomit blood, and four with scabrous skin boils impervious to any oils. All seven have been ostracized by the others for fear of spreading disease. They beseech the Most Treasured Lady to remember them in her prayers.

4. It is requested that the Most Treasured Lady implore the Emperor to take pity on Concubine Thị Bích, Grade Eight, and allow her to speak to a family member across the partition, because she is inconsolable after having had a dream that her parents had drowned. At night she cries and pulls her hair and disrupts the sleep of others.

5. Châu personally requests permission to make a list of the concubines between the Fifth and Ninth Grade, of which there are forty-two, deserving of an upgrade, for the consideration of the Most Treasured Lady and the Son of Heaven, as he prepares to bestow honours on the occasions of the Lunar New Year. This is with the intention of avoiding the vitriol and wailing of the previous year when only five upgrades were awarded.

6. The earthen teapots in the Sixth Pavilion are a decade old, chipped and grubby. On behalf of the twenty-three women residing there, it is requested that a new set be provided.

"You're a brave woman to petition the Most Treasured Lady without receiving any request from her first," Eunuch Vinh said, but Châu ignored him and asked briskly, "How soon will she see the list?"

"Probably not till tomorrow afternoon. Her mornings are too busy, even though she rises well before sunrise, at the Hour of the Tiger."

"To be carried to the Cấn Thành Palace to serve the Son of Heaven his breakfast?"

"At her age, it's the only personal service she can render her husband. She pays her daily respect to the Queen Mother and returns to her Residence by the Hour of the Cat to receive the morning greeting of her servants and breakfast alone. When the sun clears the ramparts at the Hour of the Snake, she hears complaints and petitions. I'll give your list to one of her senior eunuchs. They'll advise her which grievances to reject as trivial and what punishment to mete out."

"Maybe some good will come for the distraught women," Châu said weakly.

"For now, take some comfort in the knowledge that you've tried to make their lives easier. Do you know, when I was first assigned to the Women's Compound, a senior eunuch warned me that I was going to the lions' den. Because there were no children, the women could not be grouped or labelled according to the fruits of their labour — those who have borne a royal son cherished and given their own quarters, those frequently summoned and expected to bear a son in the second tier, the ones who have given births to daughters dutifully cared for, and the older and the never-summoned virgins caring for their more fortunate sisters and their babies. 'Without this hierarchy, they squabble like cats. You'll see,' he told me."

"We are all together, yet so alone."

"At least you've found a substitute 'daughter.' I have no one," Eunuch Vinh said mournfully. "Last night, I dreamt I was floating face-up in a pond and a giant white cormorant plunged from the cloud and repeatedly pierced my chest with his beak. Blood was gushing from the sieve of my body but I could not get away because I cannot swim. When I woke up, my back was pressed against the mat, my chest was leaden, my legs as stiff as two dried-up bamboo trunks. I coughed to bring back my breath and was petrified to realize that if I died right then, without a progeny, there would be no one to worship me after death and my soul would roam the earth for eternity."

Châu struggled to say something hopeful, but couldn't. She felt great sorrow for Eunuch Vinh, for herself, for all the barren, wronged women and maimed men in the Citadel. She put her hand in Eunuch Vinh's and felt his fingers interlace with hers. She longed to snuggle in his arms and let him cuddle her — to cuddle him in return — but they were sitting by the wall of her Pavilion and it was daylight.

1866

This was the year of Châu's first grey hair. Thu Hiền noticed them when massaging Châu's head one morning and pointed them out to her gently, offering the consolation that it was a validation of her seniority. But Châu felt no sorrow. She had grown into wisdom and stature, and had come to believe that she could handle any turmoil in her life and in the Compound.

Until the morning she realized that breakfast was an hour late. She walked to the gate to see if the ladies-of-the-palace were on their way and found it locked. At the Hour of the Dragon? By noon, there was still no food but now sounds of thuds and clangs and cries of pain flew over the wall, followed by the booms of walls collapsing into ruin. Terrified, Châu ordered the women to the far corner of the wall where they cowered there for the rest of the day.

Just after sunset Eunuch Vinh strode through the gate, a burning torch in his trembling hand. He told Châu that the Citadel was under attack by the son of the brother passed over for succession nearly twenty years earlier. The rogue Prince had conscripted a hundred labourers toiling to build a Mausoleum for the Son of Heaven some distance from the Capital. Learning that the men were being worked hard, and poorly fed and paid, he had fed them, given them coins, and promised more rewards if they helped him seize the throne from his uncle. In a surprise night attack, the motley band, armed with hoes, rakes, and mortar pestles, had overpowered the sentries of the Citadel, scaled the walls of the Forbidden City, and occupied the Royal Theatre right next door to the Son of Heaven's Cấn Thành Palace. The Emperor, who was not informed till mid-morning because his guards and sentries were ashamed of their capitulation and fearful of his wrath, was summoning his Mandarins to plan resistance.

"What does the Most Treasured Lady say?" Châu asked.

"She orders you to put the women to work. And to quell any unruliness — ruthlessly."

"The women haven't had any food since last night."

"Neither have we. Let them chew on leaves and grasses. For now, let us all pray to save our lives."

Châu ordered the terrified women to squat in circles, shoulders touching for comfort, and to chisel twigs of bamboo into chopsticks for the petite hands of the Son of Heaven, for whom ivory chopsticks were too heavy. Those who had been taught to write could engrave their names on them for him to see. While they worked, they recited prayers, their tender voices barely overlaying the rumble outside the wall. Eventually some food was delivered but the nightmare continued for days. Two concubines died that week of fever spun by hysteria. Their doleful housemates wrapped the bodies in rattan mats and stored them in a makeshift grave to await proper burial. Thu Hiền trembled on her sleeping mat alone, while Châu attended to a hysterical concubine who in delirium pleaded to be put to death.

When the royal troops finally quelled the rebellion, the Son of Heaven ordered that its leader, even though he was a royal relative, be executed by the slow death of *tùng xẻo* — the extreme penalty for transgressors against the will of the Emperor. The ill-starred Prince would be tied to a tree and the executioner would cut off his flesh with a dagger chunk by chunk — a volley of drums beating between his screams. On the day of the execution the women were ordered to pray constantly that no other conspirator dare challenge the Son of Heaven's might. The deathly drums throbbed in the background for hours. Thu Hiền and several others vomited on the grass while Châu defiantly prayed in her head that the tortured man die quickly and the barbarity end.

Two days after the execution, a Chinese fortune teller was allowed into the Compound — a reward from the Son of Heaven for the concubines' loyal prayers. The women swarmed around the exotic visitor who, gowned in crimson silk and a matching turban, sat on a red-and-black-dyed cloth she had spread in front of the First Pavilion. Thu Hiền pushed her way in through the crowd and stared in awe at the dozens of red-lacquered fortune sticks bearing hieroglyphs, a cluster of colourful cock feathers, and a large gourd of *I Ching* silver coins that lay on the fortune teller's tray. A monkey sitting on the fortune teller's shoulder bared its white teeth at Thu Hiền, who suddenly felt a wisp of a dreaming stirring in her head: *I am a country girl / but my bamboo bridge is gone / and my people are also gone…* The words rang false so she shook them out of her head and started over. *I was a country girl / but my bamboo bridge was swept away / and my people have forgotten me / and my fate is buried in the I Ching coins…* She was so absorbed in her musings the fortune teller had to pinch her arm to remind her to pick a coin.

When Châu's turn came, she picked a red stick with her eyes closed. "You will be snatched from the maw of death," said the fortune teller. "You will retrace your voyage to the Citadel and arrive home an old and wrinkled woman."

Châu jerked and was about to ask, "How?" when she was pushed out of the way by another concubine jostling for her turn. She elbowed her way out of the crowd and collided with Thu Hiền waiting for her with her cheeks aflame. "I chose a coin and she told me to trust my heart… and to expect a new beginning. And just before she said that a dreaming came to me…"

Châu took in a dollop of air swiftly but exhaled it slowly, "These dreamings, you haven't given up on them yet, have you?" She did not want to hear about poetry. Thu Hiền had not composed any dreamings in years, but from time to time, when she appeared to be trying to make one up, she drew away from the world of the Compound and into a world of her own. Châu could not follow her there and felt annoyed every time. Now she said sternly, "The Chinese are full of tricks, just like the French. They should never be trusted. Never!"

Thu Hiền's dreamy face crumpled into a grimace and her cheeks flushed with anger. "You are old... You don't understand beautiful things," she said, pivoted on her heels, and marched away.

1873

Mournful cries pierced the air and echoed against the wall circling the Compound. Châu, sitting on the threshold of her pavilion threading dried berries on a twine, lifted her head. Eunuch Vinh was hurrying toward her and she asked him, "Are the French causing trouble again?"

"No, Concubine Nhật is bleeding again." Châu repeated the news to her housemates, who were threading their berries inside, away from the sun. They nodded in silent resignation. They had always expected the brazen woman's bid to fail.

Concubine Nhật had been a fecund wife of a royal cousin and in six years of marriage had given him four sons and two daughters. But life with her opium-addicted husband was miserable and she had thought to capitalize on her gift. "I am as fertile as a rabbit. I can be impregnated where the other women have failed," was the boast a eunuch she had befriended carried to the Son of Heaven on her behalf.

"What nerve and what peril!" groaned the women of the six pavilions. If she failed, either the Son of Heaven or her husband could order her killed for causing them ignominy. Concubine Nhật had been kept in the Son of Heaven's chamber for three months. Her cries that morning were the final proof of the calamity the reigning Monarch had brought onto the kingdom — one that he could not very well blame on the French.

Concubine Nhật's failure to conceive came a week after Concubine Quỳnh — the storyteller and worshipper of Emperor Minh Mạng — died in agony. The virgin woman, having reached her fiftieth year, had succumbed to desperate longing and the overtures of an aging Court Mandarin. The intimacy was brief. Eavesdroppers tattled, and the Mandarin was abruptly retired to his home district. Concubine Quỳnh collapsed in hysterical tears. Châu heard her cries and ran to the First Pavilion, where she saw her at the entrance rocking astride a stone turtle.

The Most Treasured Lady was notified and ordered that the grieving woman be taken to the isolation shed. There the Court physician stood behind a bamboo screen with two eunuch guards at his side, as Châu pushed Concubine Quỳnh's gloved hand through a crack in the screen for her pulse to be taken. Not allowed to touch the patient's skin, see her face, or talk directly to her, the physician spoke in a loud voice to be sure that Châu heard his diagnosis — the patient's pulse was normal and the usual herbal potions and a massage should be administered. But the sullen woman continued to weaken, her body withered, her burning eyes fixed on a point in the rafters. Since neither the concubines nor the eunuchs were allowed to die in the Forbidden City for fear of spreading disease, as soon as the death rattle began Châu summoned two eunuchs to carry the doomed woman in a hammock to the House of Departure, just outside the walls of the Citadel, from where her remains would later be carted to her native village. She and Thu Hiền held her hands as far as the North Gate.

Concubine Quỳnh was the fourth and most senior woman to die that cool and soggy spring. Châu and Thu Hiền, exhausted by the ailments and the passings, had become irritable and bickered about trifles. Other women locked into themselves and hardly spoke at all.

It was Eunuch Vinh who dispelled the gloom with a bomb-shell: a French military envoy was coming to pay homage to the Son of Heaven. After dinner, the exalted guest and his entourage would watch the tiger—elephant fight.

Châu was relieved beyond measure, for herself, and for all the others. "What a chance to have us celebrate and cheer again," she said to Thu Hiền, who could barely contain her fervid antici-pation of a new and stirring event to ignite her imagination.

On the day of the visit all the concubines ran to the wall to hear the growls of the wild cats as they were carried in their cages to the arena, only a short distance to the west of their Com-pound. Then the elephants were led by, the whips of the mahouts whacking the air. The giant beasts seldom trumpeted on their way. They knew from experience that the fight was stacked in their favour — they could roam the arena while the tigers would be chained to trees. Later, the palanquins of the Son of Heaven's guests were carried by and strange words and phrases the concu-bines could not understand drifted over the wall. Was it French? The guests did not speak in Việt? How unbefitting.

In less than an hour, the first roar of the crowd flew over the wall. The mahouts must have begun to prod the elephants toward the tigers and the guests were shouting to urge the giants to charge. The concubines knew the routine by heart; they had fol-lowed many previous fights by sound. At first the elephants would try to jab at the tethered tigers with their tusks, and the wily cats, more nimble but much smaller than their attackers, would try to repulse them with bared teeth and blood-curling growls that made Thu Hiền and some others cover their ears in mock fear. Whenever a tiger repelled an attack, the hum of disappointment issued from the crowd and the concubines hushed, trying to mirror the mood of the spectators they could hear but not see. They waited for calls of "Blood! Blood!" Then the mahouts would drive the elephants closer and closer to the trees, and the tigers, seeing the giants barrelling at them, would run around and around the tree trunks, their iron leashes getting shorter, the guests hollering louder till they saw the tigers throttled against the bark, at which point the elephants stamped them to death. When a victorious cry rose from the arena, Châu and her charges sprang to their feet, stamping and cheering in unison with the Son of Heaven's guests, hoping that he would hear their ovation. But Thu Hiền always cried for the poor tigers — and so she did that day. Châu saw her back and her neck becoming ramrod stiff, as if she herself were crammed against a tree.

At the Hour of the Pig Eunuch Vinh came in to do the late-night check and lock the gate to the Compound. He looked nearly overcome, not only by the excitement of the tiger fight but by seeing real Frenchmen too. The women swarmed him instantly, Thu Hiền at the forefront, her voice ringing like a bell: "What did the French look like? How was the envoy dressed? What did the Son of Heaven say to him?"

Eunuch Vinh mounted an overturned rainwater barrel and, visibly thrilled to be the one to impart the news, said, "The French envoy was very tall. The Son of Heaven greeted him from a raised dais so that their heads would be at the same height. The French military uniform is very different from what our soldiers wear. The dark trousers are pressed as crisp as a sun-scorched banana leaf. The coat is jasmine white, trimmed with golden shoulder bars and tied around the waist with a blue sash. The buttons are as shiny as frogs' eyes." The concubines purred with pleasure. "The kepi cap the French envoy wore was the shape of a betel box, except it had a peak at the front. But he, and all the Frenchmen present, removed their caps promptly... Their custom is to bare their heads." A grumble of awe rose to the sky — bare heads in the presence of their Son of Heaven? Some of the women instinctively touched their head coverings, as if to confirm that even in the seclusion of their Compound they were properly dressed. Eunuch Vinh extended his right hand to quiet the commotion, then wrapped it tightly around his left hand, and said, "The Son of Heaven shook hands with the visitors... like this. Our Monarch had practised handshakes on his Mandarins and extended his right hand very well."

The concubines murmured among themselves: "How odd to have strangers touch each other's skins at the very first meeting. How could the Son of Heaven allow it?"

Eunuch Vinh reassured the women, "The Son of Heaven was very gracious. His hand looked long and strong. The fingers of the Frenchmen looked puny. Their custom is to trim off their nails."

Châu scanned the spellbound faces around her. "They must not forget that the French are the enemy." She suddenly remembered her father, now banished from the Citadel for life, and resentment filled her heart — a confusing bitterness against him and his intransigence as she struggled to accept that the Monarch who expelled him now welcomed foreigners to his Court. Thu Hiền, sitting beside her, looked absolutely bewitched, her lips moving, her thoughts probably forming themselves into dreamings she had almost forgotten she ever had. Châu nudged her to pay attention, vaguely troubled that her chosen sister was drifting away from her into the melancholy of her dreamings.

Eunuch Vinh went on to describe the fifty-four-course state dinner, with twelve kinds of fish, a delectable pickled tortoise as well as platters of *thịt heo kho tàu* — pork marinated in fish brine and roasted on a spit. "But the Son of Heaven enjoyed the conversation even more than the food," he said, "because the honoured guest told him about a French Emperor who had conquered half the world in spite of being of short stature. The Son of Heaven was amazed; his Mandarins had assured him that all Frenchmen were as tall as pine trees."

Eunuch Vinh was now wheezing like an aroused cat because he had saved the best for last. "The ceremony of farewell was simply majestic. As the guests were leaving, our bells and drums lifted the sky. The Son of Heaven extended his right hand again and said *merci beaucoup et au revoir.*" Eunuch Vinh paused and watched the concubines hang on his every word. "Which in French means 'thank you very much and goodbye.'"

The concubines heaved a collective sigh, charmed to know that their Son of Heaven could speak French. For days afterwards, Châu heard them practise saying *merci beaucoup* and *au revoir* as they went about their chores and games. For them it was a fancy novelty. But at night, when she felt Thu Hiền's slumberous breath on her back, she kept herself awake a little longer, picturing the French envoy, in his ridiculous uniform, stamping over Imperial grounds, tainting it with his odious presence — and felt her father's hand touch her arm.

Very soon, just as Châu's father had predicted, the French were causing the Son of Heaven more grief than amusement. Within months, French soldiers, drawing on the support of the growing community of Việt Catholics, seized Thăng Long, the former capital in the north of the country. One day, Eunuch Vinh, just returned from the funeral of a royal princess and fittingly dressed in the white of mourning from his feet to the top of his turban, told Châu that henceforth the northern land of Bắc Bộ would go under the French name of Tonkin, and the foreigners would build more trading posts and garrisons there.

"So my father was correct all along," Châu cried. Eunuch Vinh just stood there, his eyes clouding over, but Châu could not hold back her anger. "Ah, the Nguyễn Son of Heaven, bringing shame on us all. May he suffer —" Eunuch Vinh pressed his fingers to her lips and, when she tried to continue, twisted her arm painfully behind her, and forced her to her knees.

1876

"Now that the French are all over our land, if one of their flying bullets pierced my chest, who would worship me after death?" Eunuch Vinh asked Châu one day.

"Your eunuch brothers would worship you right here, on the grounds of the Citadel, in that little pagoda across the stream. It was built by and for the eunuchs. You know that."

"But every man must be worshipped by a son. The Son of Heaven too."

"Well, what do you think he will do?"

"He'll have to adopt a royal relative. Make him his son. And I think I must do the same. Adopt an unwanted boy — that's what village people have been doing for centuries."

"There are no unwanted boys... or girls... or any children here," Châu said.

"But there are virgins yearning to be summoned. You tell them, you tell them today, that I'll reward — have summoned — the one who will find me a boy-child I can bring to the Forbidden City. He can be enfeebled... bedridden... but he must be able to pray."

That evening Châu carried the message to her women.

The spirit of the Compound lifted like a stork ascending the clouds. The virgins were ecstatic at the chance to shed the loathsome label of unsummoned women. They had heard of eunuchs sending rice to families back home to pay them for designating one of their sons as a proxy heir. But to bring one to the Forbidden City? They chattered well after the dinner mats had been rolled up, then settled down for a sleepless night of reckoning. Had they saved enough ligament coins or rice to pay the eunuchs to carry their message to the Mandarins? Would the Mandarins let their villagers know that a boy was wanted for sale? The recently arrived women had the advantage of fresh memories of the hungry families back home with too many sons to feed, families who would gladly castrate one son to have him raised in the Citadel.

At the first gleam of morning light Concubine Thái Bảo, barely a year in the Compound and never summoned, stood at Châu's window frame. She had remembered a boy in her village born *giảm sanh* — with his sexual organs atrophied. His father was a retired tutor of the royal cousins who had three healthy boys, and he would probably welcome the chance to get rid of the boy he called only the Fourth Son.

When Châu told Eunuch Vinh, his face lit up. "Ah, so the child would not have to be castrated," he exclaimed and promptly sent a plea to the Queen Mother and the Most Treasured Lady. After their senior eunuchs advised that a giảm sanh child would be unlikely to taint the Forbidden City with bad spirits, and might in fact provide some diversion at the Women's Compound, a Court Mandarin carried to the boy's parents Eunuch Vinh's offer to relieve them of their burden.

When the Mandarin brought the boy to the Citadel, two eunuchs brought him in a hammock to the quarters where his adoptive father waited. They lifted the child out like a limp sack of duck feathers and lowered him to the ground. Eunuch Vinh took a careful look at his son. His head, nearly hairless and with no eyebrows, distended upwards, its crest disfigured by a bump that peaked with a thin line, like the ridge of a narrow hill. His eye sockets were deep and wide-set, his ears tiny and low-set. The upper lip was invisible, the lower lip swollen red.

"Get up on your feet," Eunuch Vinh issued a fatherly command. The child stood but had to stretch out his arms to hold his balance because only his one mangled foot could lay flat on the floor. The left leg fell short, only its toes touching the ground. "What is your name?" Eunuch Vinh asked.

The boy stuttered, eyes cast down, "Master... my n... name is Fourth... Son..." Eunuch Vinh felt jabs in his chest, as if that bird from the old dream was stabbing him anew. The boy could understand and answer questions and had been taught to respect his elders. He could be taught the rites of worship. He was fit to be a son. "You'll live here with me now," he told the child, extending his arms, surprised at how clammy they felt.

An hour later, Eunuch Vinh walked through the gate of the Women's Compound, flaunting his bundle like a royal banner. Châu rushed out of her quarters, arms in the air, Thu Hiền close behind her. Châu reached out to caress the child's ankles and toes but Thu Hiền drew away when she saw the boy's face up close; the ugliness repelled her. Other concubines poured out of their pavilions to hail the marvel in their midst. The child looked frightened and his father cradled his distended head, pressing it into the folds of his coat. "He's only just arrived; let him be."

He paused long enough to allow Concubine Thái Bảo to touch the boy and to thank her for her lucky lead. She gripped the boy's arm but looked at his father. "I'll collect my reward very soon. I will! Yes?" The faces of the women around her lit up with envy. A very new virgin had won a coveted prize. And a eunuch had managed to procure a child to call his own. They were concubines; they would never be allowed to adopt.

Two days after the Fourth Son's first visit, when Concubine Thái Bảo was drying herself with hibiscus petals after the morning wash, Concubine Tuyết yanked her hair and pushed her to the ground. "Down with you, snotty cow!" She grabbed a pail of suds and sluiced it over the downed woman's face. Two other concubines kicked Concubine Thái Bảo. She spat out the suds, struggled to her feet, and tore at her attackers with her chisel-sharp fingernails, her scimitar arms slashing the air. But before Concubine Thái Bảo's fingernails could reach a face, Concubine Tuyết sank her teeth into her shoulders from behind. Concubine Thái Bảo swung around, aiming to claw her nails into her opponent's face, but lost her balance and fell again. Half a dozen women were upon her at once, kicking and punching. Other concubines ran from their pavilions shouting, "Stop fighting, stop now!"

Within minutes two dozen eunuchs charged in, swishing their whips over the heads of the fighters, pushing the naked bodies and shoving them into their pavilions, yelling, "Stay indoors!"

When Eunuch Vinh ran past her window screen, Châu called out to him through the slats, "The Most Treasured Lady must be informed at once!"

"She has been. Stay indoors."

Very early the next morning, while the exhausted fighters were still asleep, Eunuch Vinh brought Châu the news that the Most Treasured Lady's advisors had decided that the "unseemly occurrence" was grave enough to take to the Queen Mother, who was prompt with her judgment. "At a time when the destiny of the country is hanging on a silken thread, the wretched virgins are behaving badly." She ruled that Concubine Thái Bảo's unwomanly hubris and bluster was the cause of the unpleasantness and ordered, "Lock her and her two attackers in one room for a month, like three cats in heat. All outings, all singing and dancing in the Compound forbidden!"

When the three women emerged from their isolation, Concubine Thái Bảo no longer bragged about her good deed. She was tagged as a troublemaker and seen as a portent of bad luck. Eunuch Vinh could not take a disgraced woman to the Palace. Concubine Thái Bảo raged at his "foul treachery" and called him a "castrated dog."

The following year, when the Son of Heaven's thirtieth anniversary on the throne was celebrated, Eunuch Vinh received a commendation from the Palace for bringing "recognition and joy" to the entire community of the Forbidden City. Châu and Thu Hiền received upgrades, and, together with all the other concubines, gifts of silver jewellery and pearl necklaces, as well as additional allotments of rice. Concubine Thái Bảo did not. Calling her "an odious reminder of past unpleasantness," the Most Treasured Lady demoted the ill-fated woman from the Ninth Grade to the ordinary "lady-of-the-palace" and ordered Châu to have her moved to the cleaners' dormitory.

Alas, five months before the Son of Heaven's death in 1883, the Most Treasured Lady was to suffer a similar disgrace. One rainy morning, at the Hour of the Tiger, she lingered too long on the verandah of her Residence, waiting for the rain to thin before she was carried to the Cấn Thành Palace to serve her husband his breakfast. The Son of Heaven was displeased with her tardiness and promptly demoted her to a lower grade. She would not serve him breakfast again.

The evening of the Most Treasured Lady's downfall, Châu ordered the sobbing sisters of the six pavilions to spear all the Compound's torches into the earth and keep them burning all night so the disgraced woman would see from afar that she was not suffering alone. But Châu felt terribly alone, and crippled, as if her backbone had been crushed. In her head, she raged at the Son of Heaven's pettiness and her own disquiet. Eunuch Vinh had been coming to the Compound less frequently, protecting his son from the fervid women, protecting the women from learning about the growing impotence of the Court against French encroachments. Thu Hiền was growing distant in her own way, often lost in reveries Châu had never understood and had less and less patience for.

1885

In the fourth lunar month, under the high sun of the Hour of the Horse, Châu heard the sounds she had been dreading: Boom! Boom! Fearful thuds coming from afar and getting closer. French rifles. Thu Hiền and a dozen servants, cultivating the trellises of morning glory in the courtyard of the Queen Mother's residence, paused and cried out in alarm. "Get back to work," Châu ordered. "We're safe here. Our soldiers have arrows, and swords, and scimitars. They'll not let the enemy over the ramparts." She did not believe she was telling the truth.

Only a few weeks earlier, Châu and Thu Hiền, and nearly five dozen other widows of the Son of Heaven, had returned from his sprawling Mausoleum, nestled in the forest three days' travel away, where they had spent the customary two years of mourning. They had scrubbed the ornate temple and pavilions of the Mausoleum, scoured its stone walkways, weeded the gardens, and raked the lotus ponds. They had made offerings for his soul. His remains were not on the grounds of the Mausoleum, and no one would know where they lay because the 200 men who had taken his body to its grave were, upon their return, beheaded.

In their doleful seclusion, away from the Citadel, the widowed concubines heard of the calamities that followed the Son of Heaven's passing. A nephew designated as heir had taken the crown but three days later was deposed by a competing Court faction and left in prison to die. His successor was the dead Emperor's younger brother, who some months later was murdered. Châu was sitting by the lily pond of the Mausoleum, finishing a toy rattan-and-jute fishing boat and a matching fisherman's hat to send to the Fourth Son, when news of the third ruler arrived — another adopted son, barely a teenager. He too would meet a violent death.

Now the Son of Heaven's widows were back in the Citadel and the gunfire coming over the ramparts was getting louder and louder. Two eunuchs burst through the trellises, shouting "Run! Run to the North Gate!" The women sprang to their feet but did not run — they had been trained never to show haste. The eunuchs thrust their arms northward and kept yelling, "Everybody run! Run now!" The women scurried through the narrow portal, past the piercing cries of the peacocks. Running behind Châu, Thu Hiền stumbled and fell to the grass, a peacock feather fluttering just before her face. She snatched it in her fist with fearful desperation, hoisted herself up, and was swept into the frantic crowd.

At the North Gate, the women clung together in bewilderment. Should they cross to the outside? Did they have the proper escort? What dangers lay beyond? Châu kept looking over her shoulder, straining to spot the faces of Eunuch Vinh and the Fourth Son, but all she saw was a throng of Mandarins racing in panic from the Cấn Thành Palace. A brilliant speck of yellow — a young boy in the palanquin — glided over their heads. She tugged at Thu Hiền's arm, "Look!"

But a eunuch shoved her forward, shouting, "The enemy is here. Run! Run, or be killed."

Gunfire rumbling over their heads, Thu Hiền pulled Châu through the North Gate. And there, over the heads of the screaming throng, as far as the eye could see, lay rolling rice paddies, orange groves, and, at the horizon, a village screened by the woods, land like her own, whose sights and sounds and smells had long ago flocked into her dreamings.

Less than an hour later, Châu and Thu Hiền struggled to find a place to sit among a dozen other concubines crammed around them, and finally wedged themselves into a grassy furrow. Thu Hiền pulled out the peacock feather she had plucked from the Queen Mother's lawn, and stuck it in the ground to mark their place in the ditch. Several eunuchs had posted themselves along the ditch as sentries. Behind them puffs of grey smoke darkened the sky over the Forbidden City — their beautiful home. Châu thought how crushed her father would be to learn that French soldiers were now inside the impenetrable fortress. Perhaps it was better that he was not here to witness this hour of defeat and shame.

The women sat immobile for hours, numbed and hungry, hiding their faces and their fears in the folds of their soiled tunics and pantaloons. At the Hour of the Snake, with the sun dipping into the Perfume River, several village women arrived carrying large baskets of cooked rice, and sacks of sliced green mangoes on their backs. They portioned out the food on banana leaves and brought them to the escapees, looking at them with curiosity and pity, then left promptly as if chased by ghosts, taking the scent of mangoes with them. After the meagre meal, Châu rested her head on her knees, not wanting to see or hear anything.

Thu Hiền stared at the billows of smoke rising over her Compound. Obedient to an ancient quivering inside her, she opened her lips:

> The invading foe struck the kingdom with force
> The mighty ramparts yielded to France
> Flee soldiers, flee Mandarins, flee in a blaze
> Let the paddy edge
> Give you shelter...
>
> But do return...
> The swallows in the rafters will whirl
> The lotus pond will trill...

She closed her lips and smiled; for the first time since coming to the Citadel all those years ago she felt warm, and alert, and fertile, alive with words ready to be shaped into dreamings again. From her furrow in the ditch she could no longer see the wide horizon, but the impenetrable fortress was in front of her and a momentous story was unfolding there. Could she make it into dreamings for the people in the villages — maybe for the children of her brothers too — to tell them in poetry of the Citadel steeped in gun smoke, and the Frenchmen armed with their magical rifles scaling the ramparts, and the tearing down of the walls... and of the old ways? The half-moon was the sentry above as she gently swished her hand down the curve of Châu's sleeping form, plucked up the peacock feather, and started walking.

The following morning, Châu woke to find the spot next to her empty and the peacock feather gone. At the narrow end of the ditch, a lonely eunuch was shouting that return to the Citadel was allowed.

Looking wildly for Thu Hiền, she saw several more empty spaces down the line and asked loudly, "Where are these women?"

"They disappeared into the night," said a voice from farther along the ditch.

"You mean they've gone back already?"

"No, they just left."

So Thu Hiền had gone without her. Back to the Citadel or into the unknown? Either way, she was gone. Three hundred steps would take Châu to the North Gate. But she could not bear the thought of going back now that French soldiers had desecrated the sacred grounds with their presence. Fresh anger had stirred up inside her against her departed Son of Heaven, that feeble Nguyễn ruler, small in all things, who had ceded the land to France and diminished his people. He had failed to procreate, had never brought her to his chamber, and had ruined her father's life. She tried to recall what her father had looked like forty years earlier when he kowtowed to her at the South Gate. If alive, would he be a shrunken shadow now? Would he recognize her and allow her near him, and later allow her bones to rest near his bones?

A fold of dove-grey cloth brushed against Châu's cheek and three feet came to a stop in front of her. Eunuch Vinh and the Fourth Son — his good foot almost as big as his father's now — stood there, the boy's bamboo staff touching the hem of her rumpled tunic. "Don't try to make me go back. I want to go home to my people," she told them without looking up.

Eunuch Vinh spoke softly. "We're not going back either. We're going to a pagoda two-day's walk to the west. A wise eunuch built it in the forest of pines some years ago so his brothers could retire and die there. I'll take care of the graves and pray. My son will worship me there when I'm gone."

The Fourth Son said in one breath, without stuttering once, "Do you know where Thu Hiền is?"

"She is gone. I don't know where. Left without saying goodbye."

Eunuch Vinh said softly again, "We thought we saw her going back to the Citadel with some of the others, but did not want to believe it. Such a place of sorrow and death." He ruffled the folds of his coat and, as he turned to leave, said, "If you find your father alive, pass on my respects. If only we had more patriots like him."

The three feet and the bamboo staff ambled away, and when Châu looked up she saw the House of Departure, where over the years the bodies of so many of her sister-concubines had been readied for burial. The women working there would give her food and show her the way.

La femme et la mer

203

In 1930, the large mass of South East Asia that now belongs to Việt Nam, Laos, and Cambodia was an overseas possession of France. The Nguyễn Dynasty continued on the throne but its emperors had to be sanctioned by the French. The lesser men and women worked the plantations, the mines, and the construction sites of the colonizers. That year, the Communist Party of Indochina was born, and, under the leadership of Hồ Chí Minh, vowed to make Việt Nam independent. The objective was supported by the fledgling Communist parties of Europe.

AFTER THE GRUMPY DOCTORS AT *l'Hôpital Grall* had signed her discharge, with stern admonitions to avoid overstimulation and liquor, she resolved to shake off the stain of her insolvency and her breakdown without delay. She took a rickshaw to the women's *pension* that the French matron in charge of her floor had referred her to, and, once in her room, ripped off every stinging, chafing, itching piece of her clothing — the tapered brown skirt cramping her hips, the tailored jacket with padded shoulders and sleeves so narrow that they barely allowed her to bend her arms at the elbow, and the cage-like corset she loathed. She had not worn this formal ensemble in months. The young Việt nursing-aides must have pulled it from the suitcase sent to the hospital by her last landlord because they had laid it out for her in the morning, so that she would leave their care properly attired. Now the rumpled heap of wretched folds lay at her feet.

From the same suitcase she pulled out the flowing tropical favourites she had worn the day she was admitted — the red *crêpe de Chine* skirt slit thigh-high and loosely tied at the waist with a yellow sash, and the rice-paper-thin blouse with the *ligne du ciel* — the alluring V-cut neckline her Vietnamese seamstress had copied from a Parisian journal. Stepping to the mirror, she kicked the corset under the bed and hung a long string of carnelian beads around her neck and a pair of jingling silver hoops in her ears. Lastly, she smeared some vermillion on her lips.

She set out for a stroll down the streets of Saigon, barefoot and hell-bent on being her own self again and settling some scores with the city that had treated her so shabbily. Perhaps a flagrant display of defiance would silence the drums rumbling in her chest and hush the dreary shimmering in her head. As she stepped out into the street, she swung her shoulders back and forth to make her breasts sway, and swivelled her hips hard enough to let a flash of leg show through the slit. Her sash had come undone and was trailing on the ground. Her crimped chestnut hair, immured in a chignon when she left the hospital two hours earlier, was now flapping like a kite against the tussle of the wind. If any stray wisp wafted across her face, she brushed it aside.

Lit by shafts of sunlight, the street was her stage, and she was delivering a command performance to the French audience that kept coming at her all along *Boulevard Charnel*, on *Quai de Belgique*, and down the super classy *Rue Catinat*. Her flashy clothing and seductive manner were calculated to provoke and rile, to incite disdainful stares that would bear witness to her survival and to her tenacity never to allow prudish inhibitions to dampen her spirit. Let the heads turn. Let the straitlaced matrons, the surly directors, and the headmistresses of the *lycées français* — her tormentors from the past who might be walking by or sitting in the open-air cafés — be incensed again by her flamboyance, now that she was no longer *l'institutrice* and could be oblivious to their censure. Yes, they who had so lamented her lack of poise and frowned at her wayward hair seldom neatly gathered in a bun, at her bouffant blouses, frilly skirts, and open-toed shoes. The snobs who detested her coarse *breton* accent, and rolled their eyes when she allowed her two children to run barefoot with the lowly offspring of the *indigène* servants and speak the ghastly Vietnamese language with them instead of French. Let the offended hypocrites — all of them — watch her pass by and squirm in their cozy armchairs in the sprawling *café-terraces* of Saigon. *Merde!* Let them have to pay for another glass of Pernod to drown their contempt.

At the end of *Rue Catinat,* her feet raw and her energy spent, she stepped over the embankment to the silvery ribbon of the Saigon River, and gazed for a long while at the junks meandering lazily to the markets of Chợ Lớn, while a song played in her head — *Ramona, I hear the mission bells above, Ramona, they're singing our song of love...*

Only a few months earlier, she had stood barefoot on the shore of her concession in Cambodia, watching the waves crush the rocks and hearing them roar at her: *"Quittez! Quittez la folie!"* More than once she had been on the brink of quitting, of saying, *"D'accord! J'en ai assez!"* and letting the waves take her out to sea. Today there was no need to think of dying, or to go over again the other follies of her life — the teaching positions abandoned in a huff, the fickle lovers discarded, and the ruinous investment impulsively made. Yes, she had been wild but she had survived, so why despair of the future? What future anyway? Her son was dead — opium-steeped when she could not be there to stand guard. Her concession had been annulled and her savings were gone. The money she did not regret, but that she had allowed her son to slip away from her was a lingering torment, a gash refusing to close.

To her right, overlooking the river, loomed the neoclassical *Hôtel Majestic,* which held the memories of her long months of imprisonment on the piano stool before she finally got her plantation. She could almost feel again the hot current seeping from the ivory keys as she scaled them into melodies. "That wooden piano stool," she thought, "was more of a jail than *l'Hôpital Grall.*" The Việt whores, on their way to the Poker Room, used to pass behind her back and run their fingers through her hair, to tease or annoy her, and she could not scold them or shove them away because she was fearful of losing her way with the music.

Eventually, *Madame* Bijou would wave her arm from behind the velvet curtain to alert her that her son was on his way to the Opium Room again, and she would pound the keys furiously to get to the end of the tune and beg a break to run after him. At the Opium Room entrance, the *petit gendarme* would try to cut her off. There was always a tussle between them — but only a token one. She was a white French woman, a piano player in the hotel, tall and feisty, and he was a dark *indigène*, a puny Việt sentry who needed to show that he was enforcing the hotel rule that forbade employees to go there. She always won, of course, and stormed past him. By that Opium Room door she felt not like a widow with two children, not like one of the *Petits Blancs* on the skids, but like a woman of superior rank. She savoured her victory every time.

Now, on the bank of the Saigon River she could taste another victory — the horrid three years of toil in the fetid swamps of Cambodia could finally be forgotten, and the six weeks of insane din in the white pavilion of *l'Hôpital Grall* would eventually also fade away. The only memories still replaying themselves in her head were of the last time she thought she had a future, and of the last man who had asked her to dance, and charmed her, and awakened her. Was he still in Saigon or had he lost his head to a Việt woman... or maybe a crocodile? She remembered him with an ardent throb of loss and sunk her feet into the cool pebbles to ease the hurt. All at once, a gust of hot breeze tossed her into the air, and she soared like a seagull that has been beaten to the ground by a downpour, but has shaken off the raindrops and taken flight again — relishing a liberty so painfully earned.

"VOUS PERMETTEZ, MADAME?" A dark-haired head bent down and a firm hand grasped her elbow and pulled her up. The man's right foot moved back, her left foot moved forward, and she swam into the slow-slow-quick-quick step of the hotel band's foxtrot rhythm. He pressed his ear against hers and she could feel the heat of his palm flat on her back because she was corsetless. Together they sailed past the stained-glass door of the Games Room, past the Việt orchestra sweating in their tuxedoes, past the more sedate couples shuffling around the floor: his hips twisting, her skirt twirling. When the music stopped, he led her back to her table and pulled out a chair. "We did all right on the floor, *n'est-ce pa*s? I'm Jacques Martin."

She was breathless and not ready to give her name just yet, but agreed to give him the pleasure of her company for a round of Pernod. A liveried Việt *garçon* sprung to the snap of his finger, and as they clicked their glasses she said wistfully, "*Vive la France.*" He pulled out a silver cigarette case and offered her a Sobranie. She retrieved her ivory cigarette holder from her purse while he retrieved his, made of silver to match the case. His fingers were bony, the nails manicured. No wedding band and no imprint of one on the skin. She inhaled and took a long look at his starched collar and his Hermès tie. *Ah, l'élégance française.*

"I've been in Saigon all of three days. I guess it'll take time to get used to the muggy air?" he said.

"My name is Jeannine. I've also been in Saigon for three days. But altogether I've been in Indochina for twenty years, the last three with the *indigènes* of Cambodia."

"So what brings you to Saigon?"

"Business. To finalize a loan about to be approved for my property. Whenever I come, I try to catch a moment of music or a dance." She swished her palm over her hair to make sure it stayed tousled and added, "You're quite a virtuoso on the dance floor. It's a wonder that I did all right. In the jungle my dance is strictly *solitaire*."

"*Bien sûr*, but someone keeps you company over there?"

"My husband is dead, my silly daughter back in France, so it's just me and my son — he's about to come of age but needs a lot of care. The rest of the company, apart from the *indigènes*, is four-legged — wild boars and elephants, tigers and crocodiles. One day, you may want to come and meet them."

"But you must have guests... visitors?"

"I certainly do. The missionaries. I have no love for religion, but when the preachers show up in my jungle I give them a cot and feed them."

"Perhaps you should feed them to the crocodiles," he smirked but she stayed serious.

"One or two have actually fed themselves to the crocodiles. It's not difficult, you know. You take one careless step by the swamp and you're gone." She drained her glass. "And you? What brings you here?"

He tapped the ashes into the coconut ashtray, his lip curved. "I've come to Indochina to write. Maybe help in some way? Definitely not to surrender my head to a crocodile."

She fixed her eyes on his quivering Adam's apple and wondered why he seemed nervous. "You've come to the right place. There is plenty to do. The *indigènes* need to be civilized — they're ages behind... live in squalor... cholera alone takes a dozen lives a month in my camp. They need *la su-pér-iorité de notre cul-ture*," she sing-songed the syllables.

"*Eh bien, la mission civilisatrice.*" He grimaced and dropped his voice. "Do you really think we can enlighten the natives with our superior culture? Or that we should? These tawny Việt men in the orchestra, for example? They've been dressed in tuxedos, but have they converted to our ways? *La supériorité*? At the stroke of midnight, they'll go back to their thatched huts and eat rice with their sticks. If anything, we should warn them against our culture… our Catholic faith… that instrument of oppression. And our imperialism… The only European things arguably superior are our ships. They've carried us far beyond where we have any right to be."

"*Aiija,*" she blurted. "You're quite a cynic." She shifted in her seat and glanced at a *garçon* expertly balancing a silver tray of steaming plates in one hand. "Are you hungry?"

"I'm famished. Is there anything good here?"

"Yes. Every time I come to Saigon from Cambodia, I'm ravenous for French food and order *croque-monsieur — la spécialité du chef.* The chef is a Việt man but trained in France, of course. The ham is cured locally, but the *gruyere* is Swiss and he grills it to perfection."

He aimed a thin whistle toward the *garçon* standing by the wall and ordered two *croque-monsieurs* and a bottle of Bordeaux. She cringed at the *faux pas* — whistling in one of the better cafés of Saigon? — and raised her hand to her lips, her bangles jingling. He scanned the faces around him, oblivious to her discomfort.

When he turned to her again, she said, "You say you've come here to write. So what do you write?"

"Oh no, we've talked enough about me. *C'est votre tour.* I'd like to know why a beautiful young woman would leave France to start a new life on the other side of the world."

She twisted her lips into a faint smile. "Because she was suffocating in a dreary town beyond the reach of the sea breeze, trying to exist on a teacher's salary that never stretched till the end of the month. Buried among thickheaded bumpkins who had never been anywhere and — worse —" she bore her cigarette butt into the ashtray, "wouldn't have had the courage to shift their *derrières* to see any other part of the world. The north of France is like the Bastille, a prison so grim that your lungs screech."

"So who was the adventurer who brought you here?"

"I brought myself here, actually. I'd seen government posters — *A FORTUNE IS WAITING FOR YOU IN THE COLONIES!* Pictures of men and women in white linen suits leaning against coconut palms, their dark servants standing at attention. I wanted to be one of those women." She studied his face for a sign of interest, and went on, her voice coquettish. "A married man was in love with me, reckless enough to leave his wife and children for me. We boarded a steamship and joined the Crusades for Indochina. *Voilà, mon destin.*"

He stared at her skeptically. "So what kind of destiny has it been for you and your man?"

"*Pas mal.* The man is gone, and I've made a minor misstep now and then, as one does. But the best years are ahead. In a way, my life is only beginning — my new life."

"*Eh bien, la séduction,*" he leaned back as the dinner plates were put before them. "We've all been seduced once or twice."

"So, what seduced you about Indochina?" she asked between bites.

"Hunger… of a sort. To check on the colonial world… see what I can do… maybe I'll just end up playing poker seven days a week… maybe seduce a hundred women…"

"*Merde,* that's ambition!" she exclaimed, noting he did not flinch at the swear word. "You did come to the right place; you're a gambler at heart."

"My whole life has been a gamble," he said, turning his head toward the stained-glass door and the Games Room behind it, where the roulette tables were clinking, the chips swishing on the green, the Việt croupiers calling, "*Mesdames et messieurs, faites vos jeux.*" He took a sip of wine and said with a confident grin, "Betting and bluffing are my games all right."

They ate in silence for a while, and when she finished she crossed her legs under the table and wedged herself snugly into her armchair. The lonely evening she had dreaded had taken a fortunate turn. From her purse, she took out a small hand mirror, swivelled her head to examine her cheeks and eyelids, moistened her lips, and snapped the mirror shut.

He rested his knife and fork on the plate, dabbed the napkin around his lips, and took a piercing look at the colonials around them — the mustachioed men, their well-ironed white shirts unbuttoned at the neck, ties hanging loose, and the women in their lace-trimmed gowns and matching hats. She wondered if he was on the lookout for someone.

"So what kind of a gamble lured you from Saigon to the jungle of Cambodia?" he asked.

"It wasn't a gamble. I took a once-in-a-lifetime roll of the dice that can't go wrong. A free grant of virgin land by the sea-shore. To be planted by my *indigènes*. I make profits from the sale of the harvest and get full title to the property after three crops. All I need is the loan to pay for the dikes I will have my *indigènes* build to keep the sea out."

"It's still a gamble — to sink your money into the virgin land and make a profit from it."

"But I will. I wanted to do it and the time is right."

"But *Madame*, have you not heard? *La belle époque est finie.* A depression is upon us," he said.

"What depression?" She swung her arm and the bangles swished against his sleeve. "The good times are just beginning. My own plantation. A fortune to be spent when I sell it and go back to France richer than the bumpkins in my town can ever be."

"*Eh bien*, we can drink to that," he snapped his fingers at the *garçon* for another bottle of Bordeaux. "But you may be dreaming, *Madame*. The capitalist system is in crisis. Look at America. You know what happened on Wall Street last December? The stock market crashed and people were jumping out of windows."

He saw the puzzled look on her face and added, "Because they had lost their life savings and their hopes."

She took a sip of wine and rolled her fingers over her necklace. "The last painful news I heard from America was that Rudolph Valentino was dead. I adored the man. When he died — at thirty-one — I thought — *merde!* I need to take hold of my life. Seize the day before it's too late. So I signed up for a concession that will let me leave a mark on Indochina. And bring an inheritance for my son."

"Many leaders in Europe are warning of black clouds gathering over the colonies. The natives are getting tired of looking into our arrogant eyes and bending their backs to our will."

"Nonsense." She tugged at his sleeve and caught the hard metal of his cufflink. "You've not been here long enough to know. Listen! *Les émigrés, les entrepreneurs, les aventuriers* who come here are sinking their money and their blood into this place. Thanks to them, the *indigènes* eat and live better. If you look around you'll see — the schools and hospitals built with French money, the plantations and mines… the architecture… *C'est la belle colonie.*"

"And what do young people learn in those schools? How to serve their *bourgeois* masters? Shouldn't we teach them how to run their own schools and hospitals and be masters in their own house… you know, the truths that matter: *la liberté, l'égalité, la fraternité*?" He slapped the table with his fingers close to hers and the wine glasses trembled. "The Revolution has already succeeded in Russia. The downtrodden will rise —"

"*Aiija,* what do you mean? Are you talking subversion?" She put her forefinger on his hand in disbelief. "Are you talking about *agents provocateurs*? The Việt communists? When I was last in Saigon, just before Christmas, three of them had just gone under the *guillotine.*"

He winced. The dance floor was empty, the band at rest, and the rickshaw traffic in the street had died down. He lit another Sobranie off the old stump and said, "*La guillotine*, eh?"

"*Mais oui!* Law and order must be maintained. The *indigènes* kept in their place. That's what the *gendarmes* are for. It's a grim business — subversion. You should be careful who you talk to like this."

He leaned back, braided his fingers, and rested them on his waist. "Well, is there a place in Saigon to get mixed up with dazzling people? To have a really good time?"

She snapped her fingers and swayed her arms above her head. "*Certainement.* There is a dancing pool in the forest in the *banlieue*... lit at night by Venetian lanterns. The dancing floor overhangs the pool — the orchestra sits in the cavern nearby. Are you following me? Oui...? Swimmers change in a tent or in the bushes and splash in the water in full view of the dancers. But those who want to swim... *au naturel. Aiija!* They wait for the lights to dim and the music to stop, and then the dancers rush to the railing to watch the bare-skinned pranksters race from the trees and jump in — Wroommprahhh! There is a round of applause and the dancing resumes."

"*Eh bien, c'est sublime... la vie coloniale!*" He raised his glass. "*À votre santé.*"

She was almost giddy with excitement now, but put on a sad face when she noticed the orchestra packing their instruments and the *garçons* gathering the silverware from the tables. "Let's stretch the night a bit and end on a high note," she proposed and called for two glasses of absinthe verte.

"Is it legal to drink it in Saigon? It's been banned in France for years."

She brought her lips closer to his ear and whispered conspiratorially, "Shhh! Every good thing is legal in Saigon. No need to surrender to our *ennui colonial*. There is always a good drink, an opium den, and a woman — a Việt woman, if that's your choice. But watch it, they can be treacherous. Pierce your heart and stab your back all at once." She swung back and squirmed in her armchair like a kitten. He pinned her palm to the table with his forefinger. She calmed down for a moment, then squirmed again. When the *garçon* brought two glasses filled with green liquid she beat him to the toast, "*Vive la République Française, Vive l'amour!*" When he leaned forward to touch her glass she added, "*Vous êtes très sympathique, Monsieur.*"

He kissed the tips of her fingers. "*Vous êtes charmante, Madame.*"

IN THE MORNING, he left her and walked leisurely to his well-out-of-the-way *hôtel-pension*, waving away the rickshaws and horse-drawn buggies whose drivers motioned to him from right and left. He felt lightheaded and content to lose himself in a new town on the other side of the world. Not one person here knew anything about him — not his real name, not why he came, not the life he was glad to escape.

He had grown up in the slum of the *Vieux Port* of Marseille, a love child of a local *pédicure* and an Andalusian fisherman. Every day after school he made deliveries of fish for his father, using a low four-wheel dray he had stolen from the back lot of a plant that pickled *cornichons*. When he told his mother he had found it abandoned she exclaimed, "*C'est parfait!*" His father patted him on the head. He made his rounds hitched to the dray like a donkey, gave the earnings to his father and the meagre tips to his mother. At night, in the family's one-room cellar, he watched burly men in gut-stained coveralls grumble conspiratorially around the table. Sometimes, his father would strike his fist on it and holler, "*Ce n'est pas juste!*"

A week after his fourteenth birthday he found his father on the floor, rivulets of blood soaking his sleeves. When the landlord saw the medical examiner's ruling, underlined in heavy ink — SUICIDE — he ordered mother and son to leave the cellar by the month's end. His mother had to move in with her parents. They had never accepted their daughter's sinful liaison with a fugitive Spaniard who could never legally marry her in France, and would not allow her bastard son in the house. For three nights he slept in the street. On the fourth evening, he spotted a newspaper *kiosque* vendor dozing on his stool and filched enough money from his raincoat pocket to buy a baguette and a train ticket to Paris. There, he made his way to his father's sister, married to a Frenchman but childless, and immediately found himself in another cellar filled with burly men talking in great agitation. Some of them spoke in foreign tongues. His first trip with his aunt and uncle outside the neighbourhood was to the *Gare du Nord*, to meet a train bringing somebody from Russia.

Years later, when he got a job writing political commentaries for a socialist weekly, he became curious about the world beyond the borders of France and dreamed of travelling to Moscow. He had heard his uncle say many times, "Those Russian revolutionaries are on to something," and ached to see them first-hand. He could not read the foreign tomes in English, German, and Russian his aunt had hidden under the pot lids in the kitchen trunk. But he was learning enough from the old issues of *l'Humanité*, torn into handy squares and laid out on the bathroom's windowsill. The same names came up over and over again — Marx, Engels, Lenin, Trotsky — and the same message, that the world was ripe for radical change. Once, he came across a byline of Nguyễn Ái Quốc above an article on the evils of colonialism, and wondered what kind of a crazy Asian would want to get mixed up in European utopias. His uncle explained that the Vietnamese man had once lived in Paris, combining menial jobs at night and by day petitioning his colonial masters and their allies for Vietnam's independence. He was in Moscow now because that's where a better future was being built.

THAT EVENING, she waited for him in Café Lola, sitting erect and demure, casting insolent glances at the crowd of colonials sipping their drinks. She had let down her hair to make herself look more girlish, chosen a tight-fitting satin dress, and arrived on time. The *café-terrace* overlooked the rim of Saigon's *Haut Quartier*, filled with the clamour of the *indigène* language and littered with hawkers of roasted peanuts. Wearied Việt maids walked home after a day's work, carrying soiled white aprons to launder for tomorrow. Bird vendors pushed carts loaded with daintily latticed cages, the birds twittering in their ornate jails, the wobbly two-wheelers rattling over the cobblestones. On the terrace, now misted in the evening dusk, the *garçons* flitted from one linen-draped table to another like frenzied swallows before the rain.

When he walked in, he was impeccably dressed but dragging his feet a bit and looking vaguely rattled. She offered her hand to be kissed. He asked if a glass of *Crème de Cassis* would be sweet enough to compensate for his being late. She said it would and added that she was also in the mood for a taste of her childhood's favourite treat — a serving of *marrons glacés*. He told the *garçon* to bring two spoons. They lit their cigarettes from one match and turned their heads away to exhale. Then they stayed silent, each waiting to see who would speak first. After the *garçon* had brought the mouth-watering concoction of candied chestnuts and whipped cream on a fancy *porcelaine de Sèvres* plate, he said, "*Superbe!*" to the chocolatey topping and licked his lips.

"You still think that battling floods in Cambodia is the life for you? Would it not be easier to give your land back to the sea and return to Saigon?"

"Give it back? Never! If they try to take the land away — over my dead body. Life in Saigon will be very good indeed — one day. I just need to get that loan. I'll pay my *indigènes* double to push back the sea."

"*Eh, bien.* The sea is always smarter than people. How did you end up with a piece of shoreline anyway? Wasn't there any better land to be had?"

"The colonial agent said it was a prime oceanfront lot. I saw it and fell in love. Both he and the *indigènes* knew that the sea had been flooding that land for a thousand years, but they never warned me. *Les barbares!*"

"*Eh, tes illusions!* You think you can reverse a thousand years of nature?"

"*Quelles illusions?* Scores of people have made fortunes on plantations — on tea, or jute or hemp or cotton — some of it growing in swampy soil. I can do the same. I'm having my *indigènes* build me a bungalow on stilts to keep me safe from crocodiles. And once I get my loan, I'll be safe from the colonial agents."

"What if they refuse you the loan?"

"The Colonial Land Office can go to hell; I know how to deal with officials. After my husband died in France, they admitted that he'd contracted a grave disease in Indochina, but because in his final weeks he had apparently refused treatment and gone home, they would not issue the death-in-service certificate. Can you believe that? Without the certificate I couldn't collect his pension. *Aiija!* I badgered them no end about it — seven long years. And I won. The Colonial Governor and the bank need to know that I never give up. They'll see it tomorrow."

"Still, such a hard life for such a beautiful woman," he said and kissed her hand.

She twirled the dessert spoon close to his cheek. "It's not as if I'm going to rescue the land with my bare hands. That's what my coolies are for. I may have to whip them first, but they'll work. They'll stick their skinny arms in the muck and salivate at the prospect of having plenty of food to eat for once. And I can buy more of their goodwill with quinine and tobacco."

"Perhaps you were expected to offer something to the agents ... to get a more fertile location?"

"I'd rather fight officials than bribe them. Maybe some people —"

"Some people are smart. They find out how the system works first —"

"I don't care about the system. I care about my concession and intend to make it work. It would be easier if I had a partner... a man I could trust... to advise me. I have a beautiful stretch... breathtaking scenery... unbelievable." She cocked her head sideways and snapped her fingers. "You can see for yourself. Do you want to come?"

FOUR MONTHS EARLIER, she had written a five-page letter to the Colonial Governor in Saigon (not to the Governor of Cambodia, whom she understood to be a subordinate), following the accepted protocol carefully. First, she thanked the Governor for the 300 acres of land that had been granted to her gratis on condition that she put it to cultivation. She restated her intention to purchase the additional 200 acres at a reasonable price, as per the offering, as soon as she got some money from the current crop, and thus to become a major producer of rice, mangoes, corn, and pepper. She added a flowery sentence about the splendour of her area of Cambodia, and how proud and privileged she felt to own such a beautiful overseas French property.

She went on to explain that her failure to produce a crop three years after taking possession was due to the proximity of her property to the sea, which had flooded her planted fields. But the problem would be rectified soon because she was about to put her *indigènes* to work constructing a tier of sturdy dikes and fortifications. Colonial agents should not harass her with threats to withdraw the concession. Their interference was detrimental to the government's plan to encourage agricultural production.

She reminded the Governor that she was the widow of a respected colonial official and the mother of... two children, she wrote at first, and then, in a stroke of genius, added the two children from her husband's first marriage (whom she had not seen in twenty years) to make herself the mother of four. She concluded by respectfully requesting that the inspections by colonial agents be postponed, and that the Governor pronounce favourably on her application for a loan to finance the building of a sea wall to protect her property.

To strengthen her case and to move the Governor to compassion, she made the second part of the letter into a poignant description of the life of her *indigènes*.

> Your Excellency must be aware of the pitiful living conditions of the indigènes in this part of the Cambodian plains. The men plant small plots of rice, hunt, and render occasional services to visiting officials and missionaries. When such jobs are not forthcoming and the rice is not yet ready to be harvested, families live on green mangoes because they are too hungry to wait for the fruit to ripen. Most families have a baby every year. The little ones hang in cotton sacks around the stomachs of their mothers and when they begin to walk

are left naked in the care of their older siblings. All day long
they squat in the mud — starving dogs roaming in their wake
and feeding on human excrement. Many youngsters die — of
neglect, hunger and disease — their bodies dumped in a hole
like dead monkeys. Cholera and malaria claim the young and
the old with dreadful regularity in this primeval area.

It is under these circumstances that I, a patriotic Citizen of
France and a long-term resident of Indochina, am struggling
to build a viable agricultural plantation and provide
employment for the pitiful indigènes *and sustenance for*
their families. My efforts merit Your Excellency's support,
and I look forward to Your Excellency's favourable reply.

She added the customary assurances of high regard, signed her name, and placed the letter on top of two applications for a loan she had written earlier to the *Banque de l'Indochine* and the *Société financière*. She would deliver the three envelopes in person as soon as she found someone to take her to Saigon.

On the back veranda of her unfinished Cambodian bungalow, her son was grooming his laughing monkeys with a hairbrush. She told him to pour her a glass of Calvados and when he brought it to her *chaise-longue* she sank deep, crossed her knees, and lit up a 555 — the expensive English cigarette she liked. She inhaled deeply and swelled with hope. Very soon, with the loan money in her hands, she would add a veranda to the oceanfront side of her bungalow, and watch her *indigènes* build the wall of dikes all along the shore and never again see her crops under water. She motioned her Cambodian errand boy to crank up the Victrola, and set her mind to drift with the spin of the record, *"Ramona, when day is done you'll hear my call..."*

A MONTH BEFORE meeting Jeannine, he had left *Quai de la Joliette* in Marseille aboard *Cap Varella*, a sleek steamer of the *Chargeurs Réunis* line. He had held on to the railing of the lower deck, almost writhing in elation at the coastline sailing away from him. He was certain that he had buried the past and was plunging into the future lean and clean. But five days into the journey, after a madcap night of drinking and tangoing, he sat sweaty and morose on the rumpled berth of his cabin wondering whether his dicey mission in Indochina might lead him straight to perdition. He was on his way to a remote French colony, his real name struck out, his notebook filled with hastily scribbled instructions and names. What in hell had he gotten himself into?

It was not a question of him not having faith in the cause, because, God knows, he had seen enough misery in France to believe that a better world needed to be built. A world in which despondent mothers did not have to abandon their children to the gutter, and beaten-down fathers were not driven to suicide. The two families he had grown up with had taught him to believe in Karl Marx's grand design — the capitalist system was rotten and the exploiting classes should be made to pay. But to make the Asians rise against their oppressors, brave souls would need to risk their health, and maybe even their necks, to lay the groundwork for the revolution.

After his second divorce, finalized after an ugly altercation with his wife's gangster-lover (which brought him some notoriety and a suspended sentence), he went to visit his mother, who had recently married. In a back street of his native *Vieux Port* of Marseille, he ran into two of his father's old comrades who had come back from Asia inflamed about the revolutionary potential of Indochina. "The masses are dirt poor and illiterate. They need to be radicalized. The time is now," they said. Over several evenings of oysters and Marseille-style *pastis* on ice, he listened to them explain Lenin's political program for the colonies, the imperative of propaganda work, and the well-financed covert support he would receive. He owed his divorce lawyer some money, so the promise of payment was welcome. He wavered because he had never crossed the border of France before and feared he might not be up to the task. But he had grown uneasy about being just an onlooker for too long. His probation had just ended, and he was an unfettered single man again, so why the hell not take up the Asian challenge? He bid goodbye to his mother, telling her that he was catching a train back to Paris.

Upon disembarking in Saigon, he was shocked to see that the *indigènes* were very small in stature and confusingly alike — their hair, eyes, and teeth black, their garb scruffy, their postures uniformly servile. He had to blink a few times to see if he could tell any of them apart. At the hotel, even the Việt porter who spoke some French seemed terribly foreign — brash and surly. Was such a sorry lot really ready to be radicalized? Two years of having to work with them suddenly loomed like another suspended sentence. Mercifully, the Việt girl who arrived at his door bearing a nightcap on a wicker tray looked as dainty as a vase of porcelain, her teeth no less white than his, the folds of her *áo dài* of crimson silk overlapping like rose petals. She stayed the night, leaving him reassured that even for women of a different race he was a virile and captivating man.

AFTER HIS SECOND NIGHT with Jeannine, they woke up late and it was nearly noon before they settled themselves on a grassy slope behind *l'Hôtel Majestic,* both wearing white linen suits — hers with a pleated skirt and an outsized ribbon at the waist. He felt grumpy, irritated further by the cries of the naked children splashing in the river below. Above them, at the crest of the slope, a massive hedge of hibiscus bushes in yellow bloom kept the sun at bay.

"Maybe the *indigènes* have a point; maybe to succeed in life, the gods must be on your side," she mused. "If my gods flex their muscles and shake some high-ranking colonial officials out of their stupor, favours will pour down on me and the concession will be mine for life."

"You're so dramatic."

"Because my life in Indochina has been dramatic. That's the way I like to live."

"And so naïve..."

"*Aiija!* Naïve? I've been working my bones off for three years. Nobody lifted a finger to help. My daughter scoffed when she saw the paddy crabs gnaw my dikes into shreds. She couldn't care less about anyone but herself. After the first flooding, I found a nice Chinese man for her, the son of a rich exporter I knew, and begged her to marry him for the sake of the rest of us — she knew how little we had. But no, she wanted to be a writer. She's a Paris bohemian now — without a penny to her name. And my batty son would never have made a go of it at the *Lycée Chasseloup-Laubat*, even if I had the money to pay the fees. He likes his opium and his monkeys. *Voilà, mes enfants.* I take it you have none?"

He did not answer for the moment because he was beginning to wonder how far he should go with this raving colonial — so consumed by illusions, so wrapped up in her narrow world. Back in Marseille they had instructed him that settling down with a woman — a native woman or a French woman who knew Indochina — was the surest way of acquiring camouflage. But was she the right woman? A couple of years his senior, but attractive, and good in bed, she would easily draw the curtain on his messy marriages and divorces and take him over the threshold to his new life. Her twenty years in the colony were a definite advantage. But she was willful and flamboyant, and if she found out what he was up to, would she betray him? He would have to trust that, like most women, she would be happy to stand by her man so long as she was gratified in bed and got a bottle of perfume now and then.

He leaned in, squeezed her hand, and murmured affectionately, "How could we see each other if you go back to Cambodia? You belong in Saigon."

"But in Cambodia I'm Queen. My word is law. Well, maybe not with my son, but with my *indigènes*. And I can go barefoot all day wearing a cotton sack, and cut my nails to the bone. In Saigon, teaching French or playing the piano, I had to be corseted and properly manicured. I never really belonged; I was one of the *Petits Blancs*. Do you know who they are?"

His ear caught the note of resentment he had heard from the French underclass, and he turned his head to listen.

"They are the white people who live beyond the rim of the *Haut Quartier* in stifling alleys that run alongside the ratty tramway line. My first lodging in Saigon was there — on the ground floor, the tramway cars rolling by the window. A cheap eatery and a Chinese grocer took up the other front room, and a dressmaker's shop and an opium den took up the back. French custom agents were the upstanding residents on the floor above. Việt whores lived in the attic. I counted their customers as they climbed the squeaky staircase at odd hours. It was as close to a bordello as you'd want it to be, but discreet."

He was beginning to like this story of a life so different from and yet so similar to his own early days — both the poverty and the artifice. The undertone of irony and anger in her voice aroused him. When she blew out a train of smoke and picked a shard of tobacco from her tongue, he felt tenderness swelling in his chest and was tempted to kiss her cheek.

"The *Petits Blancs* are different from the snobs who've sunk their money into rubber plantations up north. On Sunday mornings they take their children down the alley in a horse-drawn *calèche,* while the *parvenus* are being chauffeured along the wide avenues of the *Haut Quartier,* and on to the racetrack or the casino... I'd watch their *Peugeots* and *Citroens* from a distance and feel my blood boil." She raked her fingers through her hair in mock despair. "*Merde.* The rich run this place, and only pretend to notice the rest of us when they need something done."

"*Eh bien,* you sound like Karl Marx. Have you read him?"

"Who is Marx?"

"A writer, a German revolutionary. He's dead now. He wrote that capitalism is doomed because the rich make profits on the backs of the poor... and one day the poor will take over —"

"Pfff... It'll not happen here. The poor can snivel all they like. This is a gold mine for the wealthy. They hold all the cards. Their destiny is to rule."

"And all you want is to become one of them, *n'est-ce pas?*

"It'd be nice; I've never been rich before."

"*Eh bien.* What if one day you found your Cambodia coolies raising their scythes against you? They've already rebelled in the mines. The rubber plantations could be next to go up in smoke. Then you'll have your destiny."

"*Aiija,* it will *not* happen. Any conspirators... *agents provocateurs...* deluded rebels — the *gendarmerie* is there to help me. And the *guillotine* is there for them."

"*Eh bien,*" he said, exasperated, his shirt soaked with sweat and pasted to his chest. "*Bonne chance, Madame!* You and I are standing on the brink of a precipice — with crocodiles waiting below. I fear for your future as much as for my own. Maybe we'll both drown in this swampy hell."

"*Ah, voilà*. So now who is being dramatic?" she cried. "Life can be good in the swampy hell. Just drop your barricades and inhale *l'Indochine*. Let it remake you."

"You know, you're so volatile," he exclaimed in annoyance. "I sensed it when I first asked you to dance. You go from being a brittle stem of an orchid to being a hardy shaft of bamboo. My mother... my aunt... they kept their feet on the ground. You soar on a wing then dive like a falcon. There's no telling what target you'll hit next."

"*C'est vrai*." she shot back. "Very soon I'll be absolutely soaring — you'll see. *Merde*." She yanked the combs from her *coiffure pompadour* and let her hair spill over her breast.

He glanced at her bare neck, at the strand of grey splayed on her sunburned neck, and spat through his teeth. Was it worth keeping in her good graces? Aversion to religion was the one stance they shared. She would never convert to his cause. But if he ran into problems and had to hide, her Cambodian hideaway would be a handy place to have. *Merde*.

THAT NIGHT SHE SLEPT alone and badly, and in the morning resolved to revisit some old haunts of her bygone Saigon days. When the sidewalk leading from the hotel came to an end, she entered an alley roofed by rows of slender cajeput trees, now shedding their outer bark in thin brown layers. The wrinkled leaves curled on the ground into tender cones that creaked and cracked like rice paper when she stepped on them. In the distance, the marshes glistened under the parasols of water-coconut palms, their fronds braided into one thick crown. The air was redolent of fetid mud and the sweetish stench of something smouldering. In a narrow passage across the road, a one-legged *indigène* was holding a shoeshine boy by the hair with one hand and using his other hand to beat him with his crutch. The youngster was punching his attacker in the stomach and wailing piteously. Finally, he broke the hold of his crippled assailant and disappeared into the dusty copse of old durian trees that — she guessed from the odour — rickshaw pullers used as urinals.

Four years earlier, when she was still living in town, she had strolled down the same road looking for her son, who had been missing for over a month. Her daughter had told her to watch for a heavy black door ornamented with a wooden lizard, its tail curled into an O. When she found it, the smell — something like burning chocolate — betrayed what was going on inside. As she entered the yard, a doormen stepped out of a dimly lit booth, arms outstretched, to block her way into what looked like a storehouse. She hit his chest with her fist so hard that he thumped against the wall. Then she stepped over the body of an *indigène* junkie, his arms raised in a theatrical plea for money. Inside, there were two big rooms with several rows of camp beds, where men in various stages of *déshabillage* lay slumped on the mats, eyes half closed. Wooden pipes leached a sickly smoke that draped them in a yellow haze.

Her son lay there stoned into semi-consciousness, curled up like a child, exactly the way he used to curl up against her and his sister in the huge iron bed the three of them shared when she worked in the north, in Vĩnh Long, a decade ago. When her contract there was not renewed — she had slapped two Việt embroidery instructors in the *École des filles annamites* where she taught French — she had brought her children back to Saigon, where she had no choice but to take her seat on the piano stool at *l'Hôtel Majestic*. Her son, almost a teenager by then, often sat by her side, and when he got bored he amused the guests with silly jokes and puzzles. When he got older, he vanished into the Opium Room with them. It took her some time to realize that his pasty skin, murky eyes, and frightful agitation — the shaking hands, the eyeballs rolling in their sockets — were all signs that he had gone without a fix for too long.

The concession in Cambodia had held the promise of a cure and of great riches. When her daughter's liaison with a rich Chinese had come to naught, she gave up on her, refused to even see her off to Paris. She insisted that her son come to Cambodia to help with the planting. He ran away. After she found him sprawled on the bed in the wretched alley, she bought him a fancy opium lamp, carved in jade, and a pouch of opium he could smoke at home. One day, when he was stoned, she drove him to Cambodia in a borrowed derelict Peugeot, thinking she would trim down his dependency there. He stayed, but within weeks she knew that her *indigène* errand boy had become her son's supplier. Her money, cigarettes, and jewellery kept disappearing. Sometimes she would wake up in the pitch-dark and tiptoe to his cot to make sure he was breathing.

That first year, watching the swelling wave on her untamed Cambodian shore, she was often swept by panic and begged the tide to take her sorrows with it and ebb them out to sea. When the gruelling drudgery in the mud got beyond endurance, when she believed she could not manage another day of hauling boulders and sand with her *indigènes* under the merciless sun, she felt feverish for a real man — a Frenchman — to work at her side by day and press against her at night. A lover who would share her burdens and her ecstasies, and be there to see her triumph in Cambodia. Every time she made a trip to Saigon, finding a man was on her mind.

Realistically, the best she could hope for was to seduce a newly arrived Frenchman before a Việt woman snared him — and even that only for the few months before his wife and children joined him in the colony. Jacques Martin was a real find. Very new, unattached, and a writer — though what he thought he might find to write about in Saigon baffled her. His *idées fixes* about capitalism were irritating, but the fervour behind his arguments was delightful. She liked the way he swayed back and forth when making a point while rumpling a Sobranie between his fingers, the way those fingers furrowed his Hermès tie while waiting for her to answer his questions. The gallant way he had swept her to the dance floor, ushered her to dinner, and beckoned her to bed. Five years of celibacy had sharpened her hunger, and Jacques had slaked it in full. Her last lover had been a wiry Chinese gardener who seduced her right after her husband had left for France to die. But going native reeked of desperation. She was lucky to have happened upon this passionate Frenchman. *Aiija!* If she could only sway him away from his theories and have him do some real work helping her build a sea wall. And make him see the passion she was ready to give in return.

She turned back from the alley of opium dens now, and headed into town along the same road of shedding cajeput trees. Down a narrow cul-de-sac she caught a glimpse of her man dashing out of a house. "Jacques," she called out, jubilant to have discovered his lair. He had been vague about where he was staying, and both their nights together had been at her hotel. He paused at the bottom of the steps and flipped through the swath of papers in his hand. "*Bonjour*, Jacques!" she called out louder, but he lurched forward without looking up and vanished around the corner. Miffed, she walked the length of the alley and up the steps to the door.

It was a very ordinary *hôtel-pension*, housed in a large family villa, the vestibule walls covered in Oriental paper prints, and a brightly tiled floor bordered with flowering azaleas against the wall. At the counter she asked for a sheet of paper and an envelope and wrote, "*Vous me comblez de beauté et de gentillesse. Salut.*

Jeannine." She printed his name on the envelope and handed the letter to the man at Reception. He slid the metal ruler down the register name by name.

"*Je regrette, Madame,* but we have no guest by that name staying with us."

"*Impossible!* Jacques Martin walked out of this hotel a minute ago..."

"*Je regrette, Madame,*" he repeated disdainfully and swung his arm as if getting rid of a fly or a floozy looking for a client. Her face flared with humiliation and she wanted to argue. But he was a Frenchman, and judging by his accent possibly also from *Bretagne.* She yanked the envelope from his hand and shot him a gelid look of contempt. But his head was already down. She hurried toward the exit, nearly knocking over a pot of azaleas, her temples and her heels pounding in unison. Past the doorstep she paused to think: had Jacques Martin found a Việt woman? He had told her he would sleep at his own hotel the coming night because he had business to attend to the next morning, and she had agreed because she had her loan to check on. Now she wondered — what kind of business was he really in?

HIS FIRST MISSION in Saigon was to report to an undercover agent at the top of the list they had given him in Marseille. The *garçon* who served him breakfast directed him to the street, which turned out to be an open sewer, and he swore when his leather shoes sank into the sludge. At house No. Twenty-Seven, the Vietnamese woman who opened the door met his prearranged password with a cautious nod. Her face was drawn, her eyes red-rimmed. She began to explain but, seeing he could not follow her French, brusquely switched to Vietnamese, shouting and waving her arms toward the horizon. Finally, she slashed her neck with the edge of her hand and slammed the door shut. The best he understood was that her man had been taken away... to the *guillotine*? He was too shaken to see his way clear and tripped in the sludge again.

He walked back fighting panic — large steps, brisk pace, head jammed down between his shoulders — beginning to realize that working as an *agent provocateur*, no matter how noble the cause, meant living with his stomach tied up in knots, watching over his shoulder for betrayal, and fearing arrest and interrogation — maybe even death. *Merde.* In the street filled with filthy, half-naked children, he thought of the boy left alone two decades earlier when his mother was evicted. This time, he had a hotel room to go back to, but in it sat two trunks of contraband materials waiting to be delivered to the right contacts. If the *gendarmes* found them there...

To avoid arousing suspicion he needed to find a *pied-à-terre* and get to work. His comrades in Marseille had already chosen his *nom de plume* and were waiting to receive his commentaries, which they would offer to periodicals looking for first-hand reports on the political developments in Indochina. Writing travel pieces would be his overt *métier*, a base from which to make forays to clubs and poker rooms, to bet on horses at the races, and perhaps — his private agenda — to seduce a woman or two. Later on, he would receive instructions from Marseille on how to build a revolutionary cell. In the meantime, Saigon seemed overwhelming, the colonial crowd arrogant and reactionary, and the Oriental customs bizarre. He badly needed a helpmate to make him a home, guide him through the maze, and give him a cover.

In the *Parc Maurice Long*, he slouched on a wooden bench, bored his elbows into the cast-iron armrests to ground himself and thought of the two women he had been with. Jeannine — flamboyant and erratic. Politically naive. Her idol was Rudolph Valentino, for God's sake. She would never accept the challenge of his mission. He shouldn't have mentioned Marx to her. She was too much of a colonial. Obsessed with landownership. And her flakey son? Opium addicts were high risk. Altogether, too much to take on.

He recalled the young visitor of his first night. The exotic nymph who, knowing no more than a dozen French words, surprised him with a wicked manoeuver *à deux* he was happy to learn and now almost blushed to remember. Perhaps a Việt woman would be a better cover? More discreet and content to keep the hearth fires burning for him? Eventually, she would open more doors to the local patriots, help with the language, and be grateful for the upkeep and small favours — although how would he know until he had lived with her for a while? *Merde*, yet another Oriental puzzle to unravel.

He checked his watch and rose to walk under the arch of tamarind trees, his head and legs heavy. From the street curb, a fortune teller — a pair of European suspenders stretched over his straw vest — called out in a blend of Vietnamese and French and waved a horoscope sheet at him. Should he ask him about his destiny in Indochina? Hell, no!

He waited for her in the *Salon Orchidée* of *l'Hôtel André*, practising his skill with chopsticks on a plate of spicy hors d'oeuvres. When his second Bourbon was served, he lit up his fourth Sobranie and puffed out smoky rings toward the orchid blooms drooping from the ceiling. Would a Việt woman keep her man waiting for almost an hour? Probably not. Restlessly he pulled the tulle curtain aside and saw Jeannine tearing toward the hotel dressed in a well-tailored suit, her hair tight in a chignon. The knob of her chin was down and her arms sliced the air like a soldier's on parade. Had she heard bad news? If she had, in thirty seconds he would have to deal with a furious woman gripped by an impossible ambition but unable to let go of her folly.

For a moment he felt pity — at another time perhaps he would have wanted to help. He had just moved his arms forward, ready to extend them in a courteous welcome, when a loud crash resounded from the vestibule. Something heavy had been shattered. Broken pottery shards rumbled down the porcelain tiles and a chorus of panicky *Aaaahhhs* rose and was drowned by her feral cry, "*Laissez passer! Merde!*" Sounds of kicking and stomping pierced the air and several voices shouted in Vietnamese, the shrill glottal syllables calling out for help.

God! Had she lost her mind? If she ran to him screaming, in full view of the colonials, he would be embarrassed — discredited — his mission compromised? Perhaps the *gendarmes*... A tingling current raced through his chest as he locked his fingers around the wooden sticks and heard the familiar voice shout: "*La Banque de l'Indochine* can burn in hell! *Merde!* Let the *Société financière* go belly up. *Les barbares!* The *guillotine* is too good for them!"

The *maître d'* ran across the room, pleading, "*Madame, s'il vous plaît, Madame!*"

"*Aiija!* Let them clutch their money. Let them choke on it. The whole bloody colony is a bordello! I've been a faithful colonial and... Get out of my way! I have a rendezvous here with one Jacques Martin... or whatever he is calling himself... *Laissez passer!*"

Her hysterical howl burst his head... She was completely out of control. What would she say next? He was a fool. He had said too much... exposed himself to a madwoman. He gripped the edge of the table, hoisted himself up, and bolted past the piano, his cigarette case abandoned. He ran to the rear exit of *Salon Orchidée* and flew down the back steps, which cascaded toward the row of waiting buggies, the echoes of his alias thudding in his head. A rickshaw pulled up, and he barked the address of a secluded *hôtel-pension* he had memorized in case he had to run, threw a large note into the coolie's lap, and whacked his back with his fist: *Vite! Vite!* The luminous windows of *l'Hôtel André* watched his back disappear in the dusk.

END NOTE: This story was inspired by the life of Marie Donnadieu, mother of the French writer Marguerite Duras. In 1984, when she was seventy, Duras published *The Lover* – an internationally acclaimed autobiographical volume in which she dramatized her youthful liaison with a rich Chinese man. Her mother had apparently encouraged the romance, hoping to finance her son's addiction to opium. There is no evidence that Marie Donnadieu was ever confined to a mental hospital or had an affair with a Communist agent. But for nearly a decade she did have a concession in Cambodia where she suffered a string of setbacks and exhausted her health and her savings. She later died in France, as did her daughter.

Dear President

The 1950s were the time of revolutionary changes. In 1953, with French rule on the wane, the Vietnamese Workers Party led by Hồ Chí Minh, which controlled the northern part of the country, moved to give "land to the tillers." Landowners saw their holdings confiscated and distributed to the peasants. Alas, a short time later, having chosen the socialist model for the economy, the Party ordered the peasants to "donate" their newly acquired private plots to state cooperatives. When much resentment and a big drop in rice production ensued in the early 1960s, five percent of the communal land was allowed back to private plots.

Dear President Hồ Chí Minh,

Please accept the warmest greetings and best wishes for good health and happiness. Please be assured that we, the workers and peasants of Vietnam, cherish your leadership as we struggle to implement the revolutionary policies of the Communist Party that will lead us to Socialism and Communism. Your wisdom, gained through diligent study and worldwide travels, is our beacon. Led by the Party Cadres, who are the most worthy members of our Fatherland, we will transform our backward peasant society into a progressive modern people. May you continue in vigour to lead us to a glorious future.

I am Nguyễn Thị Bùi, daughter of a patriotic family of peasants, born thirty years ago in the village of Yên Hà, province of Thái Nguyên, where my ancestors endured feudal and colonial oppression for generations. The village stands at the foot of a rocky range. The soil had to be pried from the flank of the mountain, irrigated with water carried from the river, and coddled like a baby to make it grow food. Father toiled on a scrap of land leased from a rich man. Mother took care of me and later worked as a midwife. She told me that she met you some years ago when she was away from home receiving training at a birthing station. In her spare time she worked as a volunteer brick layer at a hospital construction site, and you arrived, unannounced, to meet the labourers working there and to commend their selfless effort. She calls it the greatest day of her life.

It is because of this memorable encounter that she has asked me to write to you about a painful event in our district. Last month, on the outskirts of the town of Bắc Kạn, where I now live, a man's body was found with a sign that read *TRAITOR* looped on a cord around the neck. The authorities quickly took the body away, not to the local morgue but out of town, at night, because the next morning road workers saw tire tracks in the mud on the trail leading south — and only the Cadres have the use of a truck with rubber tires.

Our community is in a state of great agitation. We were hoping to talk to the two men who found the body but Cadre Vạn Xuân told us that they had been taken away to assist with the investigation and identification. People around me speculate that the body was that of peasant Giới, who had been missing for some weeks. But Mother fears that it may have been Father's. He disappeared nearly two years ago, but recently the spirits have been telling her that he is on his way back. She keeps the door unlocked day and night waiting for him.

I venture to trouble you with a personal matter at a painful time for our Fatherland. The American war has brought us unspeakable grief. When I read in newspapers about bombs falling on our towns and villages, I seethe with anger and pray for the victory of our just cause. General Westmoreland and his vile band will suffer a terrible retribution. All of us rejoice in the glorious victories of our heroic soldiers over the American aggressors in the Province of Quảng Nam earlier this week. May they continue triumphant till President Johnson and his imperialist lackeys are brought to their knees.

Many years ago, when you were in prison in Hong Kong, you wrote from your cell:

Untidy clouds carry away the moon
The bedbugs swarm
around like army tanks on
manoeuvers,
While the mosquitoes form
squadrons, attacking like
fighter planes.

I remember reciting those lines at school, and share your contempt for the pests that invade us from the sky. In our district, we are ready to confront the enemy ruthlessly while consolidating our alliance with freedom-loving people everywhere. Your writings inspire us to great sacrifices, so that future generations will have peace and a better life.

At this time of strife you must be busy in the Capital meeting foreign leaders who support our heroic struggle. But I know that you continue to read letters from common people because not long ago a woman from my town wrote to you about the beatings of women by their husbands. She received from your office a reply stating that such behaviour was a remnant of the feudal and colonial past and had no place in a socialist society. I write to you as I would to an Older Uncle, because you are the beloved Uncle of our Vietnamese family, and you have already met Mother. She still lives in our ancestral village with my paternal grandfather who, like you, is seventy-five years old and in good health, and with her brother, my Younger Uncle, who is a cripple. Mother's burden is heavy and she needs her husband at her side. She wants to know whose body was found.

Allow me to explain that peasant Giới was an ambitious and clever man who flaunted his riches. He did things that were ideologically incorrect. He may have been led astray by feudal consciousness or seduced by capitalist thinking. Before he disappeared, Father worried that peasant Giới's individualism (some called it "selfishness") would spread and sap our socialist morality. But most peasants were just envious of his success. They went hungry while he prospered. Many of them had run away to the South. Father knew, and the Party must have known too, that they took this unpatriotic step because they resented having to surrender their land to the Cooperative. Also, their pay was very low. Father, a hard worker, received as much as those who did hardly any work at all. In the second year of the Cooperative, the rice crop dropped so low that when the fall harvest was brought in and the Cadres took away the quota required by the State, very little rice was left for distribution.

One day, all the peasants were summoned to a meeting where the Party Secretary called on them to fulfill their patriotic duty of meeting the production targets set by the State Plan. "If, instead of complaining, you work harder, the Communist state of abundance will be reached sooner," he said. When some peasants grumbled, he shouted a warning, "The enemies of the Revolution will not be allowed to steer the masses from the righteous path!" He tried to shame us for not trusting the Party, but many peasants understood that there might not be enough rice to feed their families.

Shortly afterwards, the Party recognized the difficulty and allocated some communal land to private plots. All of us hailed the wisdom of the policy, never expecting that inequalities and resentments would follow. The "five-percent gardens" began to thrive even though officially they did not receive any seeds or fertilizer from the State. Father and Mother tended our plot after work, often at night — hoeing, seeding, and pruning by the light of the moon — so well did they know every furrow of our tiny property, so deeply did they care to get the most out of it. Some Party Cadres only bought vegetables grown on such plots because they saw how well tended and healthy the herbs were. They looked askance at the scrawny goods of the Cooperative.

Peasant Giới's garden was "five percent" in name only. It was much bigger than any other garden, spreading across the entire meadow to the stream that was State property. This was because three years earlier several Cadres had come to peasant Giới to buy pork to make *bánh chưng* cakes for the dinner celebrating the Lunar New Year and he did not have enough pork for all of them. They were disappointed and peasant Giới told Cadre Phạm Thanh that if he allowed him a bigger five-percent garden, he could keep more pigs and chickens, and grow sweet potatoes, or pumpkins, or watermelons, or all three, and maybe even breed dogs — to have extra meat for sale for holidays and observances. Cadre Phạm Thanh pretended not to hear a word of what peasant Giới was saying. But some weeks later, when he came to buy pork again, he told peasant Giới that he could wedge his garden into the land of the Cooperative, provided he delivered a certain quota of his produce to the Cooperative at the State price. The rest he could keep and sell privately at his price.

With his five-percent garden becoming bigger, peasant Giới had to hire a labourer. A year later, when his wedge had become bigger still, he had to hire two more. Father seethed about it in silence, but others began to rage loudly that having a private citizen hire labour for pay — exploit other citizens and grow food for profit — flew in the face of our socialist morality. "Is not peasant Giới a capitalist now?" they asked the Cadres and each other. "Is he any different from those enemies of the people in foreign countries who abuse workers and peasants mercilessly?"

In the year that followed — and Father was missing by then — peasant Giới had become rich enough to give free food to the Cadres for State occasions. His neighbours gazed at the comings and goings of his customers and wondered how long the ideological cant would be allowed to continue.

Six weeks ago, peasant Giới vanished, rumoured to have joined the army to atone for his capitalist deviation. His wife was so distraught she went into seclusion, and his labourers admitted to the ideological error of working for hire for a capitalist and fled fearing for their lives. As for the two dozen pigs peasant Giới owned — well, one night they also vanished. Many families were outraged that one man had been allowed to own that many pigs. Peasant Giới's five-percent garden was left untended. Children ran by it shouting "capitalist pig" and threw in coconut shells and other garbage as they would into a dump.

Father wanted to see peasants prosper but I know he would have been mortified to see how rich one greedy man could become. He had lived through the terrible famine of the years under the Japanese yoke and the destitute post-War years. "Socialism will bring a better life," he taught me and I believed him wholeheartedly. "Work hard and study hard," he commanded and I obeyed. That is why I am the best-educated woman of my village and the first woman ever admitted to the Agricultural College. That is why I can write to you on behalf of Mother who, like most women in the country, is illiterate.

She used to be greatly distraught to see the Cooperative produce so little. She saw how, after the spring rains, village women hurried to pick sprouting bamboo shoots, which they boiled for soup with porcupine bones saved after the meat had been eaten. Father knew that peasants grew maize and cassava in fallow ditches to make alcohol, and rice to make vodka for private sale. He watched men sit around the fire late at night drinking and chewing betel to camouflage hunger pains. With a lingering hangover, they staggered to work late, fell asleep in the paddies, and could not make the required points in their brigades. But mostly they could not work well because they were weak from hunger.

In our family, Father was the eldest son, responsible for providing votive meat to offer the gods during the celebration of the anniversaries of his Nguyễn ancestors' deaths. Some families in the village had to observe more than a dozen anniversaries a year and their dogs and cats had all been eaten. Father led these desperate men to hunt monkeys with stones and arrows. Mother helped village women make patties of snails and mice and pretend it was pork. She has told me that in most households women ate only half as much as their men — sometimes less, if they had children to feed. That is why their emaciated newborns often died. That is why she resolved to become a midwife.

It has to be admitted that Father was short-tempered and querulous. Most Nguyễn men in this district are like this. It is their nature. My grandfather was also irascible. Once, the two had a quarrel about the righteousness of the socialist path, and Grandfather chased his son — who defended the Revolution — with a knife, and forbade him to come home for the night. It was four years before we were allowed to visit Grandfather again. But Father was growing angry with the shortages, with the Cadres' speeches about the correct political path and their promises that backwardness would disappear. "When?" he began to ask.

The time came when at the end of a poor harvest damaged by pests, our local People's Committee asked the People's Council to make an urgent request to the regional Party Secretary for a truckload of manioc and potatoes. But the President of the People's Council ruled that, to grant relief, the Party Headquarters had to be satisfied that work discipline was being maintained. He ordered that an inquiry into the management of the Cooperative be held first. Now you know what the word *inquiry* means to a peasant — it means trouble. At the mere mention of it they become terrified of being accused.

A meeting was called, and I — an eager harvest-time helper at the Cooperative — sat on the ground with a hundred others in front of the threshing station. The turmoil was frightful. Agitated men crouched on the grass nervously, shouting bitter words at the Cadres when they arrived. Father jumped up and yelled over the others, "We need food, not inquiries. You talk like Mandarins. That's all done with." I tugged very hard at Father's shirt to make him sit down but he could not stop yelling. "Every lazybones in my brigade is paid as much as I am, yet I do twice as much work as they do. I've worn my hands and knees to the bone. The point system isn't worth one fistful of rice."

The man standing on the right of the President shouted back, "You're exploiting a difficult situation..." but Father was beside himself and would not let him finish. "You're exploiting us! That son-in-law you made the accountant cannot count. He doesn't know how to keep a day workbook. We don't know how to read the numbers. He can cook up any production totals he wants and we wouldn't know the difference. We have no say..."

The President pointed his finger at Father and ordered, "You sit down now!" But others stood up and shook their fists at the Cadres. The President grabbed his army hat and ran. His men followed him. The peasants remained standing, ready to chase after the Cadres.

Father was the one to calm them down. He shouted, "No! No! Stay where you are. The Party will not let us down. No one will be allowed to starve." But the President and his men had already left. They never saw Father stand up for the Revolution.

A week later Father was late for the evening meal. Mother and I waited. We covered his bowl with a grass mat and kept the fire going till darkness came and all the fires in the village had been extinguished. And then it was dawn. Could it be that Father had fallen victim of ambitious men who put their selfishness — their advancement in the ranks — ahead of the good of workers and peasants? Could it be that he had been punished unjustly? Can injustice happen in a socialist society? Please believe me when I say that Father was an exemplary worker and a progressive man. He treated me as if I were a son and allowed me to study at the Agricultural College even though I was a girl. Many villagers called him a fool and Mother argued that I should follow our traditions and be a wife and mother first. She had found me a suitor, but I refused to marry him. She punished my defiance with a harsh beating but kept silent when Father sold six of our chickens to pay for my studies.

I am writing to you because Mother and I need to know whether the body that was found was peasant Giới or someone else. When will we find out? With the American war and class struggle going on, other men have disappeared and their families have not been told. Bad things are hushed up or excused away. It is distressing for the two of us to hear people say, as some do now, that although peasant Giới may have been involved in capitalist exploitation, he did it for the correct reason — to serve the masses. He was friendly and helpful, and when food was scarce, he supplied people (including the Cadres) with vegetables and fresh pork. But Father is remembered as blunt and disrespectful. Last month, when I asked Cadre Trần Lương (not for the first time) when we would find out about Father, all he said was that Father showed rebelliousness that put everyone in danger. I sensed that he would like Father to be forgotten. I venture to ask you: how is it possible that a peasant like Giới, who hoarded food for profit, like any vile landlord of old, can find defenders, while Father — an exemplary citizen and patriot — is dismissed and forgotten? Isn't my family's ideological purity worth more than the greed of a covert capitalist? Isn't the capitalist the real *TRAITOR*? Mother and I are desperate and have nowhere to turn — we two patriotic women who have always been faithful to your teachings and to the Revolution.

Allow me to give you just one example of our ideological uprightness. Whenever I was back in my village on holidays from the Agricultural College, I would walk with Mother past an old grain storeroom where the authorities kept the families of the former landlords under guard. A sad mother often stood at the doorstep holding the hands of her twin daughters, who waved to us. The woman's father was a former landowner and her children were his grandchildren — therefore they were not allowed to go to school. Not once did we wave back to the girls or speak to their mother, knowing that fraternizing with class enemies would show an incorrect attitude. All the adults of that family were soon sent away to be re-educated and learn a proletarian attitude, but the sisters remained and were placed with a peasant family in the village. The adults never returned and the girls were eventually allowed to go to school, but village children often threw chunks of cow dung at them, shouting, "Hey, daughters of exploiters, bow your heads!" Mother and I did not stop them. We believed that having suffered so much under feudalism, the peasants had a right to vent their anger.

I know from your teachings and from remembering the lives of my grandparents that the landowning classes were cruel and corrupt. They got away with every wickedness. My family suffered when the landlord's henchmen caught my maternal Grandfather in the threshing shed. He was hiding some grains scattered on the floor in the folds of his sleeves. He had toiled in the landlord's paddies for forty years and never had enough to eat. They beat him till one of his lungs collapsed. They disliked him because he often pleaded for mercy when peasants were whipped for not being able to repay money they had borrowed from the landlord. He was a hero to the villagers. But to the exploiters and their henchmen he was just another landless hired hand — a water buffalo under yoke. I call him my family's first revolutionary because before he died he told Mother to give birth to three sons. "You teach them to take vengeance on our torturers and their children," he instructed. Mother has given birth to just one child. I am the daughter and the promised three sons all in one. I am the kernel of my family's dream.

Like a dutiful daughter I toiled with my parents in the paddies, washed tubs full of taro roots at the Cooperative every harvest-time, and picked tea leaves in the hills till my fingertips bled. I am lucky to be an only child and to have lived next door to the village teacher whose family had a baby every year. Mother helped the babies into the world and cooked for the family to give the mother time to rest and to suckle the newborn. Father drew water for our family and for the teacher's family, and the teacher repaid my parents' kindness by helping me with homework. I walked with him to school and was not allowed to miss any classes. Other girls often had to stay home and cook for the family whenever there was an illness, or planting, or harvesting. My attendance was perfect and I read aloud better than the boys. Like all Vietnamese patriots, I applaud the Party's bold literacy program that will make our country modern and give us a better life.

I am also proud to tell you that I have fulfilled my patriotic duty of punishing the exploiting classes exactly as was expected of me. When your progressive government brought in the land reform, I was almost twenty — old enough to understand the historical necessity of the Revolution. Just after the Spring Festival of 1954, which was in the Year of the Horse, half a dozen Party Cadres arrived in our district from the Capital to instruct us, correctly, that the enemies of the people had to face the vengeance of the people. Our landlords had their land confiscated, along with their furnishings, family treasures, even bronze incense burners from their Altars for the Ancestors. I yearned to avenge the suffering of my maternal grandfather and helped the others tie the exploiters to a tree. Then we took turns whipping them. The children brought cockroaches, lice, and leeches and plastered the insects onto the exploiters' skins. To cement the end of the old order and hail the new one, Father led other men to the burial ground, where they wrecked the oppressors' ancestral tombs with mallets. For that loyal act he received the Certificate of Support for the Revolution. We are a progressive and patriotic family.

Though illiterate, Mother is a model socialist woman. Last time I went home, she was called to attend the birth of twins in a village on the other side of the river. When we reached the riverbank, we found that the pregnant woman had just arrived in a junk boat. She was lying in it on a bed of leaves, moaning piteously. Her eyes were hollow and her huge belly as sweaty as her head. Her daughter, who was about eight, told us that in the last two days they had eaten only what they could find in the forest they had walked through to reach the shore. She explained that her father had quarrelled with the foreman of his Cooperative, and the foreman had cut off the family's food rations; the father was scared of him and had run away. Mother barely had time to pull out the birthing cloth before two babies gushed forth, the second one dead. She stayed with the mother as she suckled the child, and made her drink some of her baby's urine to restore her energy. She allowed her a short nap then pulled her to her feet and made her pee standing up to let the urine drip down her legs to strengthen her muscles. Mother believes that our peasant customs — which you know well — are the best remedy in labour and delivery.

She is distraught that although everybody knows that Father was taken away, nobody will talk openly about him. People are afraid to know more than what is safe to know, in case they are interrogated by the Cadres. So they snitch on their neighbours and pry into each other's past, looking for hidden vices or violations, thinking that such information will come in handy when they get in trouble and must discredit the accuser to survive.

Have we lost our revolutionary spirit? Should it not be a patriotic duty of every citizen to talk frankly about our socialist development and point out errors that make people suffer? I can tell you a lot more about goings-on in our district, things you may not know about now that you live in the Capital. And I hope you will reward my courage in speaking out against corruption and against those who defy your teachings. Some of them live in this town. The Party Cadres for example. I have watched them come go and few have behaved irreproachably. The five men who now form the Party Cell are no exception.

Cadre Trần Lương — our Senior Cadre — is a single man from the Capital, rumoured to have deserted his army post two months early. But because his Second Uncle is Party Secretary in the Quảng Bình province, no inquiry was held. He says that "women cannot understand political matters" and has dismissed all my inquiries about Father. Last year, when four children drowned in the river, he said their mothers were to blame. He was the only Cadre who did not join the search, saying his duty was to mind the office.

Cadre Phạm Thanh is a father of three boys who likes the benefits of the Revolution. Two summers ago, for the funeral banquet of his father, he roasted a ten-kilogram dog brought in from the Capital. Peasant Giới supplied corn, sweet potatoes, and strawberries, and only the Cadres and their families were invited. Father tried to tell Cadre Phạm Thanh that our custom was to invite the elders from the community, but he would not listen. Some of his relatives have escaped to the South (where they are fraternizing with the Americans) and I know that his mother wants him to go to California. Does this not make him a traitor?

Cadre Cao Trung Hiếu has two sons in the Army and four daughters at home, and he beats all of them but denies doing it. (Other men also beat their women but shouldn't the Cadres be more progressive?) He earns money on the side cutting men's hair during office hours, and has many customers because he tells them lewd stories about his wild nights in Saigon in his younger years.

Cadre Vu Đức Duy comes from a coastal province and was once in the anti-aircraft artillery, where his older brother — a medic — lost his life to an air-to-ground missile. He also knows how to benefit himself and his family. Last spring when his son came to visit, he made him the foreman of a work brigade. Many peasants complained, but Cadre Vu Đức Duy told them that with the production level shamefully low, they would do well to learn from an outsider. The production level is still low and the son is still here.

Cadre Vạn Xuân is a good man, but because he stutters people make fun of him and call him "slow mouth." He is good at printing party slogans and mounting posters on walls. His class background is incorrect, but he has denounced his landowning family in writing and severed all contact with them. He wants to be liked, so he makes promises that he seldom keeps. He told Mother that in a socialist society justice always prevails and that she would find out about Father soon. That was a long time ago.

Are these model revolutionaries more worthy men than Father was? Are they better patriots than my parents, who were born in this district and spent their lives working in their village? Most of these men were brought to our district from other provinces. They have no loyalty to us here. They know that they cannot trust us, or count on us, so they take care of themselves.

Last spring, two old buildings were levelled to make room for a new assembly hall, and all the old bricks and tiles and plumbing pipes from the demolition disappeared by nightfall. Where did they go? Only the Cadres knew the date of the demolition. Soon we learned that they had gone to Cadre Trần Lương, who had just gotten married and wanted to construct a dwelling for himself. He paid for the materials a tenth of what others would have had to pay.

When peasants see Cadres run off with perks and benefits, they become fearful for their own future and scheme to protect themselves. When the four children of former exploiters drowned (or were drowned), some people said it was a just retribution. But Father argued that the children were not responsible for the crimes of their parents and should not have been sacrificed. You would be surprised how many peasants still fear that the cruel past will return, that the children of the former oppressors, if allowed to grow to adulthood, will come back to reclaim their ancestral lands and privileges.

I am telling you all this because in the Party newspaper, *Nhân Dân*, I have read that you like to hear about people doing good deeds. "Every small act of goodwill counts and should be rewarded," you said. Many people receive your Uncle Hồ Badges — like that eighty-four-year-old woman in Hà Nội who had patched up the potholes in the sidewalk with pebbles so that passersby would not trip. She must have been so proud to receive your citation. Dare I believe that my honest account of the wrongdoings in our district also deserves to be rewarded? Was Father put in prison, or was he forced into the army to fight the Americans because he was critical of the Party harvest targets? In our revolutionary times social discipline must be strictly enforced, but should a man who lost his temper once not be allowed a second chance? Especially one who was awarded the Certificate of Support for the Revolution?

You may not realize that people like me, whose class background is correct, have to suffer derision and ostracism when the family is suspected of disloyalty. In my job at the Office of Land Resources, where I am a junior assessor, I report to my Director, who is a card-carrying member of the Communist Party. The day Father went missing, when I came to work late, he yelled at me and called me a lazybones in front of the others. Thereafter, he ignored me and my work. Yesterday, the Field Inspector submitted a report on land erosion in the area west of our town. He called the situation "catastrophic" — the soggy turf caving in and in danger of sweeping away the bridge come the spring rain. I wrote by hand two copies of the report for the Director, because I know that he likes to keep duplicates. Later, through the crack in the door, I saw him tear the copies to shreds. Today he said in front of my coworkers that such rubbish need not be copied and I was stupid not to know it. I felt humiliated.

My coworkers follow the Director's example, as they must. If you made one of your unannounced visits to our office, you would find the five of us working in a very small space beneath a palm-leaf fan. I work alone in one corner, the other four huddle together in the other. They want to distance themselves from the problem of my father. We eat the noon meal around the same floor mat, but after work they do not know me. Mother is also ostracized: the village women talk to her in the market but will not come to visit.

I know I am not stupid. I excelled in all school subjects, and the retired army colonel in charge of the Agricultural College said I was bound for a promising career. Now Father's unexplained absence has put a blemish on my family's reputation. Last month, I applied to be trained as a senior assessor, but Cadre Vu Đức Duy refused outright. "Your family history is 'complicated,'" he said. "Even the job you have is too good for you." I felt so hurt. For Mother's sake and mine, Father's fate needs to be brought to light.

There must be a reckoning. For the good of the Party, people like us must not become disenchanted with the Revolution.

A long time ago you wrote some commands for children Father had me memorize: *Love the country; love fellow country-men. Learn hard; work hard. Maintain solidarity; keep discipline. Stay hygienic. Be modest and courageous.* I have followed these virtues faithfully but often feel lost. In Father's youth there were three milestones in the life of a peasant: when he had saved enough to buy a water buffalo, when he chose a woman to marry, and when he erected his mud and bamboo dwelling. For a woman, marriage was the one all-important landmark. Is it still her only chance? People find it incorrect that I have not married. But after graduating from college I became an outcast. Mother had been right about this — an educated woman cannot be a submissive wife. No man in our district will have me.

I am writing a lot about myself but please do not think that I do it out of immodesty. I know that your family would understand our longing — Mother's and mine. You left Vietnam as a young man of twenty-one, and went across the ocean aboard a foreign ship, and stayed away for thirty years. They must have lost all hope of seeing you again. But one day you returned and they rejoiced. If Father is returned to us, our family's faith in the Revolutionary justice will stay strong, and we will work our bones off for the glory of the Fatherland.

I beg you to listen to my plea. I trust your fair-mindedness and wish you a long and happy life. Long live our glorious Revolution and the cause of Communism. Long live the Communist Party of Vietnam and its Cadres.

Respectfully submitted by
Nguyễn Thị Bùi

Orange County, Canada

259

After the American War in Vietnam ended in 1975, the victorious government in Hanoi took strong measures to unite the North and South of the country. It imposed rigid controls over the lives of all citizens and sent former U.S. collaborators to re-education camps. In 1986, with the country pacified, a program of renewal (đổi mới) eased up on state surveillance and opened Vietnam to foreign investment. Clan and family loyalties, already ravaged by the pernicious War, would soon be tested by the temptations of Western novelties and affluence.

Nguyễn Ngân Hoa knew the story of Second Uncle Lang and the pig by heart and cherished it as her rightful inheritance. When she was growing up, she had heard it in small chunks from Aunt Mai Linh, who had heard it from Third Uncle Dũng, who probably subtracted or tacked on some details to add a bit of glory to the Nguyễn clan lore. When she was an adult, she had it confirmed by one of Second Uncle Lang's wives.

No family member had seen the man since 1963, when he had been carried off by the Communists. Five years later, Second Uncle Lang's convoy had been on a mission in the wilds of the Trường Sơn Mountains. Eighteen teenage recruits, wearing green army hats and rubber sandals made of discarded truck tires, walked down the sludgy trail like goslings following their mother goose. They were carrying ammunition and spare parts for anti-aircraft posts scattered along the Hồ Chí Minh Trail. Camouflaged with leafy twigs, the heavy boxes swayed on ropes tied to bamboo poles stretched between the shoulders of the boy-men. Their commander, a little older and wearing snug army boots that had probably been pulled off an American corpse, walked in the middle of the line. He wanted to have in view all those walking ahead of him, and also be able to cast a backwards glance at those who walked behind him.

Minutes before the noontime rest they came to a downed footbridge — tangled ropes and shards of wood jutting from the foaming waters. Second Uncle Lang started to wade in to cross the river right there, but the commander called out to him, "Hey!

The rapids are too rough here. Walk up that hill and we'll cross the river on the other side of it."

Halfway up the hill the deafening roar of the time-delayed bomb the enemy had laid for them burst the earth into a hail of sod and stones. The blast hurled Second Uncle Lang into the air, where he somersaulted wildly before hitting the ground with the hollow thump of a ripened durian. His helmet and sandals blown away, he rolled over in the dirt several times and came to a stop beside a wild pig — its legs in the air, its hide scorched crisp, its belly smoking. Desperate for cover, he clamped the rigid tail between his knees, pressed his chest to the pig's backbone, and ringed his arms around the warm body, his fingers sinking in the slime oozing from the belly.

In no time and out of nowhere, U.S. sky raiders strafed and swooped at him like wild ducks. He held onto the pig, sank his chin between its ears, and kicked his heels to propel himself down the slope — his army shirt and pants shredding over the protruding rocks and rhizomes. A boulder halted his slide at the bottom. His knuckles and the pig's snout rammed against it hard and his head jerked up on impact. The sky was so lit with orange tracer tongues of artillery fire that Second Uncle Lang could see single needles on the pine tree above him. Then he blacked out.

When he came to, he was lying on a scrap of grass, the pig on his belly, raindrops drizzling down on them. Somewhere far away, birds were chattering, only — he realized soon enough — they were not birds but firefights again. In front of him a decapitated tree slumped over the ridge. Underneath it, coated in ash, lay the shrapnel-riddled body of a medic, his left arm missing. Second Uncle Lang spotted the arm under the tree by the orange band on the sleeve. He slid toward it, relieved to find that he could move, and dragged the arm back to the body so that the medic would be whole for burial.

For hours he lay holding the pig on his chest, inhaling the stench wafting from its guts, praying that the tigers would not find them first. As soon as he heard voices, he cupped his hands and cracked like a gecko — an agreed-upon signal. When the stretcher patrol found him, his chest and face were beneath the pig, and they carried them both straight to the cooking area where Second Uncle Lang's fingers were pried off the mucky hide. Later, lying under a tent in the field infirmary, he heard the soldiers chant *Thịt lợn rán, Thịt lợn rán,* savouring the promise of pork for dinner. For years afterwards, Second Uncle Lang would tell his wives and his children how he collared a wild pig under enemy fire and fed the entire platoon.

He had been an illiterate South Vietnamese fourteen-year-old when Việt Minh scouts rounded him up while he was fishing alone up the river. "Your patriotic duty is to defend your country against imperialists," they thundered, promising food and schooling. He cared nothing about schooling; he had heard his father talking about ill-tempered French teachers in colonial schools banging children's heads against the wall and calling them cretins and a dirty race. But the promise of food was irresistible. For too long he had watched his father chew on a piece of tree bark to kill his hunger pains and his mother get frailer and frailer from living on a single serving of rice per day.

Eleven years later, when discharged in Hanoi, a thousand kilometres north of home, Second Uncle Lang was twenty-five years old, weighed thirty-five kilos, and was blind in one eye. The South was now losing the War to the Communist North. A soldier's widow, nearly a decade older, was assigned by the army to cook for him and nurse him to health. Within weeks he had put on enough weight to perform the patriotic duty expected of soldiers who survived: he married the widow. A son was born and then another. When the wife began to suffer from dizzy spells and cough up blood, she also did what was expected — she found him a second wife and a third, both young, healthy, and happy to have a few grains of rice guaranteed for life on their husband's soldierly pension.

Altogether, four sons and four daughters were born to the three women. After the oldest wife died, and the younger two no longer had to care for her, they began to sell noodle soup from their kitchen, just in the morning, to earn enough for the school fees. The children brought out the steaming bowls and sometimes received crayons or small trinkets from the patrons. Before running off to school, they built towers of the dirty bowls for their mothers to wash.

Second Uncle Lang never entered the kitchen. He spent his time sitting on a plank in front of the family hut with the unruffled demeanour of a blind man. He greeted the patrons — most of them regulars from the neighbourhood — but whenever a stranger came, he would shift the cigarette to the corner of his mouth and ask his name and where he came from. Then he would point to his withered legs and empty eye socket. "I've fought for the Revolution; I've given my wives eight children who'll look after them in their old age; I've done my duty."

If asked more about his army life, Second Uncle Lang would retell the pig story and add that he had a First Class Resistance Medal hanging on the wall. Only when pressed would he admit that he had never stood face to face with an American soldier, often appending some bluster, "If I'd locked arms with the bastard, I would've slaughtered him like a hog." He seldom thought of his relatives in the South — his parents who did not survive the war, or his three brothers and a sister who did. He did not want the authorities to see him — a patriotic veteran — fraternizing with the losers.

Ngân Hoa had never met Second Uncle Lang. But she liked

to think that she understood his frame of mind. She had always lived among losers and knew that they were made of jagged twine. For Ngân Hoa, Second Uncle Lang was a ghost, but a magnetic ghost she wished to meet and bring back to the Nguyễn family fold. She was hoping to hear the pig story one more time — from Second Uncle Lang's own lips — so as to be able to correct him if he went wrong.

[THE PEOPLE OF VIETNAM STRIVE TO REDUCE
POVERTY AND INCREASE PROSPERITY TO BUILD
A HAPPY MODERN LIFE]

Ngân Hoa knew about the American Nguyễn family — her cousins in Orange County — from the letters they used to send to their illiterate mother. She knew they had lived in California for close to three decades, the parents having left Vietnam on a boat in 1976 when they were just teenagers. "They were not married to each other, and she may have been pregnant," Aunt Mai Linh had once told Ngân Hoa in a low voice. "The boy's father — a second cousin on your mother's side — was an aircraft mechanic for the Americans. The girl's father was a militiaman whose job was to turn in Communist sympathizers. After the War, both fathers were officially categorized as "traitors, renegades, and swine." They knew their children would have no future in Communist Vietnam. So they had them smuggled into a craft going overseas — somewhere."

The young couple were not heard from for five years — the letters either not written out of fear of endangering the lives of their parents, or confiscated by the authorities. The family was discussing whether to add them to the roster of dead relatives when a letter arrived bearing stamps with the gaunt face of President Lincoln. In it was a short note saying that they had made their way to America, and all was well. Enclosed was a photograph of three small boys sitting — without their parents — on a plush settee in front of a glossy canvas painted with ocean waves. Aunt Mai Linh sniffed the glue along the rim of the envelope, said it smelled suspect in spite of the fine appearance, and warned, "If you ask me, the CIA told the parents to send this. Forced them to show off their sons. One more dirty American trick to snare the Vietnamese into the foreign hellhole." Then she turned the picture around for all to see. "The climate is hot in California. So why are the boys wearing long pants? And what is this background? Looks like a painting. Aren't there enough real ocean waves in California? Anyone can see it's a set up." The neighbours scattered. They needed time to decide who would report to the District People's Committee that a village widow had received a letter from California. From a son — now a Việt Kiều — an overseas Vietnamese — a traitor and a swine. In case receiving such mail was illegal. In case the CIA had tainted the paper with chemicals to poison the recipient.

Although the three little boys in the picture were adults now, they had never set foot in Vietnam and apparently never wanted to. Over the years, the parents wrote that, while they kept the Altar for the Ancestors in their California living room, and the offering bowl was always filled with almonds and oranges, the sons prayed with them only to keep family harmony. The young men had "careers," "girlfriends," and "credit cards" — Aunt Mai Linh spat out those words like curses when she read the letters to the family. And they lived "on their own" — not with their parents!

Ngân Hoa listened, her chest swelling with compassion for the aging couple — how they must have wailed to see their sons behave like foreigners, how they must have felt abandoned when not even the eldest son chose to live under their roof.

Fourth Uncle Hiên has told Ngân Hoa more than once that his only sister Mai Linh was not their village's wise woman for nothing. Even as a young girl she had an eye for anything that was not correct — like boys ogling girls from the bushes. When she was a teenager, Aunt Mai Linh watched in dismay as Western engineers arrived to work on a highway project nearby, their bodies — so awkwardly bulky next to svelte Vietnamese men — spilling out of their giant vans. The travelling trunks the foreigners unloaded were also huge. They must have been filled with extra money, because the men's wallets already bulged out of their back pants pockets like gourds. But Aunt Mai Linh saw the bulging gourds at the front as more ominous. She watched the lustful eyes of the engineers follow village girls and was not shy to tell their mothers, who were twice her age, to keep their daughters away from the foreign menace.

That her only niece, approaching thirty and still single, worked in Hồ Chí Minh City for a company often visited by Western men, spoke English with them, and accepted gifts from them, caused Aunt Mai Linh great worry. "She fears that one of the foreigners will kidnap you into marriage, and our family will be haunted by the spirits and damned by the villagers. She's taken it upon herself not to allow such sacrilege to happen," Fourth Uncle Hiên warned Ngân Hoa before concluding spitefully, "That's how unmarried women think."

Ngân Hoa knew that a "kidnapping" had taken place some decades earlier right under Aunt Mai Linh's very eyes. A red-haired, blue-eyed, brown-freckled engineer had arrived from France. He was a freak, towering over the local men, the hair that sprouted out of his lower chin cut blunt, which made him look like a goat. But he was a foreigner and an expert in road design and his oddities had to be tolerated. Within weeks he had fallen for a thirty-year-old teacher in Aunt Mai Linh's school. In private, the staff and the students agreed that by marrying him the bride was dishonouring her ancestry and selling herself into prostitution. But she was old, and tall, and her cheeks were bony. The defect did not bode well for the groom. Bony cheeks on a woman were a portent of bad luck and bound to cause the husband early death. "No local man would have married a thirty-year-old ill-omened eyesore like her," Aunt Mai Linh explained, then added, "and now here you are, the same age and unmarried. You were such a pretty and sweet-natured girl. Instead of letting you move to the city, my brother should have married you off in the village when you were very young." Aunt Mai Linh's chin quavered because she remembered all too well her own father's negligence. "For years I was the family's cook and cleaner. Young men were leaving to fight the foreign devils and Father could have found one to quickly marry me before he left for the jungle. But he didn't want me to cook for my husband's family. He wanted me home to cook for him. And then I was twenty-five and it was too late. Do not miss your chance, Ngân Hoa. Life without a husband is just half a life; and without children, you have no right to call yourself a woman."

[LET US DECREASE THE NUMBER OF POOR HOUSEHOLDS, INCREASE THE NUMBER OF RICH HOUSEHOLDS, AND MODERNIZE THE COUNTRY]

The last time Ngân Hoa heard any news about Third Uncle Dũng — from Aunt Mai Linh before she was diagnosed — he was living in a wattle-and-mud dwelling in the central province of Quảng Trị and working as a warder in an institution that was an orphanage, a detention centre, and a reformatory all in one.

Street urchins and delinquents slept in a brick-walled ward, the convicts in the hayloft with a thatched roof but no walls. All the inmates worked together in the fenced rice paddy and in the pigsty tacked to the back wall of the administration wing, growing food to feed themselves and the staff.

Third Uncle Dũng had been a clerk in the town government till 1972, when the province fell to the troops of General Võ Nguyên Giáp. Hours before the final offensive, the Catholic couple he boarded with had packed up and fled, and so had three office coworkers whose brothers fought in the Southern army, as well as the family of a landowner whose daughter Third Uncle Dũng was hoping to marry. But he was too scared to plunge into the unknown with the runaways. "I have no idea where all these people have gone," he told the Communist interrogators as they scrutinized his eyes for signs of guile or potential disloyalty and asked about his family. "My older brother Lang is a patriotic soldier fighting for the cause of Communism in the North," he answered with military resolve in his voice.

He was offered a job that came with enough food stamps to buy 250 grams of meat per month — an unheard-of trophy. Fourth Uncle Hiên later sneered at his younger brother and the "unheard-of-trophy."

"His only political commitment was to nourishment," he said.

The new military commanders told Third Uncle Dũng that the Revolution did not need boys but men. He was to marry at once to get a foothold as a husband and adult male. He agreed. The army arranged a five-minute betrothal rite to an orphaned teenage seamstress of military uniforms who was not sure what clan she came from. An order to leave on a secret mission followed. His pay would be delivered to his wife. When Third Uncle Dũng came home three years later, the neighbours told him that his bride had been with other men. She did not deny it — she said the lonesome recruits in town had pursued her. He dragged her into the yard and beat her with the butt of his rifle to be sure the neighbours heard her screams and knew that he had done what was expected of a cuckolded husband. Then he settled down to a quiet life.

The wattle-and-mud dwelling that he shared with his seamstress wife also housed a dozen dented mannequins — slinky tailor's dummies crowding the space that should have been taken by children. Fourth Uncle Hiên disdained going there but Mai Linh, the only sister, visited once and was irritated by the nakedness around her, and by her brother's sulky wife who did mountains of sewing but no cooking. Her husband cooked. Aunt Mai Linh was so upset by the oddity that she asked the neighbours if they thought her brother had lost his mind. The neighbours said they had suspected all along that instead of sleeping with his wanton wife, the man of the house slept with the mannequins. Otherwise, why would there be no children? When Aunt Mai Linh questioned her brother, he snapped, "Look who is asking," and told her not to visit again.

Upon her return, Aunt Mai Linh raged to her niece about the misery an out-of-clan marriage can bring. When Ngân Hoa replied that she would like to meet Third Uncle Dũng's wife, Aunt Mai Linh shouted, "Never, ever go there. They don't want to see you. Find a Nguyễn husband in the city... never a foreigner." Ngân Hoa set aside her longing, but vowed to herself that one day — even if she had to wait until Aunt Mai Linh was no more — she would find a way to meet her obstinate uncle and his headstrong wife.

[PRESIDENT HỒ CHÍ MINH WILL LIVE
IN OUR HEARTS FOREVER]

Ngân Hoa saw Western men often at the T & B Joint-Stock Sea-food Processing Company, where she was floor manager. The foreigners walked through a narrow tunnel that led from the paved parking lot reserved for cars, past the work floor, and up the stairs to the boss's office. From her elevated observation booth, mounted on a high pedestal tacked to the wall, she sent the suit-and-tie men a welcoming wave, diffident but cheerful enough to make sure they remembered her lofty position as the only woman on the floor also wearing a suit.

The 700 women who worked under her rode bicycles to work. Their parking lot was a field of tumbleweeds behind the refuse bins. All day long they stood encased in blue sterilized body suits — baggy nylon trousers, equally roomy tops elasti-cized at the neck, rubber aprons always splattered with goo, and helmet-like head coverings with Plexiglas visors at the eyes. Ngân Hoa had been one of them for six years. All day long, with hands in plastic gloves and feet in rubber galoshes that came up to their knees, the women set their elbows on the edge of a table-tray filled with the day's quota of prawns. Each pasty prawn had to be peeled and deveined — lift the translucent husk with a blade, jerk it and the membranes off, slit the meaty back two millimetres deep, scrape out the bowel vein, and throw the evis-cerated pod into the straw baskets that sat in front of them. The plastic-covered table-tray ran the entire length of the hall, like a railway track. Fluorescent tubes hissed and flickered above. Giant fans mounted on walls oscillated at regular intervals. But noth-ing could disperse the stench of fish, which had stayed in every pore of Ngân Hoa's skin even after she moved to a lodging with running water where she could shower every day. Even after she had bought her first deodorant. Now, the nauseating odour seeping into the elevated booth permeated her Western ensemble.

But at least working for a fish-processing company meant standing on firm ground. Ngân Hoa's parents had been water rats, their lives boxed on a raft anchored in one of the lagoons of the Mekong River. At sunset, they laid traps to catch soft-shell turtles, mollusks, Mekong giant catfish, frogs, and fresh water snails, and at sunrise delivered their catch to market.

Ngân Hoa's father, the third son in the family and too poor to ask for a wife in the customary manner, had gone to the limestone mountains to abduct a girl. For days he stalked a goat-shepherdess who was often alone in the meadow, and one day, when she was out of sight of her people, carried her off. Instead of taking her to his village, where mountain people were scorned, and where he feared his mother and sister might conspire to send her back, he brought her to the lagoon of the Mekong River. There they scrubbed decks for a year to be able to buy their own raft. There the shepherdess bore him a daughter and a stillborn son without ever making a fuss about birthing. Her mother, who had been locked in the birth-house to deliver her babies alone, as was the mountain custom, had taught her what to do: "When the time comes, stand up, press your palms against your knees, and push until the lump falls into the basket underneath you." So Ngân Hoa fell into a seaweed-lined basket underneath her mother, while at the prow of their raft her father, mighty proud to have chosen such a hardy wife, was boiling down seawater for tea.

Ngân Hoa did not care to dwell on her parents' hardy past; she much preferred dreaming about the shining future Fourth Uncle Hiên said globalization was going to bring. When the American War had ended and the Communist government sent floating schools to the water rats, she was first in line to receive her writing tablet and one stick of chalk. But two years later, when the authorities dragged away the family who owned the adjoining raft, calling them "imperialist spies" and Ngân Hoa's father saw how easily neighbours could denounce neighbours and cause them to lose their livelihood and maybe even their lives, he decided to abandon the raft and take his family to his wife's village. He would show her villagers what good care he had taken of their shepherdess and, instead of farming the sea, farm the land. His brothers, Ngân Hoa's Second Uncle Lang and Third Uncle Dũng, had been lost to the Communist muddle by then.

That left Fourth Uncle Hiên, the youngest of the four brothers. At fifteen, he had run away to seek adventure in Saigon. Two decades later, when he came to the mountains to visit Ngân Hoa's family, he smoked Cuban cigars, wore a Western suit even around the pigpen, and reeked of a mysterious fragrance. *Eau-de-cologne*, he explained, faking a foreign accent, but nobody had any idea what that meant. His face was badly scarred with raw-meat blotches, his left earlobe was missing, and he limped, but overall he carried himself like a Mandarin of old, dismissive of curious stares. He stared Ngân Hoa up and down several times and said to her father, "If you want to be rid of her, I can use her in the city. She'll cook for me."

In the heat of the sixth lunar month and two days after her sixteenth birthday, Ngân Hoa followed Fourth Uncle Hiên to a brick building a hundred times bigger than her parents' hut and bafflingly cool. "Air conditioning," Fourth Uncle Hiên explained. On the third floor, she nearly cried out when she saw a man wearing the same khaki green uniform with brass buttons and a golden tassel on the chest pocket that had been worn by the men who had dragged away her water-rat neighbours. But she kept quiet as Fourth Uncle Hiên had instructed her. Before he said a word, Fourth Uncle Hiên offered the man an American cigarette, waited for him to take a drag, and said, "My niece has

moved here from her village to care for an ailing war veteran."
When the man lowered his eyes, Fourth Uncle Hiên pulled out
from his inside jacket pocket an envelope out of which the tips of
some green bills were showing. The uniformed man grabbed the
envelope as if something stolen from him were being rightfully
returned. Fourth Uncle Hiên kowtowed and left the American
cigarettes on the desk. A month later, Ngân Hoa's temporary
permit to reside in Hồ Chí Minh City was granted.

[THE COUNTRY MUST BE UNITED AND DEMOCRATIC TO MEET THE CHALLENGES OF THE FUTURE]

Fourth Uncle Hiên worked as a sidewalk barber. At sunrise, he
hobbled three blocks from his ground-floor flat at the back of a
bakery to the utility building just past the Reunification Palace.
A bulky satchel hung on his shoulder and under his arm he carried a folded metal bar stool he had hijacked from an American
tavern. Right about the middle of the bullet-riddled wall of the
Palace, next to the waterspout, he stopped and fumbled in his
pants pocket for a nail. With a stone he pounded the nail into
one of the holes to hang on it a mirror that he pulled out from
his satchel. Then he wiggled the stool's legs into the ground till it
stood firm, and opened a tattered snake-leather briefcase, a farewell gift from an American soldier, that held his scissors, combs,
brushes, and razors. Ready for business, he leaned against the
wall and smoked his first cigarette of the day, hoping that the
noodle-soup cart would come by before his first customer did.

When the War was ending in 1975, Fourth Uncle Hiên had
refused to board a U.S. escape helicopter because he'd been told
that in America people who were ugly and lame could not find
work and were left to starve — and his left leg was mangled and
his face badly singed. Two years later, these injuries — scars from

a bomb explosion at the Tân Sơn Nhất airport in Saigon where for years he delivered taped boxes (the content never explained) for the Americans — would save him from being sentenced to a re-education camp. For his hearing, he had hired two boys to carry him to the room in a chair, his maimed leg stretched forward. His crimson-blistered face spoke for itself. The all-powerful tribunal deliberated for less than five minutes before agreeing to let him go. Had they ruled against him, he had saved 400 American dollars, enough to bribe each of the three officials into reversing the verdict.

Now the makeshift barbershop earned him $150 a month and offered a platform to shine as a street philosopher and deal-maker. Aging veterans came daily to recall the War and let their tongues loose at the scoundrels who had allowed the Communists to "liberate the South." With only a patch of grass and no sidewalk along the fence, and with the motorized traffic roaring by, the men felt safe to ridicule in full voice the stupidity and graft of the "Confucian impostors from Hanoi." Fourth Uncle Hiên added his wisdom to theirs: "Stalin and Mao are no ancestors of ours. The global proletarian family is bunk. Money and privilege are what the bastards are after."

One of Fourth Uncle Hiên's frequent customers was a distant relative who had been a brigadier general in the Southern army and later barely survived two years of hunger, hard labour, and Communist indoctrination in a re-education camp. A year after he was released he came running to the barbering wall not to get a haircut but to share momentous news: someone in the bowels of officialdom must have ruled that he had been punished enough for his wartime treachery, because unexpectedly his daughter had received permission to write the university entrance exam. Three months later, when the results were announced, another jolt: the daughter passed. Meanwhile, the eldest son of another customer — Director of the Municipal Housing Authority — who had also taken the exam did not pass. The distressed father swore into the barbering mirror and kicked the wall.

Within minutes, Fourth Uncle Hiên detected the possibility of a lucrative deal. The same week, he brought the two fathers to the wall and reminded them that by custom and common sense an eldest son's right to higher education should trump that of a girl. The former brigadier general surrendered his daughter's university spot to the son of the municipal housing director, who in return cosigned to him a dilapidated dwelling in District One. The swap saved the municipal director from the shame of having his son's failure exposed in the community, and gave the former brigadier general's family a new home. Their previous lodging had been one room in a housing project on the outskirts of the city, with a urine-soaked staircase and outdoor latrine which vegetable vendors emptied for fertilizer at night. Fourth Uncle Hiên — the catalyst for the deal — pocketed a wad of crisp notes from both grateful families.

He was so proud of this deal that he topped it with another — he sent some of his handyman customers to help renovate the dilapidated dwelling. A year later, at the housewarming, Ngân Hoa could not turn her eyes away from the glow of the newly-tiled roof, the shine of the windowpanes, and the peachy hue of the walls. Fourth Uncle Hiên congratulated the smart daughter for honouring the ancient tradition of male prerogative: "You're the family's benefactor and can have your own bedroom now."

The young woman demurred. "They have me engaged to be married and I will not live here much longer."

Undeterred, Fourth Uncle Hiên pushed a bottle of Heineken at his niece — she had never tasted beer before — and said, "You look, Ngân Hoa… You need to learn how one smart move, one clever deal, can make many people happy. That's the American way."

Ngân Hoa also demurred. It had troubled her for some time that her father had cast her off to his youngest brother's care so hastily, so carelessly, even though he knew little about life in the city. Neither the father nor his brother had asked Ngân Hoa if she wanted to move, because, by ancient custom, such weighty decisions had to be made by men. But now Ngân Hoa wondered how much she really owed her parents for her life and her upbringing, and worried what kind of a scheme her bene-factor uncle would dream up for her. He had said many times that since he "rescued" her from the grimy mountain village, he owned her.

[LONG LIVE OUR FATHERLAND AND THE LEADERSHIP OF THE PARTY]

Fourth Uncle Hiên brought Ngân Hoa to the Motorbike Café one day after she had been cooking for him (and washing hair at a salon near his house for pocket money) for two years. He ordered a beer for himself, a lemonade for her, and announced, "Some Westerners want to open a fish processing factory in town. They need 100 women. I've told the man that you like working on your feet with your hands in water."

A Western man arrived, shook hands with Fourth Uncle Hiên, sat down, crossed his legs, and also ordered a beer. The two men began to talk in English. Ngân Hoa kept quiet as instructed and lowered her eyes to the menu. The •DRINKS• side offered the choice of Trung Nguyên coffee on ice, Heineken beer, and berry wine from Phú Quốc Island — potions totally foreign to her. The •FOOD• side was equally incomprehensible — BLT sandwich, Triple Decker, and Grilled Cheese Platter. Ngân Hoa had tried a morsel of cheese once, on the opening day of a supermarket; it smelled like raw chicken giblets and tasted like stale bean curd.

She put down the wacky menu and looked around. The café was lit with strobe lights instead of lanterns, in place of plastic stools had soft-cushioned chairs with solid metal backs, purple cotton tablecloths instead of gaudy oilcloths, and salt and pepper shakers on each table but no toothpick holders. Posters of Vespas, Hondas, and Harley-Davidsons — luxury two-wheelers she had sometimes seen in the streets — adorned the walls. A glass balustrade behind the bar was lined up with fancy bottles bearing labels in foreign tongues. "So this is what a Western bar looks like," she thought. A couple of fat Western men sprawled in their chairs, their knees open wide, their legs stretched out like logs, their T-shirts hanging out. They clinked their glasses and said "Cheers" — the first English word Ngân Hoa would master — and talked in low voices. By contrast, the local men, twig-thin and prim, kept their knees together under the table but talked in loud voices and gesticulated wildly.

Ngân Hoa did not care to dwell on these differences. She was more interested in the exchange of the two men at her table. They were discussing her future and she could not understand a word. But she hoped that Fourth Uncle Hiên was about to open the door of her cage. Working in a fish-processing plant would mean travelling daily beyond his drab quarters behind the bakery and the dim alley that for two years had been the limit of her world here. She would have to cook Fourth Uncle Hiên's dinner after work but she would be earning her own money and, although he would demand that she hand it over to him, she would find a way to keep some for herself. With a steady job, she would get a permanent resident permit. She sat primly, noiselessly, hands in her lap, so that when the Western man finally looked at her he would see what a sensible eighteen-year-old she was.

Years later, after the Motorbike Café had doubled in size and Ngân Hoa had become Westernized enough to go there alone, she would still not sit at any of the front tables that spilled out onto the sidewalk, because she feared that men — Vietnamese or Western — would take her for a slut. She sat at the very back, where she could see through the glass wall to the garage, which was always full of "motorists." They spent hours fixing their mopeds, motorcycles, and scooters, retrofitting the engines, punching the tires, fingering spark plugs and valves, and buying and selling spare parts. School-aged "helpers" from the neighbourhood, boys who did not own a pair of sandals, hung around all day in their rubber-tire flip-flops admiring the steely mules, hoping to be allowed to mount one for a moment if they promised to run an errand for the owner. When a Frenchman showed up atop a stylish Mobylette, the crowd closed in and their mouths fell open. Ngân Hoa was open-mouthed at all of it — the street, the shop, the café — the whole lavish glitter of Western goods and the people who had the money to buy them.

She was twenty-four when she became manager and celebrated the promotion at the Motorbike Café alone. To signal her entry into a new life, she asked for a grilled cheese sandwich but stopped short of ordering a beer. Three months later, an accident at work gave her a new reason to celebrate. Several peasant girls had been hired to work at the prawn table and one of them promptly cut herself badly with a peeling blade. Ngân Hoa was told to take the girl home — which was a rented room shared with another girl from the same village. She stayed with the two overnight — the roommate delivering an explanation of her absence to Fourth Uncle Hiên. She stayed the second night, and several more, then wrote to her parents, care of the village teacher who would read them the letter, that as manager she was expected to live with the women from work. After eight years, Fourth Uncle Hiên may have grown tired of her, because when she went to collect her things, all he demanded was a pledge that she would always live with other women — only a whore would live alone. She promised to visit every Sunday to cook his dinner.

A year later, with several months of English classes behind her, she could order a mug of draft with ease and chant along with Madonna — the sexy words blaring from the Motorbike Cafe's speakers — practising her pronunciation and learning more rules of life in the West.

She noticed that Western men drank green liqueur in the same tiny sips that her kin in the village drank green tea, but the village men would never hold the door open for a woman. Ngân Hoa loved to have a door held open for her even though she was uneasy about having a man walk behind her. She believed they were ogling her buttocks. She had been staring at men's buttocks all her life — that's where one's eyes went. A woman who walked ahead of a man was a cut above a woman who walked behind him. She was a woman hungry for a good life, not inclined to allow a man to obstruct her view of the horizon, bold enough to tread her own path.

Over time, Ngân Hoa became as devoted to the Motorbike Café as her parents were to their village. Every time she returned from visiting them, she would go there promptly to bridge the chasm between her two worlds. In the village world, she sat at the edge of the lotus pond wearing a hemp vest and watching her mother — meek, wrinkled, and spent — stoop over the fire to roast a sweet potato for her. She listened to the croaking of frogs and the whirring of cicadas and knew they were speaking her language. She raked her fingers through the vines of brilliant morning glory that crept among the moss-covered rocks. The terraced rice paddies zigzagging the mountains in the distance wore the gold of the sun.

Three days later she would be staring at the landslide of pedicabs rolling by the jam-packed Trần Hưng Đạo Street. She saw a Western man sitting at a table wearing a yellow T-shirt with an imprint: "Want a roll in the hay? Just ask." The question baffled Ngân Hoa. At another table, local travel agents sported well-pressed suits and shirts unbuttoned at the neck to show that even on a hot day they wore undershirts — a status symbol recently arrived from America. They crossed their legs at the knee to let one leg hang out and show off their polished leather loafers. "Their fathers still walk barefoot," Ngân Hoa thought. She had kowtowed to her own father only a few days earlier, and had looked down with faint disgust at his bare feet — grubby and misshapen from paddy slop.

It was blissful to be back in the city, to be back not in Fourth Uncle Hiên's crummy quarters and the twitter of his messy caged birds. To be sitting in the Motorbike Café where she could stare at everybody — including men — without censure. To be wearing cotton running shoes, blue jeans that tapered smartly on her narrow hips, and a plain blue T-shirt stretched tight over her flat chest. Not to be wearing the prescribed woman's look of resignation.

[WARM WELCOME TO THE REPRESENTATIVES
ARRIVING FOR THE SUMMIT OF THE
NATIONAL FATHERFRONT]

Ngân Hoa learned about the Inuit living in northern Canada from a TV program she watched in Fourth Uncle Hiên's house the day his colour TV was delivered. She was not living with him by then but was dutifully present for the grand occasion and sat with him on a settee upholstered with goat hair while a dozen neighbourhood women stood in a half circle behind them, grateful to have been invited and breathless with awe. The youngsters on the screen looked like the children on her street — their dark-skinned faces pudgy, their glassy eyes char-coal-black. But they wore colourful parkas trimmed with animal pelts and their winter wear made them look bulky, three times the girth of the children on her street. Ngân Hoa sat mesmer-ized by the fur-rimmed hoods and by the children's cheeks dusted with white speckles — snowflakes? They must have been cold. But how cold was the cold of snow? And how would snowflakes feel to the touch? Like lumps of salt? Would they melt like a gob of whale fat on a grill?

The television announcer said the Inuit were fishermen who lived on salmon and the flesh of whales, and that they trapped four-legged animals. During the warmer months of the summer, women gathered mushrooms and berries. Ah, just like in Viet-nam. And they also believed in the power of shamans to exorcise evil spirits, calm down warring tribes, and put people in touch with their mythological gods. So how were the Inuits Western? They had to keep their hands warm inside mitts, so they probably did not shake hands all the time like other Westerners. Shak-ing hands was very much on Ngân Hoa's mind because it was a Western custom she had found difficult to get used to. After half a dozen years of shaking hands with foreigners at work, she still thought it brash to touch the skin of a total stranger right at the introduction. And how uncivilized to withhold the kow-tow of high esteem. Maybe the Inuit were a lot like her Nguyễn kin. Maybe just the cold was different?

For the first time in her life Ngân Hoa mused about going to the West — perhaps to visit her cousins in Orange County? Perhaps the old people might not be the "reactionaries" Vietnam-ese newspapers claimed most Việt Kiều in America were; they might welcome a visitor from their home country. But then their American sons might refuse to shake hands with an intruder from Communist Vietnam. And what would she tell her relatives overseas? That their family in Vietnam was in disarray — four Nguyễn brothers scattered across the length of the country? A sister never married and dead set against foreigners? It would probably be easier to visit the Inuit in Canada.

She pondered the obstacles to venturing beyond the borders of Vietnam. She had no money saved, knew nothing about passports and visas, and was loath to abandon her job. She could do what many women her age had done — travel with a Western man, first to Bangkok which was not too far away, and then to Europe or to America. But what if the man turned nasty? Government newspapers had carried woeful stories of Vietnamese girls lured by the promise of luxuries and freedom but later abandoned by heartless benefactors who tired of them. Some had to turn to prostitution to save up for a ticket home, only to find that their families did not want them back. Nor could Việt Kiều be trusted. Just recently, the police had closed a brothel in town owned by the returning boat people. Was it more scary to leave, or to stay and still be owned by Fourth Uncle Hiên, still report to him how much money she made and how she spent it, still run to cook for him every Sunday, which was his housekeeper's day off but not hers?

[WE HAVE TO OBEY DECREES OF THE CITY'S PEOPLE'S COMMITTEE TO MAINTAIN PUBLIC SECURITY]

One scorching Sunday, on his third bottle of beer, Fourth Uncle Hiên sat waiting to be served the hot pot Ngân Hoa had prepared for him with fresh prawns she had brought from work. "You know," he began dreamily, "all through the War, my sister cooked prawns for American servicemen in their nightclubs. Here in Saigon, right in the middle of District One. Every second day, a couple of glum GIs, armed to the teeth, drove her in a jeep to the market in Chợ Lớn where she shopped for fresh seafood. But did they take any pleasure in her cooking? Naaah. I saw them gulp down her sea bass with lemon grass like it was hamburger; they put ketchup on it. The same with *tôm xào gừng* — prawns stir-fried with honey and ginger and I forget what else. In Father's house, they were a delicacy we could only afford once a year, for the Tết family dinner. Any local man would have laid down his life for a taste of the sauce alone. The Americans ordered it every day but chewed it sloppily, obliviously, their eyes always on a woman they wanted to take upstairs to a private room. Horny snakes. There wasn't a nighttime eatery in town that didn't double as a brothel."

"Aunt Mai Linh is a clever woman. She can put her foot down very well if she wants to. Why didn't she get a better job?"

"Ah, exactly what I've been wondering. People said it was because she had been a 'market mouth.' You know who they were? Undercover agents, women who shopped a lot in order to pass intelligence about what the Americans were up to. They'd fold a secret message inside a bill and pass it to the stall owner, who'd pass it on to his contact, the seafood supplier from another province — often stuffing the paper in the mouth of a fish — who would in turn take it to his liaison with the Việt Minh command. We had thousands of such barefoot couriers in the South. She was clever all right. She never told us the truth. She's not well, you know."

Ngân Hoa rested her chopsticks. Aunt Mai Linh a "market mouth"? Was she really that clever, that cunning? She imagined her aunt standing in front of a stall sticking a paper ball in the mouth of a fish, risking her life for her country. As heroic a soldier with the fish as Second Uncle Lang was with the pig. Equally worthy of recognition — yet she had no medal. "How is she not well now?" she asked, but Fourth Uncle Hiên was too full of beer to explain.

"To survive the War, you had to work both sides," was all he mumbled.

It was after this unfinished conversation that Ngân Hoa decided to write a letter to Second Uncle Lang, who was still living with his two wives in the North. She offered her reverent greetings first, then inquired about his health, told him about her job at the T & B Joint-Stock Seafood Processing Company, and asked about his wartime deeds. She closed with the hope that, it being more than two decades after the end of the War, the family rift could be healed, and he — as eldest son — might consider taking the first step. The reply came a month later from the Second Wife, who described the carnage of the Hồ Chí Minh trail, the heroism with the pig, and the well-deserved medal on the wall. She concluded with these words:

> Your Second Uncle Lang wishes to be left in peace, as his
> health, resulting from his wartime patriotism, is fragile,
> and his commitment to the Revolution unshaken. His three
> younger brothers and one sister live in a different world.
> As for his duties as the eldest living son, you can tell the others
> that he observes the Anniversaries for the Ancestors every
> year without fail. He has fathered four sons who will continue
> the Nguyễn lineage. We are a virtuous socialist family.

When Aunt Mai Linh read what the Second Wife had written, she pointed out brusquely that the pig story could easily be bogus and the medal a sham. She could not reconcile her brother's alleged heroism with the memory of the skinny, sickly, and needy boy favoured by his mother. And working in the bars of Saigon had made her cynical about soldierly bravado. "Every GI had his own shady tale. Some of them told me they had seen Việt Minh fighters strip uniforms from the bodies of their comrades to pocket leftover food, cigarettes — and medals. Because with a medal they could get bigger food rations or a promotion."

Ngân Hoa did not know what to believe. She flinched at the thought of her senior uncle snatching a medal from a dead comrade. She would have wanted him to salvage a thousand pigs and bring home a dozen medals. Was Aunt Mai Linh bitter or just blunt? Why would she not show reverence for her eldest brother? They all lived under one government now. Would the family loyalty ever prevail over the wartime bruises that were refusing to heal?

[WARM WELCOME TO THE DELEGATES TO THE SUMMIT OF VIETNAMESE TRADE UNIONS]

The first time Ngân Hoa saw a girl driving a motorized vehicle was two days after arriving in Hồ Chí Minh City, which was, Fourth Uncle Hiên said, the new name of Saigon. He had taken her with him to District One, where he bought some tickets for a new state lottery. They were waiting to cross the street at the Clock Tower of the Bến Thành Market when a crimson motorbike parked in front of them. The driver, not much older than Ngân Hoa, wore a dainty crocheted tank top and a tight leather skirt hiked up over her thighs and stretched taut to allow her feet to reach the pedals. Her black hair had light streaks on top of her head. The ends of the hair hanging loose down her breast were also blonde and curled up. The girl was completely different from any girl Ngân Hoa had ever seen, more beautiful than any of the glossy silk-draped dolls on display in tourist shops, which were in turn a million times more beautiful than the seaweed dolls Ngân Hoa had grown up with.

She stared at the woman, even though it was bad manners, and also at the passenger behind her who had his hands on her waist. A man! Ngân Hoa's heart skipped two beats. A woman was driving a man? He hopped onto the pavement like a rabbit and cupped his palm around the elbow of his lovely pilot, who disembarked on her spiky heels as graceful as a crane.

A few months later, Fourth Uncle Hiên took Ngân Hoa to renew her temporary residence permit. They were walking on Đồng Khởi Street, which in colonial times had been known as Rue Catinat and had never lost its French ambiance. At an open-air bar a Western woman sat on a tall stool, humming a melody and crossing and uncrossing her legs, swinging them to the tune of piped music. She wore a pair of open-toed sandals. Her toenails were painted red. Ngân Hoa stared at the crimson lacquer. She was not sure if coloured toenails would attract or repel bad spirits, but she was vaguely afraid for the woman. Fourth Uncle Hiên had told her that at the beginning of the Communist rule in the South barmaids with painted nails had had them torn out. If a Vietnamese girl had painted her toenails red, or any colour, and sat at a bar flashing her legs at the passersby, she would have been taken for a slut and carted to jail. But this woman was Western. She was exempt from censure. Ngân Hoa glanced at her own toenails. They were straw-yellow, rimmed with dirt, the edges chipped. She felt ashamed of them, and strangely drawn to the crimson flecks swinging from the bar stool, and to their Western owner so blissfully oblivious to onlookers around her.

[VIETNAM'S FUTURE IS WITH PEACE-LOVING PEOPLE EVERYWHERE]

Three years after his niece came to live with him in Hồ Chí Minh City, Fourth Uncle Hiên had to spend a week in the hospital to relieve some ongoing problems resulting from his wartime injuries. Ngân Hoa seized the short time of self-rule to take herself to a movie in the newly opened entertainment complex in her neighbourhood. In the washroom, she saw a Vietnamese girl hang the gold chain of her pearl-studded purse around her neck and hitch her emerald-green skirt high up. As she bent down to smooth out her lacy slip, her breasts spilled out of a matching camisole. Ngân Hoa followed the woman to the lobby and watched her slide her hand deep into the arm of a Western man. He pulled out a shiny red packet of cigarettes and she dipped her red fingernails into it and slipped the cigarette between her red lips. He flicked the lighter, and she leaned in close and curled her little finger around his thumb. A faint cloud of smoke enveloped her face as the man's arm reached out to loop her shoulder. By then, Ngân Hoa's armpits had gone itchy. Her father would have had her beheaded for smoking. No proper Vietnamese girl would disgrace herself with such vulgarity because no Vietnamese man would take for a wife a woman who smoked. Yet here was a Vietnamese woman, her age, smoking in public with impunity. She must have been debauched by her Western companion. Feeling tethered to the old but magnetized by the new, Ngân Hoa was baffled by the Westerners apparently not shackled by any rules, not aware of their coarse manner... so provocative... so crude... Did Aunt Mai Linh have a point about these lustful foreigners? Yet they were so disarming in their "freedom."

[WE STRUGGLE TO PROMOTE DEMOCRACY TO MAKE THIS DISTRICT MODERN AND MORE BEAUTIFUL]

In Ngân Hoa's dreams, Interstate 405 was a road to heaven — brand new, silver-grey, and without any Vietnamese potholes. There wasn't a ripple to its sheen. It meandered through Orange County in sunshine and in moonlight all the way to the horizon, and there was only one car on it — Ngân Hoa's very own silver Buick. In the morning, watching from her elevated booth the blue mummies rip the prawns with their blades, she would imagine green road signs with mileage to San Diego or to other towns with quaint Spanish names posted all the way down the work table, the big arrows pointing to the far end of it, which was the border of Mexico. Sometimes, she would grip the edge of her countertop as if it were a steering wheel — she had never sat behind the wheel of a car in her life — press the imaginary gas pedal, round the corner, slow down to figure out what YIELD might mean, and speed up again — the seascape flying by.

In her shared room she watched American sitcoms on her black-and-white TV (a twenty-fifth birthday gift from Fourth Uncle Hiên — "To help you learn English"). When her head began to spin from the chatter and she could not keep up with the American vernacular she wanted to master, and when none of the hairdos on the screen looked suitable, she would let her mind drift away and see herself gliding through San Bernardino County, which must be somewhere near Interstate 405, and watch the sun come up over the Santa Ana Mountains, which were somewhere there too. She drove her silver Buick right over the sand of Huntington Beach and into the water, scattering surfers in all directions, as reckless American teenagers did in the movies. She turned onto Interstate 5 and cruised by a giant mall where shoppers were coming out of Walmart loaded with packages. Faces that looked familiar were among them, and she wondered again if these men were still Vietnamese or already American — polite but distant and not living with their parents or their uncles. Would one of them take her to see *Forrest Gump* again, that funny movie about a cripple who let his leg braces drop away so he could run to where he wanted to be? She admired him but it puzzled her to see him protest against the War in Vietnam. How could American citizens be disloyal to their government and behave badly in the streets? Why would they risk losing their jobs and ruining their careers that way? Where were their parents to discipline them with a whip? In the evening, after work, she stretched out on her sleeping mat with her eyes closed and drove her Buick through the maze of American highways.

[WE HAVE TO TRY AND FOLLOW DECREES
OF THE PEOPLE'S COMMITTEE TO MAINTAIN
TRAFFIC SECURITY]

Aunt Mai Linh pressed her spine into her straw pillow in the twelve-bed ward of the Grall Hospital, a high-ceilinged and ornate facility French colonizers had constructed for themselves in Saigon a century earlier. Two nights before, the ward oncologist had promised to send a gofer to find some sleeping pills for her after hospital hours. When during his rounds today he passed by her with no more than a downward wave of the hand, she knew that he had not found any. The hospital had some awe-inspiring medical hardware, but it had not yet caught up with globalization. The floor tiles were not spick-and-span, the walls needed a fresh coat of green paint and the corridors stronger light bulbs. Antibiotics were in short supply and some of the equipment wore "out of order" tags. Worse, there were no painkillers or sleeping pills on demand. Russian or Polish analgesics could be had now and then, but for a price.

Ngân Hoa flew straight into Aunt Mai Linh's arms and quickly buried her closed fist in the blanket. Under its cover she opened up her fingers and let some rolled-up bills — two-weeks salary — fall out. Then she pulled out the hand and gave Aunt Mai Linh a hug with both arms. "Go to battle with them, buy your pills," she said.

"You're a dutiful child. The doctor should be coming… I cannot fall asleep with the women around me moaning and crying. Some of them walk the floor all night and call out to their ancestors to be ready to receive them. Every two hours the night nurse makes her token rounds, but few of us dare speak to her. If she helps us, she will want to be paid."

"Now she can be. Tell her… whatever you want."

"You had to borrow the money from your Fourth Uncle?"

"No, most of it is mine and the rest I borrowed from my mummies at work."

"They hardly earn anything."

"They earn enough, better than they used to. And they know I'll pay them back… they trust me," Ngân Hoa said, proud that she was making enough money to help a family elder no other family member could or would. "If you need more, send the same cleaner to tell me. I gave her a tip."

"You're a good woman. You would have made a good mother," Aunt Mai Linh said tearfully. "You know, my grandmother, just before she died, told me that all people on earth, women too, have their very own star in the sky shining just for them. When a person's last breath dies down, the star's last beam of light is also extinguished. But before it dies, the star drags its tail across the sky, signalling that it's about to fade away and calling on the other stars to give birth to a new one. So very soon there'll be a fresh and shiny star in the sky for me. When you're troubled, look for it."

Eyes stinging, Ngân Hoa ran out of the ward, down the murky hospital passageway, across the lawn, and onto the city bus that had just arrived. It was a long haul from District One to her Joint-Stock Company and she could not be late. She tucked herself into the corner seat at the very back and prayed… prayed not only for Aunt Mai Linh but for better times to come to all of

Asia. "Let my small and backward country — my Fatherland — that has driven off the Chinese, the Mongols, the French, and the Americans, defeat poverty. Let us all have a richer future." The bus sputtered down the road under the red banners with Government slogans floating overhead — *decrease the number of poor households... struggle for democracy... build a better life.* A better life. Ngân Hoa could almost see it. Sleeping pills on demand. Italian ice cream, lipsticks that did not melt in the heat, and loads of French perfumes. More women would become managers, and she would be able to leave her two mummies and find an equal for a roommate. With her she would shop for sexy lingerie. The good life of globalization would free her from having to obey Fourth Uncle Hiên just because he was her kin and her elder. It would give her courage to say "No" to any man, without fear of shame or punishment.

[THE WHOLE COUNTRY CELEBRATES THE GLORIOUS ANNIVERSARY OF THE LIBERATION OF HANOI FROM COLONIAL OPPRESSION]

"Here is something for you," said Fourth Uncle Hiên, as he pulled a large cream-coloured envelope with a bevelled edge out of the pocket of his shirt. Ngân Hoa's name was written on it in ornamental handwriting. "A house that rents out for $3000 a month."

It was Sunday, the day when his duty-tethered niece, just turned thirty-two, came to prepare and serve him dinner, wash the dishes, and often also scour the bottom tray of his bird cage. She thus continued to repay her lifetime debt to the family elder who sixteen years earlier had rescued her from the mucky coop that was her mountain village.

Ngân Hoa pretended to be unmoved by the hugeness of the sum or the shine of the envelope. Fourth Uncle Hiên tipped his chin and cast his eyebrows skyward — his command that she open it. Inside was an invitation with a dreamy landscape embossed on the front page, the crest of the hills traced with a golden thread. Ngân Hoa turned it up and down, smelled its candied scent, read it, and said, "This Mr. Jackson must be living in a golden castle. Who is he?"

Fourth Uncle Hiên filled up his chest with air. "A very important director for an international program. He's recruiting English-speaking people to help with a survey of endangered fish stocks in the lakes and rivers of Vietnam. He invites you to a reception at his home, and look at the street address. It took more than one magic trick to obtain this favour for you." Ngân Hoa did not recognize the street name but Fourth Uncle Hiên . helped. "It's a gated compound on the outskirts of the city. Gated means that a soldier, acting as a security guard, will stop you at the gate and ask for an ID. He decides who can come in — only moneyed people can. But once you're inside, you're somebody. Instantly!"

Ngân Hoa couldn't begin to imagine becoming somebody instantly, but Uncle Hiên was sitting there, his shoulders pulled back and his chest puffed up, waiting for her acknowledgement of his effort to pave her way to rich foreigners. "I thank you for being the only uncle who cares about me," she said, knowing that this was what he would like to hear.

He blinked. "I've hired a woman to make you a grand looking *áo dài*. Right away you need to slap some whitening creams on your face to lighten up your skin. You won't get far looking like a peasant woman scorched to a crisp in the paddies."

The night before the event, showing off her new áo dài, Ngân Hoa was miffed when Fourth Uncle Hiên, instead of complimenting her, rattled on about the gated housing site, which apparently had once been a swamp encircling a fishing village.

"When the government told the peasants it was taking over the land and they had to move, the peasants set to digging up the bones of their ancestors from the village graveyard. They carried the bones with them to rebury close to where they were to be resettled. But many bones were left behind in the village graveyard, remains of those whose kin died in the War or fled to America and thus left the tombs unattended. So now the Westerners live on top of the bones and will be tormented by the wrathful spirits and never know where their suffering comes from." Fourth Uncle Hiên groaned with relish at the prospect.

Ngân Hoa momentarily wondered why he was sending her to a place filled with wrathful spirits, and how he could so carelessly put her in the hands of rich foreigners.

[REVOLUTION, REVOLUTION, AND ONCE AGAIN REVOLUTION]

The entrance to the $3000-a-month house led through a glass-panelled arcade furbished with giant vases of pink azaleas. The British wife of the American host greeted her guests with a faint, "Good evening," and an equally faint handshake of her right hand, followed by a very proper, "I'm very pleased to see you." Her smile was bleak, her body rigid. Her head did not move as Ngân Hoa made a deep bow. With her left hand she steered her young guest into the living room and the merry chaos of the guests — all strangers. Ngân Hoa took half a dozen steps forward and found herself facing two Western men holding beer mugs. They extended their right hands, which she shook as she told them her name, pronouncing it very clearly, but over the clamour of the room she did not hear theirs. One of the men fixed his eyes on the neckline of her áo dài, then slid them down her body all the way to her high-heeled sandals. She cast her eyes down — her toenails were their natural straw-yellow but cut short and clean. Where else should she direct her eyes? Westerners thought it impolite to keep them on the floor. She braided her fingers, noticing how colourless her fingernails were.

One of the men spoke so loudly that he startled her into looking into his eyes. "We're with an NGO. Environmental issues and stuff... and you?"

Her head scrambled for the *engeeo* and *stuff* but drew a blank. "I work with fish... Not cut fish... executive..."

The second man said, "Very interesting. That's what this survey is about. It needs people who know fish." Ngân Hoa let out her breath.

The hostess was approaching them with two more men in tow, saying in a loud voice, "Aha, she'll tell us... Do you still have buffalo fights in this day and age?" Ngân Hoa had never seen a buffalo fight in her life and had to scramble for the necessary words.

"Since long time ago," she said. "They're name *chọi trâu* — very big, very strong. Old people like. They like very much, wait to clap hands. Before fight... many time before fight... family take care of chọi trâu, give a lot food, make strong. Four families, four chọi trâu. The fight is strong. People shout. The family of winner is great respect."

"But how do you get them to attack each other? Is it like the *corrida* in Spain?"

Ngân Hoa was lost. She caught the word *Spain* but where was that country? And what was *corrida*? Her mind had gone empty. The hostess waited for a moment, then asked another question: "Are the animals actually killed in the fight?"

Ngân Hoa's words flew out in an instant, as if wanting to make up for her ignorance of Spain. "No, never! They killed after fight. The meat for every people. All village — old people, children, eat, to make... strong... strong like chọi trâu. In our culture... make drums from skin..." She had no idea how such details had come to her.

"You mean you make drums from the hide," the hostess corrected somewhat haughtily. "That's what animal skin is called in English. You might want to remember that." Ngân Hoa moved her head up and down twice but forgot to say thank you, because she felt scratching at her toes and heard the hostess laugh. "That's our little bull fighter! Stop it, Tinker!" Ngân Hoa moved her eyes down and saw a small Pekinese dog with long feline whiskers and a palm-leaf tail sprawled on the carpet and baring its teeth at her toes. She had heard of Chinese emperors playing with small dogs indoors, but nobody she knew in town or in her village would let one into the house. But this dog had a name, which meant it was what Westerners called a *pet*. Its owner, or the owner's servant, probably fed it food some villagers would be grateful for, and bathed it to keep it flea-free. This little bull fighter would not be eaten — no matter how much muscle and fat it grew.

The hostess bent down, scooped up Tinker in her arms like a baby, tucked its tail into the hollow of her arm, and walked away. The two engeeos had wandered off, so Ngân Hoa had a moment to gather her strength and tally her exploits: she had shaken hands well and smiled as was expected of her; she had made herself understood in English and answered the questions about buffalo fights. But her nerves were frayed and her throat clenched. A Vietnamese server walked by with a tray of thin-stemmed glasses filled with froth the colour of overripe mangoes. She reached for one without asking what was in it and heard the guests standing behind her toast each other: "Cheers."

A male voice asked from the right, "Are you enjoying yourself?" She did not understand the question. What did he mean by *enjoy*? She had not come to this elegant house to enjoy herself but to pay respect to the host and hostess. "Are you having fun?"

She did not understand that question either but shook her head No, because it was safer than saying Yes to the unknown. "Not know... many people, English not very good... nice house... beautiful, but try very hard... nice to people..." She was running out of English words and had to stop to take a breath, but the man had already moved on. Her head was about to fall off from all the polite nodding but her spine was still firm.

She fumbled with her glass, too nervous to taste the drink. Strangers swarmed around her saying incomprehensible things. Through an open wall to her left she saw a white-aproned Vietnamese maid carrying a tower of dirty dishes in her arms. Ngân Hoa walked toward the kitchen, entered, and found herself in a room bigger than the one-room lodging she still shared with her two mummies from work. A white porcelain sink, with two washbasins side by side, sparkled in the sunshine that poured through the windows. On a ridge dividing the two basins was a shower-type spout mounted on a pivot. The Vietnamese maid moved the spout from side to side rinsing plates, her face shrouded in the steam rising over the left basin. So the Westerners had hot water in the kitchen. Amazing! And a movable spout. Another example of those American conveniences Fourth Uncle Hiên had raved about when he bought his first electric razor.

Ngân Hoa still did not know what to do with the tall drink and walked over to the Vietnamese maid, who pursed her lips and said, "There's vodka in it, you know. Vodka is like rice wine but much stronger — made from potatoes." Ngân Hoa leaned against the sink. It was blissful to hear her native language again. Every word stood for something real and could be understood without effort. She stared at the pile of dishes soaking in the soapy scum till the maid pushed her aside. "This is my work station. You better go back to them — where you belong." Ngân Hoa looked over the maid's shoulder into the depths of the porcelain hollow, raised the tall glass, and saluted the sink. "Cheers." Then she drank the mango liquid in one unbroken gulp, stuck the glass in the hand of the maid, and walked back to the room full of foreigners.

[VIETNAMESE TRADE UNIONS HAVE BEEN CREATIVE IN PROMOTING THE RIGHTS AND LEGAL BENEFITS OF EMPLOYEES AND SUSTAINABLE DEVELOPMENT OF THE WHOLE COUNTRY]

Ngân Hoa had just returned home from work when a teenager arrived with a message that she must go to Fourth Uncle Hiên's house at once. She wove her way on foot through the rush-hour traffic, motorbike pedals grazing her ankles, and was surprised to see him at the gate. She had assumed he was ill. He motioned her in and did not bother to fasten the latch. Inside, the scent of almond buns from the bakery next door perfumed the air, and Fourth Uncle Hiên's pets — half a dozen tiny red birds with black bellies — twittered in the wooden cage shaped like a temple.

Fourth Uncle Hiên's servant, a pan-washer from the bakery — her hair very grey and her hands very wrinkled, poured the tea and vanished behind the latticed screen. Ngân Hoa waited for Fourth Uncle Hiên to pick up his teacup first, so that she could pick up hers. But although he could see she was out of breath and must have known that she was dying of thirst, he ignored the tea and said, "The urgent matter concerns a chance to set myself up as a go-between in a deal that would benefit our family. Not including my brothers in the North, you understand. Those traitors have made their deals with the Commies and can cover their own asses."

Ngân Hoa did not flinch at the profanity but stared at the latticed screen wondering if the servant was eavesdropping. "Asses" and "balls" were her boss's choice English words. She said, "Third Uncle Dũng isn't a traitor. He just —"

"Both of them are weasels. The one in Hanoi may have lost the use of his eye but not the use of his pecker. He's fathered more children than all his siblings put together. Four Commie sons. The boy who would have been your First Uncle was still-born. It tears my guts to think of the sons he would have spawned for the family. Your father could've tried for a son with another woman — as I urged him to — but he wouldn't take advice from a younger brother. Now our lineage will continue through the Commie sons. It's a disgrace!"

"The real disgrace is that we've never seen these sons."

"Shut up and listen. I've arranged for you to meet with a Việt Kiều. His parents were boat people. He has three children in California but his wife has left him. That's the American way — women don't know their place and disobey their men. Anyway, you must be very nice to him. I mean very nice. Tell him our family history exactly the way I tell you. Convince him that we're honourable people to do business with. Don't mention the weasels from the North. Never mention them." He touched the teacup to his lips but still took no sip. "He's brought some religious books with him."

"Isn't bringing religious books illegal?"

"He's looking for someone to give them out to people — discreetly — and he will pay the distributor very well. He speaks some Vietnamese and you speak some English."

"Why should I talk to a Việt Kiều? Aren't they traitors?"

"Shut up and listen. The Government once called them traitors but likes them a lot better now — they bring in American money and American know-how. That means how things work.

Besides the Government is up north in Hanoi, and you know what those people are like — dim-witted, officious. Not good for business. This is an opportunity for me, and for you too, to earn some green money. I don't mean disrespect to my older brother, but your father's fishing for seaweed from a raft hasn't brought much dignity to the Nguyễn line. To this day he cannot read and write... You didn't know that? At least the northern weasels were forced by the Commies to learn the alphabet. This is your chance to show your parents that you're as good as a son. But don't tell them anything for now. When you give them enough money to buy a house, they'll be happy."

"I send them money every month. They're happy."

"They're not happy with you. You're not married. They have no son-in-law and no grandchildren. They know your prospects are dim because you're old. I set you up in that fish place so that foreigners would see you, but you've made nothing of it... nothing. What's wrong with you?"

"It's my life."

"Ah, talking like a Westerner. You're not one yet. First, you'll have a nice dinner with that Việt Kiều. We'll see what comes out of it. I know the new investment law from my best customer. He's a chauffeur for a Party Cadre who'll be Prime Minister one day. The law allows foreigners to set up joint venture companies. You work for one. They bring in the money; we bring in the workers. That's globalization."

Ngân Hoa stared for a while at the paraffin lamp flickering on the Altar for the Ancestors before she said, "You know Aunt Mai Linh would have hit you over the head with a broom for this. And she would have been right. I hope all of our ancestors are listening to your schemes for me."

"My unmarried sister knew her place. You must too, so don't talk back — you unmarried woman. Import–export is a cooperative business. A charmer like you can lubricate the deal. If you learn to drink a bit of wine like a Western woman, you can reverse the family's destiny. We've had bad luck enough. If you get to travel abroad, do you know what kind of money you can bring? Years back, a couple on my street went to work in East Germany. They returned with enough money to buy a house for cash. Now, when one of their daughters marries, 300 guests are invited to the Metropolitan Hotel. I can only work behind the scenes because I'm pockmarked and crippled. You are over thirty now... shame... but still can look good in front of foreigners. My woman here will make you another fancy áo dài. You know how a Nguyễn woman should look. Graceful, virtuous. I trust you've been virtuous... not a slut? Because if he offers you marriage, you bloody well say yes... and he better not have a reason to send you back. You owe it to your family."

Ngân Hoa felt faint from thirst. She needed to get away — to run to the Motorbike Cafe and pour some liquid down her throat, anything cool, anything on ice. She stood up, kowtowed — her backbone resisting a bit — and ran out to the gate.

[HAPPY NEW YEAR TO OUR COUNTRY — PEACE AND WEALTH TO ALL]

On the last night of December 2005, Ngân Hoa twirled alongside her Việt Kiều man on the marble floor of another gated mansion, her face hidden behind a mask studded with fake diamonds, confetti sparkling in her hair, a red balloon tied to her wrist, and a tall glass of bubbly liquid in her hand. Around them, Western men and women danced cheek to cheek.

Through the eye slits of the mask, she watched their children, fingers locked together, weaving snakelike among the dancers. They wore glossy outfits and giggled constantly. But she felt sorry for them: they lived so far away from their native land. Their ancestors were buried oceans away. Their grandparents lived overseas and had not been invited to the party. How inhuman. Did they know about the Kitchen God who soars to heaven on the back of a fish to report to the Jade Emperor in the sky whether they have been good or not? Did they know that we release carp into lakes and rivers for the Kitchen God to ride on, and bribe him for the voyage with pearly rice and lemon grass chicken so he will report only our good deeds? Had they been taught any of our customs at the International School?

Her Việt Kiều man had taught her well about Christmas — about the old man with a white beard who comes down from the sky bearing gifts to those who deserve them. How he rides reindeers, not carp, on his travels, and how the Westerners kill the carp and eat them. "When the two envoys pass each other somewhere along the heavenly highway," Ngân Hoa mused, "they must exchange salutes... and laugh."

Her Vietnamese Lunar Year holiday was three weeks away. She would go to her village to celebrate the Tết bearing gifts for her parents — Western things: for her mother a French hair dye to cover her grey hair, and a fragrant German conditioner so that the worn-out woman would not have to rinse her hair with citronella leaves. Two cartons of American cigarettes for her father. She would bring no husband — which was the one gift they would love to have. Her Việt Kiều man would not come because he was still tethered to a wife elsewhere. Her Communist uncles would not be invited. Fourth Uncle Hiên had for some time refused to visit what he called the "shitty backwoods" of her village. Aunt Mai Linh was gone.

She drank the bubbly liquid bottom up, put the glass down on the nearest table, and from behind her mask reached out to her absent kin. She swept Second Uncle Lang into her arms and twirled him to the rhythm of the music, his Resistance Medal flying around his neck, his two wives waving their arms above their heads from their seat by the wall, his four sons — the only Nguyễn heirs of her generation — snapping their fingers in delight. She released him into their embrace and locked arms with Third Uncle Dũng's dented dummies, leading them in a jolly prance around the floor, while he and his sulky wife laughed from the sidelines. Alone on the confetti-strewn floor, she was not dancing a crazy Western dance, but her own Vietnamese lion dance. She did not see any smirks and did not hear any snickers.

Out of breath, she had no strength to summon Aunt Mai Linh's heir-star to be with her, and in the windowless dance hall could not look to the sky to find it. But she knew that the star was up there and looking down to her. "Don't worry, Aunt Mai. I won't marry a Việt Kiều, not this one anyway. Let him think I will say yes, and let Fourth Uncle Hiên toot his schemes all he wants. But I'll have the final say."

There was froth on her lips and fizz in her head. The floor underneath was shifting. Orange County opened up on the horizon but it was in the wrong place... somewhere in Canada, because the Inuit were buying fur-trimmed parkas and their black-eyed children were sliding down the sheet of ice that was Interstate 405. How would she find her way out of this morass? Which way should she go? Something collided with her at knee level and when she pulled down her mask to see better, a child at the long end of the snake was giggling up at her. She took the child's hand, fell in step with the snake line, and glided around the floor with the young revellers — like some heavy-hearted but hopeful phantom from a faraway land.

Acknowledgements

When I leafed through the pages of the finished manuscript, great pleasure came from remembering the people who along the rugged road of writing it offered guidance and encouragement.

I kowtow with gratitude before my teachers:

Melanie Little, who in the early years of this century, in Ottawa, was my first instructor of the art and craft of writing.

Karen Connelly, who in 2005 was my mentor at the Humber School for Writers in Toronto, and later read the first lame drafts of these narratives.

Salvatore Scibona, who led the Advanced Fiction (The Novel) class at Harvard in 2010.

Julia Glass, who presided over the "Writing from the Character" class at the Fine Arts Work Centre in Provincetown, Massachusetts, in 2011.

Cam Terwilliger, who led the Master Fiction class at the Grub Street Collective in Boston in the summer of 2011.

My classmates in Cambridge, Boston, and Provincetown inspired me with their own writing and commented generously on mine. The editors of the *Harvard Summer Review* opened another door when they chose an excerpt from my manuscript for publication in their 2010 issue.

Maria Coletta McLean (no relation), herself a published writer, read my early drafts at her desk in Toronto and challenged my assumptions, my reasoning, and my characterization at every step. Her editorial scimitar finely edged and seldom off the mark, she slashed my serpentine sentences and useless adjectives, and invariably suggested a rewrite. I buckled down on my bamboo stool and wrote a better version. I cannot thank her enough.

My first reader in Hanoi was Lưu Đoàn Huynh, a retired diplomat and scholar who died in 2010. Although in ill health and working on his own book, he found time to explain the role of Confucianism and Buddhism in the Vietnamese culture, and to correct several historical misconceptions. I treasure the memory of his wisdom and his gentle civility.

The 400 graduates of the Diplomatic Academy of Vietnam in Hanoi, the renowned university training professionals for the foreign service, who were my students between 2005 and 2010, offered me friendship, welcomed me in their homes, and shared many personal stories with me. Nguyễn Đặng Lan Anh, Lê Thị Hà, and Phạm Thị Nhung were my excellent students first, and after graduating became my teachers of the language, the history, and the rituals of Vietnam.

Nguyễn Minh Phương and her daughter Đoàn Phương Mai were my second family in Hanoi. So was Nguyễn Thị Như Nguyện, a loyal friend and fellow lover of literature and good food.

Andrew Hardy, Director of l'École Française d'Extrême-Orient in Hanoi, kindly loaned me out-of-print works from his personal collection. The research centre's courteous librarian, Nguyễn Văn Tường, climbed the ladder time and again to fetch books for me.

The friendships one makes in the course of writing are for life. Lady Borton, Linda Mazur, and Sue Fleming have lived in Hanoi for years, understand the Vietnamese culture, and write insightfully about it. They have been my splendidly perceptive readers and merciful critics.

The Writers' Collective of Hanoi — Suzi Garner, Andy Engelson, Mary E. Croy, Helen Kang, Grahame Whyte, Jennifer

Fossenbell, and Kelly Morse — fine writers and encouragers all, will stay with me forever. So will Alwyne Smith of Rokeby, Tasmania, a woman of good judgment and impeccable rectitude, who read parts of the manuscript and shared her own experience of Vietnam with me. My faithful bookworms from the Beechwood Avenue Book Club in Ottawa — Gilliane Lapointe, Ingrid McCarthy, Barbara Bloor, and Gwynneth Martin — egged me on from afar.

When I thought my work was ready for publication, Barbara Berson gave the manuscript a thorough review. John Pearce, my esteemed literary agent, took one long look at the eight historical panels I had painted and knew instantly (and perfectly) how they ought to be framed.

I left for Vietnam in 2005 cheered by my children, Eric and Anna, who urged me — pushed me — to go and do what I really wanted to do. They remained a rock of support throughout my years in Asia. Returning to Canada in 2011, I settled near them in Vancouver, not knowing what to expect from the new-for-me city. Then I met Betsy Warland, Caroline Adderson, and Deborah Willis, and knew that life would be good.

An earlier version of this book, entitled *Imagining Vietnam*, won the 2011 Impress Prize for New Writers, and was published in the U.K. by Impress Books in 2013. This revised edition, retitled *The Swallows Uncaged: A Narrative in Eight Panels*, has benefited immeasurably from the erudition and superlative editing of Barbara Scott and exemplary diligence and care of Kelsey Attard of Freehand Books. I would share my last bowl of rice with them any time.

Elizabeth McLean
VANCOUVER, BRITISH COLUMBIA
JUNE 2015

Author's Note

To learn about the history of Vietnam and research material for
this volume I have looked to books written by historians and
cultural anthropologists in English and in French. From the Vietnamese side, invaluable were:

Nguyễn Khắc Viện. *Vietnam: A Long History*. Ha Noi: The Gioi
 Publishers, 2007
Hữu Ngọc. *Wandering Through Vietnamese Culture*. Ha Noi: The
 Gioi Publishers, 2005.
Nguyễn Văn Huyên. *The Ancient Civilization of Vietnam*. Ha Noi:
 The Gioi Publishers, 1995.

From the Western perspective, very helpful were:

Jamieson, Neil. *Understanding Vietnam*. Berkeley: University of
 California Press, 1995.
Taylor, Keith Weller. *The Birth of Vietnam*. Berkeley: University
 of California Press, 1983.
Templer, Robert, *Shadows and Winds: A View of Modern Vietnam*.
 London: Little Brown Company, UK, 1999.
Views of Seventeenth-Century Vietnam (Christoforo Borri on
 Cochinchina and Samuel Baron on Tonkin). New York:
 Southeast Asia Program Publication, Cornell University,
 2006.

Also very useful were the two dozen booklets on subjects ranging from *Martial Arts* to *Wedding Customs* to *Traditional Medicine* to *Royal Exams* to several other facets of Vietnamese culture, jointly edited over the last decade by Hữu Ngọc and Lady Borton. The three journals that employed me as a freelance writer — *Vietnam Cultural Window, Vietnam Heritage,* and *The Guide* (literary supplement to *Vietnam Economic Times*) — yielded many informative articles on Vietnamese customs and traditions.

For books in French, written by Vietnamese and French scholars, I relied on the excellent collection, going back to colonial times, of the library of *l'École Française d'Extrême-Orient* in Hanoi, especially the following volumes:

Maybon, Charles B. *Histoire Moderne du Pays d'Annam 1592–1820.* Paris: Librarie Plon, 1949.
Lê Thành Khôi. *Histoire du Viet Nam des origines à 1858.* Paris: Sudestasie, 1981.
Huard, Pierre, and Maurice Durand. *Connaissance du Vietnam.* Paris: Imprimerie National, 1954. (The drawings in this book are particularly instructive.)
Adler, Laure. *Marguerite Duras.* Paris: Éditions Gallimard, 1998.

¶ This book was typeset in Alda, which was created by Berton Hasebe in 2008 and published by Emigre.